MW01200479

Blacktop Cowboys® Compilation

Also from Lorelei James

Rough Riders Series (in reading order)
LONG HARD RIDE
RODE HARD
COWGIRL UP AND RIDE
ROUGH, RAW AND READY
BRANDED AS TROUBLE
STRONG SILENT TYPE (novella)
SHOULDA BEEN A COWBOY
ALL JACKED UP
RAISING KANE
SLOW RIDE (free short story)
COWGIRLS DON'T CRY
CHASIN' EIGHT
COWBOY CASANOVA
KISSIN' TELL
GONE COUNTRY
SHORT RIDES (anthology)
REDNECK ROMEO
COWBOY TAKE ME AWAY
LONG TIME GONE (novella)

Blacktop Cowboys® Series (in reading order)
CORRALLED
SADDLED AND SPURRED
WRANGLED AND TANGLED
ONE NIGHT RODEO
TURN AND BURN
HILLBILLY ROCKSTAR
ROPED IN (novella)
STRIPPED DOWN (novella)
WRAPPED AND STRAPPED
HANG TOUGH

Mastered Series (in reading order)
BOUND
UNWOUND
SCHOOLED (digital only novella)
UNRAVELED
CAGED

Rough Riders Legacy Series
UNBREAK MY HEART

Single Title Novels
RUNNING WITH THE DEVIL
DIRTY DEEDS

Single Title Novellas
LOST IN YOU (short novella)
WICKED GARDEN
MISTRESS CHRISTMAS (Wild West Boys)
MISS FIRECRACKER (Wild West Boys)
BALLROOM BLITZ (Two To Tango anthology)

Need You Series
WHAT YOU NEED
JUST WHAT I NEEDED
ALL YOU NEED (April 2017)

Lorelei James also writes as mystery author Lori Armstrong

Blacktop Cowboys®
Compilation
3 Stories by
By Lorelei James

1001 Dark Nights

EVIL EYE
CONCEPTS

Blacktop Cowboys® Compilation
3 Stories by
Lorelei James
ISBN: 978-1-945920-71-4
1001 Dark Nights

Roped In
Copyright 2014 Lorelei James

Stripped Down
Copyright 2015 Lorelei James

Strung Up
Copyright 2016 Lorelei James

Foreword: Copyright 2014 M. J. Rose

Published by Evil Eye Concepts, Incorporated

Sign up for the 1001 Dark Nights Newsletter
and be entered to win a Tiffany Key necklace.

There's a contest every month!

Go to http://www.1001darknights.com to subscribe.

As a bonus, all subscribers will receive a free
1001 Dark Nights story
The First Night
by Lexi Blake & M.J. Rose

Table of Contents

Also by Lorelei James   5
Foreword   12
Roped In   11
Stripped Down   145
Strung Up   251
Discover 1001 Dark Nights Collection Four   352
Discover 1001 Dark Nights Collection One   354
Discover 1001 Dark Nights Collection Two   355
Discover 1001 Dark Nights Collection Three   356
About by Lorelei James   358
Discover More Lorelei James   359
Special Thanks   361

One Thousand and One Dark Nights

Once upon a time, in the future…

*I was a student fascinated with stories and learning.
I studied philosophy, poetry, history, the occult, and
the art and science of love and magic. I had a vast
library at my father's home and collected thousands
of volumes of fantastic tales.*

*I learned all about ancient races and bygone
times. About myths and legends and dreams of all
people through the millennium. And the more I read
the stronger my imagination grew until I discovered
that I was able to travel into the stories… to actually
become part of them.*

*I wish I could say that I listened to my teacher
and respected my gift, as I ought to have. If I had, I
would not be telling you this tale now.
But I was foolhardy and confused, showing off
with bravery.*

*One afternoon, curious about the myth of the
Arabian Nights, I traveled back to ancient Persia to
see for myself if it was true that every day Shahryar
(Persian: شهریار, "king") married a new virgin, and then
sent yesterday's wife to be beheaded. It was written
and I had read, that by the time he met Scheherazade,
the vizier's daughter, he'd killed one thousand
women.*

Something went wrong with my efforts. I arrived in the midst of the story and somehow exchanged places with Scheherazade – a phenomena that had never occurred before and that still to this day, I cannot explain.

Now I am trapped in that ancient past. I have taken on Scheherazade's life and the only way I can protect myself and stay alive is to do what she did to protect herself and stay alive.

Every night the King calls for me and listens as I spin tales. And when the evening ends and dawn breaks, I stop at a point that leaves him breathless and yearning for more. And so the King spares my life for one more day, so that he might hear the rest of my dark tale.

As soon as I finish a story... I begin a new one... like the one that you, dear reader, have before you now.

Roped In

Acknowledgments from the Author

A 1001 thanks to the fabulous Liz Berry for all her love and patience with me—and for asking me to be a part of this amazing project.

And thanks to my readers who wanted to know more about Sutton Grant's brother Wynton, and London's pal, Mel. This love story is for you…

Prologue

Steer wrestler Sutton Grant knew the instant he threw himself off his horse he was in for a world of hurt.

He'd miscalculated the distance and his rate of rotation. The last thing he remembered before he hit the steer was he could kiss this year's world championship title good-bye.

He woke up in the ambulance, his head pounding, unable to move any part of his body but his eyes.

Fuck.

Try and move.

I can't.

Was he paralyzed?

He couldn't be.

What if he was? He'd never hurt like this. Never.

But the fact he could feel pain had to be good, right?

Maybe the intense pain is your body shutting down.

If he was paralyzed, who would shoulder the burden of caring for him for the rest of his life? He didn't have a wife or a girlfriend. Would responsibility fall to his family?

Oh, hell no. He'd put them through enough with his last rodeo mishap.

Mishap? Don't you mean accident that kept you out of commission for a year? Do you remember living at home and seeing the worry on your parent's faces?

That'd been worse than the months of physical and mental recovery. Then he'd had the added burden of seeing their happiness vanish after he'd healed and had informed them he planned to return to the sport.

His mother's voice drifted into his memory. *You're still going to do this even if it hurts, maims, or kills you?* He'd responded, *Even then.*

He still saw the tear tracks on her face, the subtle shake of her head. And he'd still gone off anyway, chasing the gold buckle, putting his body through hell.

I take it back! I didn't mean it!

Right then and there, Sutton made a bargain with God:

Please Lord, if I survive this with my body intact, I swear I'll give up bulldoggin' forever. No lie. I'll be done for good.

White lights blinded him and for a brief instant, he thought he'd died. A voice he'd never heard before whispered to him, *promise accepted.*

Then darkness descended again. The last thing Sutton remembered was wiggling his fingers and toes and whispering a prayer of thanks.

Chapter One

Eight months later...

"You ain't supposed to be out there doin' that," Wynton shouted.

Sutton looked across the paddock at his older brother and scowled. He tugged on the reins but his horse Dial wouldn't budge. Damn stubborn horse; he had to be part mule.

"I've got a ridin' crop you can borrow," his younger brother Creston yelled from atop the corral fence.

"I'm surrounded by smartasses," Sutton informed Dial. "And apparently I'm a dumbass because I never learn with you, do I?"

Dial tossed his mane.

After he climbed off his horse, Sutton switched out the bit and bridle for a lead rope. Then he opened the gate between the paddock and the pasture, playfully patting Dial's flank as the gray dun tore off.

Dial actually kicked up his hooves in glee as he galloped away.

"Yeah, I'll miss our special time together too, asshole."

Asshole. Man, he was punchier than he realized if he was calling his horse an asshole.

Sutton sauntered over to where his brothers waited for him, surprised that they'd both shown up in the middle of a Friday afternoon—with a six-pack. Wyn and Cres both ranched with their dad, although as the oldest, Wyn had inherited the bulk of the ranch work decisions. It appeared he'd changed the rule about working a full day—

every day, rain, shine, snow, come hell, high water, or wild fire.

"What's the occasion? You here to borrow money?" he asked.

"Good one. Glad to see they didn't remove all of your funny bone after surgery," Wyn said dryly.

"Hilarious." Sutton quirked an eyebrow at Cres. "Got something smart to say?"

"Yeah. You know you ain't supposed to be doin' anything that'll further injure you. When we hadn't heard from you all week, we figured you were up to no good. And I see we were right."

"It wasn't like I was bulldoggin'."

"This'd be a different conversation if we'd seen you doin' that." Wyn handed him a beer. "We ain't trying to bust your balls, but goddammit, Sutton. You almost fucking died."

"*Again*," Cres added.

"Well, I ain't dead. But don't feel like I'm alive, either." He sipped the cold brew. Nothing tasted better on a hot summer day.

"Should we be on suicide watch?" Wyn said hesitantly.

Sutton had a mental break the last time he'd been injured, so his family kept an eye on him, and he knew how lucky he was to have that support. "Nah. It's just this sitting around, healing up stuff is driving me bugshit crazy."

"The way to deal with your boredom ain't to get in the cage with your demon and go another round."

Sutton squinted at Cres. "You callin' my horse a demon?"

Cres rolled his eyes. "No, dipshit. Your demon is the need to prove yourself. Regardless of the cost."

His gaze met his youngest brother's. Growing up, Wyn and Cres joked about Sutton being the mailman's kid because he was the only one of the three boys with blue-green eyes. Both his brothers and his parents had brown eyes. Sometimes he wondered if that outsider status is what lured him into the world of professional rodeo and away from working on the family ranch.

He sighed. "I appreciate your concern, I really do. I'm just frustrated. Makes it worse when I hafta deal with Dial. He's a temperamental motherfucker on his best days. I don't trust anyone to work with him after that last go around with the so-called 'expert,' which means he ain't getting the proper workout for a horse of his caliber."

"A few months cooling his hooves shouldn't have changed his previous training that much. Breeders take mares out of bucking contention, as well as barrel racing, when they're bred. Sometimes that'd be up to two years."

"I know that. But Dial? He ain't like other horses. Gelding him didn't dampen that fire; if anything, it increased his orneriness."

"I'd be ornery too if some dude sliced off my balls," Wyn said with a shudder. Then he looked at Sutton. "So that other bulldogger, the guy with the weird name...what happened the weekend he borrowed him?"

"Weird name." Sutton snorted. "That's rich coming from a guy named *Wynton*."

"Fuck off, *Sutton*," he shot back. "I think Mom was high on child birthin' painkillers when she picked our names."

"Probably. You talkin' about Breck Christianson? He tried to help me out during the Western Livestock Show in January while I was still laid up."

"Yeah. Him." Wyn looked at Cres. "Don't know if I ever heard you talk about what went down that week you were there with him and Dial."

Cres rested his forearms on the top of the fence and his hat shadowed his face. "It was a damn disaster in the arena. Dial wouldn't do nothin'. Seriously. That high-strung bastard stayed in the damn chute. The one time he left the chute, he charged the hazer's horse. Breck traveled to Denver specifically to get a feel for Dial before the competition, but he ended up sticking with his own mount."

"Huh. Surprised you stayed in Denver for the whole stock show since it meant you had to take care of demon horse while you were there."

Cres shrugged. "I never get to see the behind the chutes action for a week-long event. It was interesting and everyone was friendly."

"So Breck took good care of you?" Sutton asked.

Cres choked on his beer.

Wyn patted him on the back. "You okay?"

"Yeah." *Cough cough.* "A bug flew in my mouth." Another cough. "Breck introduced me around."

Sutton nudged his shoulder. "Breck introduce you to his buckle bunny pussy posse?"

Before Cres responded, Wyn interrupted. "Cres wouldn't know

what to do with the ladies. The kid is all work and no play. He probably spent all his time hidin' in the horse trailer."

"I ain't a kid," Cress said tightly. "And don't assume you know what I got up to because you don't. Anyway, Breck knows everyone." He looked at Sutton. "He introduced me to Saxton Green, that other bulldogger you get mistaken for all the time. He's built like you, even looks like you, but he sure don't act like you. That man is fuckin' wild."

Sutton groaned. "Do you know how many times I've had to defend myself against something Saxton did? It sucks. That's about the only time I don't mind that the other competitors call me 'The Saint.'"

"Other competitors, and everyone else involved with the rodeo circuit, including the women, call you 'The Saint' because you're the one who acts like a freakin' monk," Wyn pointed out helpfully. "Damn man. How do you turn down all that free pussy?"

"It ain't free, trust me," Sutton retorted.

"Wyn, leave him alone," Cres said. "Stop acting like you've got it rough and ain't getting your fair share of tail. Women are lined up in your driveway to get a piece of you."

Wyn smirked and raised his beer. "It's good to be me."

Cres rolled his eyes. "Oh, and I also met the couple who raised and trained Dial before you bought him."

That piqued Sutton's interest. "Chuck and Berlin Gradsky? Really?"

"They were in the arena when Breck was having a hard time with Dial. Neither of them even tried to step in. They said the only people who had any effect on him was you and their daughter who'd trained him."

London Gradsky. He hadn't thought of her in a couple of years. The surly brunette who'd thrown a shit fit when her parents had sold Dial to him rather than just continuing to let him compete on the horse. She'd accused him of taking advantage of her parents, caring about his career above the welfare of the animal. Then she'd launched into a diatribe about how self-absorbed he was for pushing to have the stallion castrated without considering the long-term gains for breeding. After calling him a dickhead whose belt buckle was bigger than his brain, she'd stormed off.

Chuck and Berlin explained away her behavior, fondly referring to her as their headstrong filly. They were proud that she'd struck out on her own as a horse trainer rather than just expecting to get a primo position at Grade A Horse Farms because her parents owned the business. But still, London's accusations had stung. What he wouldn't give for her expertise now. Although it'd been three years since their altercation, he doubted the feisty firecracker would let bygones be bygones. "Well, it's obvious I need help."

"What about that Eli guy?" Wyn said. "Didn't you say he's some kind of Native American horse whisperer?"

"Eli is top notch. But Dial's temperament is particularly bad around other horses. He took a chunk outta the alpha horse the one time I left him there—this was after Eli put him in a pasture by himself and he jumped the fence. So Dial is no longer welcome."

"I have faith you'll figure something out that doesn't entail you bein' on the dirt with him."

Cres straightened up and moved to toss his bottle into the shooting barrel. "To be blunt, as much as we care for our animals, bro, they are tools. Tools are replaceable. You are not. This last time you nearly went into kidney failure, liver failure, and they talked of removing your spleen. Both me'n Wyn would've offered up a kidney or even a damn lung for you. You know that. We'd rather not have to face that choice again."

"We're askin' you not to do something that'll put you back in the hospital for another six weeks followed by months of recovery." Wyn gestured to the ranch house and the area around them. "You've got a nice place to hang your hat, money in the bank, the kinda looks that get any woman you want into your bed, and family nearby. Ain't nothin' wrong with that life."

Sutton watched his brothers drive off. He put the three bottles left from the six-pack into the fridge in the garage, knowing he'd be less tempted to drink them all if he had to leave the house to get them.

He changed clothes, flipped on the ball game for some background noise, and snagged his laptop. He typed London Gradsky in the search engine. The top result read:

London's Bridge To Training A Better Horse

Seriously? That was the worst fucking business slogan he'd ever heard. He clicked on the link.

Hers was a simple website. Contact info via e-mail or phone. Testimonials about her training successes. Links to horse brokers and breeders—no surprise Grade A Horse Farms topped the list—but nowhere did London list her lineage. Interesting.

Lastly, he saw a page with a schedule of summer events.

Sutton scrolled the page. Evidently, London put on training clinics on the weekends during the summer at local fairs and rodeos. For fifty bucks, she'd spend thirty minutes assessing the horse and rider before offering training recommendations.

The cynical side of his brain remembered her cutting words to him and weighed in with: *What are the odds she recommends herself as the horse trainer who can miraculously fix bad habits and riders?*

But his optimist side crawled out of the dark hole it'd been hiding in since the accident and countered with: *Her business wouldn't last long if she didn't get results, and the horse training world in Colorado would shun her if she was a shyster.*

It looked to him like she'd been putting on these summer clinics for at least a couple years. And every time slot was booked, as well as several people on standby for an open appointment. He scrolled down to the current week's schedule and his heart skipped a beat.

Score.

She'd be in Fairfax, Colorado, this weekend. That was only thirty miles from here. And score again. Her last slot of the day was still open.

With zero hesitation, he typed in D.L. A-ride and hoped liked hell she had a sense of humor.

And that she wouldn't chase after him with a horse whip when she realized who he was.

Chapter Two

Worst. Morning. Ever.

London Gradsky glared at the busted coffee maker. She'd spent twenty minutes fiddle-fucking around with the thing to try and get it to work. Giving it up as a lost cause, she'd chucked the whole works outside.

No coffee in her cozy camper meant she had to go to the exhibitors' and contestants' tent to get her morning jolt of caffeine. Since she'd just planned on quickly ducking in and out, she hadn't combed her hair, washed her face, brushed her teeth, or changed out of her pajamas.

And motherfucking, son of a bitch if *they* weren't there, Tweedledee and Tweedletwat. Making cowpie eyes at each other while people looked at them with indulgent smiles. She could almost hear the collective sigh of the women in the tent when Stitch gently wiped a smear of powdered sugar off Paige's cheek then kissed the spot.

Paige giggled and nuzzled him. Her tiara caught on the brim of his cowboy hat, which sent the newly anointed golden couple's admirers scurrying forward to help them out of such a huge pickle.

Of course no one pointed out how stupid it was that Paige actually *wore* a fucking tiara to breakfast. The man-stealing bitch probably wore it to bed. Then London drifted into a fantasy where Paige had donned the tiara when she gave Stitch a blowjob and it cut the hell out of his abdomen.

"Sending eye daggers at her while eye fucking him ain't smart, London," her on-the-road partner in crime Melissa "Mel" Lockhart said behind her.

"I'm not eye fucking him, I'm eye fucking him *up*."

"Doesn't matter, because that's not how anyone will see it. Come on, let's get out of here."

London allowed herself to be led away. As soon as they were out of screeching range, she exploded. "How in the fuck am I gonna survive this summer, Mel? When every time I turn around I see them sucking each other's faces off? What does he see in her?"

Mel didn't answer. She appeared to be hedging, which was not her usual style.

"Just spit it out."

"Fine. That girl is a bonafide beauty queen. Everyone says she'll be the next Miss Rodeo America and people treat him like he's a prince— the heir apparent to take that All Around title at the CRA Championships in a few years. They are a match made in PR heaven. What don't you get about that?"

"I don't get how that asswipe could dump me, via text message, after he does one fundraiser with her because it's true love? Bullshit. No one falls in love in a night." London paced along the metal fencing. "I wanna choke her with her stupid 'Miss Rodeo Colorado' sash and then tie it around his dick until it turns blue and falls off."

Mel's hands landed on London's shoulders and then she was right in her face, her brown eyes flashing concern. "This has gotta stop, London. What the hell did you see in him anyway? He's looks like Opie from *The Andy Griffith Show*. I think the only reason you ended up with him in the first place is because you were lonely and wanted a dog."

"He's a damn hound dog who needs to be put down," she muttered.

"Not true, because we both know that man did not rock your world or even the damn camper when you two got down and dirty. He doesn't know how to be a horndog."

London couldn't argue that point.

"Seriously sista, you're starting to scare me with all these violent scenarios you spout off like horror poetry. Stitch scratching an itch with Paige the underage is not the end of the world. I think the real issue here is you need to get laid by a man who knows what he's doing. And you're putting out this I-will-rip-your-dick-off vibe to any man who starts sniffing around you."

That wasn't true…was it?

"Find a hot guy and fuck him 'til he can't walk. Then you'll be back to strutting around with your head held high instead of acting like a whipped pup."

"You're right."

"Of course I am. Now take a minute and breathe."

London closed her eyes, inhaled for ten counts, exhaled for ten, and reopened her eyes to gaze at her friend.

The freckle-faced redhead wore a smug look. "Better?"

"Much. Thank you." Then her gaze narrowed. "Hey, you just did that thing my mother always does. Did she give you instructions on how to get me to cool off?"

"Yes, and I asked her—but she didn't offer up her magic mom trick freely."

"When were you hanging out with my mother?" London demanded.

"Uh, since she *owns* my cutting horse, I see her more than you do."

"She may own your horse, but I trained Plato so he'll always love me best."

"Even my color blind horse can see what you're wearing is all kinds of wrong because you look like a leprechaun hag. Where *did* you get those god-awful green pajamas?" Mel leaned closer. "Do they have frogs on them? And sweet baby Jesus on a Vespa…are those frogs baring lipstick-kissed butt cheeks?"

"Yep. Nana gave them to me after Stitch ditched me. Said toads like him could kiss my ass."

"Appropriate I guess, but still hideous. Come to my horse trailer. I've got coffee and everything to banish that outer hag." She smirked. "You're on your own getting rid of that inner hag."

"Fuck off."

"You love me."

"I really do." She looped her arm through Mel's. "Let's start making a 'get London laid' list of candidates." She paused. "You still got your little black book of rodeo circuit bad boys?"

"Yep. It's even color coded by cock size, which circuit they're on, and their ability to last longer than eight seconds."

* * * *

London was hot and tired, but exhilarated after six hours of working with horses and their riders. About three quarters of her clientele were kids under fourteen. It was gratifying, proving to novice equestrians that their animal was under their control. Contrary to belief, she picked up very few new regular clients at fairs and rodeos. The problems she helped with were rider related rather than horse related. The horse issues would take more than a thirty minute fix.

She checked her sign-up list, surprised to see her last opening had been filled. Weird name. D.L. A-ride. No gender or age listed. Was it a joke? D.L. A-ride. She watched the gate for a horse and rider to approach.

After two minutes she closed her eyes, breathing in the familiar scents of hot dirt and manure and livestock, with the occasional whiff of diesel fuel and something sugary like cotton candy or funnel cakes or Bavarian almonds.

"Excuse me," a deep voice said behind her. "I'm looking for London Gradsky?"

London pushed off the fence and turned around, but the *you found her* response dried on her tongue. Holy balls was this man hot. Like off the charts hot. Two days' worth of dark scruff couldn't hide the sharp angles of his face. Strong, almost square jaw, ridiculously full lips. The guy wore a ball cap and dark shades. A short-sleeved polo in ocean blue accentuated the breadth of his shoulders, the contours of his chest and... Holy smoking double barrels, welcome to the gun show; his biceps were huge. His forearms appeared to have been carved out of marble. She stopped herself from dropping her gaze to his crotch. Had Mel sent this man her way?

"I'm London. Do I know you?" *Please don't tell me you're a long lost cousin or something.*

"Yeah. We met a while back." He paused. "I signed up for the last class slot because I needed to talk to you."

Needed. Not wanted. Her skepticism reared its snappish head. "Who are you?"

He encroached on her space, completely throwing her body into shadow and tumult. Then she waited, breath trapped in her lungs for the moment when he tore off his sunglasses.

Eyes as blue as the Caribbean stared back at her.

Fuck me. She knew those eyes. She'd dreamt of those eyes. Although last time she'd seen them up close she'd wanted to spit in them. "Sutton Grant."

"I reckon a once-over like that is better than the fiery look of hatred I expected." He grinned.

That grin? With the damn dimples in his cheeks and in his chin? Not fair. She was *such* a sucker for a devil's smile boosted by pearly whites. But she'd considered him devil's spawn after his dealings with her family. In her mind she'd attributed cloven hooves, demon horns, and a forked tongue and tail to him.

Which pissed her off because the man was a piece of art. A real piece of work, too, if he thought she'd let bygones be bygones just so she could stare slack-jawed at his perfect face, spellbinding eyes, and banging body.

"You lied to get a meeting with me?" She snorted. "I see you're still the same manipulative bastard who follows his own agenda."

He took another step closer. "I see you're still the same brat who jumps to conclusions."

"Yeah? I'm not the one in a piss-poor disguise, douche-nozzle."

"Douche-nozzle...I don't even know what that is."

"Look in the mirror, pal." Her gaze flicked over him. "A ball cap, a polo shirt, and...no freakin' way. Are you wearing *Mom* jeans, Sutton Grant?"

He shot a quick look around and said, "Keep your voice down. No one has recognized me and I'd like to keep it that way."

"I'll bet your girlfriend picked this outfit because it is guaranteed to keep you from getting laid. Like ever."

He scowled. "I don't have a girlfriend. Now can we skip the insults and cut to the chase? Because I really need to talk to you."

"You scheduled the time and it ain't free." London held out her hand. "Fifty bucks for thirty minutes. The clock starts ticking as soon as you pay up."

Sutton dug in his front pocket and pulled out a crumpled fifty. "Here."

"Shoot."

"It's about Dial."

"What did you do to him?"

"It's more a problem of what I'm *not* doin' with him. Due to my injury, he's been benched the last eight months."

Now she remembered. Sutton had gotten badly hurt late last fall during his circuit's last qualifying event for the CRA Finals and ended up with life-threatening internal injuries. "What do you want from me?"

"I'll hire you to work with Dial, get him back up to speed, since I'm still sidelined."

"So he'll be in top condition when you're back on the circuit?"

A funny look flitted through his eyes and he looked away. "Something like that."

"Why me?"

"Because we both know the only people who've been able to work with him have been you and me."

She sucked in a few breaths and forced herself to loosen her fists. "This wouldn't be an issue if you hadn't browbeaten my folks into selling Dial to you outright. When the breeder owns the horse and a rider goes down, other people are in place to keep the horse conditioned. That responsibility isn't pushed aside."

"You think I don't know that? You think I'm feelin' good about any of this? Fuck. I hired people to work with him and the stubborn bastard chased them all off. A couple of them literally."

London smirked. "That's my boy."

"Your boy is getting fatter and meaner by the day," Sutton retorted. "I'm afraid if I let him go too much longer it'll be too late and he'll be as worthless as me."

Worthless? Dude. Look in the mirror much? How could Sutton be out of commission and still look like he'd stepped off the pages of *Buff and Beautiful Bulldogger* magazine?

"I hope the reason you're so quiet is because you're considering my offer."

London's gaze zoomed to his. "How do you know you can afford me?"

"I don't. I get that you're an expert on this particular horse and I'm willing to pay you for that expertise." Sutton sidestepped her and rested his big body next to hers—close to hers—against the fence. "I know it'll sound stupid, but every time I grab the tack and head out to catch Dial to try and work him, even when I'm not supposed to, I feel his frustration that I'm not doin' more. I ain't the kind of man that sees a horse—my horse—as just a tool. Your folks knew that about me or they wouldn't have sold him to me for any amount of money."

"Yeah. I do know that," she grudgingly admitted, "but you should also know that I wouldn't be doin' this for you or the money, I'd be doin' it for Dial."

"That works for me. There's another reason that I want you. Only you."

"Which is?"

His unwavering stare unnerved her, as if he was gauging whether he could trust her. Finally he said, "Strictly between us?"

She nodded.

"If it's decided I'll never compete again, you're in the horse world more than I am and you'll ensure Dial gets where he needs to be."

London hadn't been expecting that. Sutton had paid a shit ton for Dial, and he hadn't suggested she'd help him sell the horse to a proper owner, just that she'd help him find one. In her mind that meant he really had Dial's best interest at heart. Not that she believed for an instant Sutton Grant intended to retire from steer wrestling. First off, he was barely thirty. Second, rumor had it his drive to win was as wide and deep as the Colorado River.

As she contemplated how to respond, she saw her ex, Stitch, with Princess Paige plastered to his side, meandering their direction.

Dammit. Not now.

After the incident this morning, she'd steered clear of the exhibitor's hall where the pair had handed out autographs and barf bags. She felt the overwhelming need to escape, but if she booked it across the corral, it'd look like she was running from them.

Screw that. Screw them. She was not in the wrong.

"London? You look ready to commit murder. What'd I say?"

She gazed up at him. The man was too damn good-looking, so normally she wouldn't have a shot at a man like him. But he did say he'd do *anything*...

"Okay, here's the deal. I'll work with Dial, but you've gotta do something for me. Uh, two things actually."

"Name them."

How much to tell him? She didn't want to come off desperate. Still, she opted for the truth. "Backstory: my boyfriend dumped me via text last month because he'd hooked up with a rodeo queen. Because he and I were together when I made my summer schedule, that means I will see them every fucking weekend. All summer."

"And?"

"And I don't wanna be known as that poor pathetic London Gradsky pining over her lost love."

Sutton's eyes turned shrewd. "*Are* you pining for him?"

"Mostly I'm just pissed. It needs to look like I've moved on. So I realize your nickname is 'The Saint' and you don't—"

"Don't call me that," he said crossly. "Tell me what you need."

"The first thing I'd need is you to play the part of my new boyfriend."

That shocked him, but he rallied with, "I can do that. When does this start?"

"Right now, 'cause here they come." London plastered her front to his broad chest and wreathed her arms around his neck. "And make this look like the real deal, bulldogger."

"Any part of you that's hands off for me?"

She fought the urge to roll her eyes. Of course "The Saint" would ask first. "Nope."

Sutton bestowed that fuck-me-now grin. "I can work with that." He curled one hand around the back of her neck and the other around her hip.

When it appeared he intended to take his own sweet time kissing her, she took charge, teetering on tiptoe since the man was like seven feet tall. After the first touch of their lips, he didn't dive into her mouth in a fake show of passion. He rubbed his half-parted lips across hers, each pass silently coaxing her to open up a little more. Each tease of his breath on her damp lips made them tingle.

She muttered, "Kiss me like you mean business."

Those deceptively gentle kisses vanished and Sutton unleashed himself on her. Lust, passion, need. The kiss was way more powerful and take charge than she'd expected from a man nicknamed "The Saint."

Her mind shut down to everything but the sensuous feel of his tongue twining around hers as he explored her mouth, the soft stroking of his thumb on her cheek, and the possessive way his hand stroked her, as if it knew her intimately.

Then Sutton eased back, treating her lips to nibbles, licks, and lingering smooches. "Think they're gone?" he murmured.

"Who?"

He chuckled. "Your ex."

"Oh. Right. Them." She untwined her fingers from his soft hair and let her arms drop—slowly letting her hands flow over his neck and linebacker shoulders and that oh-so-amazing chest.

Their gazes collided the second she realized Sutton's heart beat just as crazily as hers did.

"So did that pass as the real deal kiss you wanted? Or do I need to do it again?"

Yes, please.

Don't be a pushover. Let him know who's in charge.

London smoothed her hand down her blouse. "For future reference, that type of kiss will work fine."

Sutton smirked. "It worked *fine* for me too, darlin'."

His face, his body, his voice—everything about him tripped her every trigger. The man would be hell on her libido.

Or you could be hell on his. Take Mel's advice. Getcha some mattress action. See exactly what it'd take to get "The Saint" all hot under the collar.

When she smiled at him, his body stiffened. "Why do you look so nervous?"

"Because that devious smile you're sporting is scary. So let's skip what it means for now. You said you needed two things from me before you'd agree to work with Dial. First is this boyfriend fake out stuff. What's the other?"

"I need a place to crash. Since I'll be working with your horse every day, I'll be crashing with you for the summer."

Chapter Three

Crashing with him?

What the bleeding hell?

He opened his mouth to protest and London laughed. "Dude, you oughta see the look on your face!"

"So you were just dicking with me?"

Her smile dried. "Sorta."

"Explain...sorta?"

"Okay. Fine. I've been living in my camper since Stitch ditched me."

"Stitch? Seriously? Your ex's name is Stitch? Is he really funny or something?"

London rolled her eyes. "No. His given name is Barclay or something stupidly stuffy. The year he turned five he was in the emergency room for stitches like ten times. The doctor said they oughta change his name to Stitch and it stuck. Anyway, I didn't have any place to go after his breakup text."

"Why didn't you go home? I've been to your house. It's huge." He paused. "Did you have a falling out with your parents?"

"No. But I'm twenty-seven. Returning home...I'd feel like a failure. I've been on my own for years. I only gave up my apartment because I was practically living at Stitch's anyway." She looked away. "I thought the relationship would be permanent. When it turned out not to be? I should've followed my mom's advice to always take care of myself first and to not give away things for free."

"Meaning...why buy the cow when you're giving the milk away for free?" he teased.

"No. Meaning I trained Stitch's horse. That's part of the reason he's done so good on the circuit this year."

His gut clenched. "He didn't pay you?"

She shook her head. "Worse. I didn't charge him." Absentmindedly, she traced the polo logo on his left pec and his nipple hardened. "I've been meaning to look for a place to live that's centrally located, but my summer schedule is busy and I don't seem to have enough time."

"But you'd have time to work with Dial?"

"Yes, especially if I'm onsite with him. I just need a place to park my camper. That's it. I won't bother you at all. My morning training appointments don't start until ten. I'm usually done by six in the evening." Her gaze hooked his. "Wait. You don't live at home, do you?"

"No. I have my own place. Why?"

"I just thought maybe your injuries were such that you moved home again so your family could help you out. I remember my mom mentioning—"

"The last time I injured myself in the arena was five years ago, and yes, *that* time I did return home. As soon as I dealt with some issues, I finished the house I'd started to build for my ex. After I'd changed the layout so it was what I wanted not what she'd demanded."

London's hazel eyes softened. "Glad to see I'm not the only one with baggage from an ex."

"You have no idea."

"Then tell me."

"Why?"

"If we're involved I'd know stuff like this. Plus, I'm nosy. So dish on the biggest bag."

Christ, she was pushy. "I met Charlotte when I started competing professionally in college. We were young. She knew what she wanted. I was too...green to see it."

"See what? That she just wanted you for your green?"

"Clever. She wanted a man who made a good living but was gone all the time. After my career setback and the injuries that required multiple surgeries...I was off the circuit. That meant no money coming in and I'd be underfoot expecting her to take care of me. She bailed on me the second week of my recovery."

"Harsh. That sucks."

Sutton let himself get a full look at this woman he'd spent a good five minutes kissing. High forehead and cheekbones. Dark eyebrows and eyelashes. Her eyes were more green than brown. With her auburn hair and fair complexion he expected to see freckles, but her skin was smooth. Flawless. Her lips, when they weren't flattened into an angry line, were pink and lush and way too tempting. If he had to describe her heart-shaped face with one word he'd say...sweet.

"Why the fuck are you gawking at me, bulldogger?"

And...not so sweet. Undeterred, he traced the curve of her neck, intrigued by how her pulse jumped at his touch. "Because it's one of the first times you've let me. And darlin', you *are* a pretty sight when you ain't scowling at me."

She blushed. But she didn't move away from his touch. "Can I ask you something?"

"Sure."

"Were you ever a player?"

"How would you react if I said yes?"

London considered him for a moment. "I'd be surprised."

"Why?"

"You seem more settled than the last time we crossed paths."

Wrong. He'd never been more unsettled, which was proof people saw what they wanted. "Not to disagree, but you were so busy painting me as the enemy back then that's all you saw. I'm not a bad guy; I was just trying to prove myself in the arena. Any of the player stuff I get accused of is because I get mixed up with Saxton Green."

She snorted. "I've met him. He doesn't hold a candle to you." London realized she'd paid him a compliment and backtracked. "Well, hate to burst your bubble, pal, but you'll still be proving yourself to me."

They realized, simultaneously, they were still body to body, face to face. But when London tried to bolt, Sutton wouldn't let her. "Steady. Don't want the people watching us to think we had a tiff after that kiss, would we?"

Her eyes widened. "Do you think there are people watching us?"

"I know there are, because darlin', that was some kiss."

Her lips curved into a smile. "Yes, it was."

Sutton pressed his lips to her forehead. "Let's head to your camper to finish this discussion in private before my thirty minutes are up."

London retreated, took his hand and said, "This way."

On the walk to where the competitors and exhibitors had set up camp, London said hello to several people but didn't introduce him, and luckily no one recognized him.

Her camper was the pull-behind kind—not fifth wheel sized, but the funky silver-bullet Airstream type. He noticed it was still hooked up to her truck. "When did you get here?"

"Late yesterday afternoon." She unlocked the camper door. "After you."

Sutton hadn't known what to expect when he'd stepped inside, so the vibrant color scheme filled in the blanks about what kind of person London was in the hours off the dirt.

Crafting stuff covered every inch of surface area across the small table. "I function in creative chaos and don't normally have visitors."

"What'd the smashed coffee pot on the ground outside do to get tossed out?"

"Quit working."

"Ah." He leaned against the wall while she packed things away. "You're lucky you've got this much space. Bad thing about bein' on the road is there's never enough room in the living quarters of a horse trailer."

"That's why my mom insisted I get this. She has no problem hauling horses, but she insists on sleeping in a hotel."

"Smart lady."

"So, Sutton, what do you do during the day at home since you aren't training or on the road?"

"Physical therapy some days," he lied. Those days were behind him. "Other days, I'm a great gate opener when my dad and brothers need extra help on the ranch."

London looked up sharply. "You don't ranch?"

He shook his head. "Growing up a rancher's kid, I never saw the appeal, just all the damn work."

"I hear ya there. I didn't date ranchers' kids because I never wanted to be a rancher's wife." She sorted beads and strips of twine into a plastic catch-all container with dozens of different compartments.

"Does this feel awkward to you?" she asked without meeting his gaze.

"What? Me bein' in your camper?"

"That, and the fact that we'll be spending a lot of time together over the next few weeks. An hour ago, we were strangers who'd spoken just one time and now we've played a pretty intense round of tonsil hockey, and here we are alone."

He laughed. "If I think too hard on it, yeah, it'd seem weird. But I approached you, London. I figured that my offer would catch you off guard."

"As I'm sure my counter offer did you."

"Yeah. Well, I ain't exactly sure how that'll work."

London's shoulders stiffened.

"That came out wrong. What I meant is we're acting like a couple only on the weekends?"

"Saturdays are my workshops, so I'd like you to be around after my sessions end."

"Not before?"

"I don't expect world champion steer wrestler Sutton Grant to stand around holding my clipboard and collecting payments."

"You'd be surprised at what I'd do to get a sense of purpose these days," he said dryly.

She smiled and kept packing stuff away. "If the rodeo finals are held on Sunday, there's usually a dance Saturday night. I'd like to put in an appearance because that'd be normal for me. And since we're together..." She glanced up at him. "Speaking of, what will we tell those nosy people who ask how we ended up falling in *lurve* so suddenly?"

Sutton scratched his chin. He really needed to shave. And make sure he didn't dress like a bum. No daily schedule meant he'd gotten lax on dressing the cowboy way, as he'd done for years. "How about the truth? I was havin' behavioral issues with Dial. I knew you'd trained him so I asked you for help. We spent a lot of time together and that's our *lurve* story."

"Perfect." She snapped the locks on her huge plastic tote. "Done."

"What is all that anyway?"

"Like I said, creative chaos. I'm the super high-energy type, which means I always need to be doing something. Making jewelry forces me to focus and slow down. It's a hobby, but since I'm so task oriented, I'm very prolific."

He could see that. "How many pieces you finish in a night?"

London shrugged. "At least two. Some nights as many as ten."

"Sweet Christ, woman. What do you do with them?"

"They're in plastic tubs in the bedroom. Hell, I think there might even be some tubs on the bed. Not like the bed has seen any action lately."

We could remedy that. Right now.

She seemed embarrassed by her confession. Before she fled, Sutton hooked a finger in her belt loop, stopping her.

"Whoa there. No running away. Especially not in here since there's no room for me to chase you, darlin'."

Her eyes blazed. "Let go."

"Nope. You're gonna tell me what you meant when you said the bed hadn't seen any action."

"That's none of your damn business."

"Wrong. Every low-down dirty personal detail about you is now my business bein's we're a couple in *lurve*." To reinforce his point, he crowded her against the cabinet. "If I remember correctly, you said your ex broke up with you a month ago. So it's been a month since that mattress has had a real pounding?"

"That mattress has been jostled and bounced, but it's *never* been pounded."

Sutton quirked an eyebrow. "Stitch too much of a gentleman to give you a good hard fuck?"

The fire in her eyes died. "Just drop it."

"How long's it been for you, London?"

"Four months."

"Motherfuckin' hell. What was wrong with that asswipe? He had sexy you in his bed and he left you alone for three goddamned months?"

"Yes. Apparently he was getting what he needed from Paige so he didn't touch me. I made excuses for his behavior. He was stressed, I was too pushy, I was too kinky. You name it, I took the blame." She sighed and studied the logo on his shirt again.

"No sirree. You ain't takin' the blame for him bein' a total douchenozzle."

That brought a smile.

"And I will tell you something else."

"What?"

"I will take complete blame for this." Sutton's mouth crashed down on hers. With every insistent sweep of his tongue, with every sweet and heady taste of her, his pulse hammered and his cock hardened. He imagined hoisting her onto the counter and driving into her, finding out firsthand where her kink started and how hard she'd let him push her. The second kiss was hotter than the first. Once the embers started smoldering, it wouldn't be long before they ignited.

She kissed him back with the same hot need. By the time they ended the kiss, they were both breathing hard and staring at each other with something akin to shock.

Then London nestled the side of her face against his chest. "Okay. Wow. Normally I'd say, whoa, let's take a step back, but all I can think is I'd rather take a running step forward straight to my bedroom."

"In due time, darlin'."

"You busy right now? Or are you just out of condoms?"

He stroked her hair and smiled against the top of her head. After a bit he said, "Yeah, I'm out of condoms. Haven't needed them."

She lifted her head and looked at him. "What? A hot, built guy like you ain't getting any at all?"

"Nope. You said it's been four months for you? I've got you beat. It's been over nine months for me. Since before my accident."

London's skeptical gaze roamed over his face. "Are you just saying that to make me feel less shitty?"

"Why would you think that?"

She slid her hands up his chest and curled her fingers around his jaw. "Because you look like this."

He blushed. "Now you're just bein' ridiculous."

"You can't honestly tell me you don't have women hitting on you all the freakin' time."

"Not lately, bein's I've been holed up at home recovering. Ain't a lot of women prowling around my place. My dogs tend to run them off."

"Sutton. I'm serious."

"So am I." He counted to five. "Women don't want to see a man struggling to put himself back together. It's easier to go it alone. I found that out the hard way the first time." He tugged her hands away from his face, sidestepping her and the topic. "So is there a dance tonight?"

His abrupt subject change perplexed her. "Yeah, but I'd decided to skip it."

Sutton angled his head toward her box of jewelry supplies. "Got other plans?"

"Maybe." London pointed to the back of the camper. "Got a mattress that needs pounding. And darlin'"—she gave him a hungry, full-body perusal—"you look completely recovered to me."

"Much as I'd love to take you up on that offer, ain't gonna happen today."

"Why not?"

"Because even before my injury I wasn't the kind of guy to indulge in indiscriminate sex." That made him sound like a total pussy. He made light of it. "That's why they call me 'The Saint,' remember? Plus, I'm gonna make you at least buy me dinner first."

"There's a box of Corn Pops in the cupboard. And the milk is fresh." She waggled her eyebrows. "I'd totally give it away to you for free."

He laughed. "Taunting me won't change my mind."

"So saintly you is leaving *just* when it's starting to get interesting?"

"Yep. I said my piece. Come by tomorrow when you get done here. I'll be around." He picked up the clipboard and scrawled his address and phone number in the last box where she'd written—*D.L. A-ride.* "Didja get my joke?"

"Dial a ride? Yes. Not funny."

"I've heard that before too."

"What?"

"That I lack a sense of humor and I'm always too serious about everything. So with that..." He headed for the door.

London grabbed his hand. "Did I scare you off by being too aggressive? Is that why you're slinking outta here like a scalded cat?"

"No." He said, "No," again more forcefully when her eyes remained skeptical. "I like that you know what you want—I'll never judge you for that. This all happened fast. You kissed me once; I kissed you once. I'm guessing the heat between us surprised us both, and hot stuff, ain't no doubt there's an inferno between us just waiting to ignite. We both need to think about it and decide how far this is gonna go before it blows up in our faces. But it's not happening an hour after we reconnected. And not ten steps from a bed."

"For the record, can I say I hate that you're right?" She plucked up the clipboard and clutched it to her chest. "I didn't even like you an hour ago. Now I'm pissy that you won't test the bounce factor of my mattress, so obviously my head isn't clear."

"Lust and reason rarely go hand in hand." Sutton let his gaze move over her, making sure she knew he liked what he saw. "Let's let reason win today."

"Fine. But it doesn't feel like much of a victory."

"For me either, sweetheart."

After Sutton exited London's camper, he headed straight for his truck. Unlike past years on the rodeo circuit, no one stopped him to chat. No one recognized him. That would've bothered him when he'd been trying to make a name for himself. Now it just drove home the point he was done with the world of rodeo.

Or he would be, as soon as Dial had regained some of what he'd lost. Only then could Sutton find an owner that saw the workhorse beneath the spirited nature.

The drive to his place passed quickly. At home he fed Dial and talked to him about London, mostly out of habit. There were times on the road when Sutton had felt his horse was his only friend—totally fucked up, but true. Dial wasn't just a tool to him. Most of the time the opposite was true. Dial needed the challenge of those moments on the dirt. Sutton needed the moments on the dirt as a means to an end.

Over the years, socialization had gotten easier for him, but in the beginning on the circuit, he'd remained in the background, barely speaking because he'd always been painfully shy. Early on most folks considered him conceited, but he couldn't help people seeing what they wanted to. Rather than hit the wild parties after a competition, he hid in his horse trailer and watched DVDs.

That's not to say Sutton didn't have friends—just none of them, with the exception of Breck Christianson, were professional rodeo competitors. Plenty of buckle bunnies had sniffed around him from day one. But he'd understood early on that it wasn't him personally those women saw, but him as a meal ticket.

After Charlotte dumped him and he'd survived his recovery, he'd returned to life on the blacktop and lost some of his reserve. He hadn't gone hog wild as much as he'd learned to separate love from sex. Being in a serious relationship at such a young age hadn't given him any experience with no-strings-attached, let's-fuck-just-because-it-feels-amazing kind of sex and he quickly became a huge fan of it. But even then, his sexual exploits were nowhere near what his fellow road dogs were indulging in. And he'd yet to find a woman willing to let him explore his darker side. So, he'd let her set the initial parameters and then he'd push the sassy cowgirl's boundaries.

As he walked back up to his house from the corral, it reminded him how much he loved being at home. His house was his one indulgence. Basic on the outside. But inside? Big rooms, open space. A man his size needed room to move around. And because he'd had the house built from the ground up, he'd installed an underground shooting range. The basement, dug a level deeper than most, was literally his fortress. The concrete bunker that ran a 100 yards beneath his house was completely soundproofed and fully ventilated. He could fire ten clips from an AR-15 and anyone sitting in his living room wouldn't hear even a small pop.

His private shooting range wasn't something he broadcasted, lest he get called a gun nut or a freak preparing a bunker for the end of days—neither of which were true. But he'd always been drawn to guns. Not for hunting, not for collecting, but for the actual skill it takes in shooting all types of firearms. If he hadn't been offered a college scholarship for rodeo, he would've gone into the army. And he'd taken perverse pleasure in turning the indoor "dog run" that Charlotte insisted on for her stupid poodles into a regulation competitive shooting range with all the bells and whistles he could legally buy.

Not only had the shooting range saved his sanity during his recovery period this go around, but being home for longer than a week at a time, he'd had a chance to hang out with other guys with the same passion.

Passion. He'd had passion for his sport and passion for his hobby, but passion for a woman had been missing long before his accident.

It'd shocked him how quickly passion had sparked to life with London Gradsky today. He liked the challenge of her. His thoughts scrolled back to that day she'd given him what-for when she'd found out he'd bought Dial. The fire flashing in her eyes, the over-the-top hand gestures. He admired that she didn't hold back her true nature.

She might be used to getting her own way on the dirt, but guaranteed he didn't get roped into this situation without planning to take some risks of his own.

Chapter Four

Winning four steer wrestling world championships must've paid well because Sutton Grant had a gorgeous house. A ranch style with southwestern elements. The corral spanned the distance between the house and the big metal barn-like building on the left side. A three-car garage on the right side balanced out the sprawling structure.

It was obvious this house had no full-time female occupant. No flowers or landscaping beyond a few bushes beneath the front windows. The reverse U-shaped driveway was unique, giving her the choice to pull up to the garage, follow the wide swath of blacktop and park in front of the house or pull up to the metal outbuilding.

Before she could decide which would be the best parking option, Sutton strolled out the front door sans shirt. When she tore her gaze away from his muscled torso and saw he was wearing pants—pity that—and that he was barefoot, she hit the brakes hard. Nothing on earth was sexier than a bare-chested barefoot man in faded jeans. Nothing.

Sutton meandered over.

She unrolled her window but gazed straight ahead at the garage door instead of his mesmerizing chest.

"Hey. I wasn't expecting you so early."

"Did I interrupt something? Because I can come back."

"Why would you think you interrupted something?"

Because you're half-dressed and I'm pretty sure if I look down at your holy fuck washboard abs, I'll see the top button on your jeans is undone. Then I'll imagine you were lounging naked in bed when you heard a car pull up and you're probably commando beneath those body-hugging jeans.

Jesus. She even sounded like a breathless twit in her head.

"London. Why aren't you lookin' at me?"

"Because you've got way too few clothes on." *And I've got way too many ideas on what to do with a hot, half-naked man.*

A rough-tipped finger traced the length of her arm down from the ball of her shoulder, pausing to caress the crease in her elbow, and continuing down her forearm and wrist, stopping to sweep his thumb across her knuckles. "You could even things up, darlin'. Get rid of that pesky shirt and bra."

"I'm not wearing a bra," slipped out.

Sutton sucked in a sharp breath. "Prove it."

London's head snapped around so fast she might need to find a neck brace. Her indignation vanished when she saw his dimpled grin.

"That gotcha to look at me."

"Jerk."

Keeping his eyes on hers, he gently uncurled her fingers from her grip on the steering wheel. "Let's start over. Good afternoon, London. You're lookin' pretty today. I'm happy to see you. There's a concrete slab on the far side of the barn where you can park your camper."

"Thanks."

"You're welcome."

Sutton continued staring and touching just the back of her hand in a manner that should've been sweet but sent hot ripples of awareness vibrating through her. "Uh, I'll just go park now."

He released her hand and her eyes. "Need help?"

"Nah. I've done this a million times." She drove along the front of the house, cutting the turn wide when she started down the driveway. Then she put it in reverse and cranked it hard, perfectly lining it up alongside the building. After she climbed out of the truck, she saw Sutton had already unhooked the camper from the ball hitch. "Thanks."

"My pleasure. You wanna grab the stabilizer blocks?"

She lifted them out of the back of the truck and set them on the ground.

Sutton had them in place in seconds. Then he stood and brushed the dirt from his palms.

Her focus had stuck on how the muscles in his arms flexed. Given his bulked up state, it didn't look like the man had spent the last eight months recuperating from injuries.

"London?"

She met his amused gaze. "Did I say something?"

"Not with your mouth, darlin', but you are sayin' a whole lot with them burning hot eyes of yours."

"Sorry."

"Don't be. You need help hauling anything into the house?"

London frowned. "No. But if you'll show me where I can plug in—"

"No." Then Sutton crowded her, trapping her against the side of her camper with his arm right by her face. "I'm a single guy with a four-bedroom house. There's no reason for you to stay in your camper."

Good Lord his muscles were even more impressive this close up. What weight exercise did he do to get that deep cut in his biceps? She could probably stick her tongue halfway into that groove. Then she could follow that groove down... Way down.

Stop. Mentally. Licking. Him.

"London?"

She cleared her throat. "I can think of a reason."

"What?"

Scrambled by his nearness, she said, "I snore really loud."

"I'll wear earplugs."

"I get up at least twice every night to use the bathroom."

"You have a private bathroom in your room."

"I'm messy. Really messy."

"I have a housekeeper."

She was losing this battle. *Think, London, because if you can't come up with a plausible reason to stay out of his house, guaranteed you'll be in his bed.*

"That's what I'm hoping for."

Her gaze zoomed to his. "What are you hoping for?"

"That you'll end up in my bed. Or I'll end up in yours."

Jesus. She'd said that out loud.

Grinning, he pushed back. "Come on. I'll show you the guest room."

She followed him inside. The entrance opened up into a big foyer with tile floors. Beyond the pillars separating the entrance from the hallways going either direction, she saw a great room with a fireplace, a man-sized flat screen, and puffy couches. Windows overlooked a patio. The living area melded into an open kitchen and small dining room. No bachelor bland in Sutton's abode. The colors were masculine; rust, dark brown, and tan, yet the coffee table, dining room table and chairs, and end tables were light rough-sawn wood.

"What a gorgeous space. Did you decorate it?"

"Not on your life." He snagged a black wife beater off the back of the sofa and yanked it on over his head. "I told my mom what I wanted, well, mostly what I *didn't* want, and she supervised since I wasn't around much."

"She lives close by?"

"A few miles up the road. This house is actually on the far corner of the ranch."

"Handy."

"My brothers each have their own places too."

"There are worse things than having your family as your closest neighbors."

Sutton flipped a switch and light flooded the hallway. "We've never had a problem with it. What about you? I don't remember how many siblings you've got."

"Two. My older brother, Macon, is an attorney in Denver. My younger sister, Stirling, received her masters' degrees in biology, genetics, and animal science." London held her breath, waiting for the inevitable question. *What's your degree in?* Yeah, she bristled at being the lone Gradsky kid without a college education. Instead, she'd chosen the "school of hard knocks" route.

"So you're a middle child, too?"

She slowly exhaled. "Yep."

"My oldest brother, Wynton, ranches with our dad, as does my younger brother, Creston."

"Wynton, Sutton, Creston; masculine names for strapping western ranching sons."

He leveled her with a look. "I'd think a woman named London wouldn't poke fun."

"I'm not. What are your folk's first names?"

"Jim and Sue. Mom wanted something unique for us, but personally I'd rather be Bill or Bob or Joe." He took a few steps down the hallway. "Here's the bathroom."

"At least your mother didn't go with a theme. My dad's full name is Charleston Gradsky, and he hates it so he goes by Chuck. But that didn't deter Mom from picking a southern city as my brother's name."

"So you're London because she's Berlin? Why didn't she name your sister Paris?"

She whapped him in the arm. "Too easy. She narrowed her choices to Stirling, which is a town in Scotland, or Valencia, a town in Spain. She hated the idea that Valencia could be shortened to Val. God forbid one of her kids would have a somewhat normal name."

"Wynton never uses his full name. He's gone by Wyn since he started school. Same with Cres. But ain't no way to shorten Sutton."

"Or London."

They smiled at each other.

Sutton opened his mouth to say something then shook his head. He turned and started down the hallway. They passed two closed doors and he opened the third. "This is the guest room." He pointed. "Bathroom is through that door."

"This is really nice." The space was simple, tan walls with oak trim and oatmeal colored Berber carpet. Centered on the longest wall was a big brass bed sporting a Denver Broncos bedspread. Next to it was a nightstand with a matching orange and blue desk lamp. Opposite sat an antique dresser with a TV on top. Shades covered the windows, leaving the room cool and dark—just like she liked it. Some summer nights her camper was like sleeping in a tin can. "You've convinced me to crash here, although I'll point out it's a good thing I'm not a Kansas City Chiefs super fan."

"Bite your tongue, darlin'. Them's fightin' words."

She peeked into the bathroom. Same Broncos theme. When she looked at him again, she casually asked, "Where's your room?"

"At the other end of the hallway. There are two bedrooms on this side and two on that side." He smirked. "So yes, your room is as far from mine as it gets."

How was she supposed to respond? Good? Or that sucks?

"Need help unloading your stuff?"

"No. My stuff is scattered throughout my camper, and I need to dig it out first."

"Okay. If you need anything, holler." Then he left the room.

London used the facilities and figured out the bare minimum of what she'd need. She practically tiptoed down the hallway, leaving the front door unlatched so she wouldn't disturb Sutton with the door slamming.

She had packed a suitcase—full of dirty clothes—and set it outside hoping laundry privileges were included in her guest status. She unearthed a duffel bag and shoved the few clean clothes inside along with her makeup bag. Her laptop bag held all of her electronics and charging cords. Then she figured she'd need her boots and hat, which were in the back of her club cab. Since she'd be dealing with Dial, a notoriously stubborn horse, a crop would come in handy. She rooted around under the seat until she found it.

Looking at the pile, she wished she'd taken Sutton up on his offer of help. She slipped the strap of the duffel over her left shoulder and the laptop strap over the right. Hat on her head, boots teetering precariously on top of the zipped duffel, she reached for the suitcase handle.

"You'd rather sprain your damn neck than accept my help?"

She whirled around. Her hat, boots, and crop went flying. "Don't sneak up on me like that!"

Sutton picked up her riding crop and muttered, "I oughta use this on you."

"Okay."

He shot her a look.

She didn't break eye contact. Neither did he.

Then he offered her a mysterious smile, grabbed the suitcase and rolled it to the front door.

Whew. Talk about a hot moment. Scooping her hat onto her head, she trudged behind him. She met Sutton in the hallway. "When you're done getting settled, I'll be in the kitchen."

I don't know if I'll ever be settled around you.

Not only was he…oh, a fucking dream man with those looks, those eyes, that body, enough amazing attributes to make any man cocky, he rarely acted that way. If she didn't know better, she'd swear the man was…shy.

Nah. He couldn't be.

Why not? Why do you think you know him? You've met the man one time. You've heard your parents talk about him, but you've had exactly one hour-long conversation with him.

But he hadn't shied away from kissing her or from accepting her challenge to act like her boyfriend. And he'd all but told her she was crashing in his house, not her camper.

Those were the actions of a self-confident person, not the shy, retiring type.

Since when are those traits mutually exclusive?

Maybe she should stop staring at the closed door like an idiot, clean herself up, and go talk to him.

London changed from shorts into jeans. Hopefully the flies weren't bad and she wouldn't regret wearing a T-shirt instead of switching to a long-sleeved blouse. She tried to run a comb through her hair since she'd had the windows down on the way here, but the brush got stuck so she finger-combed it into a low ponytail. Not the best look, but she was headed into the pasture for the next couple of hours and bad hair days were why God had invented hats.

As she wandered down the hallway, she expected to hear the TV or maybe music, but the house remained quiet. She turned the corner into the kitchen and saw bags of groceries strewn across the quartz countertops. Whoa. That was a lot of food.

Sutton slammed the cupboard door and spun around. He seemed startled to see her. "Oh. There you are. That was fast."

She shrugged. "I travel light. And I'm not much of a primper anyway." Which is probably part of the reason her ex upgraded to a more feminine model. "What's all this food for? You having a party? Feeding an army?"

He ran his hand over the top of his head in a nervous gesture. "The food is for you, actually."

"All of it? Do I look like I eat like a fucking Broncos linebacker or something?" she asked sharply.

"No. Jesus." Bracing his hands on the counter, he hung his head. "Look. I suck at this kinda stuff, okay? I never have anyone stay with me, say nothin' of a woman. I figured I oughta stock up on girl food—yogurt, salad, fruit, diet soda, double-stuff Oreos—but I reached the checkout and realized I'd bought nothin' for me. Then I worried maybe you didn't like the stuff I'd picked so I ended up buying more. Now I'm staring at it, embarrassed as hell, knowing you'll see all this food and think I'm some kind of freak for assuming we'll eat together at all."

Oh yeah. The man really was shy and unsure. And very, very sweet, worrying how *she'd* take *his* thoughtfulness in providing food for her. Impulsively, she ducked under his arm and set her hands on his chest. "Sutton Grant. You are a saint and a total sweetheart, and forgive me for acting like a thankless dick."

"You're not upset?"

"Only that you'd assume I eat girl food. Dude, I'm meat and potatoes all the way." His heart thumped beneath her palm but he didn't touch her. "Then again, I eat salad and other healthy stuff so I can eat Oreos."

"I also bought cookies and cream ice cream."

She licked her lips. "Another fave of mine. I always say I'll have a little taste, but it never works out that way. I end up wanting more."

"I know how that goes," he murmured.

His gaze seemed stuck on her mouth.

As much as she wanted him to kiss her, she knew he wouldn't. Not without a clear sign from her. "How about I help you put these groceries away?"

He retreated. "I'd appreciate it."

"Then I'll head out and catch Dial and see where we're at."

Chapter Five

Dial proved to be his usual dickish self to London.

Which was a relief. Sutton half expected the gelding would make him look like a fool by being compliant.

London suggested Sutton stay on the outside of the corral that way Dial knew she was in charge.

It took her thirty minutes to catch him and put a halter on him. Dial didn't fight the saddle, but he needed the riding crop to get him moving.

For the next hour, he watched, mesmerized as London worked Dial over with a combination of firmness and a loving touch. He'd expected her to reward the horse with oats after she unsaddled him, removed the training bit and bridle, and thoroughly brushed him down. But she merely looked into his eyes and stroked his head as she spoke to him.

For once, Dial stood still.

Yeah, Sutton wouldn't move either if London had her hands all over him as she murmured in his ear.

Since the moment she'd driven up, her interest in him still apparent after he'd given her some time to think it over, he realized that pretending they were crazy about each other wouldn't be a problem.

London bounded across the corral, her dark ponytail swinging behind her. She was long and lean—it looked like a strong wind could knock her over, so it was hard to imagine her forcing her will on animals five times her size. He'd watched as she'd approached Dial, and her presence exceeded the size of her body.

She exited through the gate and he walked over to meet her halfway. "You all right?"

"Sore."

"Where?" he asked, alarmed.

"Don't worry. Just my arms and neck, nothing serious. Dial gets it in his head to resist and he pulls like a damn draft horse."

"You're welcome to use my hot tub if you think it'll help loosen your muscles."

London tipped her head back and squinted at him, raising her hand to block the sun. "You being a nice guy ain't an act, is it?"

"You run into guys like that? Where it's an act?"

"Guys who are assholes beneath the slicked up public persona? Yep. That's how most of them are."

Sutton started walking toward the house. "I didn't see the point in maintaining a public and a private face. If it wasn't for sponsor's requirements, I wouldn't have any public presence in the world of rodeo."

"So the perfect day at the rodeo for you?"

"Do my runs. Take my turn as a hazer. Collect my check and visit with the rodeo officials and coordinators. Hop in my truck and haul my horse home. Then have a beer on my back patio and reflect on my performance—whether I win or lose." He shot London a sideways glance. "Pretty boring, huh?"

"Not at all." When she looped her arm through his, he managed to keep his feet moving instead of stumbling over them. "Attitudes of entitlement among the rodeo participants is why I rarely take jobs with them. They want me to fix a horse in a day, when the problem's usually been years in the making. They've watched 'The Horse Whisperer' way too many times and they believe that shit is real."

"You mean that one session with Dial didn't cure him?"

"Not. Even. Close."

"Dammit. Way to dash my hopes. You're fired."

London hip-checked him.

They fell silent on the rest of the short walk, but London didn't pull away until they reached the patio. "This is such a great space. No neighbors, no traffic noises, no cattle. I could sit out here for hours and just enjoy the solitude."

"Hang tight. I'll grab us a couple of beers."

"Sounds good."

When Sutton returned, he saw that London had ditched her hat and her boots. With her face aimed toward the sky, her dark hair swaying in the breeze, a slight smile on those full lips and the sexy way she spread her toes out in the patch of sunshine, he was absolutely poleaxed. Not only by lust, but by the premonition this would be the first of many times they'd be together like this.

You wish.

When she opened her eyes and smiled at him, lust muscled aside any feelings of destiny. He ached to see her mouth wrapped around his cock. He wanted to see the diamond pattern from the metal table imbedded in her skin after he pinned her to it and fucked her hard.

"Sutton? You okay?"

"Yep." He handed her a Bud Light.

"This is perfect. Thank you."

He sipped and asked the question that'd been weighing on him. "So what's the deal with Dial?"

She expelled a long sigh. "He's got deep-seated anxiety about his ability to perform, not only to the level he's reached, but on any level at all. He feels he's being punished for a mistake that clearly wasn't his fault. And in horse years, that punishment seems like years instead of months. So he's resentful of you and the only way he can show that resentment is by not doing what you ask or demand of him."

Sutton's jaw dropped. "Are you freakin' kidding me?"

London laughed. "Of course I'm bullshitting you, bulldogger. Sheesh. That kinda psychobabble about a horse's psyche is a bunch of horseshit—pardon the pun. Dial hasn't been worked with for months. He's rusty. He's ornery. Does he miss being a workhorse and doin' what he was trained to do? No idea. Alls I can do is hope the training we both did over the years kicks in at some point." She swigged her beer. "It ain't a one day fix. But hell, maybe he'll snap back to it and he'll be ready to hit the dirt in a week."

There was his nightmare scenario.

She leaned forward and pulled a folded piece of paper out of her back pocket and dropped it in front of him. "Take a look at those numbers."

"What's this?"

"My rates."

He unfolded the paper. Stopped himself from whistling when he saw the amount. London Gradsky commanded a pretty penny for working with pretty ponies.

"Of course, I wrote that out yesterday before you offered me room and board."

"So do you need a pen so you can refigure the amount?" he teased.

"Nice try, but no. The dollar amount stays the same, but I'll double the amount of time I work with Dial until there are results."

"Sounds fair." He offered his hand and she shook it.

A meadowlark trilled and she smiled. "Your house is centrally located to how far I have to drive to my clients. I will be so glad not to have to leave my camper at a campsite."

"I'll be a snoopy bastard and ask why you've distanced yourself from Grade A Farms. Your folks know about you living in your camper, parking at different campsites every night?"

"No. And please don't tell them." She paused. "My parents are great people. No complaints on the familial relationship. But their business goals are different than mine. They breed horses and sell them. They're shrewd in that they demand stud and genetic shares from those sales, but refuse to get into the sperm collecting and artificial insemination portion of the business. For a while they were trying to fit each high-end horse to the specific rodeo discipline. I was all for that."

"They don't do that anymore?"

"Nope."

"What happened?"

"My big shot lawyer brother stuck his nose in. He created a spreadsheet that showed how much money they lost in a five-year period by doing it that way and cross referenced it with the number of national champions who were using Grade A livestock to compete. They were losing capital for a few lousy bragging rights. They revamped their policies, which is why they had no issue selling Dial to you."

"So you weren't really pissed off at me for suggesting they castrate Dial?"

"Oh, I was plenty pissed off at you about that. I'd had my sights set on breeding him with a gorgeous paint. She was sturdy, sweet-tempered, and would've done fine with the beast mounting her. Anyway, that was when I knew I had to fully strike out on my own. While some aspects of what I do are still the same, I'm not in the same place, day in, day out. My clients are varied, not just monied rodeo stars. Plus, I've tried other training disciplines, not just the ones my dad used." London nudged his knee with her foot. "You played a part in me making that decision."

"Then I think I deserve a deeper discount on your services."

She laughed. "Don't push your luck."

Sutton stood and held out his hand. "Time to earn your keep, whip cracker."

London took his hand without hesitation. "Which is what?"

"Helping me get supper on the table."

* * * *

Later that night they sat side by side on the swing on the patio, watching the flames crackle in the fire pit.

They'd shared a meal together, cleaned up together, and talked about everything under the sun, except rodeo and horses. Sutton expected she'd bring up the other part of their deal, acting like a couple. One thing he hadn't been clear on was whether they were telling their families they were involved or if the only place they were "out" was on the weekends at the fairgrounds. The other thing he needed to know? If London was trying to get Stitch back. He was onboard to help London save face, but he wouldn't be happy if she planned on returning to her ex. He'd played the chump before.

But as the evening wore on, he hadn't asked because it'd been easy—ridiculously so—how well they got along.

Maybe because they were both on their best behavior. Maybe it was something else that Sutton was too superstitious to name. Tempting to let this easy camaraderie lie, but he needed to know exactly where he stood with her. "Did you see Stitch and Paige last night or today?"

"No. I pretty much avoided everyone. Stayed in my camper and worked on some jewelry."

"Why?"

"I figured a few people saw that kiss at the rodeo grounds and I didn't want to explain it. Or you. I wanted to make sure we were on the same page—hah! Poor word choice, being on *that* Paige since that's now Stitch's job—before we put ourselves out there in public."

He nodded.

"So I'm really grateful you opened up your home and we can get to know each other as friends."

Fuck. There was the word he'd feared. "Friends?" he repeated. She sure as fuck hadn't wanted to be friends when she'd practically tackled him to her bed.

"Yeah. I mean you were right to put the brakes on us yesterday. I'm more impulsive in my personal life than I should be. Just like you said, you're the calm, quiet voice of reason. So if we spend this week getting to know each other, on, ah—another level, our relationship will seem less suspicious this weekend when we're together."

"Less like we're literally doin' a horse trade to get something that each of us wants?"

She laughed. "Exactly. Being friends puts us more at ease."

"Because it's all about appearances." That came out with a bitter edge.

"It has to be. I don't want to get caught in a lie. Wouldn't that be the most mortifying thing you can think of?"

No, the most mortifying thing I can think of is getting friend-zoned by you in the first four hours of play.

Damn. No wonder he didn't put himself out there. Good thing he'd asked about their parameters before he'd made a move.

But Sutton had to respect her for taking the time to consider her boundaries when she clearly had none yesterday. Yet, the bottom line for him hadn't changed. He needed London to work his horse—no matter how much he wanted to work her over in his bed nine ways to Sunday.

Friends. He could do that. Hell, he oughta be used to it by now.

But fuck if he wasn't tired of denying himself, even when it was his own damn fault. Demanding she stay with him in his house. Cooking for her. What people said about him was true. He was too damn nice and accommodating, but he did have an ulterior motive—hot kinky sex. But he didn't want London to feel obliged to fuck him, which sounded ridiculous in his head and would sound even more idiotic if he said it out loud. He needed to retreat, regroup, before he stuck his boot in his mouth.

Sutton forced a yawn and then stood. "Sorry. It's getting late."

London's eyebrows shot up. "Late? It's only eight-thirty."

Shit. "Huh. Well, it seems later than that which is a sign I should call it a night."

"Oh. Well. Sure. Do you mind if I stay up and wash some dirty clothes?"

"Help yourself to whatever you need."

"Thank you. I was afraid I'd be walking around naked tomorrow morning since everything I own is dirty."

Do not think about naked and dirty and London in the same sentence.

Friends, remember?

Repeat it. F-r-i-e-n-d-s.

Still, this was gonna be a long damn week.

Chapter Six

Now London understood why people called Sutton Grant "The Saint."

She'd been trying to get under his skin—okay mostly she'd been trying to get into his Wranglers—for the past four days and the man hadn't been tempted even once, as far as she could tell.

They spent their free time together. She stuck close while he cooked supper, tasting and touching and forcing him to feed her little tidbits. She wore pajama short shorts and a camisole that showed a lot of her skin when they watched TV. When he'd mentioned suffering from a sore neck, she'd offered to give him a massage, but he'd spoken of the personal massager his therapist had lent him. When she'd noticed his razor-stubbled face and volunteered to shave off the scruff, he'd just smiled and said he'd pick up razors next time he went to town.

A saint.

But...London knew he watched her. He watched her work with Dial—from a distance. He watched for her truck to pull into the drive at the end of her workday—from a distance. He watched her doing beadwork—from a distance. But he watched her watching TV up close and personal. He watched her all the damn time.

But that's all the man did. Watched.

What the hell was he waiting for?

Maybe he's been watching you for some sort of sign.

She'd had a huge fucking neon sign over her head from the

moment they'd met that flashed "Available Now!" What more did he need?

Maybe he's not attracted to you.

Wrong. She'd felt his attraction when he'd kissed her. It'd been hard to miss or ignore as it'd dug into her belly.

Maybe he wants to stick to your business deal.

So he was saving his performance for the weekend when he'd have to be all over her?

Performance. Why did that word turn her stomach? Because she wanted it to be more? To be real?

It'd felt real on Saturday as those amazing eyes of his had eaten her up the way she knew his mouth wanted to. It'd felt real on Sunday, seeing his shy, flirting side behind the serious persona. But Monday morning he'd acted buddy-buddy—she'd half expected him to give her a noogie—and it'd been that way between them ever since, no matter how much she tried to turn the sweet saint into a red-hot sinner.

After London parked at Sutton's place, she opted to keep her sour mood to herself and headed straight for the corral rather than stopping inside the house first.

The day had turned out to be a scorcher. She stripped out of her long-sleeved shirt to just her camisole. Grabbing her tack out of the barn, she draped it over the metal railing. She looped the rope around her neck and whistled twice, surprised when Dial came trotting over. They played catch and mouse for a bit, not in an ornery way, but playful and she was happy to see the reappearance of that side of the horse.

This first week she'd planned on earning Dial's trust. He'd balked but each day he made a baby step. Pushing too hard too fast caused backsliding into familiar behavior.

Maybe that's what's going on with Sutton. You're pushing a man to get what you want. What if that's not what he wants?

She'd get to the bottom of it tonight.

Since Dial had shown improvement, London decided to treat him with some oats. She'd sprinkled too many in the bucket and reached in to scoop some back out when Dial tried to crowd her to get his face in the bucket.

"Hey, rude boy, back off." She turned to move the bucket aside and she felt a sharp, hard nip on her upper arm. "Motherfucking son of a whore!" She swung the bucket up and dropped it on the other side of the fence. Something hot and wet flowed down her arm. She expected to see horse slobber but it was blood.

So much for the old wives' tale about horses bolting at the scent of blood. Dial just stared at her, unmoving, his tail flicking back and forth, trying to intimidate her.

Fuck that.

London rose up, making herself as big as possible, staring him right in the eyes. "Back off," she said sharply. "Now."

Dial backed up.

She walked over to where she'd left her shirt. Her arm stung. Small, hard horse bites hurt worse than anything, tender flesh caught between that powerful jaw. It'd been a while since a bite had broken the skin.

"London?"

Shit, shit, shit. She'd hoped she could get inside and cleaned up before seeing Sutton. No such luck.

"What's wrong?" He tried to grab her injured arm to spin her around and she hissed at him, cradling her elbow with her hand. "What the hell happened?"

"Dial bit me."

"Lemme see."

"Not a big deal. It'll be fine once it's cleaned out."

"Let me fucking see it, London. Now."

She glanced up at him.

Fury blazed in his eyes when he saw the blood. "Let's go inside and I'll take a closer look." He gently lifted her arm until it was parallel with her shoulder. Then he grabbed her shirt from her free hand and held it beneath the bite to catch the blood. "Hold it like this. Did he get you anywhere else?"

"He's not like a wolf or a dog with sewing machine teeth that just keep attacking. One chomp and that's it."

Muttering something, he looked over at the corral then back at her. "Come on."

Sutton kept his hand on top of hers beneath the wound as he led her into the house through the patio door. She expected he'd stop in the kitchen but he directed her down the hallway opposite of her wing, into his bedroom. She got an image of heavy wood furniture before she found herself in a large bathroom.

He seated her on the toilet—the lid had already been down, an extra point for that—and propped her forearm on a towel on the countertop. "How bad does it hurt?"

"You don't need to make a big deal about this. And don't worry. I won't cry."

Then Sutton was right in her face. "You don't have to be the tough chick with me. Now tell me how bad it hurts."

"It stings. Worse than my foot getting tromped on but not as bad as getting bucked off and landing on my ass."

"That's a starting point." He pushed a loose hank of hair behind her ear. "Sit tight while I dig out my first aid kit."

While Sutton rummaged in a tall cabinet, she checked out the space. No bland white fixtures, tiles, or vanity in here. Gray cabinets with black accents. The countertop was black, the sinks were gray. The walls of the glass-fronted walk-in shower were frosted, but behind that she could see the walls were speckled with the same color scheme. The space was wholly masculine yet classy.

"You ready for me to clean this out and gauge the damage?" he asked softly.

"Shouldn't I ask for your medical qualifications first?"

"Helicopter medic in 'Nam. Did two tours in the medical corps during the Gulf War, then a stint in Iraq and Afghanistan."

London smiled. "And some people say you don't have a sense of humor. Wait, is it considered bathroom humor if you actually crack jokes in the bathroom?"

"Now who's the funny one? So it's okay if I poke around?"

"Take off your belt so I have something to bite down on."

She watched as he uncapped a bottle of antiseptic. Every muscle in her body tightened.

"You weren't kiddin' about needing the strap, were you, darlin'?"

Whoa. She could take that the wrong way—but so could he. She said nothing and shook her head.

"Maybe you'd better look away and focus on something else."

London locked onto the visage that'd distract her—Sutton's handsome face. She knew he'd shaved this morning but dark stubble already coated his cheeks, jaw, and throat. She'd fallen into a fantasy where he left beard burns on her throat as he ravished her when he said, "Doin' okay?"

"I guess." She hissed at the stinging spray.

"This stuff will kick in soon and it has a numbing agent."

"How bad does it look? Is the skin flapping so I'll need stitches?"

"No. The bleeding's mostly stopped now." He pressed a gauze pad over the mark.

"Fuck that stings."

"Almost done."

The way he said it... "No, you're not. And if that's the case? I'd rather sit on the counter than the toilet. Then you won't have to bend down and get a crick in your neck." She stood before he could argue. But he curled his hands around her hips and hoisted her up. She automatically widened her knees so he could step between them.

When he reached for her arm, the backs of his knuckles brushed the outside of her breast and her nipple immediately puckered. Because Sutton had his head angled down, she couldn't tell if he'd noticed or not.

But she noticed everything about him. The scent of clean cotton mixed with the darker scent of oil emanating from beneath his starched collar. His full lips were parted as he concentrated on his task, but his breathing stayed steady. She wanted to run her fingers through his dark hair, trap his beautiful face in her hands and suck on those lips until his mouth opened for her kiss. Whisper secrets in his ear while his hair teased her cheek.

Mostly she wanted to ask the question that'd been burning on her tongue for days.

Do it.

"Are you ever going to make a move on me?"

That caught his attention. "What?"

"That wasn't a question to be answered by another question. Just tell me the truth."

Sutton lifted his head. "Where's this coming from, *friend?*"

Hey, was that sarcastic? She squinted at him. "It's coming from the fact we're supposed to be acting like boyfriend and girlfriend and you haven't kissed me or touched me beyond a friendly pat since we were in the camper, and I'm pretty sure kissing and petting is something we need to practice. A lot. So to recap, you haven't touched me since Saturday. It is now Wednesday."

"I know what day it is, London," he said testily.

"Oh yeah? Do you know what I call it? Hump day."

Silence as Sutton taped a chunk of gauze over the bite.

"I thought you'd at least crack a smile at that."

"It's really fucking hard to smile when you're bleeding in my bathroom because my douche-nozzle horse took a bite of you. Sometimes I think that nasty motherfucker deserves to spend his life isolated, and I don't know why I give a shit that he's properly trained since I'd like to ship him off to the damn glue factory."

"He didn't do it on purpose," she said softly.

His angry eyes finally met hers. "The fuck he didn't."

Seeing that fierceness? For *her?* Immediate lady boner.

"Can I tell you a secret, Sutton?"

"What?"

And then she couldn't do it. Couldn't tell him that Dial had shown remarkable progress in just four days. Because if she told him that...then what was his incentive to keep her here?

None.

She couldn't take that chance.

Even if she just had one quick run-in with Stitch this weekend, he'd see firsthand that she wasn't crying in her camper over him. That she'd hooked up with a hot man who sometimes stared at her—when he thought she wasn't looking—like he'd already stripped her naked and was fucking her over the back of his couch.

If it made her a douche-nozzle to fantasize about the shock on her ex's face when he realized his loss was a better man's gain, then so be it; she'd take it.

"London?"

"I like the way you say my name. Classy and dignified, with a hint of sexiness. Makes me wonder how it'd feel to have your mouth on me when you moan it."

"Jesus, London, knock it off."

She frowned. "Okay, that wasn't sexy at all."

"I'm not trying to be sexy with you right now," he snarled—in a decidedly sexy way, not that she'd point that out.

"You should be!" She poked him in the chest. "We're in *lurve*, remember? We are in the throes of a new relationship and that means we oughta be talking about fucking all the time."

"Do you always say the first damn thing that pops into your head?" he demanded.

"Pretty much. No reason to beat around the bush when you could be touching my bush, if you get my drift. See, alls I'd have to do is scoot my butt to the edge of this counter and you could slide inside me. After we're done eating supper, you could spread me out on the dining room table and have me for dessert." She allowed a small smile. "Or I could have you."

"Is there a point to your teasing?"

"That's the thing," she mock-whispered. "I'm not teasing."

While he stood staring at her—*through* her really—she saw his eyes darken as he imagined the exact scenarios she'd just detailed. Then his eyes turned conflicted and a little frosty. "Bullshit."

"What?"

"You're bein' a cock tease. You said you wanted to be *friends*, remember? Wasn't what I wanted, wasn't what I thought you wanted, but I've stuck to those parameters. So we're friends. But every damn time you touch me or get close to me and say such blatantly sexual things, the last goddamn thing I'm thinking about is bein' your friend. I'm a man, not a fucking saint, as I've heard you mutter loud enough for me to hear. You bein' all cute, flirty, funny, and sweet ain't helping me keep the parameters *you* set Sunday night."

Her jaw dropped. "*That's* what you got from our conversation Sunday night? That I just wanted to be friends with you?"

"How else was I supposed to take it?"

"Like it was the talk you demanded we have *before* we got involved on any level! That we'd discuss it. I said *friends* because I didn't think you'd appreciate me saying I'd rather ride *you* all damn night than your horse. And you jumped to the conclusion that *all* I wanted to be with you was friends? Bullshit. You ran away and pouted, bulldogger, when you jumped up and went to bed."

"What should I have done instead?"

"This." London curled her hand around the back of his neck and pulled his mouth to hers. No sweet kiss, no teasing. She fucked his mouth with her tongue like she wanted him to fuck her body. A hot, wet, drawn-out raw mating.

Sutton clamped his hand on her ass and jerked her to the edge of the counter, pressing his groin to hers. Kissing her without pause, holding her in place so he could ravage her mouth and her throat.

After his lips blazed a trail to her nipple, and he sucked on it through the fabric of her cami, she pulled back. "Tell me, bulldogger. Does that feel like I just wanna be friends with you?"

"No. Now give it back. I'm not done with it."

She started to laugh, but it turned into a moan when he pinched the wet tip with his fingers as his mouth reclaimed hers.

Holy hell could the man kiss. And touch. And rub and grind and get her so hot and bothered with her clothes on that she might've had a teeny orgasm right there.

Four loud raps sounded on his outer bedroom door, followed by, "Sutton? Come on. Dad's waiting in the truck."

Sutton froze. Then he broke the kiss and gazed into her face. Any chance she'd had of making light of the situation evaporated when she saw the sexual heat smoldering in those turquoise eyes.

When he brought his thumb up and traced the lower swell of her lip, the intensity pouring from this man might've set off another mini O.

"Sutton? Who's at the door?"

"Cres. We're taking Dad out to the Moose Club for poker night."

"Shouldn't you get going?"

"Yeah. In a minute." He pressed a kiss to her lips, then her chin, then her cheeks. "I'll be back late."

That's when she knew they were done for tonight—all night. She hopped down from the counter. "Thanks for the first aid. I'll go lie down now, but have fun with your family and I'll see you in the morning."

London pushed him out of his bathroom and locked the door.

Let him meet his brother with a hard-on. It'd serve him right for being an idiot.

Friends. What the hell had he been thinking?

* * * *

Sutton's cell phone rang on his nightstand early the next morning, yanking him from a hot dream where he'd taken London up on her offer of an after-dinner treat—except in his version they were on the rug in front of his fireplace, him having his dessert while she also had hers. Sixty-nine usually didn't appeal to him, but in his dream, he didn't have to concentrate on both giving and receiving pleasure—just being naked with her was the pleasure. Warm skin beneath his hands, her skilled mouth, the long trail of her hair teasing up the inside of his thighs...

His phone kept buzzing.

He answered, "Yeah?"

"Grant? It's Ramsey."

Ramsey? Why the hell was his shooting buddy calling him so early? "Do you know what the fuck time it is?"

"Seven. I thought you ranching/cowboy types were up when the cock crows."

"I'm not a rancher, as you well know, so fuck off."

Ramsey laughed.

"What's up? Is your shooting range under fire?"

"Ha. Ha. You're fucking hilarious first thing in the morning."

"Why else would you be calling me? Wait. Are you offering your favorite customers free day passes?"

"You wish. And you're more than just a customer." Ramsey paused. "Look, this might seem like it's coming outta the blue but the truth is we both know that we've skirted this subject for months, so I'll just say it straight out. You're dealing with some heavy shit as far as getting back on track with your career. I recognize restless, man. So I'm not convinced that you want to return to that life on the road."

Sutton had no idea where this conversation was coming from. Wasn't like he'd gotten shitfaced with Ramsey and spilled his guts.

Maybe your lack of enthusiasm about returning to rodeo isn't as disguised as you believe. Your brothers mentioned the same thing in passing. More than once. "Now you've got my attention."

"I appreciate every time you've pitched in and helped out at the gun range. I've hinted around that I could use you on a part-time basis. You've been polite but vague on whether you'd seriously consider it. So maybe you won't give a damn, but I've run into a tricky situation, hence the early morning call."

"What situation?"

"My full-time range master, Berube, got orders and he's being deployed in a month. His deployment will last a year. That leaves me short a range master."

"Which makes me feel your pain as a customer and your friend, but why are you telling me?"

"Because you're an expert shot. You're very knowledgeable about guns without being a know-it-all asshole or a reckless dick."

"But I'm not a range master."

"You'd be a shoo-in to pass the range master's exam—the firearms range testing portion anyway. There's also a written test, but since you've earned a college degree, I'm sure that won't be a problem either."

Ramsey didn't hand out praise lightly, and Sutton found himself feeling proud of something for the first time in months.

"It's short notice, I know, but I'd planned a boys' night out for my instructors at my cabin to discuss the future growth of the gun range. Every guy who works for me will be there, so if you're even remotely interested in the position, this'd be the ideal time to get answers directly from the ones who work with me."

"Just one night? Or an all weekend thing?" He couldn't flake out on London. She expected him to play his part as her boyfriend.

"Just one night. Weekends are our busiest time so we'll be back at work tomorrow."

Two knocks sounded on the door. Then it opened and London walked in.

More like she sashayed in, wearing a see-through flimsy black thing that left nothing to the imagination. He could make out every muscled inch of her toned legs, the slight flare of her hips. Her flat belly and defined abs. Strategically placed bows hid her nipples but not the sweet curve of her tits.

"Sutton? I hope I'm not interrupting. I heard you talking in here so I assumed you were up. Look, I can't figure out the coffee pot. It keeps beeping at me every time I hit start."

Mostly Sutton heard, *blah blah blah* which translated to, "Look at my perky tits," followed by *blah blah blah*, "look at these naughty red panties that barely cover my pussy," and then *blah blah blah*, "look at my sexy bedhead and imagine holding this tangled hair in your fists while I suck your cock."

Fuck me. *Fuck me twice.*

"What the hell? Did you just tell me to fuck off?"

His rational train of thought had hit a fucking brick wall named London Gradsky.

"Sorry, no, I didn't say that. Gimme five minutes and I'll call you right back." Sutton tossed the phone on his bed without checking to see if he'd actually ended the call. "What. In. The. Name. Of. All. That's.

Holy. Are. You. Doing. Half. Fucking. Naked. In. My. Bedroom?"

"I told you! Were you even listening to me?"

Not the words falling from your mouth when your body is speaking its own language loud and clear. He cleared his throat. "I was on the phone, so I missed most of what you'd said. What's the problem?"

"Your coffee pot hates me. I can't figure it out."

"I'll be right there after I slip some pants on." And after he whacked off so she didn't see how hopeful his dick was at seeing a hot, half-naked woman in his room first thing in the morning.

"Fine."

She turned to flounce out and he noticed she wore a thong. So she treated him to a full look at that perfect ass of hers before the crabby, horny man inside him yelled out, "And you'd better put some damn pants on too!"

Even with morning wood it only took him a minute to rub one out in the shower. He brushed his teeth and packed his overnight bag before he exited his room.

In the kitchen, he was both relieved and annoyed to see London had donned a robe.

"Took you long enough," she groused. "You've had coffee ready for me every day this week, so I don't think you understand the importance of coffee in my life. I'm a bitch on wheels without my morning caffeine fix."

"I saw the poor, unfortunate coffee maker that failed to do your bidding, so I'm aware of your demands. Watch and learn." He dumped the beans in and set the lid on the filter basket. "Line up these arrows. This is a grind and brew model. If the arrows aren't lined up, then it won't work at all."

"Oh. Thanks. Now it makes sense."

He smothered a yawn. "You're welcome."

"What time did you get home last night?"

"Late. Dad likes to cut loose on poker night. Especially if he wins. If I'd gotten home earlier, I planned on..." His gaze swept over her, from bedhead to pink-tipped toes. "Never mind what I'd planned 'cause it's a moot point now. That phone call earlier was a reminder that I have a prior commitment. So I'll be gone all day and tonight."

"But you *will* be back by tomorrow? You're coming to the Henry County Fair and Rodeo with me this weekend?"

"Yes. But I'll have to meet you there."

"Promise?"

He scowled. "I'm a man of my word, London."

She scowled back at him. "You'd better be. And where are you going on such short notice anyway?"

Away from temptation. At least for one night. While I figure out why in the hell I like you so much and I've only known you five days. And why that make-out session last night in my damn bathroom was more erotic than any sex I've had in years. "I'm headed out for a retreat."

"A spiritual retreat? Is that why they call you 'The Saint?'"

Sutton rolled his eyes. "I'm called 'The Saint' because I carried a Saint Christopher medallion my grandmother gave me when I first joined the pro tour. The guys saw it and ragged on me endlessly."

"Good to know. I'm assuming the name fit your lifestyle back then?"

"At first they tried calling me 'The Monk' but it didn't stick."

"Why not?"

He pinned her with a look. "Because there's a big difference between bein' a saint and a monk. And newsflash, darlin'... I'm neither."

Flustered, London poured a cup of coffee while the pot still brewed.

"How's your arm today?"

She faced him and shrugged. "Doesn't feel too bad."

"So you're working with Dial this morning?"

"That's what I get paid to do."

His cell phone rang again. He checked the caller ID. Ramsey. Impatient bastard. He tucked his phone in his pocket. "I've got to go. Do you need anything before I do?"

"No."

"You're sure? No issues locking up?"

"I've been in a house in the country by myself before, Sutton."

If she'd shown any fear, he'd open up the locked door and assure her that she was far better protected than she could fathom.

"Wait. There is one thing I want."

When Sutton's eyes met the heat in hers, he knew exactly what she wanted. To avoid temptation, he curled his hands around the straps of his duffel bag and took two steps backward. "I can't. Not now."

"Why not?"

"Because the second I put my hands and mouth on you, we ain't goin' anywhere for the rest of the day. And night. We may even miss the entire Henry County Fair."

A sexy smirk curled her lips. "Then you'd better get going."

Chapter Seven

After London had loaded up her camper and hit the road toward Henry County Fairgrounds, she'd had way too much time to think. And all her thoughts were focused on one super-hottie, Sutton Grant.

Like...what did he do during the day? He wasn't involved in his family's ranching operation. Did he obsessively work out, trying to speed up his rehab and return to competition form? Because heaven knew, the bulldogger had the most banging body she'd ever seen up close and personal. Well, sort of up close and personal. Not that she'd gotten to do more than drool over his sculpted chest, arms and abs, even when the tempting man walked around his house half-naked.

She pondered other things Sutton could be doing with his time. Doing pay-per-view porn in his bedroom? Yeah, she'd pay to see that. Or maybe he was just watching XXX Websites all day. Maybe he played video games. She'd met her fair share of guys who were addicted to their X-box or PlayStation.

Why don't you just ask him?

Yeah, that'd go over well since he'd been so forthcoming about where he was going.

London froze. Wait a damn minute. Had Sutton been purposely vague because he'd set up a bootie call and didn't want her to know? Every time his cell phone rang this week, he'd excused himself to take the call in private.

But hadn't he told her that he hadn't been with a woman since his accident?

And you believed him? A harsh, sarcastic bark of laughter echoed in her head. *Because no man has ever lied about sex.*

Dammit. Had he played her?

Since Stitch had dumped her, she'd second-guessed everything about her attractiveness to the opposite sex, her personality, her sexual skills, and how she conducted herself on a professional level. In her twenty-seven years she'd never been the type of woman who needed validation from a man or a relationship to feel worthy of either.

Sutton Grant had better fall in line. Because he needed her more than she needed him.

* * * *

London had arrived early enough to score a primo parking place in the area specifically marked for rodeo contestants, stock contractors, exhibitors, and vendors. Being part of "tent city" was one of her favorite things about summer rodeo season. Nothing like sitting in front of a bonfire, drinking beer, laughing and talking about horses, rodeo, and the western way of life with other likeminded souls.

She tidied up the camper, deciding if Sutton showed, she'd let him sleep in the bed tonight since his big body wouldn't fit on the convertible sleeping area up front. But she'd be lying if she wasn't hoping they'd share that lumpy mattress sometime this weekend.

Then she changed into an outfit that made her feel sexy and desirable—a sleeveless lavender shirt embellished with purple rhinestones, her beloved b.b. simon crystal encrusted belt, her Miss Me jeans with black studded leather angel wings on the back pockets, and a pair of floral stitched Old Gringo cowgirl boots. She fluffed her hair, letting it fall in loose waves around her shoulders. After applying heavier makeup and a spritz of tangerine and sage perfume, she exited the camper.

The heat of the day hung in the air but the lack of humidity made it bearable. Still, an icy cold beer would make it better. London bought a bottle of Coors and wandered through tent city to see who was around.

The second person she ran into was Mel. "Hey, girl. If I'd known you were already here I'da brought you a frosty beverage."

Mel smiled and kept brushing down her palomino. "It's okay. I've gotta run Plato a bit so I'll take a rain check."

"Deal." London sipped her beer and looked around.

"Please don't tell me you're here so you can spy on Stitch and Paige."

London snorted. "As if. I don't give a hoot about them."

"Since when?"

"Since you told me I needed to get laid. A new guy barged into my life and swept me off my feet last weekend."

Mel stopped brushing Plato's back. "Are you kidding me?"

"Nope. He's hot, he's sweet, and he's crazy about me." London said a little prayer: *don't you let me down Sutton Grant, or so help me God I will superglue your dick and balls together in your sleep.*

"Uh-huh," Mel said skeptically. "But this guy that's so hot for you isn't from around here, is he? So I can't meet him."

"Wrong. He'll be here." She hoped.

Before Mel could demand more details, Stitch's best friend Lee— nicknamed Lelo on the circuit because of his association with Stitch— meandered over. He still wore his back number from the slack competition. "Hey Mel."

"Lelo. How's it hanging?"

"They ain't dangling low at all when I see you. They're high and tight and raring to go."

Mel muttered something.

When it became obvious to Lelo that Mel didn't intend to banter with him, he looked at London. "Hey. What's up?"

"Not much. What's up with you?"

"Askin' around, seein' where the parties are tonight."

A challenge danced in Mel's eyes. "Really, Lelo? Because I heard that Stitch and Paige were having a *huge* party at their campsite before the fireworks kicked off."

Lelo's mouth opened. Then snapped shut.

"I thought maybe you'd come by to invite me personally," Mel continued.

He looked between Mel and London. "Well, I, ah—"

"And since London is here, it'd be rude of you not to include her in that invite, doncha think?"

Jesus, Mel was a shit-stirrer sometimes. And precisely the reason they got along like gangbusters.

"I don't know if that's such a good idea, Mel, bein's they...dammit, you know why I can't invite her," Lelo blurted.

"Because London and Stitch used to date?" Mel flashed her teeth at London. "Water under the bridge, Lelo, since my girl here has herself a new boyfriend."

Shut your face, Mel, shut it right fucking now.

Lelo's eyes went comically wide—as if he hadn't considered that a possibility.

Which pissed London off. Big time.

"You don't say?" he said to London. "I thought you were still—"

"Hung up on Stitch?" Mel supplied. "Huh-uh. That's some bullshit Stitch and Paige have been spreading around so people don't hate him because he fucked London over."

"Mel," London warned.

"What? I'm sick of Opie and Dopie hinting around that you're some broken-hearted chump. Girlfriend, you are hot as lava and you were always way, way above Stitch's pay grade."

Lelo's focus bounced between them like he was watching a volleyball match. Then he said, "So who is this fella you're seein'? Anyone we know?"

Just then someone shouted her name. Someone with a deep, sexy voice.

London sidestepped Lelo and looked down the walkway between the horse trailers. There he was. The quintessential cowboy. And he stood less than fifty yards away. "Sutton?"

"Whatcha waiting for, darlin'? C'mere and gimme some sugar." He held his arms open.

Grinning, she ran toward him. He caught her and spun her in a circle before settling his mouth over hers. She twined her arms around his neck and gave herself over to his kiss.

And what an intoxicating kiss it was. His mouth teased, seduced, inflamed. By the time he eased back to brush tender kisses over her lips and jaw, her entire body shook.

Sutton whispered, "Sorry I'm late."

She nuzzled his neck, wishing she could pop open the buttons on his shirt and get to more skin. "You're here now."

"Did you think I wouldn't show?"

"The thought had crossed my mind."

He forced her to look at him. And her knees went decidedly weak staring into those crystalline eyes of his. "I said I'd be here. I'm a man of my word, London."

Sliding her arms down, she flattened her palms on his chest. "But when you left yesterday morning, you acted pissed off. So what was I supposed to think?"

"That I'm a man of my word," he repeated. He curled his hand around her jaw, denying her the chance to look away. "Ask me why I left my own damn house."

"Why'd you leave?"

"Because my willpower to finish the 'friends' conversation vanished the instant you showed up in my room wearing them baby doll pajamas that oughta be illegal, looking so fucking cute and sexy I had to sneak into my bathroom and whack off before I taught you how to use the coffee maker."

Her mouth dropped open.

"Surprised?"

"Very. You've seemed so...unaffected."

A growling noise rumbled from him before his mouth descended and he kissed the life out of her. She was so damn dizzy when he finally relinquished her lips, she had to fist her hands in his shirt just to keep from toppling over.

Then his breath was hot in her ear, sending shivers down the left side of her body. "Does that seem unaffected to you, sweetheart?"

"Ah. No."

"Good. Maybe you oughta offer me a little reassurance this ain't one sided."

London wreathed her arms around his neck and played with the hair that fell to his nape. "I've left my door cracked open every night, hoping you'd see an open door as an open invitation. I imagined the look on this gorgeous face if you caught me diddling myself."

His eyes darkened. "What did you imagine me doin' if I caught you?"

"Barging in, tying my hands to the brass headboard and driving me crazy with my vibrator before you pounded me into the mattress like you'd promised."

Another low-pitched growl reverberated against her skin. "You and me are gonna get a few things straight tonight. But probably not until after I fuck you hard at least once and swat your ass for you ever doubting me."

Sutton swallowed her gasp with another bone-melting kiss.

When he finally released her lips, she murmured, "You know, I'm not busy right now."

He laughed and pulled back slightly. "How about you introduce me to your friends first? Then I'll feed you."

"You don't have to do that."

"What? Meet your friends?"

"I want you to meet my friends, but you don't have to feed me since you cooked for me all week."

Sutton traced the bottom edge of her lower lip with his thumb. "I've liked having you around this week, London. More than I thought I would." After another kiss, he stepped back only far enough to drape his left arm over her shoulder.

They started toward Mel and Lelo. Mel wore a look of shock only less obvious than Lelo's.

"Did you tell your friends about me?" he asked softly.

"Just that I'd met a hot man. I didn't give them your name in case you didn't show up and I'd have to find me a new guy on the fly."

His arm fell away briefly so he could slap her ass. He grinned when she yelped. Then he whispered, "Oh ye of little faith. 'Fraid I'll have to punish you for that lapse."

"A hot lashing with your tongue or a spanking? Luckily, I'm good with either."

He nipped her earlobe. "Good to know. But it's not like I'm gonna let you choose which one *I* prefer."

"Funny."

"I wasn't joking. Now that you've shared your rope fantasy, I'll add it to mine that involves…you'll just have to wait and see, won't you?"

Holy. Hell. Heat licked the inside of her thighs.

Mel and Lelo stood side by side in front of Plato. Before London could offer introductions, Lelo blurted out, "Man-oh-man, you're Sutton Grant."

Sutton extended his hand. "Yes, I am. Who're you?"

"Lee Lorvin, but everyone calls me Lelo. It's so great to meet you. I'm a huge fan."

"Thanks."

Lelo stared and just kept pumping Sutton's hand until Mel

shouldered him aside.

"Hiya handsome," she cooed. "I'm Mel Lockhart, London's fellow road dog. I too am a huge fan. I watched you win the CRA championship in Vegas the year Tanna Barker also won for barrel racing."

"Nice to meet you, Mel. Glad you were entertained that year."

"Uh, *yeah*, hard not to be jumping up and down outta my seat when you set the record for the fastest time."

London glanced at him, and the man seemed embarrassed by the focus on him. And she wanted to rub Mel's face in the dirt to see if that'd erase her expression of lust.

"So you're a barrel racer?" he asked Mel.

"No. I'm in the cutting horse division. Not as glamorous as the rodeo events people pay to see, but I do well."

"Bein' able to cut cattle out of a large herd is far more challenging and entertaining than any scheduled rodeo event," Sutton said. "It's a real skill that's needed in ranching."

London inwardly sighed at Sutton's sweetness in making sure Mel knew her competitive event was appreciated. What kind of man did that?

"Are you about healed up and ready to get back to competing?" Lelo blurted out, interrupting the conversation.

She felt Sutton stiffen beside her, but outwardly he stayed cool. "I'm in the 'wait and see' stage right now." He turned and kissed London's temple. "Luckily, I sweet talked London into working with my horse again while I'm at loose ends."

"That's right," Mel said. "I remember Berlin told me that London initially trained your horse at Grade A Farms."

"I knew she was the only woman for the job. I just had to convince her to take me on."

"You do have some interesting methods of persuasion, bulldogger."

He laughed. "You're gonna give your friends the wrong impression of me, darlin'."

"Not me," Mel quipped, "because I'm sure hoping you've got a dirty-minded, sweet-talking single brother."

"I've got two."

Mel's lashes fluttered. "They as big and good-looking and charming as you?"

"Mel!" London said with fake admonishment.

"What? It can't hurt to ask." She scooted closer to London to whisper, "You decide to get laid and the next thing I know you've hooked up with the smokin' hottie known as 'The Saint?' Girlfriend, I'm so proud of you I might just bust a button."

Lelo made a noise and they realized he was still staring slack-jawed at Sutton.

"Lelo, you're gonna catch flies if you don't shut your big trap," Mel drawled.

"Sorry. It's just...Sutton Grant. Your runs are damn near perfect. That's why folks call you 'The Saint' because you never screw up."

"Oh, I wouldn't say never. And that's not the only reason I've been called that." He sent London a conspiratorial wink. "But it doesn't apply this week, does it darlin'?"

"Stitch is gonna flip his shit when he meets you."

Ooh, mean-girl London clawed her way to the surface. "Pity then that I'm not invited to Stitch and Paige's party, isn't it?"

Lelo's mouth opened. Closed. Opened again. Then he cleared his throat. "Uh, well, maybe I spoke outta turn. I'm sure Stitch don't have no hard feelin's if you don't, London."

Sutton sent her an amused look. "Up to you darlin', what we do tonight. You know if I had my way we'd head to the camper right now and wouldn't leave until..." His heated head to toe perusal was as powerful as an actual caress. "Until tomorrow. Late tomorrow."

"Looks like you're shit outta luck, Lelo," London said breezily, laughing as Sutton started pulling her away.

Behind Lelo's back, Mel mouthed, "Call me you lucky bitch."

"You know where we'll all be if you change your mind," Lelo shouted after them.

* * * *

"That was fun."

Sutton draped his arm over her shoulder. "How far's your camper?"

She hip-checked him. "Friends first, then food, remember?"

"Right. And I'll bet we aren't skipping Stitch's party?"

"You bet your sexy ass we're not. It's not like we have to stay long, but you do need to put in an appearance for your adoring fans."

"And rub it in Stitch's face that you're no longer pining after him and you've moved on with me?"

London stopped, forcing Sutton to stop.

He faced her. "What?"

"I don't want you to get the wrong impression, Sutton."

"I'm not."

"Are you sure?"

"I don't know darlin', maybe you'd better spell it out for me."

London inhaled a fortifying breath and let it out. "About this deal. After seeing Lelo's reaction to you—to us—I'm glad that other people who've been looking at me with pity will be looking at me in a completely different light when they see us together."

"But?"

She inched closer and twisted her hand in the front of his shirt. "But my reason for wanting you to fuck me until I can't walk isn't for anyone's benefit but mine."

"And mine," he said softly. His eyes searched hers. "So I didn't misread the situation?"

"That what's been happening between us in private the past six days is only to make us look like a real couple in public?"

"Yeah."

"Until I saw you today, I wasn't sure. No, that's not true. I wasn't sure until after you kissed me and told me you'd had to go away because you couldn't *stay* away from me. That's when I knew there's nothing fake about the heat between us."

Sutton curled his hand around the side of her face and gave her a considering look.

"What?"

"You have good insurance on that camper? Because we're gonna set the inside on fire tonight."

The inferno in his eyes nearly torched her clothes. Right there in front of the white tent proclaiming "Jesus Saves." Tempting to shout, "Can I get an amen?!" and then crack jokes about her burning bush.

Instead she slipped her arm around Sutton's waist and pecked those delectable dimples. "Feed me first, bulldogger, then we'll get naked and test the combustible point of the mattress."

Chapter Eight

Sutton couldn't take his eyes off London. He'd catch himself staring at her mouth or those long, reddish-brown curls, or the flex of the muscles in her arm even when she just lifted her fork to eat.

She'd catch him gawking and as a reward, or hell, maybe it was punishment, she'd eye fuck him and run her tongue around her straw until his cock swelled against his zipper.

He leaned forward and grabbed her hand, bringing her knuckles to his mouth for a soft kiss. "You really think we'll make it through the party and the dance?"

"Who said I wanted to go to the dance?"

"You did. Last weekend. You said you always go."

"To the Saturday night dances. It's Friday night."

He raised his hand to the waitress. "Check, please."

London laughed. "Down boy."

"Been a while for me, darlin', and I'll need a round or five to build up my stamina."

"Don't scare me. I do have to climb on a horse the next two afternoons."

"Too bad for you. I plan on making you plenty saddle sore." He smirked. "I'm looking forward to kissing it and making it all better."

She turned her hand, threading their fingers together. "We need to get our minds off sex at least for a little while. Tell me something about you that's surprising."

Besides that I've been cleared to ride and I've been lying to everyone the past four months?

"No pressure. I'll rephrase. I'll go first. I've never been pierced. Your turn."

"Okay. I don't have any ink tattoos."

"But you've had a few rodeo tattoos."

"Yep. Your turn."

"I don't like anything butterscotch flavored."

"I do. Bring on the flavored body paint, baby. I'll lick you clean."

She groaned. "You are killing me. This was supposed to take our minds off sex."

"Darlin', I can't look at you and not think about all the ways I want to make you come. And if you'd prefer that I smear the body paint on your nipples or between your thighs?"

"Both." Her eyes heated. "I'm guessing the application would be as pulse-poundingly erotic as the removal."

"No reason to rush a good thing." He nibbled on the inside of her wrist. "It's your turn."

"My brain is stuck on whether I'd finally start liking the taste of butterscotch if I sucked it off your tongue after you licked it off me."

"Let's test that theory."

"Now?"

"I saw a bottle of butterscotch syrup at the ice cream place. I'll distract them. You swipe it and shove it in your purse."

"'The Saint' contemplating a heist for a dirty sexual scenario? I'm shocked. And more than a little turned on."

"Excuse me. Are you Sutton Grant?"

His gaze reluctantly moved from London's molten bedroom eyes to the guy standing at the end of the table. "That's me."

"I thought so, but I knew you were on the injured list for this season, so I was surprised to see you. Especially here at such a small-potatoes rodeo." He paused. "Are you competing?"

"Nope. I'm here with my girlfriend." He angled his head at London. "She runs a horse clinic."

The guy glanced over at London, and she gave him a finger wave.

"Oh. Wow. Sorry. Didn't mean to interrupt," he said with zero sincerity. "But as long as I'm here, can I get you to sign this?" He shoved a piece of paper at Sutton.

"Sure. What's your name?" Sutton made small talk as he scrawled his name and the date across the program. As soon as he finished, he saw there were several more people who'd lined up. He smiled and kept signing. This was part of the gig for a man in his position, with four championship buckles—the very buckle most of these guys would give their left nut to have a shot at.

After they were alone, he stood and threw some bills on the table. Then he offered London his hand. "Come on."

It'd gotten completely dark. The musical and mechanical sounds from the midway echoed with distortion and the bright lights sent the entire area aglow. "You wanna hit some of the rides before we crash the party?" He swung their joined hands. "Might be romantic to grope each other at the top of the Ferris wheel."

"Not romantic at all because I am a puker. No spinning rides for me."

"Poor deprived girl," he whispered. Then he tugged her into a darkened corner between two storage sheds, pushing her up against a modular home. "How about if I try and get that pretty head of yours spinning another way." Sutton kissed her, starting the kiss out at full throttle. Not easing up until she bumped her hips into his, seeking more contact.

God, she made him hard. He'd never wanted a woman this much, this soon. What sparked between them might be fueled by lust but it also went beyond it—which is what'd sent him running.

For now, he'd focus on that lust.

His hands squeezed her hips and then moved north to her breasts. He broke his lips free from hers and dragged an openmouthed kiss down her throat. When the collar of her shirt kept him from sampling more of her skin, he tugged until the metal snaps popped.

No bra. Nothing to get in the way of taking every bit of that sweet flesh into his mouth to be sucked and licked and tasted.

Her breath stuttered when his teeth enclosed her nipple. She knocked his hat to the ground as she clutched the back of his neck, pressing his mouth deeper against her.

Sutton shoved his thigh between hers. Immediately she rocked her hips against that hard muscle.

"Yes. Right there."

He lost track of all sanity as he nuzzled and suckled her sweet tits, stopping himself from jamming his hand down her pants and feeling her hot and creamy core as he got her off with his fingers. Choosing instead to get her off this way, because fuck, there was something primal about making her come nearly fully clothed.

"Harder."

London's head fell back against the building and she softly gasped his name as he gave her what she needed.

She'd clamped her thighs around his leg so tightly he felt the contractions in her cunt pulsing against his quad. He felt the matching pulse beneath his lips as he drew on that taut nipple. Felt her short nails digging into the back of his neck.

Fucking hell this woman tripped all his wires.

When she loosened her grip on him, he planted kisses up her chest, letting his breath drift along her collarbone, smiling when gooseflesh broke out beneath his questing lips.

"You are no saint, Sutton Grant."

"Nope." He nuzzled the curve of her throat.

"Mmm. Keep kissing me like that while I fix my shirt."

"I'm happy you didn't wear a bra."

"No need for me to wear one, well, probably ever."

"Lucky me."

She rubbed her lips across his ear, raising chills across his skin. "Brace your hands on the building by my head."

"Why?"

She nipped his earlobe. "Because I wanna kiss you."

As soon as he complied, he angled his head so she could better reach his lips.

But London dropped to her knees and started working on his belt.

"Sweet Christ, woman. What are you doin'?"

"Giving you a kiss."

"My mouth is up here."

"That's not where I wanna kiss you."

Any blood left in his head surged to his groin. The one teeny part of his brain that wasn't giving him mental high-fives managed to eke out, "What if someone comes up behind us?"

"You really care about that?" *Pop* went the button on his Wranglers. *Zip* went his zipper. She pulled back the jeans and shifted his boxer-briefs so his dick slid through the opening.

"Fuck, not really. Just giving you an out—holy fucking hell," he said when her hot mouth closed around his cock.

When she eased back and off him, he actually whimpered.

"Oh, bulldogger, you're just big all over, aren't you?"

Before he formed a coherent sentence, she sucked him to the root.

Again.

And again.

And again.

His body throbbed with the need for release. God. It'd been so long.

"London," he managed, "I'm about to…" That warning tingle in his balls lasted barely a blip before his cock spasmed and unloaded. Each hot spurt jerked his shaft into her teeth.

Her mouth worked him until he was utterly spent. He started to feel lightheaded, realizing he'd held his breath. After gulping in oxygen, the fuzzy sensation faded, but he still felt rocked to his core.

Then London was in his face. "Sutton, you'd better do up your jeans."

"Sure." Still in a daze, he pushed off the building. He kept his gaze on hers as he tucked in, zipped up, and buckled. Then he leaned in and kissed her. "Thanks."

"My pleasure."

"Fair is fair though, darlin'."

Her eyes widened. "What do you mean?"

"I wanna taste you. Undo your jeans."

"Sutton—"

"Now."

London's obedience surprised him as well as pleased him. Excitement tinged with fear danced in her eyes as she loosened her belt and unzipped, peeling the denim back. "I don't think—"

He slammed his mouth down on hers. Kissing her with a teasing glide of his tongue and soft licks, he pressed his palm over her belly, slowly sliding his hand over the rise of her mound and into her panties. When his middle finger breached the slick heat of her sex, he smiled, breaking their kiss. "You're wet," he said, his breath on her lips.

"Yes."

"It's so fucking hot that you're wet after blowing me." He followed the slit down to her center where all the sweetness pooled. After swirling his fingertips through her cream, he worked his hand out. Then he pushed back so only a few inches separated their faces and brought his hand up, letting her see the wetness glistening there, hyperaware they were close enough she could smell her own arousal.

Sutton slipped his fingers into his mouth and sucked the sweet juices, briefly closing his eyes to savor this first taste of her.

Before he completely pulled his fingers free, London was right there. Licking his fingers, tasting herself on him, sucking on his tongue. The kiss could've soared past the combustible stage, then neither of them would've been able to stop. But something made him hold back, turn the kiss into a promise of more to come as he dialed down the urgency. Easing back, he let his hands wander, wanting all of her but willing to wait until he could have her the way he needed.

London sensed the shift too. She fastened her jeans and fixed her belt. Her gaze finally hooked his, but he couldn't read her.

He traced the edge of her jaw. "What?"

"You pack a powerful punch, Sutton Grant."

"Same could be said about you, Miz Gradsky." Knowing they needed a break from the intensity, he reached down and grabbed his hat and settled it on his head. "You still wanna hit the party?"

"Of course. Now we've got a really good excuse for being fashionably late."

"So if someone asks where we've been?"

"I'll say we were messing around and lost track of time." She smoothed her hands over her hair and straightened her clothes. "It's the truth."

They returned to tent city hand in hand. The party wasn't hard to find.

Several guys stopped London to chat, and he had a surge of jealousy even when she introduced him right away. But they both discovered it wasn't necessary since he knew a lot of the people hanging around. Except the kids in line for the keg all looked younger than eighteen. Seemed like so long ago that he'd been the new kid on the circuit. Back then, seeing guys who were the age he was now had seemed so ancient.

Finally, they reached the spot by the fire where the couple hosting the party held court.

Sutton had only seen the pair last week from a distance. Stitch was a substantial guy—although Sutton had him by a couple inches—and he appeared to be four or five years younger than London, which is why Sutton didn't do a double take at seeing his baby-faced girlfriend. She was cute, miniature in stature. But her blonde hair, as big as the state of Texas—a phrase his friend Tanna used to say—added some height. He wondered if someone had warned the young thang about the perils of standing too close to the fire doused with that much hairspray. Or about the fuse-like dangers of the synthetic beauty queen sash she wore loosely draped across her chest.

Besides, Sutton was way more interested in this Stitch guy, the douche-nozzle dumb enough to dump long, lean London for pint-sized Paige.

Like most bulldoggers, Stitch was solid, but he'd gone a step further, bulking up to the point he'd lost his neck. Nothing else about him seemed remarkable, save for the fact the guy was bow-legged. Probably made Sutton an ass to wish the dude was cross-eyed, with buck teeth and nearly bald beneath his cowboy hat too, but there it was. Sometimes he wasn't a nice guy.

London's hand tightened in his. "Sutton."

"What?"

"Stop growling."

"Sorry." *Not at fucking all.* "Just feeling a little territorial, darlin'."

"I can see that. So can everyone else."

"Good."

Lelo elbowed Stitch and his entire body stiffened.

Then Stitch dropped his arm from Paige's shoulder and skirted the fire pit, heading toward them. He offered his hand first and Sutton automatically followed suit. "I can't believe *the* Sutton Grant is here at my campsite. I can't believe I'm meeting you. Man, I'm such a huge fan! Your run in Vegas was legendary. It was a dream to get to watch history being made."

"I appreciate you saying so."

"When Lelo said you were here, I thought he was pulling my leg. He's such a prankster."

"Maybe *his* name oughta be Stitch," Sutton deadpanned.

Stitch's eyes clouded for a second. He didn't get the joke.

Sutton kept his expression cool. As much as he appreciated Stitch's enthusiasm, it bothered the crap out of him that neither the man nor his girlfriend had acknowledged London.

Paige pushed her way between them and offered her hand, while keeping a proprietary hand on Stitch. "Hi. I'm Paige. We're happy you could stop by our party."

"We appreciate the invite."

Paige glanced at London, then refocused on Sutton. "I'm sure London has told you all about us, but we had no idea she'd met someone new."

Sutton smiled at London. "Don't know where you got the impression that London and I just met. I've known her for three years. We reconnected when I asked her to work with my horse, since she'd trained him at Grade A Farms." He brought their joined hands up and kissed the back of her hand. "And what a reconnection it's been."

London let her secret smile speak for her.

"Good to see you, London," Stitch said politely. "You're looking well."

"Thanks, Stitch."

Then Stitch launched into a barrage of questions that normally would've amused Sutton, but he was just so damn distracted by the woman by his side. The scent of her. The tiny taste of her still lingering on his tongue. The bonfire had nothing on the heat that rolled off her body. Then she started feathering her thumb across the inside of his wrist. Back and forth. Pressing into the vein to feel his pulse, teasing the sensitive spots as if it was his cock.

Enough. He wanted the real thing.

When Stitch took a breath, Sutton bent his head to whisper. "Let's go."

"We haven't been here ten minutes."

"I can be inside you in under ten minutes," he countered with a silken growl.

"We just wanted to drop in and say thanks for the party invite," London announced to Stitch and Paige, "but we've gotta get."

Sutton didn't bother masking his grin.

"But you just got here!" Stitch protested. "You haven't even had a beer yet."

"Thanks for your hospitality, but maybe next time. Nice meeting you."

"Maybe we'll see you at the fireworks?" Stitch said hopefully.

Sutton glanced into London's heavy-lidded eyes. "We'll be far too busy making our own fireworks to care about someone else's, won't we darlin'?"

"Yeah, baby, we will." She reached up and touched his cheek. "I missed you last night."

Looking into her eyes, Sutton knew none of this was for show—this moment, although played out in front of dozens—belonged only to them. "Same here. Let's go."

Chapter Nine

London felt Sutton's hot breath on the back of her neck as she fumbled with the key to unlock the camper. She closed her eyes, trying to calm down because this was it, this was where all the sexual teasing and banter had led to...being naked with Sutton Grant.

Holy fucking shit was she ready for this?

"London?"

"I'm sorry. I'm shaking so hard I can't get the key in the lock."

"Let me." He didn't grab the key, he just curled his body around hers, steadying her, making his hand an extension of hers. Metal clicked and the door popped open. He pressed a kiss below her ear and murmured, "After you."

She shuddered at the deep timbre of his rough and sexy voice.

"Should I be concerned about your hesitation?"

"No. Just stop whispering in my ear. It's distracting me."

"Mmm. Sweet thang, I'm gonna have so much fun telling you every dirty little thing I plan to do to you." He made a half growl against the side of her throat. "Then doing it." He sank his teeth into her skin and growled again. "At least twice."

That prompted her to take that first step inside. The door slammed behind them.

Sutton kept his hands on her shoulders as she led him to the bedroom. She'd cleaned off her bed but it hadn't improved the area much. Suddenly, she worried this might not be the best idea.

Then that liquid sex voice melted into her ear again. "Stop."

"What?"

"Whatever negative thoughts that're keeping us from climbing in that bed and crawling all over each other." He pressed his hips into her backside. He tilted her head to the right and moved his hands over her collarbones to the front of her blouse and popped the buttons. One. At. A. Time.

As soon as he'd undone the last button, he slowly turned her to face him.

Keeping her eyes focused on her task, she undressed him in the same leisurely manner, enjoying the feel of his hot skin and contours of his muscles beneath her hands. All she could think about was feeling the press of his weight against her, feeling the musculature in his back with her fingers as he moved above her.

"You're killing me with that look in your eyes, London."

"The look that makes it very clear I want to lick you up one side and down the other?" She angled her head, breathing on the tight tip of his nipple before her lips circled it.

"Ah, Christ."

"You like that."

"Mmm. I'd really like it if we could speed things up." His hands followed the contours of her sides to the curve of her hips.

"What's the rush?"

"You," he whispered across her bared shoulder. "I wanna feel you—all of you—around me. Been wanting that for days."

That's when Sutton took matters into his own hands. He stepped back far enough that she could see him yank off his boots and socks. Then he unbuckled his belt and unzipped his jeans. He lifted one, sexy dark eyebrow, silently asking why she wasn't stripping.

London had an overwhelming rush of shyness. It was one thing to want him so desperately, to want to rip off his clothes and feast on him, to get lost in passion, to reach for each other in a haze of lust...so how had they gone from that to...this? Lowering her chin, she allowed her hair to fall over her face.

Rough-skinned hands cupped her shoulders. Then his fingers were beneath her chin and his avid mouth landed on hers, reigniting that passion. He kissed her with authority and greed while he stripped her out of her remaining clothes. His hands were everywhere, pinching her nipples, squeezing her hips, clamping onto her ass. They fell back onto the bed with Sutton on the bottom, breaking their fall.

His cock had gotten trapped between their bodies. Raising herself up on all fours, she automatically started rocking against it, kissing him frantically as the tips of her breasts rubbed against the hair on his chest.

Two sharp slaps on her ass burned like hell—but it caught her attention. She gasped, "What—"

"Scoot up."

Confused by another abrupt halt to their intimacy, her eyes met his. "Why?"

"I want your pussy on my face."

She blushed.

"London," he said with a sharper tone than she'd ever heard from him, "get on up here girl, before I smack that fine ass of yours again."

"B-but I've never—"

"Don't care. That little taste of you wasn't near enough." He held onto her inner thighs, pulling her up his body while he pushed himself down the bed. He slid his hands around to her butt cheeks and pressed her mound against his mouth.

Any thoughts London had about awkwardness vanished the instant that tongue came out.

A relentless tongue that licked her up one side and down the other. Probing her folds. Swirling inside the opening to her sex and then plunging deep. Teasing her clit with alternating soft flicks and licks.

His hands were hard, his fingers digging into her skin. The wet lapping noises of his mouth on her sex mixed with her soft moans and echoed in the tiny space.

Sutton pulled back to kiss the inside of her thigh. Then he nipped it hard and she cried out. It startled her more than hurt her, but even the tiny sting sent a shot of heat through her.

He made that sexy growling noise against the stinging spot. "Shoulda known a tough woman like you would like a little rougher play." Then he nipped the other thigh a bit harder.

London's gasp turned into a groan when he settled his hot, sucking mouth over her clit.

It'd been so long and he was so freakin' good with that naughty mouth of his. The tingling sensation immediately radiated down her spine, sending every hair from the back of her neck to her tailbone on full alert.

She threw her head back and said, "Oh-god-oh-god-oh-god don't stop! Please. That's so..." The orgasm hit—then it expanded and exploded. Each hard contraction had her knees quaking and her arms shaking.

When she opened her eyes, she realized she'd lowered herself completely onto Sutton's face and was probably smothering him. She tried to scramble back. "I'm sorry—"

Another hard whap landed on her butt and he scooted out from beneath her to stand at the end of the bed. "Never apologize for coming like that. Sweet heaven that was so damn sexy."

Next thing she knew he'd caged that big, strong body around hers. She arched into him. She might've purred.

Sutton's lips skimmed her earlobe. "I want you." His hot breath burrowed inside her ear. "Want you like fuckin' crazy." Then the tip of his tongue traced the shell of her ear. "Want you hard and fast this time." He kissed the hollow below her ear and her pulse skyrocketed. "Next go will be slow, sweet, and sweaty, okay?"

"Okay, yes, please."

He pushed back and she heard the crinkle of a condom wrapper. Then his knees moved between hers and work-roughened hands traveled the back of her thighs, stopping to tilt her ass to a better— God, hopefully deeper—angle. The tip traced her slit once before he wedged his cock inside her fully in a steady glide.

She'd held her breath, waiting for a hard thrust. So when Sutton layered his body over hers, all heat and muscle and strength, the air left her lungs in a long groan. He nudged aside her hair and planted openmouthed kisses from the nape of her neck to the ball of her shoulder and back.

Gooseflesh rippled across her body.

"You're so sexy, London. You drive me out of my ever-lovin' mind." Sutton curled his hands around her hipbones and pulled himself upright. His slow withdrawal lasted two strokes before he was ramming into her.

As much as she'd envisioned their first time together being face to face with their mouths fused and their hearts racing in unison as he rolled his body over hers, this was better. More intense. She rocked back into him. The slap of skin on skin and the rhythmic squeak of the bed created a sexual cadence that had her clenching around his pistoning shaft. Each time she bore down he'd make a deep, sexy noise of masculine satisfaction.

After about the fifth time, he said, "London. I can't hold off."

"Just a couple more. Please, I'm so close again."

Sutton quit moving, but he stayed buried balls deep inside her. He leaned over and murmured, "I'll getcha there. Squeeze me hard, baby. Really hard."

As soon as she released her tightened pussy muscles, his hand cracked on her butt and her cunt spasmed on its own.

She cried out, not in pain, but because that extra stimulation shoved her closer to the edge.

"Beautiful. Again."

London did that four more times, bore down, then felt the heat of Sutton's hand as she let go of her clenched inner muscles. Her body took over and she started to come wildly. The orgasm radiated out from her core, electrifying every inch of flesh. Every nerve ending flared to life.

That's when Sutton moved, plunging into her in the same tempo as the blood throbbing in her sex. Once her peak waned, he ramped up his pace, holding her steady as he shouted his release. Such a rush, feeling his big body shuddering behind her and the hard jerk of his shaft against her swollen pussy walls.

Then he went completely still.

Once he'd caught his breath, he caged her body beneath his again, pressing his chest against her from shoulders to hips. He nuzzled the back of her head and expelled a sigh. "You okay?"

"Way, way, way better than okay, Sutton."

"Me too. Lemme ditch the condom. Be right back." He kissed her again and withdrew.

She withheld a hiss, but her arms gave out and she collapsed on the bed.

Gentle hands turned her over and two hundred plus pounds of hot, hunky cowboy loomed over her. His kiss was so sweet and packed with such gratitude that she couldn't help but reach for him, twining her fingers in his thick hair. Running her palm down his spine and getting a handful of his muscled ass.

This man was full of surprises. Over the past week she'd learned to appreciate his quiet sense of humor, as well as his stillness. He was thoughtful and deliberate—such a welcome change from the rash and selfish assholes she'd dated in the past. He listened instead of jabbering on, but he could knock her down a peg if she needed it. He had a protective streak and yet he could soothe her with a simple touch. He loved animals. He was close to his family.

All those things would be more than enough to capture her interest. But add in his stunning good looks—although he tried to downplay them—his holy fuck body, and now learning he had a raunchy, bossy side behind the bedroom door, and she'd lost any hope of not falling madly in love with Sutton Grant.

Love. Jesus. What was wrong with her? No one falls in real true love in six days.

So this overwhelming sensation of satisfaction and excitement had to be a lust high, the happy discovery of sexual compatibility...not the kind of life-affirming love she wanted.

True to his intuitive nature, Sutton immediately sensed the change in her mood. He didn't do anything by half-measures. She should've recognized that right away. While that trait usually had her running the opposite direction, now she clung to it and to him.

"London. Sweetheart. What's wrong?"

Tell him.

Don't be an idiot.

She squeezed him more tightly. "I like being with you like this. And I'm kicking myself we haven't been doing this at every possible opportunity all week."

Soft lips brushed her forehead. "I was thinking the exact same thing."

"Oh yeah? What else were you thinking?"

He rolled them until she was on top, straddling his groin. His hand grabbed a fistful of hair and he tugged her head back, baring her throat. "I'm thinking I watched you riding my horse this week—and I've never been so jealous of a horse in my life. So after I get a chance to taste these sweet tits, I'll wanna see how well you ride me."

"That right?"

"Mmm-hmm. And baby, if you're really good, next time you can be guaranteed I'll wanna try out that riding crop on you."

Chapter Ten

Sutton towel dried his hair and watched London sleeping. Not a graceful sleeper. She was a sprawler. And she hadn't lied about being a snorer. She'd twisted the sheets into a knot, exposing her bare leg, allowing him to see the love bruises he'd sucked on the inside of her thighs. Damn if those red and purple marks didn't look sexy against her pale skin. Before they'd called it a night, he'd checked her ass to see if he'd left marks there from the whacks he'd given her. But he'd just found a few reddened hot spots and thumb and finger shaped bruises on her hips, cheeks, and the backs of her thighs.

A wave of want rolled over him, staring at the beautiful siren he'd worn out last night and who'd wrung him out. He'd never been fully able to explore his kink with any woman, besides a few slaps on the ass here and there—rarely during sex—and some limited rope play, one hand tied to the bed sort of thing. But London wanted more.

And heaven help him he wanted more too, and couldn't wait to see where the need for more would lead them.

Her arms moved overhead in a long morning stretch. She sighed softly and opened her eyes, zeroing in on him first thing. She smiled. "Hey, handsome."

"Hey yourself, gorgeous."

"How long have you been standing there watching me sleep?

Because if I'm drooling, I swear it's a new thing since I finally had a drool-worthy man in my bed last night."

Sutton returned her smile. "I've been up fifteen minutes. Took a quick shower. I've been watching you because it's so fucking hot how you just give yourself over in bed whether you're asleep or awake."

London glanced away.

"Did I say something wrong?"

"No. You said something exactly right." Her hazel eyes were alight with happiness when she looked at him. "Last night was amazing. Beyond anything I ever imagined. But what I always wanted. I wasn't sure how you'd react this morning. Make sense?"

"Perfect sense. It's that way for me too. That's why I've been standing here watching you."

"Seriously?"

"Yeah."

She brushed her hair from her face but didn't attempt to cover up her breasts as she waited for further explanation.

But Sutton was done talking. For now. "I imagine you want coffee?"

"Mmm. A man who will spank me during sex, make me coffee the next morning, and looks that damn good in a floral towel?" She sighed gustily. "Score one for team Gradsky."

He laughed. "Coffee will be done by the time you get cleaned up."

While London took a quick shower, Sutton called Ramsey at the gun range and asked the sample tests be e-mailed to him right away so he could study for the range master test. If he failed, he was out nothing. After he hung up, he really wanted to share the possible change in his life with someone, but his excitement dimmed when he realized he couldn't tell anyone. Especially not London. Things were on an uphill swing with them—not just because they were burning up the sheets. And besides, she'd been working with Dial less than a week. Doubtful the horse had made great strides in such a short amount of time.

As soon as London stepped out of the back room, fully dressed, Sutton wrapped his arms around her. She melted into him, sharing the sweet type of morning kisses he craved. "You smell great and I know firsthand that you taste even better."

"Stop blocking my access to coffee."

They sat at the small table in the front, which he noticed for the first time had been completely cleared. "Where's all your jewelry stuff?"

London blinked at him as she gulped coffee.

"London?"

"It's around."

"Not around here. Where is it?"

"Don't get mad."

He fucking *hated* when women said that because it was guaranteed to blow his top. "Where is it?"

"You had way more room at your place and I knew you'd be staying here this weekend, and we needed the space, so I hoped it wouldn't be that big of a deal if I moved it into your house. Temporarily."

"Why would I be mad about that? You've already brought some of it in."

"I don't know. Most guys get weird about their latest squeeze infringing on their space."

"I'm not most guys, sweetheart." His gaze hooked hers, silently asking, *calling yourself my latest squeeze is insulting to both of us, doncha think?*

She turned away to pour herself another cup of coffee.

He let it go. "What's on the agenda today?"

London snagged a clipboard before she sat. "I'm booked solid but I did leave myself two hours for lunch."

"What did you and Stitch used to do during breaks?"

That surprised her—almost as if she'd forgotten about him. "We didn't get breaks at the same time very often. But he always wanted to wander through the crowds. See and be seen." She shrugged. "As long as I get fed, I don't care what we do."

"Need me to hang around the corral and help you out today?"

Another look of surprise. "Why would you wanna do that?"

"It's gotta beat sitting alone in the camper."

"Don't you want to go...?"

"To watch the rodeo contestants and stock contractors? Nope. To the midway? Nope. Go chat up all my great buddies still running the blacktop? Oh, right. Hanging with them guys never was my scene." Sutton leaned over and tugged on her ponytail. "Looks like you're stuck with me."

She smiled and stole a kiss. "Looks like. Let's hit it."

* * * *

It should've been boring, watching London working horses, conferring with young riders and their parents. But there was such enthusiasm surrounding her, as well as strength and confidence that he couldn't focus on anything else except her. Wanting her, needing her, taking her.

The instant her break started, he herded her toward the camper. She fumbled with the keys again, but in her defense he did have her body pressed up against the door leaving her little space to maneuver.

"Sutton. What are you doing?"

"I'm about to fuck you right here against your camper door in broad daylight if you don't get us inside."

"This door is flimsy. If you wanna fuck me hard, I'd suggest we hit the floor."

The door flew open. Somehow they managed to get it shut and locked before they were on each other.

And the floor held up just fine.

* * * *

Afterward, they strolled hand in hand through the exhibitors' hall. If Sutton would've had his way they would've spent the last hour of her break alone inside the camper. It bothered him that even after their intimate connection, which London admitted she'd never had with another lover, that she was still on the *look-at-my-new-man* kick with Stitch.

That's what you signed on for. Showing her you are the better man is the best way to combat any feelings she might still have for him.

London stopped at a jewelry stand. She chatted with the owner, asking about square footage rental charges, revenue, venue commission percentage kickbacks. All the while Sutton stayed so close behind her he could feel the rumble of her laughter vibrating against his chest.

Finally she said, "Thank you so much for your time."

As soon as they were out of earshot, Sutton said, "Do you know her?"

"No. But I'm interested in whether running a seasonal jewelry storefront is profitable."

"You thinking about starting one for the jewelry you've been making?"

London stopped and faced him. "Do you think it's a frivolous venture? A waste of my time and energy?"

He framed her face in his hands. "No. If you love making the jewelry you'll keep doin' it regardless if it's profitable. You're savvy enough to talk to the people in the trenches before you make any decisions. Sweetheart, that is just smart business. Anyone who tells you otherwise needs their head examined before getting their ass kicked."

"You are so..."

"What? Don't leave me hanging here."

"Surprising. You're smart, with the perfect mix of raunchy and sweet."

Sutton leaned forward to graze her lips, tasting her and breathing her in. "Will it scare you off if I admit I'm really crazy about you?"

"No. Will it scare you off if I say I really need you to kiss me right now like you are that crazy about me?"

"C'mere and gimme that mouth." He deepened the kiss, keeping the passion simmering below the surface.

She kissed him back with the single-minded absorption in the moment he'd come to expect from her. Everything but her faded away.

He had no idea how long they'd been lost in the kiss until he heard a throat clearing behind them.

Reluctantly releasing her lips, he let his hands fall way.

London opened her eyes and stared at him, equally dazed.

"No offense, but you two are kinda blocking the aisle."

Sutton looked over his shoulder and saw Stitch standing there, his hands in the front pockets of his jeans, his gaze on London.

His suspicions kicked in. Had London asked him to kiss her like that only because she'd seen Stitch?

Dammit. None of what'd been happening between them was playacting on his side. Was it on hers?

London wrapped her arm around Sutton's waist and they faced Stitch. "Oh, hey, sorry. We'll get out of the way."

"No, no that's okay. I had a few questions for Sutton anyway, if he's got time."

"Gosh, that'd be swell, but we were headed to the midway so I can win my lady a prize." Sutton leaned forward and confided, "London has this theory that faithful men are as mythical creatures as unicorns, so I'm gonna prove her wrong. And win her the biggest stuffed unicorn I can find as a daily reminder that I am the man she can count on."

Poor kid looked confused as hell.

Over the course of the weekend, Stitch wore that expression a lot.

Chapter Eleven

The second week that London shared Sutton's living space was markedly different than the first week.

They spent a large portion of their time naked—in every room in the house. London never knew what to expect from Sutton either in bed or out of it. The first afternoon back from the Henry County Fair, he'd borrowed one of his brother's horses so they could ride together. Which had been fun, even when she kept an eye on Sutton to make sure he didn't show off, act all macho and hurt himself—not that the man seemed injured at all. He was in better physical condition than any man she knew. It also meant that she'd met his brothers, who'd been equally shocked to meet her.

Then the following night he'd grilled steaks and they'd sat outside beneath the starry sky and had fallen asleep entwined together on his puffy outdoor chaise lounge.

The one night he'd left her alone because he had mysterious "other commitments" she found herself watching the clock as she crafted eight necklaces, anxious for him to come home. The man had been so impatient to have her he'd practically swept all her beads off the kitchen counter like in one of those romantic movies. But the way he'd fucked her on the counter had been hot and nasty—X-rated—not a romantic thing about it, thank god.

They'd watched TV together. Cooked together. Danced around the house and the patio in the moonlight together. They'd made love in every position imaginable. Sometimes their interludes included kink—London still remembered the high from when he used ice on her after he'd bound her hands and how he'd heated up all the cold spots with his hot mouth. Sometimes their interludes were just hot and fast—new lovers who couldn't keep their hands off each other. Sometimes Sutton woke her up in the middle of the night, loving on her with such tenderness she wondered if she'd dreamt it. Which was a real possibility because not one night in the last week had he spent the entire night in her bed.

London continued to work with Dial, but she'd cut the horse's training sessions short because there wasn't much more she could do with him. Not that she could tell Sutton that yet. Partly because just after two short weeks she wasn't ready to close the deal she'd made with him. For one thing, whenever she asked the bulldogger if he'd been cleared to compete, he changed the subject, so she knew he was hiding something. But what? Did it have anything to do with her?

The one wrinkle in their intimacy was Sutton hadn't invited London to move into his bedroom. If they made love in a bed, it was hers in the guestroom. Even if Sutton fell asleep with her afterward, when she woke in the middle of the night or at dawn, the man was gone. That didn't mean he'd just crashed in his bed. No. That meant gone—she couldn't find the man in his house.

She hadn't tried to track him down, figuring if he needed time alone outside or wherever, then it wasn't her place to disturb him.

In the last day he'd become restless, but in a brooding manner. London suspected mindless chattering would get on his nerves so she...did exactly that. Jabbered on and on until he'd threatened to gag her. She'd retorted if he gagged her, he'd better plan on spanking her too.

That's how she ended up gagged with her own thong, her hands roped up with pigging string, bent over the back of the couch as Sutton whacked her bare ass until she came. Twice. Then he replaced the gag with his cock and she'd sucked him off, loving the sharp sting as he pulled her hair, which countered the gentle caress of his thumb on her jaw as he released in her mouth.

Afterward, he'd carried her to her bed and spooned her. She'd soothed him, but he still wasn't quite himself.

Right before she dozed off, she murmured, "Sutton, baby, you know you can talk to me about anything."

"I know. I just...can't. Not yet."

When she'd awoken in the morning, Sutton was gone.

As the weekend loomed, she didn't give a damn if they ran into Stitch and Paige or not. After being with Sutton, she knew even if Stitch came crawling back on his hands and knees she wouldn't take him back. She didn't want him. Hell, she'd never wanted him like she wanted Sutton. So any time Sutton asked about a specific plan to make Stitch jealous, she changed the subject.

Tit for tat, my man. You tell me what you're hiding and I'll admit you ruined me for all other men and I'm milking the training in the hopes you'll fall for me as hard as I've fallen for you.

* * * *

These late nights were killing him.

Sutton had agreed to help out his family by haying the field closest to his house. Cutting and baling was tedious work and left him more tired than if he'd run a marathon.

But he couldn't say no to his brothers—they'd pulled his ass out of the fire plenty of times. He couldn't say no to London—being with her was always the high point of his day. So the only time he had to practice the shooting requirements was after normal people went to bed. Add in the practice written tests, which weren't as easy as Ramsey claimed, and he'd been skating by on two hours of sleep a night.

Since last weekend's county fair was only forty-five minutes from his place, London decided to make the drive to her clinics every day rather than stay overnight.

Sutton had breathed a huge sigh of relief because it gave him the extra time he needed to study and prepare for the range master test. It also indicated that London had moved on for real in the make-Stitch-jealous game.

They'd entered the third week of their deal, trade—whatever it was. If he could make it through the next ten days, he'd be golden. Hopefully he'd pass the test, then he could come clean to London and his family about his future career plans and settle into a real relationship with his hot-blooded horse trainer. She'd seemed a little distant the past couple of days.

He'd managed to get two hours of dead-to-the-world sleep. Upon waking, he crept into the guest bedroom, intent on putting his wide-awake state to good use—waking London up with his face between her thighs. Nothing revved his engines like sucking down her sweet juice first thing in the morning.

The first time she came, she'd arched so hard against his mouth that his teeth had pressed into her delicate tissues. The tiny bite of pain had her fingers gripping his hair as the orgasm pulsed through her. Then he'd instructed her to grab onto the headboard and hold on.

The wait for orgasm number two, when she couldn't direct him at all, was much longer. Sutton took his time exploring her reactions. Suckling just her pussy lips. Jamming his tongue into her hole. Lightly flicking the skin surrounding her swollen clit but avoiding direct contact with the pulsing bundle. Slipping two fingers into her wet cunt, he spread her open and feasted until she begged him to let her come. When he relented and focused entirely on her clit, London's body quivered and she'd screamed her release.

Her pussy walls were still pulsating when he rammed his cock in deep. He paused for a moment, watching the sunbeams fall across her face. Probably, he should've made love to her with a gentle wake up.

But Sutton was too far gone. "The Saint" that London teasingly called him was still sawing logs; his beast was ravenous for a hard morning fuck. The headboard banged into the wall as he relentlessly hammered into her, sweat dripping into his eyes, his jaw tightened in anticipation with every stroke into that tight, wet heat. His fingers curled over hers on the brass bars, the backs of her thighs pressed against his chest. Her calves on his shoulders provided extra resistance as he drove his cock into her over and over.

After he'd spent himself—physically and emotionally—he unhooked their hands from the headboard and placed a soft kiss on each of her anklebones, then slowly lowered her legs to the mattress. He planted more kisses up the center of her body. Looming over her, he pecked her once on the lips. "Good morning, beautiful."

"Helluva way to start the day, bulldogger," she said with a satisfied feminine sigh. Her fingertips scraped the stubble on his cheeks. "I like the way this feels on the inside of my thighs."

When she kept petting him but didn't speak, he said, "Something wrong?"

"No. I was just happily surprised to have you in my bed this morning."

Sutton suspected this question would come up. He wasn't sure how to answer it. "We shared a bed in the camper for two nights on two different weekends." And it'd killed his back.

"But we didn't get much sleep. Oh. Now I get it. That's why we're in separate bedrooms? So you're not tempted to fuck me all the time and we can rest between rounds to keep it hot and exciting?"

"Smartass."

Her eyes clouded. "Why don't you want to sleep in the same bed with me? Do I snore? Did I fart?"

"Why're you taking the blame?" He kissed the frown line between her eyes. "I don't wanna fight with you. It's not a big deal that our sleep patterns don't mesh."

London slid out from beneath him and perched on the edge of the bed. "You're right. It's not a big deal. And it won't matter tonight because I won't be here."

"What? Why not?"

She stood and slipped on her nightgown. "Commuting from here will work most days, just not today."

Sutton studied her. Something else was going on with her. "And tomorrow? Are you coming back here before we head to the Jackson County Fair?"

London fiddled with the bow on her nightgown strap. "We'll see."

The idea of her not being here, not talking to her, not touching her, kicked him into sort of a red rage. She was not inserting herself into his life so completely, making him fall for her, and then just walking away, leaving him so crazy about her that he'd do anything to keep her.

Anything except telling her the truth.

He yanked his sweatpants on and pulled his T-shirt over his head. "We're not doin' this."

"Not doing what? Being honest with each other? You're the one who's keeping to himself. If I didn't know better, I'd think you were sneaking off and trying to rope and ride in the middle of the damn night. But since I haven't seen you out in the barn at all in the last weeks since I started working with Dial, I know that's not where you've been keeping yourself.

Sutton hesitated all of ten seconds. "You really wanna see what I've been up to and where I've been?"

"Yes!"

"It'll change things between us."

London cocked a hand on her hip. "Some things need to change between us, Sutton."

"Fine." He snagged her hand. "Don't say I didn't warn you."

They stopped in front of the door at the far end of the hall. He opened the little box next to the doorframe that looked like a thermostat and punched in a code. The locks disengaged and he turned the door handle.

"After you."

London said nothing as she ducked inside.

After the door shut and latched behind them, he flipped on the main lights and led her down the stairs, keeping his back to her.

The space had been completely finished. Textured walls, acoustic ceiling, tile flooring, a built-in gun vault, locking cabinets for ammo. Tall benches lined the walls with a pegboard between the bench and the cabinets. The corner held a reloading station.

Sutton loved the absolute silence in his hidey hole. Once that upper door closed, he was vacuum-sealed in. The apocalypse could happen above him and he'd be oblivious. For that reason, so he didn't venture into "survivalist" territory, he didn't keep so much as a can of soda down here, say nothing of cases of weanies and beans and plastic jugs of water.

The actual range had been built from huge circular sections of concrete culverts. The targeting system was on an electronic pulley that ran along the top and bottom, allowing him to change the size, angle, and the distance of the practice targets with the push of a button.

It'd been an unconventional choice, foregoing a traditional basement family room, but he never regretted creating this for himself.

"Omigod! What is this place?"

Sutton hated—*hated*—London's wide-eyed look of horror as her gaze encompassed the space, as if she expected to see electrical tape, mini-saws, an array of pliers, dental instruments, and other devices of torture. "It's a gun range."

"*Inside* your house?"

Technically it was under his house, but he said, "Yeah."

"You have a fucking *gun range* inside your house?" she repeated.

It wasn't like she hadn't been raised around guns—her dad was a huge gun collector. He'd even invited Chuck to come over and shoot. He forced himself to keep his tone cool. "So? Some people have photography studios or theater rooms or a woodworking shop." He shrugged. "Shooting is my hobby. So I had a regulation range put in."

"But...isn't that illegal?"

"Jesus, London. You think I'm the law-breaking type? You think I would've showed it to you if I was trying to keep it on the down low?"

"Don't get snappy with me. I didn't realize people could have a gun range inside their house!" she snapped back.

"It's not that uncommon," he assured her. "I had dozens of designs to choose from. I first got the idea when a guy on my college rodeo team showed me his dad's inside shooting range."

"I assume the guy lived in a rural area like this?"

Sutton shook his head. "In town. Don't know what the building code restrictions are there, I know I had to jump through some hoops here to get approval and to pass inspection afterward."

London marched up to him and jabbed her finger into his chest. "Why didn't you tell me about this?"

"Because—"

"This is where you've been disappearing to at night?"

"Mostly. Some nights I work out. And I didn't think it'd be in my best interest to tell my houseguest that I was down here target shooting while she slept."

Her eyes narrowed. "What if I would've stumbled down here in the middle of the night? Would you've shot me as an intruder?"

"For Christsake, London! I'm not a fucking trigger-happy rube! And you can't just *stumble* down here because the area is secured with a coded locking system and a self-closing door. That means even if you get pissed off, know the code and come down here looking for my Smith and Wesson .460 to do some real damage to me, unless you chop off my thumb to get biometric access to my gun vault, you ain't getting nothing but even more pissed off."

"Don't even joke about that."

"I'm not. And see that?" He pointed to the red ambulance light on the ceiling. "If someone opens the door while I'm down here, it triggers an alarm. I cannot be caught unaware." Then he pointed to the range itself. "That enclosed space is bulletproof. I can't shoot out, no one can shoot in. I also have a secret panic alarm that goes straight to the sheriff's department."

"God. It's like I'm in Dr. Evil's underground lair."

He clenched his jaw and bit out, "Dr. Evil? Seriously?"

"No. But goddammit, Sutton, you had to expect I'd be freaked out by this."

She had him there.

"This"—she gestured around the space without breaking eye contact with him—"is an important part of who you are, isn't it?"

"Yeah."

"Why didn't you tell me? Not just about the James Bond underground thingy, but that you—"

"Had something in my life besides bulldoggin'?"

"Yes."

Not accusatory or hurt, but more curious. So he really felt like a total fucking heel for keeping this from her, too. "Because shooting has always been just mine in a way that bulldoggin' never will be. I do it for enjoyment. It's the one thing that's kept me sane during this last recovery."

They were nose to nose, breathing hard, staring at one another.

"Are you a good shot?" she asked softly.

"Darlin', I put a gun range in my basement. What do you think?"

Then she took a step back and her gaze roamed over him, head to toe, the return journey much slower as she seemed to catalog every inch of him, as if she was seeing him for the first time. When their gazes met, something had changed in London's eyes.

"Jesus. What now?"

"Do you ever wear those special military clothes when you're down here shooting?"

He frowned. "You mean like camo?"

"No." Her eyes were firmly on his chest. "The kind of clothes that black ops guys wear. A tight black T-shirt and black cargo pants tucked into biker boots, and a belt with a place for your gun, ammo, and maybe a pair of handcuffs? Ooh, and those mysterious wraparound sunglasses."

Sutton watched as she bit her lip. Then it dawned on him. She was turned on by the idea of him packing heat.

His cock went as hard as steel.

This was a far better reaction than fear. And if she wanted to play gun range taskmaster and novice shooter? He'd give it a whirl.

"When's the last time you fired a gun?" he asked gruffly.

"It's been a long time. And I never was very good at it."

He crowded her. "We'll change that right now."

"What? I'm in my damn pajamas!"

"So? Gimme your hand."

"Sutton—"

"In here I'm the teacher, and darlin', you *don't* get to argue with me." He snatched her hand. "A Glock will be too big for you. Let's start out with a thirty-eight."

"Thirty-eight what? Shots?"

"Thirty-eight caliber." His eyes searched hers. "You really don't know anything about guns?"

"Besides they're loud and dangerous? No."

A slow grin spread across his face. "That's what makes them so fun."

Her palms slid up his chest. "So the question is you gonna show me how to handle your big gun?"

In that instant, Sutton knew total acceptance. He knew those voices in his head telling him what he felt for her had gone beyond just lust and amusement and straight to love hadn't been taunting him. Still, he kept his tone light. "The one I want you handling has some heft to it. It heats up real fast."

"Show me."

He bent down and brushed his lips across the top of her ear. "You will listen to me and do exactly as I say."

She swallowed hard. "Yes, sir."

"Feel free to look around while I get out the guns and ammo." Sutton opened the safe and removed one gun—a thirty-eight Ruger revolver. When he turned around, London was staring at him. "What?"

"You are the most fascinating man I've ever met. And I've just touched the tip of the iceberg with you. I wonder what other secrets are beneath the surface."

"It's always the quiet ones you have to worry about," he joked.

"Sutton. I'm serious."

"Me, too. Come on. Let's load and shoot." He unlocked the gun cabinet and took down the box of bullets. He flipped the cylinder out and shoved in six bullets. "This first round I'll have you watch. Then I'll get you situated to shoot." Sutton snagged his ear protection and the plastic eye protection from the pegboard. There were half a dozen other sets of ear and eye protection hanging there, and he handed her the smallest set. "You can stand behind me and watch. And pay attention, sweetheart, 'cause there's gonna be a test."

Sutton ducked into the shooting area and started the ventilation system. He chose a target, picked the range, and hit the button that sent it back to his coordinates. He moved his neck side to side, shrugged his shoulders, and dropped them down as he widened his stance. Once he'd picked up the gun, he inhaled a slow breath and released it before he fired. Six times. He punched the button and the target returned. He'd clustered his shots, pretty damn perfectly if he did say so himself. Practice was paying off for him. He faced her.

Crazy woman smiled and gave him a double thumbs-up.

After he left the shooting area, London said, "I know you want me to have a turn, but I'd really like to see you do that again."

"Fine. Let's reload. You're doing it this time. And be careful because the barrel is hot."

"Why don't you just take the box of ammo in with you?"

"It's a safety protocol. Don't reload where you shoot. Full clip going in, empty clip going out. I follow that even when I'm down here by myself."

"Such a rule follower you are, Mr. Grant."

"On most things? Yes." He let his hot gaze sweep over her sexy, pajama-clad form. "But I wanna break all the rules when it comes to you, darlin'."

Sutton shot another round. Then he brought London into the shooting area and did the clichéd instructor move where he stood behind her, his arms alongside hers as she pointed the gun. He adjusted her stance. He whispered instructions in her ear. She wasn't easily distracted, which was a good sign. But she was aware of his hard cock nestled against her ass as he maneuvered her into position.

Gun loaded, he stood behind her as she sited the target. She fired off all six shots in rapid succession. The target showed five hits, so one shot had gone wild.

"Let's go again. That's not bad."

By the sixth round, London had become more comfortable.

But Sutton's pleasure receptors had overloaded. He was in his gun range with a sexy woman who wore very few clothes and delighted in making "big gun" and "quick on the trigger" and "hot barrel" jokes while sending him—and his cock—smoldering looks. Add in the scent of gun smoke that hung in the air around them and the buzz in his ears from the gunfire, and he was in bad shape. He needed her right fucking now.

"Sutton? Are you okay?"

When his gaze collided with hers, she gasped. "Baby, let's do something about that. But you've gotta put away your toys first."

As soon as he'd locked away the revolver and box of bullets, he was on her. Kissing her desperately, fumbling with her clothes, needing her skin beneath his hands while his body covered hers. Owned hers.

Sutton took her down to the floor on her hands and knees on the rug in front of the lone easy chair, his cock, head, and heart pounding. The violent need for her had him hiking her hips in the air, pinning her shoulders down with one hand while the other guided his cock between her legs.

But something stopped him.

He glanced down at London, the sexpot who was always up for anything, and he knew she deserved better than this. She liked it as rough and raunchy as he did, but right now he wanted to give her more of himself. "London. Sweetheart. Turn over."

A haze of lust had already clouded her eyes. "What's wrong?"

"Nothing. I just wanna look into your eyes when I'm loving on you." He levered himself over her. Those muscular thighs of hers automatically circled his waist. He tilted her pelvis and pushed inside her slowly, feeling her snug pussy walls relax to let him in. His hand shook when he brushed her hair off her face. "You are so beautiful." He kissed her with awe. The gentle mating of their mouths sent warmth flowing through him. "Beautiful and sexy. Sweet and nasty. Is there a more perfect woman on the planet for me?"

"Sutton."

"I think not. I can say it, but I don't think you believe it. Let me show you."

He kissed and touched and tasted her, dragging out the pleasure until their bodies were both slick with sweat.

Her fingers dug into his ass and her back bowed off the floor when he kicked up the pace. "Please, I can't take any more, this is..."

"For me too. Move with me."

She did. They were in perfect synchronicity.

When he hit that tipping point and the first wave of pulsing heat erupted, he'd been tempted to close his eyes.

But London's whispered, "Look at me and let me see you let go," had him locking eyes with her.

It was one of the most startlingly intimate moments he'd ever experienced.

His entire being shook in the aftermath. He nuzzled and kissed her, needing that grounding contact with her warm skin. "Thank you," he murmured against her lips.

"Can we just stay like this for a little while?" London nibbled on his jawline. "I'm not ready to return to the real world yet."

"Of course." He rolled so she was on top, wishing he had a blanket to cover her.

After a bit, she said, "You know, these benches would be a great place for me to work on my jewelry."

"Yeah?"

"Yeah. Then sometimes I could be down here and keep you company while you're shooting."

"I'd like that." More than she knew.

Chapter Twelve

London glanced at her watch. Where was Sutton? He should've been here fifteen minutes ago.

The funnel cakes were tempting. Rather than give in to her desire for fried dough covered in powdered sugar, she wandered to the next vendor site. The tent blocked the heat of the day and a fan from the back blew the first cool air she'd felt since she'd sat in her truck this morning.

She stayed there, pretending to look at the racks of handmade jewelry.

A familiar voice said, "London?"

Don't turn around. Maybe he'll go away.

"Never thought you were into jewelry. I'da bought you stuff like this if I thought you'd wear it."

I didn't need you to buy me stuff like this. I made stuff like this, dipshit, or don't you remember?

"You got your earplugs in or something?" Stitch clapped her on the shoulder, forcing her to face him.

"Oh hey, Stitch. What are you doin' here?"

"Killin' time until tonight."

"Without Paige?" came out a little snotty.

"Yeah. I wanted to surprise her with a little something." He paused. "Probably be wrong of me to ask for your help, huh?"

Do you think, fuckwad?

London shocked even herself when she said, "She'd probably like anything with sparkles or rhinestones."

"Paige does like her pink stuff."

They stood side by side, looking at jewelry—for her ex-boyfriend's new girlfriend. Talk about bizarre. London spied a lapel pin with a rhinestone crown on it. Tacky, but perfect for a princess. "I think she'll dig this."

Stitch nodded. He fingered the points on the crown. "So you and Sutton Grant, huh?"

"Yep."

"He's a good guy."

"That he is."

"I've always admired him. A lot. I watch his performance tapes all the time. His runs are picture perfect." He chuckled. "Except for that one last year. I was happy to see he didn't have permanent injuries. Man, he wrecked bad. You normally only see that in rough stock events."

"Sutton is fortunate."

Silence stretched between them. Then Stitch blurted, "Dammit, London, I'm so sorry that things ended up the way they did between us."

She looked at him, half expecting to see him wringing his hat in his hands. His blue eyes were filled with wariness; his cheeks were red with embarrassment. That's when she remembered why she'd fallen for the cute cowboy in the first place. Stitch was a sweet guy. Their four-year age difference hadn't mattered to her, but now she realized they'd always been in different places in their lives. While she patted herself on the back for lighting a fire in his Wranglers, in truth she'd been more his teacher for sex and dealing with his horse than his girlfriend. As much as it pained her to admit it now, she understood why he'd wanted something different.

They'd had some good times together. But if she really thought hard about it, she'd always known in her heart that they weren't right for each other for the long haul.

So was she repeating the pattern with Sutton? Training his horse and having hot, kinky, wild sex with him?

No. There was an emotional connection she'd never had with a man before. And she suspected Sutton felt it too. But since she'd blurted out her love for Stitch within the first month, this time, when it mattered, she'd be more cautious.

"London?"

She realized she'd gotten lost in her thoughts. "Sorry. I just wish you'd talked to me instead of sending me a lousy text message. Was that your idea or Paige's?"

He blushed. "Mine. Paige knew I was with someone when she and I first started hanging out. When we realized we wanted to be more than friends...I just ended it right then so we could be."

"You didn't think I'd be upset? Or that I deserved an explanation?"

"What was I supposed to say? Especially since we'd spent more time apart than together those last couple months."

"Is that when you and Paige started seeing each other?"

"Yeah, but as friends. And just so you know, because we never talked about it, Paige and I didn't... I mean we weren't...We hadn't..." He blushed harder.

Good lord. How had she ever ended up naked with this guy? "You and Paige weren't bumping uglies while you were still with me?"

"No! I'd never do that." His fist closed around the piece of jewelry. "I liked you, London. A whole lot. But meeting Paige... I never felt anything like it. She's just the one. And she feels the same way about me." Stitch's blue eyes met hers. "This ain't a fling with her."

"Like it was with me."

He nodded.

Just then, something inside her shifted. If she had to lose out—although now she suspected it was just getting dumped that'd had her seeing red—she'd rather lose out to true love.

"So are you gonna be mad at me forever? Cause we'll be seeing each other for years yet if we're both working the circuit."

She grudgingly said, "No. But I'd be happy if you talked to Paige about keeping her animosity leashed. She doesn't have anything to worry about when it comes to me."

"I'll talk to her about backing off."

"That'd be good. I'm..." *Just say it.* "Happy for you finding the real deal."

"You are?" His eyes nearly bugged out of his head.

"Hard to believe, but yes. Because now, after being with Sutton for such a short time, I know it can happen."

Stitch grinned. "Cool." Then he pulled her into his arms for a hug.

He whispered, "Thank you for the forgiveness, London. I never meant to hurt you."

"I get that now." Before she could step back, they were ripped apart.

An infuriated Sutton demanded, "What the fuck is this?"

"I, ah, well, London and I—"

"Tryin' to get back into her bed and into her life, weasel? Guess what? It ain't ever happening because I'm there now and I take up a lot of goddamned room, and I'm not goin' anywhere. *Ever.*"

"Sutton!"

He got right in Stitch's face. "Are you one of them guys who only wants what he can't have?"

Stitch stumbled back. .

London could tell that Stitch's vocal cords had frozen in mortification from being dressed down and physically intimidated by his idol. So naturally she jumped in to protect him. "Leave him alone."

Sutton's gaze snapped to her. "Why are you defending him?"

"Because you are bein' an ass. And in public."

"Tell me I didn't just see this man with his arms around you."

"Oh, for Christsake."

"I saw it. I watched you and him all cozied up, chatting like it was old home week." He glared at Stitch. "Where's your girlfriend?"

"Uh, she and I—"

"Broke up?" Sutton supplied. "So that leaves you free to—"

London covered Sutton's mouth with her hand. "Shut your face before you say anything more ridiculous than you already have." When he tried to jerk away, she twisted the fingers of her other hand into his shirt and hissed, "Asshat." Then she looked over her shoulder at Stitch. "Sorry. I'm pretty sure he's been at the bar all afternoon."

"Oh. Well, then, I'm gonna git." He sent Sutton an odd look then threw his shoulders back. "Treat her right. She deserves it."

Sutton growled something.

London didn't move her hand until after Stitch had paid for his trinket and left.

They glared at each other.

He opened his mouth and she held up her hand. "Me first. You really thought I'd start up with him again?"

He loomed over her. "You were fucking *hugging* him, London. And it wasn't a bro hug, it was a lingering hug."

"Lingering hug," she repeated. "Wow. I didn't know there was a scale that denoted what kind of hug it was by its length. And double wow that you have somehow memorized that scale."

"I know what I saw," he said stubbornly.

"Then you need fucking glasses."

"Hey, you two get outta here," the woman behind the tables yelled. "You're scaring off my customers."

"Fine." London spun on her boot heel and stormed out of the tent.

Of course Sutton followed. His hand circled her biceps and he turned her back around. "I deserve a goddamn explanation."

"And I deserve a goddamn apology for your lack of faith in me."

He laughed. "Lack of faith? Sweetheart, the only reason we ended up together was to make that man jealous. You succeeded. Every time I've asked you if you'd go back to him if he showed interest again, you've hedged."

"Because it's a stupid question."

"No, it's a legitimate question."

"No, this is a legitimate question. You really think the only reason I'm still with you, four weeks after we made the deal, is because I'm trying to lure Stitch back? Everything we've done and said when no one's been around us was us playing a part? None of it was real?"

"You tell me," he said coolly.

Just like that, London stepped back. "How about when you figure it out you come find me." She stormed away from him.

"How about I'd better find you in my damn corral, working with my horse," he shouted at her.

For the love of God. Seriously? They were shouting at each other like angry teens now?

And she'd never understood the phrase *the devil made me do it*, but at that moment she was so mad that she lost control of rationality. "Don't hold your breath because I'm done with your horse."

"Explain what the hell that means."

"Dial is as trained as he's gonna get."

"And you just decided that right now when you're pissed?" London shook her head.

"How long have you been keeping that from me?"

"Since the end of the second week."

Shocked, he said, "Why?"

"Because I didn't want to leave you, jackass," she snapped. "I've been in this situation before. After you got what you wanted from me I figured you'd boot my ass out."

"You really think the only reason I wanted you around, four weeks after we made the deal, is because I want you to train my fucking horse?" he shot back.

How dare he throw her words back in her face? "You tell me. If you'd bothered to come out and watch me work Dial, you would've known two weeks ago that I was done. But you stayed away because you never intended to get back on that horse and compete again, did you?"

He bit off, "No," with zero hesitation.

"When were you gonna tell me?"

"When I had some other things squared away in my life."

"Was I one of those things?"

A muscle ticced in his jaw. "Are you gonna let me explain or just jump to conclusions?"

"Like you did with Stitch?"

"This is getting us nowhere. Can we—"

"No. I need to cool down before I say something out of anger that I don't mean."

"London. If we don't do this now—"

"Then we'll do it later." She jabbed her finger at him. "Don't you give me an ultimatum, Sutton Grant."

"I'm not. But please wait."

She didn't. She kept walking until she reached her camper.

Once inside, it was tempting to break into her emergency bottle of tequila.

Instead she breathed slow and deep to stave off her tears. Part of her expected that Sutton would come barreling into her camper, snarl about putting her over his knee to get her attention, but he didn't show.

She held out on checking her phone until after opening ceremonies—but no missed calls or text messages.

In fact, she didn't see him or hear from him that night.

Or the next day and night.

Or the next day.

Since London had a key to his house, she headed there first after the rodeo ended Sunday afternoon. No sign of him. But she could tell he'd been there. She could tell it'd been at least a day since he'd tended to Dial because the headstrong gelding came right up to her. He didn't make her chase him down.

Once she returned inside, she punched in the code and entered his private domain, ready to read him the riot act if he was hiding from her. If Sutton had been in his underground shooting range, she couldn't tell because the place was always spotless. Granted, she hadn't expected Mr. Responsible to suddenly leave firearms lying about, but there wasn't even an empty ammo box in the garbage.

After locking the door, she wandered into the kitchen. But she was too melancholy to fix herself food. Wasn't long before anger replaced her melancholy. The man's avoidance was ridiculous. Did he really think she'd just pack up and leave because she didn't have a conversation on *his* time frame? Did he really believe she'd let this issue stand between them when she was in love with him?

Wrong.

She might be hardheaded but she wasn't a fool.

The man had one more day to come to his senses or she was calling in the big guns.

Chapter Thirteen

Sutton was running late—a rarity for him, so he hoped she didn't give him grief for it. He scanned the tables in the restaurant. When he saw her, he smiled. There'd been a time when his pulse would've quickened, but now that his heart belonged to another, he just had a genuine sense of happiness at seeing her.

He wandered to the back booth where she'd set up camp with a stroller, a car seat, and a diaper bag.

As soon as he loomed over her, she drawled, "Forgive me if I don't get up, but as you can see my hands are full."

"I see that. Will your bruiser of a husband punch me in the face if I kiss your cheek?"

"He's not here right now. He'll be back in a bit, so kiss away, hot stuff."

Sutton kissed Tanna's temple. "I've got you all to myself, Tex-Mex? Well, besides this little guy." He peered at the face peeking out of the blanket. "Handsome papoose you birthed."

Tanna whapped him on the arm. "Papoose. With Fletch's Native American background and my Mexican, August Bruce Fletcher has gorgeous coloring." She sighed and stroked her baby's chubby cheek. "He has gorgeous everything, doncha darlin' boy."

He slid in the booth across from her. "So his full name is August Bruce Fletcher?"

"After his daddy and his grandpa. But we're calling him Gus."

"How old is Gus now?"

"Three months."

"How are you doin' with the new mom thing?"

Tanna's entire face lit up. "Fantastic. I had a rough pregnancy and ended up having a C-section because the kid weighed in at a little over ten pounds, but he's such a good baby. Such a joy in our lives." She looked away from Gus long enough to say, "If you think I'm smitten with our boy, you oughta see his father with him."

Sutton grinned. "I'd give anything to see the big, bad animal Doc baby-talkin'."

She snorted. "Not happening."

The waitress stopped by to refill Tanna's coffee and take Sutton's order. "Just a Coke," he said, "but keep them comin'."

"Wild night?" Tanna asked.

"Nope. Just a long one. Lots of tossing and turning."

"Well, you look good, if that's any consolation. But you always look like you stepped out of a magazine ad trying to sell rugged men's aftershave to men who have no hopes of ever lookin' like you."

"Stop flirting with me Mrs. Fletcher."

Tanna laughed. "Sorry. Habit. So what's up? Not that I wasn't happy to hear from you, but I was surprised."

"I figured you would be. Is it weird I considered it a sign that you'd be in Denver visiting your brother right when I needed to talk to you?"

"Not weird at all." She reached over and squeezed his hand. "I was lost and in an unhappy place three years ago. Thanks to you—and Fletch—I'm now happier than I've ever been. So anything you need from me, name it."

He squeezed her hand back. "I just need the same thing you did—to talk to someone who's been there."

"What's goin' on? Start at the least confusing place for me."

"My accident late last fall? When I came to in the ambulance and I couldn't move, I was scared out of my mind that I was paralyzed. I made a deal with God that if I didn't end up a permanent cripple that I'd never compete in steer wrestling again."

Tanna whistled.

"Obviously I recovered. I've been recovered for a helluva lot longer than anyone knows. My docs gave me the all clear four months ago. My family thinks I'm still on physical restrictions—because that's what I've led them to believe. I've pulled through two bad wrecks and some heavy emotional shit, so yeah, I'm keepin' my heavenly promise. But that's left me in limbo, not knowing what to do with myself if I'm not bulldoggin' for a living."

"I hear ya there." The bundle on her lap squirmed and squeaked and she rocked in the booth. "What else?"

"Dial has been shunted aside since the accident. I figured he'd be okay taking it easy for a couple of months. When the docs gave me medical release, I immediately took him out and tried to put him through his paces."

"How'd that go?"

"Not well. Mostly because my brothers happened to come by and check on me, saw me racing hell bent for leather on my horse, and lost their minds. At that point I coulda told them I'd been medically released and I was fine to resume training. But in the back of my mind? That little voice reminded me training was pointless because I'd promised to give it up and I had no freakin' idea what to do with my life."

"And this tug of war has been goin' on since that day?"

"Yep."

"It's gone beyond you faking a limp and constantly complaining about your sciatica to your family?"

"I see you ain't lost that smartass humor."

"Gotta take my shots when I can." She smirked. "But I'll behave. Go on."

"I hate that Dial became a problem horse because of my lie. I even went so far as to hire London Gradsky to help me get Dial back on track." He didn't want to tell her this next part, but in for a penny, in for a pound. "And I've fallen head over heels in love with the woman."

Tanna stopped moving and didn't start again even when Gus fussed. "Are you shittin' me, Sutton Grant? You and the horse trainer? I thought she hated you for convincing Chuck and Berlin to sell Dial to you."

"She did. But she's a horse woman to the core, Tanna. She trained Dial in the first place. At first she had uh...other reasons for agreeing to help me."

"Should I ask about them other reasons?"

"That's more her deal than mine. But it was a deal I agreed to. Spending all our time together...she's practically livin' with me. She's sexy, sweet, funny, and that girl has a mouth on her that don't quit—evidently that's a trait in a woman that attracts me"—he laughed when Tanna flipped him off—"and damn if I don't like playin' house with her. A lot."

"Does she know you're in love with her?"

Sutton smiled. "Talk about déjà vu."

"What?"

"I asked the same thing of Fletch that day he came to watch you race around barrels at full speed."

"What'd he say?"

"That you couldn't be around him and not know how he felt about you."

Her brown eyes softened. "I was crazy in love with that man then too, but I wouldn't admit it to him either. So the question is, has the tough babe wielding the horsewhip softened up some and is she in love with you?"

"I have no idea. This all happened so damn fast. Who the hell falls in love in a couple of weeks?" Agitated because he didn't do this spilling his guts thing, Sutton let out a slow breath. "Go ahead and laugh."

"Not on your life. But I am gonna play devil's advocate for 'The Saint.'"

He blinked at her. "Okay."

"I have to err on the side that says the horse whisperer—or should I say horse whipper?—is madly in love with you too. How could she not be? You are the real deal, a genuine gentleman and one of the greatest guys I've ever known." She winked. "Even if you are a little shy and reserved for my taste."

"I'da given my left nut to hear you say that to me years ago." He'd been so crazy about Tanna, even when she'd been crazy about Fletch, but he hadn't harbored illusions that they'd ever be together. That just reminded him he had a long history of betting on the wrong horse—when it came to women. Reading more into situations and relationships that weren't there. So he erred on the side of caution. "I just...worry that if London had feelings for me, they'll change like Charlotte's did when she realized I'm no longer interested in living life on the road pursuing another championship."

Tanna angled forward. "You listen to me, Sutton. Charlotte was a star-fucker; she doesn't deserve a thought beyond that. I take it London found out you're putting 'former bulldogger' on upcoming resumes?"

"We had a big damn fight and I didn't even tell her that I knew in the hospital I'd never intended to compete on the circuit professionally again. She asked why I hired her. I saw it in her eyes, she thought everything was lies and manipulation—and she stormed off refusing to discuss it."

"Ever?"

"No. She said she needed to cool down. Then I had to go out of town and everything is just fucked. Been a long couple of days."

Fuck. He needed to get the hell out of here. What made him think this was a good idea? He drained his soda and stood. "Sorry. Wasn't fair to dump all this on you when you've got so much on your plate already."

"Sit your ass down, Sutton. Now."

He sat.

"You came here because you want my advice, not to hear me condone or condemn what you've been doin', right?"

"Right."

She smiled at her baby when he grunted and squeaked. "My precious boy here has changed my life and the way I look at every little thang. So *he* was my promise to God, so to speak. Fletch and I tried for a year to get pregnant. I swore that if we were blessed with a child, I'd slow down. Take a year off from the circuit."

"Are you rethinking that?"

"Right now, I couldn't give a damn if I *ever* compete in barrel racing again. On any level." Tanna looked up at him. "I have four world championships. The number of women who can lay claim to that can be etched on the head of a pin." She bit her lip. "Okay, that ain't true. I still tell tall Texas tales if I can get away with it. The point is, the deals we make with ourselves, the promises we break, all lead to one question: how many championship gold buckles are enough?"

"My brother asked me that same question."

"Did you answer?"

"Nope. Mostly because I was trying to downplay the truth."

"Which is?"

"Even without the injury and the promise I made, I was ready to move on from the road to rodeo glory bein' the only life I had."

Tanna said, "Aha!" loud enough to startle Gus. The baby screwed up his face and wailed. "Sorry my sweet." She brushed her lips across his forehead. After the baby had settled, her gaze met Sutton's. "Once you stop faking your injury, what are your options as far as a career? Ranching with your brothers?"

"They'd let me be part of the operation if I asked."

"But you ain't gonna ask."

"No. I like living close to family and having some acres to spread out on and helping them out in the busy season, but the day to day grind of ranching ain't for me."

She raised a brow. "Still didn't answer the question, bulldogger. What's your college degree in?"

"Business. Not ag business, just an associate's degree in business administration." He sighed. "My dad wanted me to have something to fall back on after I stopped chasin' points and purse."

"And do you?"

He shrugged. "Maybe."

"Don't make me come over there and box your ears to get an answer. Beneath the baby spit up, I'm still a born and bred Texas cowgirl, ready to kick some ass."

"I never doubted that for an instant, Tex-Mex." He took a moment to gather his thoughts. "A buddy of mine is waiting on whether I'll pass the tests that'll clear the way for me to come to work for him at his gun range."

"That's great! See? You've got options."

"First I have to pass my range master certification."

"So? Eli told me you're a deadeye with any kind of weapon."

"It helps when you have a shootin' range in your basement," he said dryly. "Not much else for me to do while I was laying around, lying about going to rehab and stuck in my house. I told myself I was killing time, but—"

"You were preparing for the future," she finished. "So get your shit together, Sutton. Talk to London. Talk to your family. Talk to your friend. Don't put any of it off any longer."

"She givin' you some of that tough love that you gave her a few years back?" Fletch said.

Sutton jumped. How had he missed the big man approaching them?

Fletch reached down and plucked the baby from Tanna's arms—

after he gave his wife a steamy kiss. A long, steamy kiss.

Sutton laughed. "Still marking your territory?"

"Always." He cradled the bundle to his chest. "Hey, little man. You been good for your mama?"

"An angel, like always," Tanna said, smiling at her husband and son.

"I can walk around with him if you guys wanna finish your talk," Fletch offered.

"Nah, man, that's okay," Sutton said, standing up. "Your wife set me straight, which is what I needed."

"You did me a good turn. I'm happy to pay it forward," Tanna said softly.

"Agreed. Anything I can do, just ask," Fletch said. "I owe you, too."

"There is one thing..." He laughed when Fletch groaned. "Since my bulldoggin' days are over, I'll need to find a good fit for Dial. So if you know anyone who's lookin', send 'em my way."

Fletch pinned him with a look. "Chuck and Berlin Gradsky wouldn't buy him back?"

"Doubtful. He'd been a thorn in their side for a few years—before you castrated him—and since he and I were well matched they were happy to get rid of him."

A pause hung in the air. Then, "Sweet Jesus, that's something else that London doesn't know," Tanna said. "That you didn't pressure her folks into selling Dial to you. They wanted to get rid of him."

"Yeah, well, she wouldn't have taken that well since she trained him. It'd be a double blow for her."

"Sutton. You have to tell her that too, when you're telling her everything else."

"It's not my place."

"It is. Does she know you're planning on selling Dial?"

"She does now that she told me Dial has been done training for weeks and the only reason she stayed around was because of me."

"Sounds like she loves you, which means this is fixable," Tanna said, standing to hug him and then give him a quick shove. "So go fix it, dumbass."

Chapter Fourteen

Barn therapy.

That's what she needed.

London pointed her truck toward her parent's place and drove. Half an hour later she was in the shed, slipping on waders, an apron, and gloves. She loaded her tools in the wheelbarrow and started in the stall at the farthest end of the barn.

Two cleaned stalls later, she realized she wasn't alone. She turned toward the gate and rested her arm on the handle of the pitchfork.

Her mom hung over the gate. She smiled. "Barn therapy?"

"Yep. Learned it from the best."

"When you're done slogging through the shit—real and imagined—come on up to the house."

"Will do." London returned to her task. After she finished another stall, she called it quits. She cleaned up in the barn bathroom. Since the barn at Grade A Horse Farms cost on the high side of five million dollars to build, it boasted cool amenities, including a full-size shower in both the women's and men's restrooms.

After London drove the mile between the training facility and the private Gradsky family home, she wasn't surprised to see her mom waiting on the porch.

"Would you like tea?"

"That'd be great, Mom." She flopped on the canopy swing and sighed.

"I'd say I was pleasantly surprised to see you, but I haven't heard from you in a while so I figured you'd visit soon." She handed London her tea in her favorite rainbow swirl and polka dot glass.

"Thanks."

"You're welcome. Thank you for tackling those stalls. They always seem to need more maintenance than the others."

"Some kids do too," London muttered.

"Yes, your brother is always harassing me for legal advice for his toughest cases."

She smiled.

"Talk to me, sweetheart. What's the problem?"

"Sutton Grant is the hottest, sexiest, sweetest, most wonderful guy on the planet."

Her mother sipped her tea. "Doesn't seem like much of a problem to me. So I'll ask how does this affect you?"

"Because he's also the most exasperating. And I'm kinda, sorta thinkin' that I'm half in love with him, maybe a little bit."

"Kinda, sorta, maybe?" she repeated.

London blew out a breath. "Okay. Completely, totally, hat over boot heels in love with that man."

When London kept brooding, her mom said, "London Lenora Gradsky. If you don't start talking right now and give me every detail a mother needs, I will bend you over my knee."

She froze. Hard to believe how much she liked it when Sutton had spanked her. He'd been so...intense. So in tune with what she needed and wanted she hadn't even had to ask. And then afterward, so sweet and loving.

"I'm waiting," her mom singsonged.

Where to start? "After Stitch dumped me for that tiara-wearing terror, everyone thought I was suicidal. I wasn't. Yes, I was pissed, but what kind of freakin' jerk breaks up with the woman he's practically living with via text? Jerks like him. I got tired of the pitying looks and wondered how I'd survive the summer since I'd see them every weekend, and then Sutton showed up at one of my seminars. He hadn't been working Dial at all since he'd gotten out of the hospital after his accident."

"Dear Lord. I bet Sutton was fit to be tied because he's all about that horse."

"He was and I initially told him no way because I hated how he pestered you and Dad to sell him Dial. Part of me was thinking 'what goes around comes around, pal' but another part of me was feeling cocky because he had come to *me* for help." She gulped her tea. "This is where it gets tricky." After she gave the rundown about their "deal," she looked over at her mom.

Berlin Gradsky wore a smile that scared London.

"What?"

"That's my girl."

"You're not...upset?"

"That you used your brains to get revenge and make money and getcha some of that hot man honey?"

"MOTHER!"

"What? Sutton Grant is built, good-looking, thoughtful, and genuine. How could I be upset with you getting with a man like him? In fact, I'm thinking tears of pride and joy are gonna start flooding the table at any moment."

London rolled her eyes.

"Keep going because I suspect we hit the problem part of this talk."

"Yeah. So he insists I move into his guest bedroom. He's all cool and laid back, which bugged me to be honest. I wanted him to want me for real. So I put it aside and worked with Dial. And our first official appearance as a couple was so convincing that behind closed doors..." She sighed. "Sutton hasn't forgotten how to ride entirely."

Her mom lifted her glass for a silent toast.

"The more time I spend with Sutton, the more Stitch and that whole thing just fades away. It seems Sutton and I are headed into real relationship territory, but I feel he's holding something back from me."

"I imagine he's tired of that same old question of when he'll start competing again."

London nodded. "He didn't ask me how the training is going with Dial. Which I took as I wasn't doin' a fast enough job and he feels he can't push me because we're sleeping together. But now...the man admitted he won't be competing again and he's been having me work with his horse so he can get rid of it."

"Oh dear."

She drained her tea and chomped on a piece of ice. "He can't sell

Dial. I didn't train his horse for someone else, I trained it for *him*."

Her mother shook her head. "I know you've got an independent streak, sweetheart, but there's where you've stepped over the line. You trained Sutton's horse. Period. Whether he sells it or rides it himself is immaterial. He's paying you for a service." Her eyes narrowed. "He *is* paying you?"

"Of course." Not that she'd cashed the checks.

"There's your answer for that part of the problem."

London locked her gaze to her mother's. "You have no ill feelings toward Sutton at all for him demanding you sell Dial to him three years ago?"

"You somehow got your wires crossed because your father and I don't give in to demands—be they horses', kids', or customers'. We sold Dial to Sutton because they complemented each other. Dial was a nightmare horse, sweetheart. I don't know why you don't remember that. We were over the moon that Sutton wanted to take him off our hands. Sometimes I think your father would've paid Sutton to take him."

London's mouth fell open. "What? But *I* trained him."

"We're aware of that."

"So you're saying the reason Dial is such a nightmare is because of me? Of how I trained him?"

"No." Her mom set the glass on the tray and took London's hands in her own. "You and Sutton were the only two people we'd ever run across who could control that horse. The only two. We even had Dial castrated in an attempt to change his behavior and that changed nothing. We were at a loss. You know how we handle a horse like that."

"You get rid of it."

"Exactly. Sutton offered to buy him and we accepted. We knew you'd take it personally, honey. But we all know that a well-trained horse isn't always a well-behaved horse. That's Dial. When he's on the dirt he's focused, a champion, ready to do what he's been trained to. But the instant his hooves are out of the arena? He's difficult. You would've kept trying to change that behavior to the exclusion of training other horses. We had to get rid of him." She squeezed London's fingers. "I know that situation was the catalyst for you to strike out on your own entirely. Your father and I couldn't be more proud of you."

"While I appreciate that...it is sort of embarrassing that I've been wrong all along."

"About us resenting Sutton Grant? Absolutely. *You* resented him. And I worry you've gotten sucked back into that cycle of trying to fix a horse that has limitations."

She'd never considered any of this and it sent her reeling.

But didn't Sutton ask you that very first day if he couldn't utilize Dial after he'd been retrained, if you'd be willing to help find him a new home?

Yes. But she hadn't believed him. In fact, she'd done exactly what her mother claimed she'd done: she'd set out to prove Sutton wrong.

"Damn. I am a fucking idiot."

"No. You just added the complication of love to an already complicated situation."

"What do I do now?"

"Talk to Sutton. Tell him you know that we happily handed over Dial to his care. Tell him you'll help him find another bulldogger to sell to who can handle a horse who performs well but won't ever acclimate to a normal environment outside the arena." She cocked her head. "What about Stitch?"

"Oh sure, Mom, suggest that Sutton sell a horse with behavioral problems to my *ex-boyfriend*. There's no chance that Sutton would oh, hope the horse would hurt Stitch because he hurt me?"

"Sounds like Sutton is pretty protective of you?"

"Yes. Which is sweet and sorta hot, in a Neanderthal way. Sutton and I had words about a freakin' hug Stitch gave me. That's when it came out he wouldn't be competing anymore. I was mad; he was annoying as fuck. I asked for some time and I'll be damned if he didn't give it to me. It's been four damn days! He's not answering my texts or my calls. I don't know how to fix it."

"He hasn't been to his house?"

"Not when I've been there."

"Does he still have that underground shooting range?"

Again, London was shocked. "You *knew* about that?"

"Of course. It's his pride and joy. He invited your dad over to shoot." A sneaky and slightly evil looking smile spread across her mom's face. "I know one way to get a man back home, and you won't even have to get on your knees."

"MOTHER!"

"What? I mean getting on your knees to beg him. Good lord. You have as dirty a mind as your father. Anyway, call Sutton and leave him a voicemail."

"I've tried that."

"Ah ah ah. But you haven't told him that you feel so bad about what happened between you two, and you know he's upset, so you've decided to do something nice for him to open those lines of communication."

"Like what?"

She paused for effect. "Polish all his guns."

"Oh shit."

"Then tell him you've used a Brillo Pad to shine up the metal parts, but you aren't sure if you should use furniture polish or car wax on the wood parts. I guarantee you'll get his attention."

"Mom. That is brilliant. Twisted, but brilliant." Totally impossible to do with the biometric locks on the vaults, but it'd get her point across. London leapt up and hugged her. "Thanks for listening. But I'll admit you scare me sometimes."

Berlin Gradsky delicately sipped her tea. "I have no idea what you're talking about."

Chapter Fifteen

Shining his gunstocks with furniture polish?

That woman had a warped sense of humor. Seriously fucking warped.

Which was probably why he was seriously fucking in love with her.

Sutton didn't bother pulling into the garage. He parked on the concrete slab and barreled into the house. Shouting wasn't his style, but he found himself doing it anyway. "London Gradsky, you better not have put a single spritz of Lemon Pledge on my shotguns or so help me God I'll—"

"You'll what?" she said from the living room where she was sprawled out on the chaise, drinking a beer.

His eyes narrowed. Hey, wait a second. London was knocking back the special brew he'd brought back from Germany two years ago.

"Still waiting," she said and then took a big swig.

"Where are my guns?"

"Safely locked away in their velvet lined, dehumidified gun cases I presume."

He crossed his arms over his chest. "Then why'd you send me that threatening text?"

"Threatening text? When I said I was gonna help you out by cleaning up your guns? That was me being nice, asshole."

"If that's you bein' nice, darlin', I'd hate to see you when you're bein' nasty."

London leapt to her feet. "You're about to find out."

"Bring it, cowgirl. And bring me that damn beer you stole. I haven't had a taste of it."

She smirked. Then she tipped the bottle up and drained it. She wiped her lips with the back of her hand and belched.

"You are the most annoying fucking woman on the planet."

"So does that mean you missed me?" she asked softly.

Here was the moment of truth. "Yeah. I missed you like a limb."

"Sutton."

"London. I know we need to talk, but c'mere and gimme a kiss 'cause the last few days have sucked without you."

He didn't wait for her to come to him. They met halfway, and he wrapped her in his arms for several long moments, reminding himself of how well they fit together, in so many ways.

"I missed you too, bulldogger."

Sutton twisted his hand in her hair and tipped her head back to get at that sweet, hot mouth of hers. The kiss heated up, and he paused to say, "I like how that beer tastes on you."

"Stop talking and kiss me some more."

He did just that. But as much as he wanted to let the passion between them expand, letting it show her how he felt about her, he needed to say the words. "London," he murmured against her lips.

She flattened her hands on his pecs and pushed, putting distance between them. "Uh-oh. That's your serious voice."

"I have different voices?"

"Yep. There's your *Jesus, woman* tone, which means you're exasperated with me. There's your *Hey, sweet darlin'* rasp that means you're about to strip me naked. Then there's your *C'mon, sweetheart* taunt that means you're teasing me. And there's the softly spoken *London*, which means...I'm never exactly sure what I'm in for with that one." She raised her gaze to his. "So if you do plan to tell me something good that'll make me smile, weep with joy, and throw myself into your big, strong arms, let's get through the bad stuff first." She touched her lips to his. "There's things we both need to get off our chests."

He pressed a kiss onto her forehead. "Sounds fair. Kitchen or living room?"

"Living room. That way if you really piss me off I'm farther away from the knives and you have time to run."

Yep. He so loved this woman.

London held his hand and led him to the sectional couch. After he'd settled himself in the corner, she immediately stretched out on top of him, nestling the side of her face against the center of his chest, pressing her hip between his legs. Being body to body, where he could touch her at will but wasn't staring directly into her eyes as he made his confessions, would make those confessions come easier.

Sutton ran his hand down her arm. "Is this okay for you?"

"It's perfect for me." She kissed his pectoral. "Start when you're ready."

He reflexively tightened his hold on her hip. "You won't take off?"

"Nope. Unless you tell me you're part of some religious sect where they allow you to have as many wives as you want, because I don't share well at all."

"Me neither." He marshaled his thoughts and decided to get the worst over first. "The reason I have no intention of ever competing as a professional steer wrestler again is because I made a deal with God that if I survived the wreck, I'd walk away from the sport for good. I'm keeping my word because in that moment I finally realized how lucky I am." When she didn't laugh or call him an idiot, he told her the story. "So no one knows what really went down. Not my family, not my sponsors, not the CRA."

"How long have you been medically cleared?"

"Four months. My brothers busted me trying to work with Dial right after I'd been released. I chose to perpetuate the lie. No idea why I did. Seemed smart at the time. Then it just steamrolled. But you know better than anyone what happens to a highly trained horse when it's allowed to run amok. Needing your help with Dial was completely sincere."

She traced the edge of his shirt pocket. "I know. I knew when you didn't balk at pretending to be my boyfriend as a stipulation of me helping you that you were desperate."

"Not the word I'd use..."

"After the first time we kissed, I knew I was in big trouble with you."

"Why?"

"Because I didn't give a damn about Stitch anymore."

"But I thought you did and I kept pushing us into bein' more visible as a couple—"

"When all I wanted was alone time with you, my hot man. So you believe me when I say Stitch means nothing to me? That conversation you interrupted—"

"That overly friendly hug," he corrected with a growl.

"Was just a hug between friends. I didn't only ask you to pretend to be my boyfriend to make Stitch jealous. I needed my ego bolstered after being dumped. I never wanted Stitch back. I guess I didn't make that clear."

He sighed. "How did this get so fucked up?"

"Because we both kept following our own agenda. How long did you plan to keep me training Dial?"

"Until you said he was back to normal or that you couldn't get him there." His hand traveled back up her arm and he brushed her hair from her shoulder. "Then I remembered why your folks agreed to sell me Dial in the first place—because you'd keep working with him to the exclusion of every other animal in their stable. So I was selfish, hoping it'd take you a long damn time to retrain him."

"Because...?"

"Because I fell in love with you. I hoped if you had more time with me, you'd fall for me too—when I wasn't second guessing myself that no one really fell in love in a week." He felt her smile against his chest.

London lifted her head and looked at him reverently—and they weren't even naked. That had to mean something, right?

"Talk to me."

She ran her fingertips over the stubble on his cheeks. "I expected you to say you didn't think this was real because you were my rebound man."

"Shit. I should've been worrying about *that* too?"

She laughed. "No." Then she sobered. "Here's the truth. Dial is as good as he's ever gonna get. At least under my training. I've been pretending that he hasn't made much progress because I didn't want to leave you."

He grinned so widely it hurt, then he wondered if he might've pulled a muscle.

"I've been milking this job. But not for money. Every check you wrote me is uncashed. I also suspected you weren't being truthful because you let me be. You weren't gauging Dial's progress. A guy antsy to get back on the dirt would've been out there every day harassing me for faster results."

"You didn't take my hands-off approach as that I trusted you to do the job I'd hired you for?"

"Nope."

"Damn."

"But I'd hoped that you were keeping me around because you were starting to feel things for me since I'd fallen in love with you."

Sutton kissed her then, knowing he'd remember this moment for the rest of their lives.

"So what now?"

"You move in with me."

"Like we're roommates?"

"Fuck no, we won't be roommates. And we ain't playing house either. This is for real."

"I can move my stuff into your room?"

"Woman, half your shit is already in my room—don't think I didn't notice." He held her chin and feathered his thumb over her lips. "Dream come true having a woman like you in my bed every night."

"A woman like me?"

"A hot, feisty, sexy cowgirl who loves me for me. Not because of the championship buckles, the fame, or the money. "

"The money is a nice bonus. But will you be in our bed with me every night? Because that's been another thing we haven't discussed. Your need for space."

"Baby, it's not about me needing space; it's about me needing more time. For the past month I've been haying with my brothers, and keeping you thoroughly fucked to entice you into staying with me forever, and that wears a man out. So the only time I could study for the test I'm taking to become a range master was in the middle of the night. The only other thing that's been constant in my life besides bulldoggin' is my love of guns. My buddy Ramsey owns an indoor/outdoor gun range. The first week you were here he told me one of his range masters is getting deployed for a year. He asked if I'd be interested in taking the test and filling in. Then when the guy returns from deployment, he'll find me a permanent position if I like working there. So that's where I've been the past two days, taking the written test, which wasn't fun at all, and sharpening my skills here and at the range for the firearms qualification portion, which will be the fun part."

"It's a really exciting change and opportunity for you, Sutton! How awesome you get to do another thing that you love to make a living."

That shit-eating grin spread across his face again. She got it. She got him in ways he didn't have to explain. "Thanks. I planned on telling my family after I told you."

"Will you make an official announcement about retirement from the CRA?"

"Most likely. I've been avoiding my PR person, so I'll talk to her about it."

"That leaves just one thing left to deal with." She paused. "Dial."

He brushed her soft cheek with his knuckles. "I asked my buddy who's a veterinarian in Wyoming to keep his ear to the ground for anyone interested in a championship bulldogging horse. Dial needs to work, so I prefer he went to a qualified candidate. Payment, lease, whatever is all secondary to me at this point." He paused. "Why? Do you already have someone in mind?"

"No, but I agree it's better to wait than just shipping Dial off and cutting your losses. As long as folks in the rodeo world know you're serious about finding the right competitor for him, you *will* have interest. Whether it's the right interest? Dial is the best judge."

"I'll defer to my expert horsewoman. But I'll point out you didn't think Dial had the best judgment when he chose me."

"You'll still be harping on that years from now, won't you?"

Sutton liked that London was already imagining a future for them. "Maybe. Unless you agree to keep working Dial until he's found a new home."

"Hell no. He's *your* horse. You can put him through his paces every day. Besides, I'm officially not your horse trainer any longer."

"Mmm. But you will keep that ridin' crop? Cause I have a feeling you're the type of woman who'll need a whack every once in a while to keep things interesting."

Epilogue

Three months later...

"I can't thank you enough." Stitch kept pumping Sutton's hand as he spoke. "He'll be in good hands. You'll never have to worry he ain't bein' well taken care of."

"That's why we're letting you take him," London said sweetly. Then she laughed. "Well, not *take*, exactly."

Stitch nodded, his gaze zipping to his horse trailer as if he couldn't believe what it held. Then he met Sutton's eyes again. "You're really okay with payments starting in January?"

"This year is a loss for me, at least professionally"—he sent London a wicked smile—"on the personal front, it's been a bang-up year." London melted when he wrapped his arm around her shoulder. "I've no problem waiting until you're starting a new season."

"That's just...awesome, man. Thanks." Stitch smiled at London, his gaze zeroing in on the big sapphire ring on her left hand. "I heard you two got engaged. Congratulations."

"Thank you," London said, sneaking a peek at the ring Sutton had given her just one short week ago. In typical Sutton fashion, his proposal had been a little offbeat; he'd tied the ring at the end of a fancy ribbon and looped it around the barrel of her new shotgun, begging her to make an honest man of him.

"Have you set the date?"

London said, "No" the same time Sutton said, "Soon."

"Good luck." Then Stitch climbed in his rig and drove off.

Sutton kissed her temple. "Whoda thunk, huh? That Dial would take to Stitch and vice versa?"

"Stitch is a good guy."

"Just not the guy for you," Sutton said with a growl.

God, she loved that possessive tone. She loved that the shy man wasn't shy at all about showing her every day, in so many different ways, how much he loved her and how happy she made him.

And she was more than happy to return the favor. To be the woman he could count on to love him through the good times and bad.

He draped his arm over her shoulder. "What's on the agenda tonight?"

"We could pick up and clean the shell casings for the new line of bullet jewelry I've started."

"Pass. I get enough shell casing clean-up duties at my day job. What's my other option?"

"Hanging out in front of the fireplace. Playing cards."

His eyes lit up. "Strip poker?"

"No, you cheat."

"Me?" he said innocently. "I'm 'The Saint,' remember? I don't cheat."

"Ain't no one calling you that anymore, bulldogger."

"Thank God." He pulled her closer and his lips grazed the top of her ear. "To be honest, I don't care what we do just as long as I'm with you."

She sighed. "I'm so crazy in love with you."

"Same goes, sweetheart."

Stripped Down

Chapter One

"Weddings make me horny."

Best man Wynton "Wyn" Grant turned to look at Melissa Lockhart, the curvy redheaded maid of honor. Today was the first time they'd met, so the comment threw him off—as had the other sexual remarks she'd made over the past two hours. Wyn wasn't sure if she was playing him...or if she wanted to play. He offered her a nonchalant, "Really?"

She smirked at him. "A strapping, handsome rancher such as yourself doesn't have anything to say to that besides...*Really?*"

Enough. He angled his head and put his mouth on the shell of her ear. "Gonna get yourself in trouble, you keep teasing me."

"You think I'm teasing?"

"Only one way to find out, ain't there?" He traced the rim of her ear with the tip of his tongue. "Words don't mean nothin' if you can't back it up with actions. And darlin' I *am* a man of action."

That caused a quick hitch in her breath.

He smiled and backed off.

After the last guests passed through the receiving line, Wyn's younger brother Sutton, aka the groom, snagged his attention. "The photographer wants a few shots of us alone, so can you—"

"Make sure the wedding party gets to the head table?" Wyn supplied. "No problem."

"Thanks."

Wyn's new sister-in-law, London, whispered something to Melissa.

Melissa leaned over, giving Wyn a peek of her magnificent tits. She attached the train to the back of London's wedding dress so it didn't drag on the ground. Then she straightened up and looked at Wyn.

He offered his arm. "The party waits."

She slipped her arm through his. "Such a gentleman."

Cres, Wyn's youngest brother, snorted. "Gentleman, my ass. He's been pullin' one over on you, Mel. My big brother is the biggest manwhore in three counties."

Little did his baby brother know that Wyn had been damn near a monk the past eight months, but he didn't bother to try and mask his playboy reputation. "Actually, I prefer the term man-slut," Wyn replied. "Manwhore implies that I take money for something I do very well. For free."

Melissa laughed. "You and I must be slutting around in different counties, Wynton Grant, because I don't have your name in my little black book of bad boys." She paused. "Yet."

They stared at one another with identical "bring it" challenges in their eyes.

And that's when he knew, without a doubt, his sexual dry spell was about to end.

"Oh for the love of God. You two have been eye-fucking each other all day. Just sneak into a horse stall and get it over with already," Stirling, London's sister, and the other bridesmaid, complained.

Cres's annoyed gaze flicked between the best man and the maid of honor. "Take Stirling's advice. And don't even think about givin' one another head beneath the head table. Tonight ain't about your uncontrollable urges." He paused. "Got it, Super Man-Slut and his new sidekick, Slut-Girl?"

Wyn struck a superhero pose and Melissa snickered.

After heaving a disgusted snort, Cres muttered to Stirling and they started the trek to the reception hall.

"I do believe I'm offended," Melissa drawled. "My sidekick name should've been *Amazing* Slut-Girl at the very least."

He laughed. "Come on, Melissa. Let's see what kinda dirty,

dastardly deeds we can get away with."

"Deal. But call me Mel."

"Mel? Nope. Sorry. No can do."

"Why not?"

"Mel is the name of a line cook. Saying, 'Suck harder, Mel,' or 'Bend over, Mel,' brings totally different images to my mind than 'I'm gonna fuck you through the wall, Melissa.'"

"I see where you're coming from, cowboy." She paused outside the sliding wooden doors that led to the lodge. "But that just means I'll be calling you Wynton—even when you're not making me come so hard that I scream your name."

"Darlin', you can call me anything you like as long as I get to bang the hell outta you tonight."

"Oh, there will be banging. But I'm gonna make you work for it to see how bad you really want it." Her eyes danced with a devilish glint that tightened his balls.

"That ain't gonna scare me off." Wyn let his gaze move over her, taking in every feature. From her cinnamon-colored ringlet curls to the broad angles of her forehead and cheekbones. From her bee-stung lips to the pointed tip of her chin. Then down her neck, noting the smattering of freckles across her chest and the plump breasts. Moving down her torso, imagining softness and curves beneath the long, emerald green dress. He took his time on his visual return, mentally shoving her dress up to her hips, pinning her against the wall, feasting on her skin from neck to nipples as he drove into her over and over. Finally his eyes met hers. "I love a challenge."

Inside the lodge, it was obvious London's parents had gone all out for their oldest daughter's wedding. The ceremony itself had taken place in a meadow on the Gradsky's land. One of the few places—according to London—that wasn't a horse pasture. Even the weather, always iffy in October, had cooperated, filtering autumn sunshine across the meadow grasses, creating a dozen shades of gold against the backdrop of a clear, vivid blue sky. After the simple ceremony, the newlyweds had hopped into a horse-drawn carriage. The wedding guests were loaded onto flatbed trucks—a fancier, classier version of a hayride—and returned to the lodge for the receiving line and reception.

"Isn't this magical?" Melissa said with a sigh. "It fits London and Sutton so perfectly."

"That it does," he murmured. Strands of lights were hanging from the rough-hewn log rafters and twisted around the support poles. Centered on each table was a lantern bookended by mason jars filled with flowers in earth tones ranging from gold to russet. Shimmery white tablecloths were tied at the edges with coarse twine—a mix of elegant and rustic.

He glanced at the far corner of the enormous room and saw a band setting up behind a large dance floor. A makeshift bar had been erected in the opposite corner, coolers stacked on top of hay bales and bottles spread across a wooden plank. Long buffet tables stretched along the wall. Beneath those serving dishes was beef raised on the Grant family ranch. Wyn had checked out the slow-cooked prime rib prior to leaving for the ceremony. Between family, friends, and Sutton's rodeo buddies, as well as the Gradsky's big guest list, he suspected there wouldn't be many leftovers.

"Whatcha thinking about so hard?" Melissa asked.

"Food. I'm starved."

"Me too. I hope the photographer doesn't keep the newlyweds forever. At least being in the bridal party, we get to eat first."

Cres and Stirling were standing in front of the head table with guests crowding around them.

"Looks like our receiving line duties ain't quite over yet."

Wyn steered Melissa to the other side of Cres so any well-wishers would have to talk to them first—even after the bride and groom slipped in.

It turned out that these few stragglers had skipped the receiving line and were looking for a private word with the newlyweds. Wyn kept his smile in place as he repeatedly told the guests that the bride and groom were finishing up with pictures. He had no patience with people who didn't listen to the announcements or thought they were above the rules.

"I hear you growling between guests," Melissa whispered.

"I don't like the unspoken sense of entitlement. Every one of these people should've just waited in the damn receiving line like everyone else."

"Agreed. I'm glad Sutton and London aren't being bombarded with this. They deserve a little time alone, away from the maddening crowd."

Melissa's smile tightened when the last couple approached them.

Breck Christianson whistled. "Mel, you're lookin' fine. Damn girl. I thought maybe you'd turned into one of those binge and purge kinda chicks at the beginning of the rodeo season. Skinny as a wild dog. Then here you are. Back to all those plump curves."

Wyn didn't bother to bank his annoyance with this blowhard. He'd never liked Sutton's rodeo buddy and he liked him even less after that bout of verbal diarrhea. "I don't know if you're already drunk or what, but sayin' that bullshit to her ain't gonna fly with me."

Breck's eyes narrowed. "Who the hell are you to tell me what I can and can't say to an old friend?"

"I'm a man who won't put up with your disrespect because from what I hear, you do this all the time. So it ain't happening at my brother's wedding."

"Jesus, Mel, are you dating this guy?" Breck asked.

"Doesn't matter," Wyn said coolly. "What does matter is telling Melissa you're sorry for bein' a loudmouth."

"Or what?" Breck challenged. "You gonna pound on me, tractor jockey? I throw down steers bigger than you every damn day."

"Breck," Cres said sharply. "You're bein' a jackass. Knock it off and move on."

Breck leveled Cres with a dark look, but Cres didn't back down. Then Breck dropped his arm over his date's shoulder. The miniature-sized bleached blonde barely reached the center of Breck's chest. Her sneering gaze rolled over Melissa and Wyn from head to toe. "They're not worth your time, Brecky."

Melissa held in her reply until the obnoxious couple drifted away. "How the mighty have fallen. It looks like *Brecky* had to buy a bargain basement escort to the wedding. The idiot has lost a lot of friends in the past year." She stood on tiptoe. "Thank you for calling him out on his lack of tact." She brushed her mouth over his ear, sending a shiver down the left side of his body. "But you didn't have to do that to impress me, because Wynton, I am a sure thing tonight."

Wyn nudged her chin with his shoulder, forcing her to look at him. "I did it because he was outta line. Had nothin' to do with how crazy I am to taste the freckles on the back of your neck as I'm driving into you from behind."

Desire turned her light-brown eyes almost black. "Gonna be hot as a brushfire between us, Super Man-Slut."

"For right now we'll have to settle for a slow burn, Amazing Slut-Girl. Shall we take our seats?"

* * * *

The bride and groom finally made an appearance half an hour later.

Evidently Sutton was starving because he pushed back speeches, reception games, and dancing until after everyone had eaten.

Then Wyn was so busy shoving food in his mouth and seeing to his best man duties that he didn't have a chance to talk to Melissa privately until over an hour later.

He grabbed a beer and sat beside her. "Hey. Did you get enough to eat?"

"Too much. The food was great." She propped her elbow on the table and rested her chin on her hand. "When you disappeared for so long I thought maybe there was an emergency that only Super Man-Slut could handle."

"And not invite my trusty new sidekick, the Amazing Slut-Girl? Not likely." He sipped his beer. "Why? Did you miss me?"

"Yes. We had a very...promising conversation going and then the Injustice League split us up."

He laughed. "I don't know what the hell Cres's problem was." Wyn and Melissa had taken the two chairs on the other side of the groom's seat at the head table. But Cres and Stirling insisted the setup was groomsmen next to the groom and bridesmaids sat on the bride's side. So it *had* seemed like they were purposely being separated. "Anyway, great toast."

"Yours was good too."

"Glad it's over. I ain't much on public speaking." He set his forearms on the table. "And while you were talkin', I noticed you have a hint of a drawl. Where are you from? Texas?"

"As if. I'm from the great state of Kentucky."

"That didn't sound real sincere."

"I used to be all *Rah! Rah! Go Wildcats!* But I grew up, moved away, and haven't been back to the Bluegrass State for more than the occasional weekend since I graduated from college."

"A Kentucky college girl. So what's your degree in?"

"American literature with an emphasis on twentieth century

authors."

"Huh." Had she noticed his eyes glaze over? "So uh, what do you do with that degree?"

"Exactly."

Wyn blinked.

"I would've liked to teach—I still would—but earning a degree was secondary to why I attended UK."

"And why's that?"

"I went to school there to be part of their equestrian team. Train with the best, win a team collegiate championship, compete individually, and qualify for world finals with the end goal of competing in the Olympics." She sipped her drink. "Bored yet?"

"Are you kiddin'? Lord, woman, you're a Kentucky blueblood from a horse training dynasty or something, aren't you?"

"I was, now I'm not. Now I..." She shook her head as if to clear it. "This year, I've been teaching at Grade A Farms. Chuck and Berlin Gradsky have...shall we say, affluent clientele who prefer their children train in the English style rather than western."

"Well, Kentucky, I'll bet your horse cost more than my house."

"But you own your house. I never owned my horse. My parents' corporation did. And when I was competing I leased my horse from Gradskys."

"You're not competing anymore?" He didn't remember what her rodeo specialty was. Since she'd gotten the horse from Gradskys, he'd put money on her being a barrel racer.

"How did I end up blathering on? It's your turn." Melissa stared at him expectantly.

Wyn shifted in his seat, feeling uncomfortable with her for the first time since they'd met.

"Don't." She squeezed his knee beneath the table. "This is why I don't tell people about where I came from. I'd rather they see me as a rodeo road dog who gives it the almighty try year after year but never *quite* makes it to that top tier."

"That's intentional, isn't it? Not competing on the highest level?"

"I had enough of that. Now I drift from town to town and occasionally toss out a Sylvia Plath quote or a passage from William Faulkner to keep people guessing about me." She squeezed his knee again. "You were about to spill all of your secrets to me, Mr. Grant."

"That's one thing I don't have are secrets. I grew up a rancher's kid and never wanted to do anything else. When it became obvious that Sutton was better than average with his rodeo skills, I knew he wouldn't want to ranch full time, so I stepped up and learned everything I could. Figured it'd be up to me'n Cres to keep the ranch goin'. My folks did insist on shipping me off to vocational school for three years."

"What's your degree in?"

"Associate degrees in engine repair and veterinary science." He sipped his beer and smirked at her. "Granted, it's no Elizabethan poetry degree, but it's helpful around the ranch knowin' how to doctor up machines and animals."

"Elizabethan poetry? Nice shot, grease monkey."

He laughed. Damn he loved her sense of humor. "You had that comin', Kentucky."

Her eyes turned serious. "Why is this so easy with you?"

"Because we're both easy?" he offered. "It's easier knowin' how things are gonna end between us tonight."

"You two look awful cozy over here," a cooing female voice broke the moment.

Wyn looked up at Violet McGinnis. Then he leaned back and draped his arm across the back of Melissa's chair. "Hey, Violet." After spending one night in Violet's bed, she decided they were destined for each other. Not because the sex was off the charts explosive. Not because she was crazy about him and wanted to spend the rest of her days with him. Her sudden interest happened after she'd turned thirty and decided to settle down. He'd never been interested in that with her, or any other woman, and hadn't hidden that fact from anyone. But she hadn't taken the hint. Evidently it was time to broaden that hint.

"We are very cozy," Melissa said, pouring on a thick drawl. "In fact, we may not move from this spot all night, it's Super"—she caught herself and amended—"that me and my best man are hanging."

Violet crossed her arms over her chest. "I hope that's not true because Wyn promised me a dance."

"When did I promise you a dance?"

"It's a figure of speech, Wyn, meaning I want to dance with you."

"Ah. Well, I wouldn't want you turnin' down all the other fellas who're eager to squire you around the dance floor on the off chance I'll tear myself away from this lovely lady's side tonight. Because I doubt that's gonna happen."

Violet didn't know how to respond. She spun on her boot heel and stormed off.

"Recent conquest?" Melissa asked.

"Eight months ago or so."

"She lousy in bed?"

"Not that I recall."

"So why no repeat?"

Wyn watched Violet move to the back of the room. "That'd give her the false expectation there might be a three-peat. I'm not interested in settling down with her. Or anyone else."

"That's another thing we have in common. But there seems to be…a few haters, here, Super Man-Slut. So how many women in this place have you nailed and bailed?"

He scanned the tables. "Six?"

"You're not *sure* how many women have slicked up your pole, grease monkey?"

"Funny, Kentucky. You say that like you didn't admit, two short hours ago that you're equally as slutty as me."

"Fair point."

"Lots of people from the world of rodeo here. How many guys have you mounted and discounted, Amazing Slut-Girl?"

"Mounted and discounted." She snickered. "That's a new one. I might have to steal that." Melissa tried to discreetly crane her neck to scan the area. After several moments, she said, "Four. Five if I'm counting the same guy but two different times."

"Nope. Still only counts as four. But I *am* interested on what he did that earned him a second go."

"He was breathing."

Wyn choked on his beer. "What the hell?"

Melissa shrugged. "All right, it was more boinking from boredom. We ended up at the same after party. Other people started hooking up so we were like…you'll do. How close is your horse trailer?"

"Has he been eye-ballin' you?"

"Some. But I'm not interested in ballin' him, because that'd be a three-peat rule violation and like you, I don't raise false hopes." She cocked her head. "But I'd make an exception to that rule for you."

"You know what I like about you so far, Kentucky? You don't

make excuses for bein' a highly sexual woman."

"And?"

"And you said you were gonna make me work for it. Since we're bein' open about everything else, explain how. Because I want a piece of you like you wouldn't believe." Wyn pushed to his feet. "I'll be right back."

Chapter Two

Mel, you are in deep with this man and you've known him less than half a day.

She watched Wynton Grant amble off. And she couldn't help but notice other women sizing up the rancher hottie too.

From the moment she'd set eyes on him she had that overwhelming punch of want—a feeling that happened to her so rarely lately. So seeing the identical look of lust sizzling in his eyes? The balls to the wall woman of action who'd been in hiding for the past six months had awakened with one thing on her mind.

Sex.

Lots of it.

Hot and dirty sex.

Fast sex.

Slow sex.

And it turned out the very sexy best man was more than happy to oblige.

This was turning out to be the best wedding ever.

The object of her lust stopped to speak to an older woman, giving Mel ample opportunity to study him. The man had it going on. His shoulders were so broad that he blocked the view of the woman entirely. Pity he hadn't taken off his western cut suit coat so she could check out his ass; she'd bet his buns were grade A prime beef too. Not only did he have a big physical presence, he carried himself with confidence. He had an easy smile—which was a sexy-as-his wicked grin. From the back she noticed his dark hair brushed his collar and held more than a little curl. The groom and groomsmen had removed their cowboy hats as soon as the wedding pictures were done. As much as she appreciated a man in a hat, Wynton looked better without it.

Hands landed on the back of Mel's chair and a soft rustle of fabric tickled her neck.

"Staring at him that intently won't make his clothes disappear," London murmured in her ear.

"That obvious?"

"Yes. But if it helps, my brother-in-law is staring back at you the same way."

"Then maybe I'll get lucky on your wedding night too, Mrs. Grant."

London plopped down in Wynton's chair. Her wedding dress was a stunning mix of ivory satin and chiffon. Intricate beadwork of rhinestones and pearls stretched across the bodice of the off-the-shoulder dress. Folds of satin were ruched below her breasts and then floaty, filmy panels of chiffon fell in a column to the floor. It was simple and elegant—exactly like London herself.

"So you'll get a kick out of this, but you cannot tell anyone." London leaned in close enough that a long tendril of her hair touched Mel's cheek. "Earlier, when Sutton said the photographer wanted pictures of just us? Total lie. My husband insisted we have some alone time. And by alone time I mean us in the ready room, with my wedding dress pushed up to my hips, Sutton's tux pants around his ankles as he proved how much he loved me by immediately consummating our marriage."

Mel grinned. "Sounds like him."

"He said he didn't want to wait hours to finally claim what was legally his forever."

"If I didn't love you so much I'd hate you. That's so freakin' romantic."

"I know. I'm so lucky. I am such a sucker for that man. He keeps trying to get me..." She sighed. "Look, I need you to do me a favor."

"Anything."

London tucked a key into Mel's cleavage. "Keep this away from me. And definitely keep it away from Sutton."

"What is it?"

"The key to the ready room where we already rocked the countertop. I have to tell him that I lost it because if he had his way we'd be in there right now. I understand this is a celebration for everyone else, so I can share him for a few more hours. But I promise we ain't gonna be here all night."

"Everyone will expect you to take off."

"Speaking of expectations…You've been such a huge help to me throughout the wedding planning. Mom and I couldn't have done it without you."

Mel teared up. "My pleasure. But if you would've turned into Bridezilla at any point, I would've bitch-slapped you."

"And that's why I love you." London hugged her. "But don't think for one second that I'm not aware there's been some serious shit going on with you the last six months. You can talk to me about anything. So I'm telling you that you *will* be spilling your guts to me as soon as I return from my honeymoon, got it?"

"Yes, bossy-pants."

"That's *Mrs.* Bossy-pants to you." London whispered, "Thank you for being my maid of honor, Mel. Thank you especially for being the sister of my heart."

The tears she tried to hold back fell freely. "Same goes."

"You have your own special chair, my darlin' sister-in-law, so get outta mine," Wynton said behind them, "and quit hoggin' my wedding partner."

"I'm goin', I'm goin'."

After he sat, he noticed Mel's damp cheeks and he looked at London sharply. "You made her cry?"

"They're happy tears, I promise," Mel said with a sniffle.

"So you weren't here warning her off me?" Wynton asked London.

"I should, because you're a serious pain in my ass. But I kinda like you, Wyn, so I'll take the high road and not fill her in on your many conquests." London winked. "His little black book rivals yours, Mel. So I'm thinking you two might be a match made in heaven."

He laughed after London flounced off. "Love that girl."

"Me too."

A voice boomed over the loudspeaker. "Let's kick off the festivities with the bride and groom's first dance as a married couple. Sutton and

London, take the floor please."

Wynton scooted his chair closer. "Will you cry when you hear the song he chose?"

"Maybe. This part and the father/daughter dance always make me cry." Her eyes narrowed. "Wait. What do you mean the song *he* chose?"

"Sutton asked London if she trusted him to pick a first dance song and surprise her."

"So you know what it is?"

He nodded. "And trust me, Kentucky. You're gonna need more tissues."

Turned out, he was right.

* * * *

Ten minutes later, when she and Wynton were on the dance floor with Cres and Stirling, the newlyweds, and both sets of parents, Mel still had a lump in her throat thinking about the song Sutton had picked. Billy Joel's "She's Got A Way."

"You all right?" Wynton murmured.

"No. I'm just so happy that London found the perfect man for her. Sutton...gets her. I never would've pegged him as the romantic type."

"Yeah. Me neither. He told me she makes him a better man. I guess that's something to aim for in a relationship." Wynton smiled against her cheek. "I'm happy for him too." He paused. "Maybe a little jealous."

"Jealous? You? Mr. I'm-not-settling-down?"

"From a strictly competitive point of view," he explained. "I'm the oldest. I should've gotten married first."

Mel tilted her head back and stared into his eyes. "I call bullshit on that. Nut up and admit you want that." She pointed at the happy couple.

"Fine. I want that. Someday. How about you?"

"Of course I want it. When I'm lucky enough to find the one."

The DJ called for all the guests to join the wedding party on the dance floor. And although people crowded around them, it seemed as if they were the only ones in the room.

"What makes a man 'the one' Melissa?"

The husky way he rasped her name sent a slow curl of heat through her. "Not wanting anyone else. Everything you do, everything you are with that one person is enough."

"I never thought of it that way."

"It's logical. The literature degree allows me to break anything down to its most basic component. Even love."

"No, baby, that romantic notion of 'one true love' is all you, and logic won't play into it at all when you find him."

And...she melted. "I really want you to kiss me right now."

"I really want to take that pretty mouth you're offering, but not here." He brushed his lips across her ear. "Dance with me. Let's both of us take the time to enjoy the journey for a change. Since it sounds like we both jump to the good part first."

Mel was beginning to believe being in Wynton's arms *was* the good part.

The tempo changed to a fast tune and he eased them into a two-step. They danced four songs together. When it came time for the father/daughter dance, he draped his arm over her shoulder and wordlessly pulled a tissue out of his pocket when she started to sniffle.

He excused himself to dance with his mother, and Cres whisked her back onto the dance floor when he saw Breck approaching her. After that, Mel danced with London's dad, London's brother, Macon, the wild bulldogger Saxton Green, and Sutton's boss.

By the time she returned to the head table for a drink, she realized the dizzy feeling wasn't just from dancing and she needed a quick snack to keep her blood sugar in check. She cut to the bar and downed a glass of orange juice. She turned around and Wynton was right there.

"I saw you slam that."

"I was thirsty."

"So it appears." He drained the contents of his lowball glass and set it on the tray. "I like dancing with you, Kentucky. Come on." He clasped her hand in his and led her to the dance floor.

She nestled her face against his chest and murmured, "I like dancing with you too, cowboy."

At the start of the second slow song, Wynton said, "Most dangerous place you've had sex, Amazing Slut-Girl."

If it was anyone else, she'd be surprised by the question. "Against the pen that housed the bulls after a rodeo. I kept waiting to get rammed in the back by a horn. It didn't last long, if I recall. How about you, Super Man-Slut?"

"In my high school girlfriend's parent's bed. We'd just finished when we heard the front door open. We had no choice but to dive into the closet. But her parents were in the mood and they ended up goin' at it on the floor—on the other side of the bed so we didn't get a floor show, thank God. But my girlfriend was horrified. She was even more horrified when her dad said if he caught us doin' it, he'd cut off my cock and send her to a convent. We broke up the next day."

Mel laughed. "The one time I remember getting caught I almost bit off the guy's dick. He assured me that he and his girlfriend had called it quits. I'm in his camper, giving him a blowjob, and the 'ex' girlfriend walks through the door—turned out they weren't broken up. She's pissed, I'm pissed, the dude is about to piss himself, so of course he suggests he's willing to share himself and maybe we both oughta blow him at the same time and then do each other."

"While he watched."

"Of course."

"Jesus. Some men are idiots. What happened?"

"I apologized to her and she broke up with him on the spot. We went to the bar, ended up doing blowjob shots all night and became fast friends."

"I call bullshit on that." Wynton tipped her head back and gazed into her eyes. "Aw, hell. That's how you met London, isn't it?"

She smirked. "I'll never tell."

"So have you been in a threesome?"

"Yes. More than one. You?"

Wynton smirked back. "Yes. More than one."

"Well, shoot. We *are* evenly matched in slutting around." Mel decided it was time to kick up the competition. "Ever fucked a famous person?"

"Define famous."

"If you said the name I'd know it."

He shook his head. "How about you?"

"Yes, I have. But I will qualify that by saying he wasn't famous when we fucked, and it lasted like thirty seconds."

"Who was it?"

"Sorry, cowboy, I don't kiss and tell details. But I have no problem giving a general overview of my sexual exploits."

"Same. But to be honest, I don't have anyone in my life who wants to hear about the kinky things I did. So I've stored up all my happy endings—"

"In an impressive spank bank?"

A beat passed, then Wynton threw back his head and laughed.

That single, spontaneous expression of joy moved her. Given their raunchy subject matter, she expected he'd toss out a few lewd vibrator references, but his laugh seemed a more genuine response than trying to one-up her.

"What's so damn funny over here?" Sutton asked.

Mel and Wynton had been so deep in conversation they hadn't noticed the bride and groom dancing right next to them. With very curious expressions on their faces.

"We're just swapping bad sex stories," Wynton said without hesitation. "Why? Did you need us to do something official?"

"Shots of tequila!" London said, pumping her arm in the air.

Sutton grabbed her arm and returned it to his neck. "Behave, wifey-mine, or I'll have to take you over my knee."

"Were you two talking about bondage games?" London asked. "Because while I appreciate my husband's rope expertise, I think turnabout is fair play, don't you? Shouldn't I get to tie him up sometimes?"

The groom blushed and whispered in London's ear. Whatever he said made her eyes glaze over and put a cat-like curl on her lips.

Mel glanced up at Wynton, expecting to see amusement in his eyes, but the longing she saw made her ache. He wanted that same connection his brother had more than he wanted to admit.

Don't you too?

"We came over to remind you that the bouquet toss and garter removal is happening soon," Sutton said. "We'll stick around for maybe an hour and then we're takin' off."

"We're at your command," Wynton deadpanned. "But there's something I've got to do first." He kept ahold of Mel's hand as they exited the dance floor.

She had no idea what was going on. When it appeared they were headed to the bar, she started crafting excuses on why she couldn't do shots with him. But Wynton strolled right past the bar and out a rear exit.

It had gotten chilly since the sun had set. Mel shivered, wishing she'd grabbed her wrap.

Then she found herself absolutely burning up, pressed against the side of the building by two-hundred pounds of hot cowboy. Good Lord. The heat in Wynton's eyes nearly set her skin on fire.

There was no speech about how much he wanted to kiss her. He just did it. Lowered his head and planted his mouth on hers.

He didn't have to prove he was a passionate man by thrusting his tongue past her lips and into her throat. He proved it with tender nibbles and teasing licks. A gentle pass of his mouth. Again and again. As if he had all the time in the world.

Each time Mel parted her lips ever so slightly, breathing him in, she felt his tongue softly licking into her mouth. So when he finally kicked up the heat into a full-blown soul kiss, it seemed as if they'd been kissing for hours.

Wynton wrapped one hand around the back of her neck; his thumb stroked the bone at the base of her skull, sending tingles down her spine. He'd stretched his other arm across her back and clamped onto her right butt cheek. The hard wall of his chest pressed against hers, leaving no place to put her hands except to grip his biceps.

She was just glad she had something solid to hold on to because the way he kissed her left her breathless, boneless, and mindless.

And wet.

His mouth left hers to drag kisses down the column of her throat. "If we weren't needed inside in like a minute, I'd already be inside you." He stopped and breathed heavily against her skin. "Goddammit, Melissa. What you do to me. Kissing you is ten times better than fucking most women. I don't think my brain can process how fantastic the real deal will be."

"Listen to you sweet talk me."

Wynton lifted his head. "Meet me back here in ten minutes."

Mel forced her arms to work and slid her hands across his shoulders. "I have a better idea. There's a private room for the bride to get ready around the back of the lodge." She brought his mouth down to hers for a teasing kiss. "I just happen to have a key. And a condom."

His smile lit up his whole face. "Is it too soon to say I think I love you?"

She laughed. "Save that for after I blow your...mind, cowboy."

The DJ invited all the single ladies to the dance floor for the bouquet toss.

"That's our cue."

Right before they walked into the lodge, Wynton murmured, "These next ten minutes might actually kill me, Kentucky."

"Don't worry. I know CPR. I'd revive you."

Chapter Three

Wyn watched London toss the bouquet. He thought it was telling—and maybe a little sad—that Melissa didn't even try to catch it.

Then he stood in a circle with the other guests as Sutton removed London's garter. He thought it was telling—and an indication of how smitten his younger brother was—that he refused to toss the garter and kept it for himself.

The events dragged out much longer than he'd expected and his gaze was continually drawn to Melissa. He couldn't wait to have his mouth on her skin. He couldn't wait to have those wild curls crushed in his hands. He couldn't wait to hear the noises she made as he touched her. When Cres elbowed him and muttered, "Dude. Quit eye-fucking her," Wyn actually blushed.

So what if he felt like a teenage boy locking eyes with his crush; his heart raced, sweat prickled on the back of his neck, and his dick started to harden. Melissa appeared to be in the same lustful state. Her cheeks were flushed and she alternately bit and licked her lips. The best part was when her eyes kept darting to the door.

He couldn't remember the last time he felt this level of anticipation. Maybe...never. It wasn't bragging that he didn't have to work too hard to find a hookup. Not because he was a smooth-talking Casanova. He just liked women, he liked sex, and he didn't pretend he wanted anything more than a good time.

So why haven't you gotten laid in months?

If his smartass brothers knew how long this dry spell had lasted, they'd claim it was because he'd bedded every available single woman in the area. The truth was, he'd gotten more selective after he'd watched his brother fall in love.

Finally, the newlyweds were ready to leave the reception. Cres pulled Sutton's truck up to the entrance. Earlier, they'd decorated it with dozens of tin cans and beer cans tied to the tailgate and dragging on the ground. They'd written "Just Married" along both sides in huge white letters. They'd filled the inside with rolls of toilet paper and paper streamers. Cres had even tracked down an old pamphlet "What To Expect On Your Wedding Night" and taped it to the steering wheel. But Wyn's favorite part was the two-dozen rainbow-colored condom packages he'd affixed to the hood in the shape of a bow.

As soon as the happy couple pulled away, Melissa was beside him. "Did you save any of those fun-colored condoms?"

He faced her and smiled. "Nope. I had to special order them. Hard to find a place that carries extra small rubbers."

She laughed. "You didn't."

"I did. He'd do the same damn thing to me."

They stared at each other. Moved toward each other.

He dropped his gaze to her lips. "You have the sexiest mouth I've ever seen."

"It's yours. However you want it." Her soft fingers circled his wrist. "We're doing this now?"

"Unless you've changed your mind?"

Melissa brought his hand to her mouth and sucked on his pinkie. "Does that *seem* like I've changed my mind?"

"Christ. Give me the key to the room."

She took two steps backward and an evil smile curled her lips. "Now...Where *did* I put that key? It's on me someplace. Guess you'll have to pat me down or feel me up to find it." She disappeared around the corner.

Wyn followed half a step behind her and he was on her, pushing her up against the door as his mouth crashed down on hers, kissing her with hunger and desperation that seemed totally foreign to him. His hands landed on her hips and he flattened his palms over her abdomen, traveling up her ribcage. Then he cupped her tits, sliding his fingers across the top of the dress and pulling the material away from her skin so he could reach into her cleavage.

Score. The pad of his finger brushed a metal ring.

Rather than scooping it out that way, he broke the kiss to bury his face between her breasts. Licking those full swells of flesh, inhaling the scent of her skin, snagging the key ring with his teeth and pulling it out.

"My, what a talented tongue you have, Super Man-Slut," she said breathlessly.

He grinned and the key dropped into his hand. Snaking his left arm around her waist, he yanked her against his body and jammed the key in the lock. The door popped open.

Once they were inside, he gave the place a cursory look. A single lamp lit the entire room. Three folding chairs were spread out in a semicircle, a low countertop and mirror took up one wall, and a loveseat had been shoved in the corner. Good enough.

He slammed the door and pressed her against it, fusing his mouth to hers again.

She tasted sweet. Like juice and wedding cake. He kissed her until he felt drunk just from the pleasure of it. His hands roved over as much of her as possible, but he needed more.

Wyn ran his hand up her spine until he found the zipper tab at the top of her dress and eased it down to the small of her back.

Melissa broke the kiss on a gasp. "Thank heaven. Now I can breathe."

"Pull the fabric down to your waist," he murmured against her throat.

Hooking her fingers into the side panels, she shimmied it down, baring her tits completely. "The bra is built in—"

Whatever she'd been about to say was lost in a soft moan as he dragged his fingertips over the upper curve of her breast. He locked his gaze to hers. "You want pretty words? Or you want my mouth sucking you here"—he swept his thumb across her nipple—"until I get your pussy wet enough to fuck?"

"That. Yes. Please."

Wyn palmed and caressed her while he feasted on her nipples. When her squirming forced him to release that rigid tip before he was ready, he said, "Hands above your head, gripping the top of the door frame."

She complied with barely a whimper of protest.

His dick was so damn hard it hurt. He didn't have to drag this out, but that's partially why he wanted to; she wouldn't expect it.

So he sucked and bit and licked her tits, even gifting her with a suck mark on the fleshy outer edge that nearly sent her through the roof.

His mouth drifted back up to her ear. "Do I fuck you sitting down or standing up? Choose."

"Standing up."

Wyn pulled a condom out of his pocket, holding it to her mouth with a husky, "Hang on to this for a sec."

How fucking sexy was it to see her teeth sinking into the plastic. He undid his suit pants, shoving them and his boxer briefs to his knees. He took the condom from her mouth with his own. Then he ripped the package with his teeth and reached down to roll it on.

That's when he noticed Melissa's hands were still above the door. Her chest was heaving. Her eyes...Christ her eyes were heavy-lidded and expectant.

The satiny fabric of her dress brushed against his bare thighs as he lifted the material up and tucked it behind her. He inched his fingers down until the tips connected with the waistband of her panties. "Hold still." As he pulled the panties down her trembling thighs, he crouched slightly, needing to know her scent before he fucked her. Wyn ducked his head and placed an openmouthed kiss on the curve of her mound. "A natural redhead," he murmured against that fragrant flesh.

Once her panties were off, he pressed his body to hers again. He grabbed behind her left thigh and lifted it up to wrap around his hip. Wyn planted his mouth on hers as he aligned his cock to her wet center. He pushed in slowly the first couple of inches and then snapped his hips, filling her in one fast thrust.

Melissa's moan vibrated in his mouth. She rolled her hips forward in a signal for him to move.

Keeping one hand around her thigh, he slid his other hand up her arm, pulling it away from the wall and setting it on his shoulder. He flattened his palm above her head on the door to brace himself as he started to fuck her.

The slow, steady pace didn't last long, even when he wanted to savor every glide of his cock into her tight, wet heat. But as the sensations built, he sped up.

The kiss had become frantic—thrusting tongues and hot, fast breath exchanged in openmouthed kisses.

When he kicked up the pace again, Melissa let her head fall back, leaving her neck wide open.

He nipped and nuzzled. Used his teeth. Lost his mind whenever she released a throaty sigh when his tongue connected with a hot spot.

His cock rammed into her faster and harder, but he kept his mouth gentle. If he didn't consciously think about it, he feared he'd turn into an animal, leaving bite marks and broken flesh in his wake.

"Wynton."

"So fucking perfect, how you feel around me."

"I'm close," she panted.

"Tell me what'll get you there."

"Move side to side. Yes. Like that." She groaned. "Don't stop."

His grip tightened on her thigh. "Your pussy's squeezing me like a fucking vise. Take it baby, it's right. There."

That did it. She began to come immediately, her body bucking and grinding against his. The sexiest noises he'd ever heard echoed around him, taunting him to join her. But he gritted his teeth and waited until the last pulse pulled at his cock and she slumped against the wall.

Wyn couldn't hold off. Six hard strokes later, he buried his face in the curve of her neck, his hips pumping as his cock erupted.

Her lips in his hair roused him. He raised his head and feathered his mouth over hers. "That was… Hell, I'm pretty sure we *are* super fucking heroes."

She smiled.

"I don't want that to be it for tonight, Melissa."

Her eyes clouded.

"What?"

"Let's see how the rest of the night plays out."

"Got someone else lined up?" *I'll beat the fuck out of them if you do. Because no one is getting a taste of you. No way. No how.*

"No, and way to ask me that when your cock is still buried inside me. I promised London I'd keep an eye on the reception. Make sure people were still having fun. As soon as this ends, I'm all yours."

Wyn relaxed and slipped out of her. He lowered her leg to the floor and took his time kissing her before he forced himself to take a step back—mentally and literally—to get dressed and remind himself he had best man duties to fulfill too.

After they exited the room, Wyn slung his arm over her shoulder. "I could use a drink. How about you?"

"I have to drop off the key so we're not tempted to misuse the ready room again." She gave him a smug smile. "And then I'll meet you inside on the dance floor."

* * * *

Wyn had knocked back a couple of celebratory shots with Cres and Sutton's coworkers, when Melissa appeared a half hour after they'd parted ways.

"Is everything all right?"

"I had a few things to do that I'd forgotten about. Why?"

"I would've tracked you down if you'd tried to turn this into a fuck and run encounter."

She hip-checked him. "You rocked my world, Wynton Grant. I'm ready for more."

A Pitbull song started and she grabbed his hand. "You didn't think they'd play only country music tonight?"

"I could hope."

* * * *

Two songs later, Wyn and Melissa were leaving the dance floor when he saw his dad stumble back. Then he clutched the left side of his body and hit the floor. Wyn's mother, always the picture of calm, screamed and froze in place.

Wyn raced across the dance floor. That last shot of tequila threatened to come back up when he noticed the ashen tone his father's face had taken. And the fear in his dad's eyes sent Wyn's alarm bells ringing louder.

"Dad? Can you hear me?"

He nodded.

"Stay still. We'll get you some help."

By that time Cres was next to him, as well as Mick, one of the guys Sutton worked with at the gun range.

Mick said, "I have medical training. Let's focus on slow and steady breathing until the ambulance arrives."

Jim Grant nodded.

Then Mick glanced at Cres. "Can you deal with your mother please?"

"Of course."

"Stay with me, Jim," Mick said soothingly.

Wyn listened while Mick asked basic questions that didn't require more than a nod or a head shake. He vaguely heard Melissa advising guests to return to their tables because everything was under control.

It seemed like an hour passed before the EMTs arrived. Wyn pushed to his feet and looked around while medical personnel assessed his father. He sidestepped them and moved to stand beside his mother and Cres.

"What's going on?" his mother demanded. "Is it a stroke? A heart attack?"

"I don't know. They'll get him stabilized enough to hand him off to the docs in the emergency room."

"How far is the hospital from here?"

London's mother, Berlin, stepped into the circle. "About twenty minutes. The staff is top notch. But if the issue is out of their level of expertise, they'll Life Flight him to Denver." She slipped her arm around his mom's shoulder. "Take a deep breath, Sue. We don't need you passing out too."

The EMT interrupted. "Is anyone riding in the ambulance with him?"

"I am," Wyn said and took his mother's hand. "Cres and I have both been drinking so we can't drive to the hospital. You haven't. So I'll need you to drive Cres so we have a vehicle there, okay?"

She blew out a breath. "Okay." Then she turned to Berlin. "Could you—"

"Chuck and I will handle everything here as far as explaining to the guests. No worries."

"Thank you."

Wyn walked alongside the rolling stretcher, his entire focus on his father. Although he had been drinking, the instant they closed the ambulance doors, he was stone-cold sober.

* * * *

As soon as they were through the emergency room doors, the medical team whisked his father off, leaving Wyn to wait for the rest of his family to arrive. He couldn't fill out anything regarding his dad's medical history. That helpless feeling he'd experienced riding in the ambulance expanded. He'd watched in near shock as his dad had become completely unresponsive. His skin had turned the same gray color as his hair. And beneath the oxygen mask he wore, Wyn thought his lips looked blue.

He paced in the waiting room for a good thirty minutes before other family members arrived.

His mother seemed calmer. The staff immediately took her back beyond the swinging doors, leaving him and Cres alone.

"How is he?" Cres asked.

"He was unconscious the entire way here."

"They give you any indication of what might've happened?"

"I overheard heart attack when the EMT was on the police scanner."

Cres removed his suit jacket, then his bolo tie. He unbuttoned the top two buttons on his white dress shirt and rolled up the sleeves.

"How was Mom?" Wyn asked.

"Doin' that freaky-quiet Mom thing. I suspect Dad's siblings will show up within the next hour. They caught me on the way out and asked which hospital. I explained we were lucky there was even one this far out. They just don't get it."

Wyn sighed. His dad's family hadn't understood why he'd left California and used his inheritance to buy a cattle ranch in rural Colorado. And the times the Grant family had visited their relatives in Santa Ana, they didn't understand why anyone would choose to live among so many people. But despite their differences, they remained close.

Several long minutes of silence passed between Wyn and his brother, which wasn't unusual since they worked together and didn't yammer on from sunup to sundown. When Wyn glanced at the clock he was surprised to see thirty minutes had gone by.

The emergency doors opened and a whole mass of people walked in. His uncle Bill and his wife Barbie, his aunt Marie and her husband Roger. Cousin April and her husband Craig. Plus Ramsey, Sutton's boss from the gun range, Mick, and Melissa.

Uncle Bill approached first. "Any word?"

"No. They let Mom go back there as soon as she got here."

"That's good," Uncle Bill said, absentmindedly patting Wyn's shoulder.

"It was great of all of you to come, but you don't have to stick around. Cres and I can call you with updates."

"Nonsense. You boys don't need to deal with all of this yourselves. We're here. Besides, the forty years I spent as a nurse will come in handy," Aunt Marie said.

"She has a point, Wyn," Cres said.

"It'll likely be another hour at least before you know anything, so maybe we could all do with a cup of coffee to keep us alert." She signaled to her husband, daughter, and son-in-law to accompany her to the beverage station.

Ramsey moved in. "I'm assuming you haven't called the groom on his wedding night and let him know what's up?"

Wyn shook his head. "No sense in disturbing him when we don't know a damn thing about what's goin' on."

"We're heading back to the hotel. So if anything changes and you need someone to wake up the bride and groom, just call me and I'll knock on their door."

They exchanged numbers.

As Ramsey and his head instructor walked away, Wyn caught Cres looking at Mick with regret. He leaned over and murmured, "So much for your post-wedding hookup tonight, huh?"

"Fuck off."

"Is that the kind of guy you go for?" Wyn asked. Since Cres had come out to his family, they'd avoided talking about their sexual conquests. But when Wyn thought back, any talk of hookups had always come from him, not his brother.

So it shocked the hell out of him when Cres said, "The dude's a cowboy. A hot cowboy. A hot military cowboy. He knows his way around guns and he knows how to ride."

"Point taken. I'd probably wanna tap that if I swung that way."

"Christ. I cannot *believe* we're havin' this conversation." Cres snorted. "Speaking of hookups..."

Melissa wandered over. And Wyn didn't pretend he wasn't checking her out. Her dress wasn't excessively wrinkled from their smokin' hot encounter. He smirked, knowing she had a suck mark on the inside of her right breast. His gaze moved up to her lips. Oh, hell yeah. Her mouth was smooth and plump from the insane amount of time they'd spent kissing. When his eyes connected with hers, that spark of desire remained.

"How are you doing?"

"As well as can be expected without knowing anything," Wyn said. "I'm surprised to see you here." Shit. That'd come out wrong. "I mean—"

"I know what you meant, Wynton. I had your family members follow me here since I've been to this hospital a number of times."

"You were okay to drive?" Cres asked. "I swear I saw you knocking them back too."

Melissa shook her head. "Sleight of hand. I avoid things that put my judgment into question. Alcohol certainly does that."

"Amen, sister." Cres stood and stepped right in front of him. "I need caffeine. You want a cup of coffee, *Wynton?*"

Since Melissa couldn't see him, Wyn mouthed "fuck off" at the snarky way Cres enunciated his full name. "I'm fine."

"Suit yourself." Cres lumbered off.

Melissa plopped down beside him. "Did I interrupt something?"

"Nah. We're both a little punchy."

"I imagine."

He braced his forearms on his thighs. "So you weren't drinking tonight? Or you don't drink ever?"

"I did the champagne toast, but that's it. I drank sparkling water with lime or juice the rest of the night. I've learned if you don't want people to catch on to the fact you're not drinking, then don't talk about it and no one notices."

"But London said you guys were gonna do tequila shots."

"*London* did a tequila shot. I reminded her that me and tequila were on a permanent break."

Wyn smiled. "Gotcha." His smile dried. "I want you to know I was sober when we locked ourselves in that ready room."

"I know or I wouldn't have gone with you."

He reached out and brushed a few stray hairs from her cheek. "You are so freakin' sexy. I'd planned on takin' you back to my hotel room tonight—"

The doors to the back of the hospital opened.

His grim-faced mother was followed out by a man wearing a white coat and a stethoscope.

Wyn's stomach churned. He rose to his feet and Cres was instantly beside him. "Mom? What's goin' on?"

"Dr. Poole will explain."

"Bluntly put," Dr. Poole started, "Mr. Grant suffered a heart attack. To what extent the damage is, we're not sure yet. I've ordered blood tests that measure levels of cardiac enzymes, which indicate heart muscle damage."

"Whoa. You can tell that with a blood test?" Cres asked skeptically.

"Yes. The enzymes normally found inside the cells of the heart are needed for that specific organ. When the heart muscle cells are injured, their contents—including those enzymes—are released into the bloodstream, making it a testable entity."

"Thanks for the explanation," Wyn said. "What else?"

"After discussing the symptoms with Mrs. Grant, I suspect Mr. Grant's heart attack started before he hit the dance floor. We know the heart attack was still ongoing when they brought him in here. We immediately medicated him."

"But?"

"But the medicines aren't working so he's been sent to the cardiac cath lab."

All this medical terminology was making his head hurt. "What's that?"

"A cardiac catheter can be used to directly visualize the blocked artery and help us determine which procedure is needed to treat the blockage."

"You're telling us this because you've made the determination there is a significant blockage?" Wyn asked.

Dr. Poole nodded. "Once Mr. Grant has been stabilized, we'll send him to Denver, via ambulance."

"Not medevac'ing him now?"

"No."

"That means...it's not that serious?" Cres asked.

"Oh, it's serious. But given that he was brought here immediately, if we observe him overnight, we'll have a full assessment to give the cardiac team in Denver tomorrow, which will save time."

"But by keeping him here and not sending him to a cardiac hospital, you're not takin' unnecessary chances with his life? 'Cause I ain't down with that at all, doc."

"Wynton," his mother softly chastised.

"I'm with Wyn on this, Mom," Cres inserted. "If Dad needs to be in Denver, fire up the helicopter and get him there. Pronto."

"I understand your concerns," Dr. Poole said. "And you have every right to question my recommendation. But I spent a decade in the cardiac unit in Salt Lake City, so I am more qualified than your average country doc."

That gave Wyn a tiny measure of relief. "Okay."

"Any other questions?"

"Can we see him?" Cres asked.

"Not right now. We'll see how the night progresses. It's up to your mother whether she stays back there with him or out here with you all."

Sue Grant lifted her chin. "My husband has suffered a major health trauma. Of course I'm staying with him." She stepped forward and offered Wyn and Cres each a hug. "As soon as I have any news, I promise I'll be out here to tell you."

Then she and Dr. Poole walked back through the swinging doors.

Wyn turned around and searched for Aunt Marie. "Did you catch all of that?"

"Yes. From the sounds of it, Jim will be out for the rest of the night. And since there's no reason for us all to be exhausted tomorrow, we'll head back to the hotel. But I promise we'll be back first thing in the morning." Her gaze winged between Wyn and Cres. "I don't suppose I can convince either of you to return to the hotel and get some rest?"

They both said "no" at the same time.

"That's what I thought." She, too, gave them both a hug. "Any change, you call me." She pulled a deck of cards out of her purse. "To pass the time."

Wyn kissed her cheek. "Thank you. You sure you're okay to drive?"

"Sober as a judge, my boy." Her brown eyes narrowed. "Last question. What about Sutton?"

"What about him?"

"He deserves to know his father is in the hospital."

"He deserves a wedding night with his wife," Wyn retorted.

"So you're suggesting we don't tell him that Dad is in the ER and headed for Denver tomorrow, possibly for surgery?" Cres demanded.

"That's exactly what I'm sayin'."

"But—"

"End of discussion, Cres."

Arguments started—and all seemed to be directed at him. So Wyn tuned them out and wandered over to the window.

He'd glared at the juniper bushes lining the sidewalk for several minutes when he felt a soft touch on his arm. He saw Melissa's reflection in the window. "What?"

"You have to tell Sutton about your dad being in the hospital, Wynton. It's his decision whether he leaves on his honeymoon tomorrow or stays here, not yours. By not telling him, you're making it *your* decision. That's not fair to him, to you, or to your father. If something unforeseen happens, and Sutton returns home to the worst news imaginable...he'll blame you for a multitude of things—starting with him not getting to say good-bye. That's too deep a burden for you to undertake."

"Do you have any idea how much this honeymoon means to my brother?" For months, Sutton had planned the four-week getaway in the tropics. Wasn't out of sight, out of mind better in this instance? Would Sutton even be able to relax and enjoy this special time with London if he was constantly calling home to check on Dad?

"I'd venture a guess...it doesn't mean as much to him as your father does."

"Jesus, Melissa."

"You need someone to be the bad guy and you don't want it to be you. But by letting Sutton know what happened and giving him the choice of what to do next, you are doing the right thing."

"It doesn't feel that way."

"I know." She swept her hand across his shoulders. "But trust me because I speak from personal experience, not telling Sutton is worse."

Wyn turned and looked at her. "This happened to you?"

"My sister had an accident while I was at camp. And instead of bringing me home, my parents let me finish out the full two weeks. We weren't allowed to have cell phones, so I didn't have a clue she almost died until after my dad picked me up. And naturally, my sister thought I wasn't there because my training camp was more important than her. It was ugly."

Before he could ask what kind of accident, Cres strolled up.

"You done bein' unreasonable?"

"Yeah."

"So you're in agreement that Sutton needs to be told?"

"Can we do it early in the morning? And at least give him the rest of this night with London? The doc pretty much told us nothin' will change tonight anyway."

"Makes sense. You cool with Aunt Marie bein' the one who knocks on the honeymoon suite door at six a.m. and tells him what's up?"

"That'd be best. He won't punch her. And she does have that calming nurse demeanor."

Right then, Aunt Marie yelled at the receptionist.

"On second thought..."

Cres chuckled. "She seems feistier than usual. I'll walk them out." Cres headed to the desk.

Melissa squeezed Wyn's arm. "She followed me here, do you want me to lead them back to the hotel?"

"If you wanna go, that's fine."

"That's not what I asked."

Wyn studied her. "Why would you want to stay? We just met today. For all you know I could be a total dick."

"A total dick usually doesn't know he's a total dick, so that argument doesn't apply. Try again."

"Do you *want* to stay?"

"Yes."

He exhaled. "Good. Because to be honest, I didn't know how to ask you to stay. This is"—he gestured to the hospital and to her—"screwing with my head."

She stood on tiptoe to whisper, "I'd rather be screwing with your body, but since that's not in the cards..." Then she stepped back and pointed to his hand. "Speaking of cards...playing strip poker would be a great way to kill time."

"Strip poker, huh?"

"Virtual strip poker, beings we're in public."

"How's that work?"

"We keep score. The next time we're alone together, we'll have a specific order in how we remove our clothes."

For the first time in two hours he had a sense of hope about something—it sounded like Melissa didn't want this thing with them to be a one and done either. "You keep score, baby, and I'll deal the first hand."

Chapter Four

Mel laid down her cards. "Full house, jacks over sevens."

"Damn. I thought I had you this time." Wynton spread out three twos, a six, and a ten.

"Three of a kind with deuces?" she tsk-tsked. "With two players that's never a good gamble." She eyed his shirt collar and imagined peeling that pristine white shirt off his broad shoulders and down his muscular arms. Her gaze caught on the thick column of his neck. She wanted to sink her teeth into that hard flesh. Taste the salt and musk on his skin. Fill her senses with the overpowering maleness of him.

"Melissa, darlin'? You okay?"

Her focus snapped back to him. "I'm fine. Why?"

"You moaned like you were in pain."

She leaned forward. "That moan was your fault. See, I imagined stripping you out of that pesky shirt and my mind wandered south from there."

"You're already kicking my ass at poker and now you gotta give me a hard-on in the waiting room?"

"Just keeping you updated on how eager I am to get my greedy hands all over your naked body. You had way too many clothes on before."

"The feeling is mutual."

But he was distracted when he said that so Melissa turned toward the front entrance when he muttered, "I'll be damned."

The good-looking military guy who'd first offered Jim medical assistance at the wedding paused inside the doors and scanned the waiting area. At the end of the row, Cres straightened up and ran his hand over his hair before he stood.

The guy saw him and smiled. Cres met him halfway and they shook hands, but not in the usual way guys shook hands. Their connection lingered.

Holy crap. Cres Grant was gay.

She sent a sidelong glance at Wynton. Did he know?

He watched the two men, not exactly circumspectly, as he shuffled the deck.

"Is that a friend of your brother's? I saw them talking at the wedding. And he left with Sutton's boss when I got here. Think he came back to see how your dad's doing?"

Wynton said nothing but then she felt him staring at her.

When their eyes met, she got her answer—wariness. Like he was afraid she'd pass judgment on his brother.

As if.

Other people's sexual preferences weren't her concern—she had enough issues with her own sexual needs to worry about someone else's. "How long have you known that Cres is...?"

"Gay?" he said softly. "He came out to us last year. Right after Sutton and London got engaged." His eyes narrowed. "But it's not common knowledge."

"Those two keep looking at each other like that in public and it will be," Mel said dryly. She picked up her cards without really looking at them. "I'd never take it upon myself to point out the obvious to others who can't see it."

"Thank God for that."

"Were you surprised when he came out?"

"Honestly? Yeah. I guess the signs were there if I cared to look. He hadn't had a serious girlfriend...ever really. Hadn't dated any girl since high school. He didn't like trolling the bars with me. Even before I hit pause on my libido last year, he preferred that we hang out and play video games on the weekends."

What did he mean...*hit pause on his libido?*

"And he always did love men's wrestling a little too much."

Mel's gaze snapped to his. "Seriously?"

He smirked. "Nah. Just seein' if you're paying attention."

"Jerk." She tossed her cards down. "This hand is crap. Re-deal."

Wynton shuffled again. Surprisingly, he kept talking. "As an adult, Cres has always seemed preoccupied. When I think back...I just wish he would've told us sooner. Because right after he told us, it was as if a giant weight had been lifted from him. I hated that he carried that weight at all."

You sweet, thoughtful man. He was a good brother—did *his* brothers appreciate that? "So your family is fine with everything?"

"Cres has always been tight-lipped. But like I said, it filled in some of the pieces about Cres that hadn't fit before. So he's got our acceptance, and I think that's all that really worried him. Who else he chooses to tell ain't my concern. It sure as hell ain't my business who he dates. I'm just happy he can be himself and date who he wants."

Mel held her fist out for a bump. "Amen. I'll just throw it out there that we wouldn't be having this conversation if Cres was on the rodeo circuit. If there's even a whisper of that kind of relationship, they're unofficially blackballed."

"That's what Sutton said too." Wynton dealt them each a new hand. "So tell me about your sister. You said she had an accident. What happened?"

How did she explain this? The few times she'd bothered, she worried she'd come off sounding like a poor little rich girl or resentful, which wasn't the case. So she usually avoided the topic entirely with men by just dropping to her knees.

A rough-skinned hand skated up her arm. "With all that we've been through today, I hope you won't start holdin' back on me now."

She inhaled a deep breath and let it all spill out. "My parents are loaded, okay? One of those requirements of being a Lockhart was making sure I excelled at riding, horsemanship, dressage, the whole package. The camp I attended when my sister Alyssa was injured was an exclusive, by-invitation-only camp at a training facility for Olympic athletes. The best trainers in the world were there. So in my parent's eyes, pulling me from camp would've been viewed in the same horrifying light as dropping out of the program because I couldn't cut it. And the Lockharts couldn't have anyone believing that of them or their human progeny." She closed her eyes. The ache of that time had lessened but hadn't disappeared completely.

Wynton cupped her jaw in his hand and lifted her face to his. "Hey. If it bothers you too much to tell me—"

"It doesn't. I just haven't talked about it in a while."

"Then I'm flattered you're sharing all this with me."

"Anyway, throughout my entire life I'd been groomed to win the gold medal in the Olympics while riding a Lockhart horse, thereby increasing its worth and mine."

"Harsh assessment, baby."

"But it's true."

"How old is your sister?"

"Alyssa is six years younger than me."

"What happened?"

"She was at a birthday party. There were go-cart races and she crashed through a fence. The fence crushed her legs and she ended up paralyzed from the waist down."

His jaw dropped to the floor. After he picked it up, he said, "Keep goin'."

"My parents focused completely on my sister—as they should have. Alyssa was really awful after the accident. She especially hated the sight of me. She resented me. Not solely because I wasn't by her side immediately after the accident, but because I was…whole, if that makes sense. As accomplished a horsewoman that I was, Alyssa was better. I'd always known if I'd failed to meet my parent's expectations, the Lockharts had another shot of having an Olympian in the family with Alyssa. I stopped riding and training after her accident because I wanted to be there for her. But she didn't want me anywhere near her. After enduring two solid months of her screaming at me to get the hell away from her, the doctors and my parents asked me to stop coming to visit her, at least until she wasn't so angry. And because it was in Alyssa's best interest, I left."

Wynton picked up her hand and kissed the inside of her wrist.

"So while my sister recovered from a near-fatal accident, I reset my priorities."

"Ran away with the rodeo, did you?"

She smiled. "Something like that. I continued to check on her, but since I was out of sight, I wasn't on my parents' minds. And don't think I was resentful because I wasn't. I was an adult. Alyssa needed them so much more than I did."

"Did your sister come around? Stop resenting you?"

"Yes. I never held the way she acted against her because she suffered a horrible life-altering ordeal at such a young age. Eventually we mended all fences. But I had no interest in going back to that world and competing on the level I'd been at before her accident. After two years, Alyssa set her mind to competing again. She trained for the Paralympics and won several national equestrian championships. She's competed in the international Paralympics, winning a silver and a bronze medal. She's so determined to succeed for herself—not just for our parents—that she won't quit until she's won a gold medal. I'm so proud of her. She's turned out to be an inspiration to so many people."

"I wish I had your attitude. I'm ashamed to say I didn't. Not either time Sutton was injured. The second time I was so mad at him when he opted to go back into rodeo. It seemed selfish of him to continue. And when he was in the hospital, I stayed away. I claimed I had extra ranch work to do because Dad was at Sutton's side, but that wasn't the reason. I just couldn't handle seein' my brother like that. I don't do well when it comes to illnesses and hospitals."

She experienced that familiar punch of sadness. She'd heard that so many times—not only over the last six months, but whenever she talked about her sister's struggles. She'd walked away for her sister's benefit—not because she couldn't deal with it. Now their relationship was solid, but she hadn't even considered calling Alyssa when she'd gotten her diagnosis—especially not after how their mother had reacted when she'd finally told her.

"Hey, Kentucky, where'd you go?" he said softly.

Mel returned her focus to him. The man had the most expressive face. More rugged than handsome, if she had to put a name to it. His features weren't as sharply defined as either of his brother's—Sutton Grant defined gorgeous and Cres Grant was almost pretty—but Wynton's raw-boned features gave him an equally striking look. His hair, in the vivid brightness of the fluorescent lights, held a dark red hue, which made the pieces curling around his ears more boyish looking.

"Darlin', you keep lookin' at me like that and I'm gonna start searching for a supply closet."

"Don't toss out suggestions you won't follow through with," she said.

He cocked a dark eyebrow. "Why don't you think I'll follow through?"

She threaded her fingers through his. "Because even with all this flirty and sexy banter, and me trying to convey my complicated past to try and take your mind off the present, I see the strain in your eyes. You're worried about your dad. But you're also worried about your mom. You feel guilty that you have someone out here with you—even if I wasn't here you'd still have Cres to kill time with—whereas your mother is back there alone."

"You caught all that?" He paused, brooding look in place. "What else?"

"I figured you'd play another two hands of poker with me, letting me believe I was successful at distracting you, before you wandered to the front desk to see if you could go back there and check on your mother, or try to get some kind of message to her to see how she's doing."

"How do you do that?"

"What?"

"Read my mind. It's a little spooky."

"Why?"

He frowned. "Because we've only known each other for a few hours."

But I've known about you for almost a year. The man London claimed had sadness behind his perpetual smile. The man who used sex to combat loneliness, just like I do. The man I refused to let my best friend set me up with—and yet somehow, she did it anyway, without even knowing it.

"Melissa?"

She glanced up from staring at his hard-skinned knuckles. "But in those few hours we've fucked, swapped life stories, and shared some brutal truths, so we're beyond the 'what's your favorite movie?' first date type of bullshit." She brought his hand to her mouth. "So go do what you have to. I'll hang around in the off chance I can continue to be a distraction."

He kissed her. "Thank you. I'll be back."

* * * *

While Wynton was in the back with his mother, Mel did a little exploring. The hospital wasn't very big and most of the private areas were in the back beyond the swinging doors, so that put a wrinkle in her plan.

When Wynton appeared about fifteen minutes later, Mel couldn't help but watch him saunter toward her—his tall, muscular body a visual feast even covered in clothes. He exuded confidence, despite the worry wrinkling his brow, and it made her realize all the guys she'd been playing around with were just boys compared to this man.

Cres intercepted him before he reached the sitting area, and she tried to decipher their grim conversation. Cres nodded, clapped Wynton on the shoulder and stepped aside.

Then Wynton's eyes met hers and she was on her feet by the time he stood in front of her. "No change."

"Sorry." She touched his cheek. "You look like you could use some fresh air."

"That I could." He squinted at the thin wrap covering her shoulders and shrugged out of his suit jacket. "Needing to clear my head don't mean I want you to freeze, darlin'." He draped the coat around her.

His scent enveloped her and his gesture warmed her more than the actual coat. "Thanks."

"Let's take a walk." They exited through the emergency room doors and paused outside the building. The October air had a sharp bite. When Wynton exhaled, she saw some of the tension leave his shoulders. The rancher definitely didn't like to be cooped up.

He dropped his arm across her shoulders and pulled her close so he could kiss her temple. "If I haven't said it enough, I appreciate you bein' here, Melissa."

The security lights lit the sidewalk as they walked around the building. They didn't speak, but the silence didn't seem forced or awkward.

When they reached the edge of the parking lot, Mel said, "My coat is in the car and I'd really love to change out of these shoes."

"Of course."

She hit the unlock button on the Jeep Cherokee and skirted the front end to slide into the driver's side. Wynton slipped into the passenger's seat. She started the engine. "No need for us to sit in the cold." She felt his questioning gaze when she turned the dashboard lights off.

"This is a nice SUV," he said. "It's got enough horsepower to pull your horse trailer?"

"This isn't mine. It belongs to the Gradsky's. I borrow it when I'm not on the road." Mel twisted around to dig on the floor behind Wynton for her athletic shoes. "It gets considerably better gas mileage than my Chevy Tahoe." She kicked off her high-heeled boots and slipped her feet into athletic shoes.

"I never asked how much you're on the road?"

She skirted his question with, "Give me the play-by-play of your multiple ménages, Wynton. Girl/girl/guy?"

"Yep."

"Girl/guy/girl?"

"That too."

"What about guy/girl/guy?"

"Yep, and before you go on, never been in a guy/guy/girl threesome."

She grinned. "That's funny because that's the only type I've ever been in. And talk about scorching hot, watching the two guys together, their hands, mouths, and bodies all over each other. It was fucking powerful."

Wynton reached over and tucked a flyaway curl behind her ear. "Same thing with the girl on girl action. Those soft hands and mouths exploring all that smooth and supple skin. I still remember the sucking sounds. The feminine squeaks and sighs. Then how hot it was to have them turn all that focus on me. Only time I wish I'd had a cock and a strap-on so I could fuck them both at once."

"Put that in your spank bank, did you?"

"Hell, yeah." Even in the dark she could see his eyes glittering when he ran the back of his knuckles down her jawline. "That encounter in the ready room is gonna go in there too."

"I'm flattered." Mel turned her head and rubbed her lips across the base of his hand. "Unzip your pants and pull your cock out. I'll give you something else to file away for a future round of self-love."

Those amazing eyes of his burned black with desire. He kept his gaze locked to hers when he unbuckled his belt. When he lowered the zipper. When he lifted his hips off the seat. When he tugged his pants and his boxer briefs to his knees. Then he eased the seat back and folded his arms behind his head.

Mel dropped her gaze to his groin, not surprised to see he already sported a full-blown erection. She shifted in her seat, angling forward across the console. Bracing one hand on his muscular thigh and the other on his chest, she parted her lips—after kissing the head—and let that hard satin heat pass over her teeth and tongue. She held her breath through the gag reflex when the tip connected with her soft palette and bumped the back of her throat.

Wynton made an inarticulate moan.

Encouraged, she started the long glide up and down his thick shaft, the wetness in her mouth easing her way, each pass progressively lower until she was deep-throating him every time. She didn't use her hands. Just the wet heat of her mouth, the sassy flick of her tongue, and the suctioning power of her cheeks.

She shouldn't have been surprised when his hand landed on the top of her head and held her in place the moment his cock was buried deep. Her eyes watered and her pulse whooshed in her ears, but she still heard him say, "That's it, baby. Take it all. Now swallow. Fuck, yeah. Do that again."

She did what he asked because she had no problem taking direction—except when she didn't. But this wasn't one of those times. And she didn't intend to tease and drag this out. She knew they didn't have much time, so she'd make this fast.

"You could own me with this mouth," he said gruffly when she began bobbing her head, using shallower strokes and stopping to suckle on the tip.

The heater finally kicked out some warmth, turning the inside of the car sultry.

Mel felt that rush of primal satisfaction when he started to pump his hips up to meet the downward motion of her mouth. His grip tightened in her hair. He muttered something about her never fucking stopping when she earned her reward.

His cock got harder yet. In the next instant, it jerked against the roof of her mouth in hot bursts, sending his seed flowing down the back of her throat. She swallowed repeatedly, the mantra in her head *gimme, gimme, gimme* as he shot his load until he had nothing left.

Even when Wynton attempted to pull her head away, she sank her teeth into the base of his cock, keeping him in place so she could suck and lick as his dick softened.

Before she released him completely, she nuzzled his pubic hair. She loved giving head. Every man reacted differently—well, they all acted grateful—but besides that, she reveled in their reaction in the aftermath. Some men wanted to kiss her and taste their come on her tongue. Some men avoided kissing her mouth entirely. Some men wanted to return the favor and practically dove between her thighs. Some men actually stared at her in awe and spent several long moments just tracing her swollen lips. Some men wanted to cuddle. The men with phenomenal recovery time were ready to fuck. So her heart raced when she glanced up to see how Wynton would act.

As soon as he had her eyes, he fisted one big hand in the front of her dress and curled his other hand around the back of her neck as his mouth crashed down on hers in a blistering kiss. He sucked her tongue hard, as if trying to take his essence back from her.

Oh. That was hot as hell.

The kiss made her dizzy and who knows how long it would've gone on if the seatbelt latch hadn't jabbed her in the side, causing her to break away.

"What? You okay?" he asked.

"It's ironic that I'm at the wrong angle now."

"There sure as hell wasn't anything wrong with the angle you were at before." He followed the upper bow of her lip with the pad of his thumb. "That was awesome. Thank you."

"Spank bank worthy?"

"Definitely."

Mel gave him one last lingering kiss before she returned to her seat so he could adjust his clothing. When she reached back for her coat, he grabbed her hand and brought it to his mouth.

"Are you wet?"

"Very."

"I could slip my hand up your dress and get you off." He kissed her palm again. "Or I could stay like this and watch you get yourself off. That'd be hot."

"It would be. But I didn't blow you because I expected something in return."

His eyes searched hers. "Why *did* you blow me? To take my mind off the family medical stuff?"

"No. I blew you because I wanted to get up close and personal with your cock."

"That's it?"

"You were expecting a more dramatic reason?"

"Maybe a more believable one."

Do not get angry. "Explain."

"In my experience, most women don't mind givin' blowjobs, but when they do it's definitely in expectation of me spending time between their thighs."

"So is eating pussy just a reciprocal thing for you?"

"Meaning I only do it when it's expected of me?" He paused and shook his head. "If I'da had my way at the reception? Before we fucked I would've been on my knees with your thigh wrapped around the back of my neck until I ate my fill of you and made you come at least twice."

Her pulse leapt at the image of Wynton's head beneath her dress and his hungry mouth showing her what he'd learned during his years as Super Man-Slut.

"I ain't proud to admit this, but I've had women blow me in hopes of getting an introduction to my world champion bulldogger brother, Sutton. I've had women blow me after an expensive dinner because they felt they owed me." He scowled. "How I kept my dick hard after hearing that is a mystery. I've had women blow me because I've asked them to put their mouths on my dick. Have I ever had a woman blow me because she just likes sucking cock and she's good at it?" Another pause, another soft kiss to the center of her palm. "No, ma'am."

Mel laughed. "Glad I'm unique and brought something new to the table."

"That you did. And while I love spending time with my cock in your mouth, I'm happier that you showed up at the hospital and have given me a chance to get to know you beyond that."

Not for the first time, Mel thought it was a shame they didn't live closer to each other because she'd like to explore this connection for longer than one night.

"We'd better go inside. I doubt anything has changed, but I need to be there in case something does."

She kissed him. "Let's go."

Chapter Five

Wyn awoke with a start when someone jostled him. Melissa immediately sat upright.

Sutton loomed over him. He didn't look pleased. London hung back behind him, covering her mouth with a yawn.

"Mornin' newlyweds."

"While I appreciate that *someone* told me the news about Dad this morning, I ain't too happy that I wasn't told last night."

"Well, excuse the fuck outta me for not wanting to interrupt your wedding night," Wyn snapped.

Cres ambled over and squared off against Sutton. "Both of you need to chill out. Nothin' has changed in the six hours that we've been here so there was no need for you to be here, okay? Mom's the only one allowed back there. We've seen her one time. We'll know more when the doctor makes rounds this morning."

"Any idea when that'll be?"

Wyn shook his head. "But even last night the doctor indicated they'd be sending Dad to Denver via ambulance. Whether they're doin' surgery or what is up in the air." He watched his brother try and get control.

Guilt and sadness crossed Sutton's face when he looked at his wife. "I hate to say this, sweetheart, but you'll have to go on the honeymoon by yourself so we don't lose the deposits. I'll catch up if—and when I can."

Beside him, Melissa sucked in a soft breath and muttered, "Wrong answer, bud."

"Go on our honeymoon by myself," London repeated. "Because that's what I care about, more than making sure your father is okay, more than making sure I'm there for you so *you're* okay, that we don't lose the fucking deposits?" London got in Sutton's face. "Let me tell you something, asshat. I am your *wife*. I am part of this family. Do you think I could just kick back on the beach with a fruity drink in my hand when your dad is fighting for his life? Do you think I'm so—"

Sutton covered her mouth in a silencing kiss. Then he said, "Point taken."

"Good. If we have to cancel the honeymoon—"

"You don't need to cancel the honeymoon," their mom said from behind them. "You might have to delay it a few days, that's all."

Wyn stood. "Mom. Sit. You look exhausted."

"I am exhausted but I've been sitting all night." She looked at each one of her sons and her daughter-in-law, giving Melissa and Mick both a quick, questioning glance before she spoke. "Dr. Poole has already been here this morning. The damage from the heart attack wasn't as bad as they'd originally believed. All that means is your dad most likely won't need surgery, but the cardiac unit in Denver will make the final determination. They'll be transporting him soon. What hasn't changed is the fact that he had a heart attack, and even if they just check him out in Denver for a day or two and then send him home, he is out of commission for at least eight weeks. Eight weeks in which he is to do nothing but recover. Not a half-assed 'I'm fine, the doctors don't know shit' kind of recovery that he *thinks* he might get away with."

Cres laughed.

"So what I need from you boys is your promise that you won't let him do diddly squat for the next two months. You won't let him get in his feed truck. You won't even let him ride along and open fences."

"Harsh, Mom."

"I have to be harsh, Wyn. I'm not going to lose that man because of his stupid pride." Her chin wobbled and Wyn wrapped an arm around her.

"We've got your back. We promise not to let him pull any crap," Cres said.

"Easier said than done because you're shipping cattle in the next two weeks," his mother said. "Yesterday, before any of this happened, your dad mentioned being shorthanded with Sutton off on his honeymoon. So you know his first response will be to climb on his horse and round up the herd to help you boys sort cattle."

"That ain't happening," Sutton said. "If you can put off shipping even for a week, we can cut the honeymoon short so I can come back and help."

Wyn shook his head. "Because of the wedding, we're starting this a week late as it is. The last thing we need is to lose all our calves to an early blizzard or freezing rain like happened in South Dakota and Wyoming last year."

"If you've got no one that can fill in for Dad, then we'll postpone the honeymoon." Sutton sent London a pleading look. "Sorry, sweetheart."

But London was studying Melissa. "Mel, what do you have going on the next couple of weeks?"

"Not much. I have a break in teaching."

"Good. Then you can help out at the Grant Ranch."

Wyn, Cres, and Sutton all said, "What?" simultaneously.

"Oh, for God's sake. Mel is a cutting horse champion. You guys all know what the main skill is for a cutting horse, right? Sorting livestock. Her horse is at my folk's farm. She can load Plato up and spend the next couple weeks in the field doing what she's trained to do."

Wyn looked at Melissa, who seemed equally shocked by the suggestion.

"London, doll, as much as I love you, you can't go offering Mel's help without askin' her first," Sutton drawled.

"You heard her. It's not like she's got other plans. And Wyn has an extra room where she can stay. So does Cres. That way your mom"—she flashed Sue a smile—"can be with your dad all the time so there's no chance he'll go against doctor's orders and jeopardize his recovery."

"That would be a huge relief to me," his mom admitted.

"Plus, not only is Mel a cutting horse champ, the past five years she's been working as part of a penning team. Shoot, I'll bet she can cut your sorting time down to nothin'. Am I right, Mel?"

All eyes zoomed to Melissa.

"About the sorting time? No. The Grant boys are ranch born.

They'll ride circles around me. But if you need an extra horse and rider, I'd be happy to help out in any way that I can."

"Then it's settled," London declared. "You all can figure out where Mel is staying later."

Wyn knew exactly where she'd be staying for the next few weeks.

Everyone started talking and Wyn leaned down to speak to Melissa privately. "You really okay with this?"

"I was thinking to myself earlier that I wished you and I had more time together, and now I've got my wish." She smirked.

"What?"

"This wasn't as altruistic of London as you might believe."

He chuckled. "Yes, it *is* fortunate that they won't have to miss more than a day or two of their honeymoon, isn't it? Because the ranch matters are handled."

"That and you know she's been trying to fix us up since she and Sutton got engaged."

That took Wyn by surprise. "Then why is their wedding the first time I met you?"

Melissa looked away. "I have no idea."

Like hell. He'd find out more about that later. "The circumstances suck, but I'm glad you're staying with me."

"Me too. I'll be happy to bunk in your guest room."

"I'd rather have you in my bed, but I'll leave that up to you."

* * * *

Wyn gave Melissa his address and the key to his front door. She had a few loose ends to tie up before she made the two-and-a-half-hour trek to the Grant Ranch, and she wouldn't arrive until late tomorrow afternoon. Normally, he didn't like people in his house when he wasn't there, but she didn't feel like a stranger. He might've obsessed on that if he hadn't been obsessing on coordinating family and vehicles as they caravanned to Denver.

Before the orderlies loaded "Big" Jim Grant in the ambulance, the doctor allowed Wyn and his brothers to see their dad for a short visit. The old man looked better than he had the previous night. Sometimes Wyn forgot that his dad was in his late sixties. He didn't look his age, nor did he act it—having a heart attack while dancing to "La Bamba" pretty much summed that sentiment up perfectly.

Now they watched the ambulance pull away and Wyn felt a pang of worry again.

"Mom seemed more relaxed about all of this," Cres commented.

"She puts on a good front in front of Dad."

Wyn looked at Sutton. "I suspect you're right."

"I ain't a doctor, but if Dad's condition was a life or death matter, they would've airlifted him last night. Hospitals don't fuck around with that stuff," Sutton said.

"You would know."

London nestled her head on Sutton's chest. "We are all staying in the same place tonight?"

"Sounds like. It's within walking distance to the hospital."

Cres looked up at the grayish cast to the sky. "I'd better get. Sure hope it doesn't snow."

"I hate that you're goin' home to check cattle by yourself." This time of year and this close to shipping, the cattle couldn't be unattended for even a day. Wyn had stayed behind yesterday morning when everyone else had gone to Gradsky's to get ready for the wedding. Today, one of them had to go home and take care of the herd, and Cres had volunteered. So it'd be at least eight hours before he got to Denver.

"Mick has offered to help me, if that's all right."

Wyn looked at the deep red flush on his brother's face. This was the first time since Cres had come out that he'd shown an interest in a guy around his family. Normally, Wyn would give him a rash of shit, but this was new territory for all of them.

"That's great," Sutton answered. "Mick mentioned when we were workin' at the range that he grew up on a ranch in Montana before he joined the service."

"Yeah, so he ain't just a pretty gate opener."

Both Wyn and Sutton's jaws dropped. They said nothing. What the hell could they say?

London laughed. She dug out ten bucks, crumpled it into a ball, and tossed it at Cres. "Remind me never to bet against you." She nudged Sutton. "Cres bet me he could say something that'd leave both of you tongue-tied."

"Bettin' against me on the second day we're married, Mrs. Grant, is gonna get you in a whole passel of trouble," Sutton warned.

She murmured something to him that made him grin.

"Jesus. Can we just go already?" Wyn complained.

"Yep. See you guys later. Without bein' a dick, I hope I don't hear from you at all until I walk into the hospital in Denver," Cres said.

"Amen, brother. Drive safe."

* * * *

Late the next afternoon, Berlin Gradsky asked Mel, "Are you sure you'll be all right?"

Berlin mothered Mel way more than her own mother did. "I'll be fine. I'm actually really excited to put Plato through his paces."

"London was right about one thing. This is what Plato was trained for."

After Mel climbed in her truck, Berlin rested her forearms on the window jamb. "Nosy question."

"Hit me."

"Is there a reason why you're staying at Wyn Grant's house and not house sitting for London and Sutton while they're on their honeymoon?"

Yes, because I plan on riding Wynton Grant as hard as Plato for the next three weeks. "Sutton said something about liability issues because of his indoor gun range. I didn't question it. And given my...condition, it's probably smart."

Berlin squeezed Mel's shoulder. "No one knows, do they? Not even my daughter?"

She shook her head. "London didn't need that extra stress during her wedding planning. We both know she would've stressed about that too." But her friend wasn't dumb. She'd asked Mel several times if she was avoiding her. She'd asked if something had happened on the circuit to make Mel drop out. Mel would tell her the reason she'd been distant the last six months as soon as her bossy-pants BFF returned from her honeymoon.

"You're right. I'm happy for my daughter and son-in-law, but I'm glad the wedding is over." She smiled. "Now I just have to worry about you."

"I promise not to take any chances with Plato if I'm not feeling up to it. You know I'd never risk his safety. I'll be fine as long as I follow the rules."

"I've watched you get a handle on this, sweetie, so I trust you with him."

"Thanks for everything."

"You're welcome. Drive safe. Text me when you get there."

"I will."

Berlin stepped back and Mel slowly pulled the horse trailer down the long road leading away from Grade A Farms.

The drive to the Grant Ranch was a little over two hours, and Mel didn't have any reason to hurry. Chances were good she'd beat Wynton there. The family had been in Denver since yesterday, and today they were getting the final diagnosis on the Grant patriarch. She'd stalled as long as she could at Gradsky's. She'd even driven into town and loaded up on groceries because she wasn't sure what type of food a bachelor rancher would stock.

In the last six months, after being diagnosed with type 1 diabetes, Mel had no choice but to monitor every morsel of food that went into her mouth. She also had to reduce her physical activity because she was still learning her limits—which weren't even close to the same as they'd been before her diagnosis.

She hadn't been lucky enough to "get" type 2 diabetes, which allowed her to control her blood sugar levels with modifications to her diet. Her regulation came in the form of daily shots of insulin. Keeping snacks within reach for those times when she felt her glycemic index was low. Carrying glucose tablets with her. Making sure she always had her blood glucose meter, glucose strips, lancets, her needle disposal container, and insulin with her. Thankfully, she could inject herself with an insulin pen, and the type of insulin it used didn't have to be refrigerated.

Even after six months, she wasn't sure she'd ever get used to any of this. It still seemed surreal.

After fighting fatigue, excessive thirst, and weight loss for two months, when she was in LA she finally went to the ER because she thought she might have mono. She'd had it once before and the symptoms seemed similar. The doctor hadn't been convinced her body would react that way to the stress of being on the road, so she'd ordered a battery of tests. When the blood and urine tests had come back positive for diabetes, and further testing indicated type 1 diabetes—a rare diagnosis in a thirty-two-year-old—Mel had literally passed out.

After she'd come to in the hospital, she'd learned the meaning of diabetic shock. She learned her life would never be the same. Ironically, she'd chosen a hospital that had an entire department devoted to dealing with diabetic patients. She learned how to inject herself with insulin. She'd taken a two-day course on proper nutrition, the dangers of excessive physical activity, and how to monitor her blood sugar. She'd soaked it all in. The only time she'd outwardly balked was during her appointment with a counselor who blathered on about emotional changes affecting the body.

Mel had been numb to that. The physical changes concerned her because she realized she'd have to quit competing. It wasn't just her and her horse in the arena, like a barrel racer, or a bulldogger, or a tie down roper. No, in the cutting horse division, it was her, her horse, and ten or more cows. During team penning competition, there were two other riders on horses and up to thirty calves. In other words—mass chaos. She couldn't take the chance that she'd have a low glycemic moment and pass out on top of her horse.

Again.

It had happened to her during a competition, prior to her diagnosis. At the time she'd blamed it on excessive heat in the arena, or being overly tired. She was lucky she hadn't injured herself or someone else.

Especially since she hadn't remembered anything that had happened.

Mel had withdrawn from all competitions. She'd been in limbo, trying to figure out what to do with her life now that her life had changed. Being a trust fund baby did have some perks—she didn't have to decide immediately.

The scenery kept her interest for the remainder of the drive. When she turned down the dirt road that the GPS indicated led to Wynton's house, she envied him and this view every day. Hills and flat land and those gorgeous snow-topped Rocky Mountains in the distance.

His house wasn't what she expected. It was an older ranch house with one old barn, one enormous new barn, and loading pens off to the side of the corral. She pulled the horse trailer up to the pasture Wynton had recommended. She'd keep Plato segregated for a few days until he became acclimated to the area and the other horses.

Since she'd exercised Plato first thing this morning, she checked him for any new marks after being cooped up in the horse trailer. Sometimes the temperamental horse would kick the walls and she'd open up the back end to see him bleeding. But he didn't look worse for the wear, so she fed him and turned him loose.

The next thing Mel did was open the house and cart all of her stuff inside, dumping it in the guest bedroom. She wanted to set the parameters from day one. She couldn't wait to fuck Wynton in every way she'd fantasized about—okay, maybe she had actually written down a list of all the positions and scenarios she wanted to try with Super Man-Slut—but she would be sleeping and waking up alone every night.

You are such a chicken-shit. Why don't you just tell him the truth?

Because she didn't want to blow a good thing. Sexually, they seemed to be on the same page, and that was all that mattered.

She stowed her insulin in the back of the closet. She hid her blood sugar meter in the same drawer as the Glucagon emergency kit. She filled the nightstand drawer with her new best friend—a constant supply of snacks. Then she unpacked her clothes and put them away. She set up her laptop, her cell phone charger, and her e-reader. She spread her toiletries out on the counter in the bathroom across the hallway, including the brand new, unopened jumbo-sized box of condoms.

Then she allowed herself to explore.

Wynton's house was a four-bedroom ranch with a decent-sized living room, and a kitchen that opened into the dining room. Off the dining room was a patio that was completely enclosed by an eight-foot tall fence. The space was homey, although a few things didn't fit. Like the rooster-imaged ruffled curtains in the kitchen and the peach-colored walls in the living room. But the gigantic TV and gaming system, and the oversized recliners and couch did scream bachelor.

One place she didn't even peek into was the closed door at the opposite end of the hallway from her room. It seemed…intrusive to check out Wynton's bedroom when he wasn't here.

And since she had no idea what time he'd arrive, she carried in the groceries she'd packed in the cooler and took stock of his pantry. Good thing she stopped at the store.

Mel had just finished the chicken stir-fry when she heard the front door open.

* * * *

The wait for the doctor's diagnosis today had been nerve-racking. But the good news had been such a relief. His dad had a new diet and exercise regimen. He had eight weeks off to recover because he would make a full recovery.

Before they'd had a chance to celebrate, Jim Grant had announced to his family that he intended to retire from ranching entirely. Starting immediately. Then he'd given Wyn and Cres the option of dividing the land in half. They could each run their own operation, or they could continue to ranch together. He'd take his cut of the cattle sale from this year and then after that, he was out. He planned to fulfill his promise to his wife to see the world. And as soon as he was healthy enough, they'd be off to have the adventures they'd waited a lifetime to experience.

Talk about floored.

Wyn was glad to have several hours to try to sort through everything. But by the time he pulled into his driveway just after dark, he was more than ready to put it all aside and focus on the sweet, hot and sexy redhead he hadn't been able to get out of his mind the past thirty-six hours. The sweet, hot and sexy redhead who was in his house right now. The sweet, hot and sexy redhead who had left the porch light on for him.

Warmth spread through him. It made him a fucking sap, but he hadn't had anyone leave the light on for him since he lived at home. And if the woman had cooked supper? He might just propose to her.

He was so eager to see her he didn't haul in his suitcase. He took the steps two at a time and burst through the door. From the foyer, while he took off his boots, he yelled, "Honey, I'm home." When he rounded the corner, Melissa stood in his living room, her wild curls pulled back into a ponytail. She wore a workout top that showcased her tits, yoga pants—thank you baby Jesus for the genius who invented *those* motherfuckers—and her feet were bare. She looked completely at home in his home.

"Hey. How was the drive?"

"Long."

"How's your dad?"

"Better than we thought, on the road to a full recovery and makin' big plans." He started to stalk her. "Tell me, little redheaded riding girl, what's that delicious smell?"

"I cooked stir-fry but the rice isn't done yet."

"Good. We have time."

Melissa took a step back. "For?"

"For you to tell me why you were trespassing in my kitchen."

"Are you the big bad wolf, Wynton?"

"Yes." He continued slowly moving forward. "Here's where you say, 'Oh my, what big teeth you have.'"

Her gaze zeroed in on his mouth. "Why are you licking your lips?"

"Because you look mighty tasty."

"But I cooked!"

"Don't want food, Red. I want you." Then he was looming over her. The sexy glint in her eyes widened his predatory grin. "Strip off them britches."

Her half-hearted "No" had him wrestling her to the floor. He hovered on all fours above her. "Don't be scared, Red. My big teeth and long wicked tongue are all the better to eat you with. Now take off those pants or I'll tear them off."

Ten seconds later, her bottom half was completely bared to him.

"Drop your knees open. Show me all of you."

Her hesitation vanished.

"My, what a pretty pussy you have." Wyn lowered his head and lapped at the sticky, sweet goodness at the entrance to her body. "I want to fuck you with my mouth, Melissa."

"Yes."

He saw no need to hurry. He explored, mapping her folds with his tongue. He licked fast, then slow. He suckled her pussy lips together, then separately. He grazed her clit with his teeth. By the time he knew the taste of her and the shape of her beneath his mouth, he also knew what maneuver his tongue could do to get her to buck her hips up. Now it was time to know what she sounded like when she came against his face, just how hard she could pull his hair, and how many times he could make her come before she begged him to stop.

Ten minutes later, he had the answers to those questions, and more.

Melissa made a timeout sign.

Wyn chuckled against the top of her thigh.

"You are a menace with that mouth," she panted.

"Come on, Amazing Slut-Girl, you can take some more."

She shook her head. "Not with that lizard-like tongue, Super Man-Slut. But that cock of yours?" She smirked, fished a condom out of her cleavage and flicked it at him. "Bring it on home, baby."

He'd never gotten undressed that fast. He was suited up, on her, and in her. She was hot, slick, tight, and perfect. As he rocked into her, she licked and nipped at his lips, searching his mouth for a taste of herself, which was so fucking sexy, he couldn't stand it.

Then her hands were in his hair, clutching his ass, reaching between them to cup his balls—Christ that felt good.

Melissa arched her back and moaned, "Harder. As hard as you can. I'm close again."

A dozen more deep strokes that sent her sliding across the carpet and she came undone.

Her moment of bliss was a beautiful thing to watch.

When that moment came for him, the last thing he saw before he closed his eyes was the same greedy look on her face that he knew had been on his when she'd unraveled.

After he was spent, he buried his face in her neck. And blew a raspberry until she shrieked and pushed him away.

She'd left the light on for him, jumped onboard for hot, welcome home sex right on the damn carpet, and she'd cooked for him.

This cohabitating thing might be better than he thought.

Chapter Six

After they finished eating, Wyn said, "Level with me. You haven't been competing this year."

Melissa wiped her mouth and set her napkin on the table. "Not since March. Partially because I burned out on it. Partially because London wasn't on the circuit anymore. Partially because I realized my life hadn't changed in the past seven years. I decided to take a break."

"That's understandable. But why did you hedge when I asked you about it?"

She shrugged. "It's gotten to be a habit. I'm really glad for the chance to try something different."

"And I can't wait to show my appreciation for all your hard work." He waggled his eyebrows.

"So can you give me an idea on what to expect, rancher man?"

"We've left the cattle in the summer grazing areas as long as possible. Starting the day after tomorrow, we'll move them into pastures closer to home. That's always traumatic for the cattle, so they'll need five days to get back up to a saleable weight. Then we'll start separating and loading them. We have different places that take them, and they have set times when they'll accept shipments, so the shipping process seems endless."

"So we'll all be on horseback?"

"For the cattle drive, we'll take the horse trailer and horses to the edge of the summer grazing area. We'll unload the horses and start driving cattle out of there. One thing that sucks is we'll have to cross two roads, but they're not paved roads and we've never had a run-in with a car. Then after the cattle are settled, we'll come back, ditch the horses, and two of us will drive out to retrieve the horse trailer. Usually Dad is the one who does that. He also drives ahead and opens the gate so we don't have to stop the cattle and make them wait. But we'll have to figure something else out since we're shorthanded—even with our hot, new cutting horse expert helping out."

Melissa smiled at him. "Flattery will not get me up at the butt crack of dawn to open gates for you, cowboy."

"Maybe I'll make so much noise in the bedroom that you'll have no choice but to get up."

"I have zero problem locking my door at night to ensure that doesn't happen."

Wyn frowned. "You locking me out of my own bedroom?"

"No, because I won't be sleeping in your room, Wynton."

"Explain that."

"I'm set up in the guest bedroom. I have no problem fucking when and where the mood strikes us, but when it's time to sleep…to be blunt, I want my own space. You've lived alone long enough that you'll probably need your own space too—you just don't know it yet. I'll be here three weeks. I don't want to wear out my welcome on the third day because I've strewn my girl stuff all over your bedroom and bathroom. And some nights I can't sleep, so I'm up late reading."

She had an excuse to cover all the bases. He couldn't argue with them, but that didn't mean he wouldn't try like hell to change her mind. He pushed his empty plate back. "So what are we doin' the rest of the night?"

"Dishes first." She kissed his nose. "Ain't domestic life bliss?"

* * * *

The next morning, Wyn hauled his ass out of bed at first light. He and Cres did chores without saying much besides mumbling every once in a while. They stopped by their folks' place to see how Dad was faring. He was tired—and annoyed by the "no ranch work" edict—so for the first time in years, they talked about other things over lunch. Wyn didn't leave in a rush because he was dodging his mom's questions about his relationship with Melissa, he was just anxious to hang out with her the rest of the day.

Once he got back to his house, he felt stupid, coming home early, expecting she'd drop everything and want to spend time with him. She was here as a favor to them to do ranch work. Since her help wasn't needed yet, he had no right to assume she'd want to spend her free time with him.

She sat cross-legged on his couch with her laptop and looked up, beaming a smile at him. "Hey. You done already?"

"For now. Why?"

"Because I want you to take me for a joy ride across the ranch in your truck, cowboy."

His heart simultaneously stopped and exploded with hope. "For real?"

"Unless you want to ride horses to show me the sights?"

"Nope. Let's go." Wyn would drag this afternoon out. Show her every nook and cranny, every field and stream, every rocky ridge and meadow of this place he loved.

Melissa proved to be an excellent gate opener, and she was properly awed by the ranch. That earned her brownie points when he parked in his favorite secluded spot and undressed her.

The times they'd been intimate had been fast and intense. For this go around, Wyn wanted slow. Maybe a little sweet.

His new roomie proved herself to be excellent at slow and sweet, with lazy kisses and lingering caresses.

Afterward, when they were both sweaty and spent on the seat of his truck, he kissed her chest as they spiraled down from the orgasmic high together.

"We're going to wear each other out," she murmured in his hair.

Wyn didn't see a problem with that. "Is that a challenge?"

She groaned. "Not today. I wouldn't mind going back. I need to make a phone call and then I want to exercise Plato."

"Okay. But, baby you gotta move off my lap and let go of my hair so I can drive."

"Oh. Right."

He loved that dazed look in her eyes, knowing he'd put it there.

* * * *

Two nights later, after another nutritious—and surprisingly delicious meal—Wyn broke out the PlayStation 4 and they played Borderlands.

"I'm surprised you're a gamer," he said.

"There's not a lot of other things to do on the road once I get the rig parked for the night."

Wyn smirked at her. "You ain't out rounding up a one-night rodeo for yourself every night? For shame, Amazing Slut-Girl. I'm disappointed."

"My cooter is way more selective these days." She shifted on the couch. "And dude, I've never had this much sex, consistently with the same guy. My cooter is clapping with joy, at the same time she's like…you expect me to take the ground and pound twice daily *and* get chafed in the saddle all day? Pass the ice pack, please."

He laughed. Christ. She made him laugh like no other woman he'd ever met. And laughing with her so much felt damn good. "You sayin' you want me to dial it back?"

"No fucking way, Super Man-Slut. My cooter does not speak for me."

Really, really crazy about this woman already.

"So what else did you do to kill time?" Onscreen he dodged a flurry of arrows and slid beneath a boulder.

"I listen to audiobooks when I'm driving. When I'm at an event, I'm out among the contestants and rodeo people because I spend enough time by myself getting to the destination."

"Do you have an apartment that's a home base?"

Onscreen, Melissa chopped a monster's head off with a broadsword, then snagged the jeweled necklace off the corpse with a, "I'll take that, sucker," before she answered. "I had a place in Kentucky. Once I stopped going there…I put my money into the nicest horse trailer I could buy. I have everything I need. I've upgraded it twice. But since I've been working at Grade A, I rented a place in town to see if I liked living in one place again."

"What's the verdict?"

She shrugged. "Still out. At least for there. Why?"

Wyn maneuvered around a patch of quicksand onscreen. "Sutton made great money when he was winning. Bulldogging paid for his house, and he's never been short on cash for anything else. But I heard other guys talkin' like they don't make a living at it."

"You asking how I support myself because you're looking for me to pay you rent while I'm here?"

"No, smartass." He bristled. "Forget it."

Melissa hit pause on the game and faced him. "Let's get this out in the open. I have Kentucky blueblood parents, remember? I have a trust fund. I use it when I need to. I'm not one of those 'Oh, I have to make it on my own even if I have to live in a hovel to prove I'm independent' kind of women. My grandparents set the trust fund up for me at birth. I was a one hundred percent scholarship recipient for college, so I didn't touch my college fund. I made enough money competing to support myself, but I'm lucky enough to have a financial cushion that allows me to not worry that I'll have to eat Ramen noodles for a month so I can afford to fill my truck up with gas to get to the next event."

"You don't have to get defensive."

"I'm not. This is just another example of why I don't tell anyone my background."

He twined a long, red curl around his index finger. "Doesn't that get lonely? Not letting anyone see the real you?"

She laughed harshly. "Being on the road and competing is the *real* me. The girl I was before? She's long gone." She tried to get away from him and succeeded, despite that he'd nearly pulled her hair out in the process.

"Come back here."

"Why?"

"So you can look into my eyes when I tell you this." He stroked her jawline with his thumb. "I like the real you. A lot. And not just because you're the sexiest woman I've ever been with, or that you have a lewd sense of humor, or that you like to fuck as much as I do."

She raised a dark red eyebrow. "You *are* going somewhere with this, right cowboy?"

"Yep. You're the first woman I've invited to stay at my place for longer than a few hours. You're the first woman who's played video games with me. You're not the first woman to cook for me, but you didn't create that meal like it was a wife audition."

"Dude, if I was auditioning to be your wife, I'd cook naked."

Wyn smiled. "See? You're so goddamned funny. I just wanna sit here and talk to you for hours. And this is all new to me, okay? And yet, it's so damn easy. You just slipped in here like you belong. But without permanent ties to anything, I worry that you'll slip back out just as easily." Jesus. Did that make him sound whiny?

Melissa stared at him. "I don't know where this will go, Wynton. I feel like I've known you for years when it's just been days. But I can't promise you anything when I'm taking things—my life—day by day."

Not what he wanted to hear, but it'd have to do for now. "Fair enough." He kissed her forehead. "Let's get back to the game. I believe you were about to pillage the village."

* * * *

For the next week, much to Wyn's annoyance, Melissa had stuck to her guns and locked the door to the guest bedroom after she went to bed. Alone. Every night. It was still locked in the morning—and his need to check that every morning just pissed him off. So prior to them saying good night, he felt entitled to poke her—promising he'd never lock her out of his room and he'd welcome any late visits from her.

He banked his disappointment that she hadn't taken him up on his offer even one time in the last seven nights.

So when a warm body crawled in bed beside him, he figured he was dreaming.

Soft hands floated over his arms and across his shoulders. Cool lips landed on the back of his neck, sending a shudder through him.

"Wynton? Are you awake?"

He groaned. "I am now. What time is it?"

"Three."

Christ. "You know what time we have to get up to start loading cattle?"

"Yes."

"Then what are you doin' in my bed, Miss I-Lock-My-Doors? Did you have a bad dream or something?"

"No. I had a good dream." She licked the vertebra at the base of his skull. "A sexy dream." She blew a stream of air across the damp spot she'd created. "A dirty dream. Starring dirty-minded, hot-bodied you." She sank her teeth into the nape of his neck.

It was as if that particular spot had a direct line to his cock, and it immediately went rock-fucking-hard.

She whispered, "I came in here to see if you wanted me to act out the good parts of my dream."

"Fuck, yeah."

Melissa rolled him to his back. "It's handy that you sleep naked, cowboy."

He kept his room so dark he could only make out her shape in the greenish glow from the digital clock on the side of the bed. "So you're waking me up to reward me with sex?"

"Are you sure you're awake? Or is this a dream starring the sleep sex fairy?" She slid down his body and beneath the covers.

Then her warm, wet mouth engulfed his cock. He clenched his hands and his ass cheeks to keep from bowing up.

By the time she quit teasing—deep-throating him, licking just the head of his cock with the tip of her tongue while she jacked him—his entire body vibrated.

She rolled a condom down his shaft and straddled him, burying his length inside her hot and slick cunt an inch at a time.

"Melissa."

She stretched her body across his and put her mouth on his ear. "I want to fuck you slowly and send you soaring without all the thrusting and straining, so when you do tip over the edge into the abyss, you'll wonder if it all had been a dream."

Wyn sank into the pillows and let her have her way with him, as she sucked and nibbled on his neck, his ears, and his chest. She rocked his cock in and out in the dreamy rhythm she'd mentioned. He trailed his fingertips up and down her spine, pleased to feel gooseflesh erupting in their wake.

When his balls drew up and he felt that tingle at the base of his spine, he grabbed onto her ass and let her body pull the orgasm from his.

She feathered kisses over his lips and disconnected their bodies. She even removed the condom. After one last kiss she said, "Reality is always much sweeter than dreams," and slipped from his room.

The next morning he might've believed it *had* all been a dream…but the hickey above his left nipple was proof she'd been there.

Maybe she was coming around. Maybe next time she'd be in his bed all night.

Chapter Seven

Over the past two weeks, Mel had become a decent ranch hand. After spending long days in the saddle and long nights christening every surface in Wynton's house, she was dragging serious ass today. Ranch work wasn't for wimps.

Luckily, her years of cutting competition had proved useful when keeping stray heifers in line. Seemed those stubborn cows always made a beeline for the creek. She could understand it if it was hot, but the weather had cooled off considerably, and it was always colder down by the water.

She shivered in her borrowed Carhartt coat. She couldn't believe how fast the time had gone. It seemed like yesterday that she'd unpacked her things, half-worried/half-excited to share living space with Wynton. She'd learned so much about him—not just his sexual preferences.

Now she knew little…domestic things. He brewed his first two cups of coffee in the morning as thick as tar. He ate lunch with his parents and brother most days. He read the newspaper from front to back before supper. He liked the scent of laundry detergent in the air so he did one load of clothes every day. He preferred sitcoms to dramas on TV. He shaved every day—not just because she was there.

Now that she also knew the core of him—his fierce love of his life as a rancher and being around his family, his connection to his animals and the land—she realized she'd never find another man like him. She hated that their time together was coming to a close. Wynton had been vague when she'd asked about his plans after the shipping was done, so she hadn't brought it up again.

Plato did a little crow-hop and she absentmindedly reached down and patted his neck. "Easy. I know you wanna work, but we gotta let the boys do their stuff."

Boys. That was almost a derogatory term for the masculine perfection of Wynton and Creston Grant. Seeing them work together was like watching a ballet. Each move and counter move perfectly choreographed. Ropes thrown in unison or in opposition. Both of them taking off on their horses at the same speed. Wynton cut left, while Cres cut right, and the herd was immediately back on track, going where the Grant boys wanted them to go.

She looked around at the pine trees lining this valley that dipped below the rock outcroppings. Some of the grass still had the barest hint of green, but even the brown stalks added to the visual appeal of vastness and serenity. She truly loved it here. It was so peaceful.

When her fingertips tingled and she knew it wasn't from cold, she dug into her pocket and took out a box of raisins. The first few days she hadn't done much strenuous activity—unless lots of hot sex, a couple times a day counted—and she had good blood sugar numbers. She felt great. Better than she had since before the diagnosis. She felt...normal. When her daily activity kicked up the past two weeks, she'd adjusted quickly and had no adverse effects. So she was beginning to think that finally after six and a half months, she had a handle on living with diabetes.

And since things were going better between her and Wynton than she ever imagined, she hadn't seen a need to test their relationship to see if telling him about her condition changed things. A smarmy voice in her head said, *Great plan, Mel. Tell him about it the first time he acts like a total jackass.*

Wynton whistled, drawing her attention to the loading chutes.

Damn, damn, damn but that man was fine. Hard-working, determined, thoughtful, funny, interesting. What you saw with him was exactly what you got. And in her eyes that made him damn near perfect.

You have fallen for him.

Who wouldn't?

She let her gaze scan the panoramic view. She could get used to this life. Working side by side—or at least in close proximity to her man. Raising cattle and maybe a few kids.

Whoa.

Whoa, whoa, whoa.

Putting the cart before the horse, much? Get through the next week with him before you start picking out baby names and knitting fucking booties.

"Melissa!"

Her head snapped up.

All Wynton had to do was point and she knew where she was supposed to be. Her gaze zeroed in on the problem cow. She clicked at Plato.

But before they reached the edge of the herd, the cow headed for the stock tank. On the other side of the pasture.

Then they were off on a wild cow chase.

Plato's withers quivered with excitement. He was in his glory as a cow horse. By the third day, he was penned with Charlie, Wyn's horse, Petey, Cres's horse, and Ringo, Jim's horse. By the fourth day in the field with the Grant horses, Plato had taken over as the leader.

The cow was fast. But Plato was faster.

Mel cut around and Plato's back end slid out so they were almost parallel to the ground. But Plato righted himself and they were in front of the cow, Plato moving back and forth as he tried to gauge which way the cow intended to bolt.

The cow heard the herd mooing behind her. Seeing no escape, she slowly turned around and lumbered back to the corral.

Plato kept on her until she was back where she belonged.

Something was spooking the herd today. Mel had to chase over a dozen runaways. So it took twice as long to sort and load. She'd depleted her secret store of snacks in her pockets and her water bottle was empty.

Wynton wasn't on horseback today. He slammed the back end of the livestock hauler and then jogged up to the driver's side to talk to Cres, who was delivering the cattle.

Mel dismounted. The cold seemed to have settled in her bones, so she led Plato into the barn to warm up as she removed the tack and brushed him down. She had to give him his special blend of oats out of the view of the other horses so they wouldn't fight for their share.

She'd just sent him out into the corral and locked the gate, when a wave of dizziness overtook her. She patted her hand along the fence, trying to squint through the white spots dancing in front of her eyes for the outside pump. There. Red handle. Once she reached it, she pulled up the handle. She had to hold on to the metal pipe as she held one shaking hand out to the stream of water. Very little liquid was flowing into the plastic; it was just getting her hand wet.

Fuck it.

Mel bent down and gulped water directly from the gushing stream. Water had pooled in the rocks, but she didn't care. She was so damn thirsty.

When she'd had enough, she yanked the handle down and cut off the flow. She pushed herself upright and wiped her face on the sleeve of her coat.

Of course that's when she noticed Wyn standing in the doorway of the barn.

He raised both eyebrows. "Thirsty?"

"Very."

"You hydrated now?"

Mel watched him stalk closer with that look in his eyes. A look that said he was about to strip her down and rock her body to the core. "Yes I am."

"Good."

"So, what's going on?"

"You."

"What about me?"

"You are driving me absolutely fucking crazy."

She waited.

"Do you have any idea how sexy you are on a horse? So regal? So intuitive? Fuck, I love to watch you make lightning quick adjustments when you're on the outside of the herd." He moved closer. "I'm surprised I can get any work done at all because I can't take my eyes off of you. For the past two weeks I've watched you. Watched that crazy red hair tossed by the wind as you're chasin' down strays. Watched your cheeks turn pink with color. Watched your eyes dancing with excitement and concentration. You're beautiful, Melissa. But when you're so focused on your task, doin' what you're so goddamned good at, you take my fucking breath away."

Her heart raced. Even when she'd just gulped water, her mouth had gone dry. While he was getting closer, she'd started backing up in a circle, retreating into the barn.

"And every day, when my cock is so fucking hard I could pound horseshoes with it, I tell myself to wait until I can take you in my bed, or on my couch, or on the damn washing machine. But today, Cres is gone, and it's just you and me. Today, I ain't gonna wait."

His eyes were hot and dark and focused one hundred percent on her.

"No foreplay. No sweet kisses or tender touches. I want you, hard and fast and rough. I wanna bend you over and fuck you until the ache of wantin' you doesn't consume me like this."

Two more steps back. "Wynton."

"You want this. I can see it in your eyes. I bet your nipples are hard. I bet your pussy is already wet."

"So?"

"So, stop movin' so we can get on with it."

"Or what?"

"There is no *or.* Don't make me chase you down."

"Think you can catch me, cowboy?" God. Why was she taunting him?

His deep, rasping, sarcastic laugh might've been the sexiest thing she'd ever heard. "Oh, yeah? How about I'll even give you a head start. I'll count to five."

Mel turned and ran.

From behind she heard, "Onetwothreefourfive."

She managed to get out, "That's cheating!" before an arm banded around her waist and she was airborne. She shrieked.

"That's it, baby," he growled in her ear. "Get those vocal cords warmed up because before I'm done with you, you're gonna be screaming my name."

Wynton carried her—one-armed no less!—into the tack room. He pulled a saddle blanket out of the stack and draped it over a workbench. Then he set her on her feet and stripped off her coat. His voice was back in her ear. "Chest on the bench, ass in the air is how I want you. Hold on to the bench with your left hand and drop your right hand beside your leg."

Her need for him overtook any thoughts of arguing. Wynton had been the most spectacular lover she'd ever had, but he'd never been like...this. Desperate to have her and sort of pissed off about it.

At first he didn't touch her besides undoing her jeans, shoving them and her underwear to the tops of her boots, then kicking her feet out to widen her stance.

She heard his labored breaths as he shed his clothing. She heard the crinkle of a condom wrapper. She felt his satisfied grunt on the back of her neck when he pressed his chest to her back and reached between her legs to find her dripping wet.

One finger entered her. Then two. God. He had such long, thick fingers. She made a soft gasp when the callused pad of his thumb connected with her clit.

Wynton kept her immobilized on the bench, his breath hot in her ear as he finger fucked her. And he knew just where to stroke inside her pussy walls and for how long. He knew how much direct contact her clit could take. He knew how to light the fuse and how long before she detonated.

"It's mine, Melissa. Give it to me."

She did cry out when the orgasm blasted through her.

He kept pumping and doing that flicking thing on her clit, dragging out her pleasure. When the last pulse ended, he stilled and pulled his fingers out of her. Then he whispered, "Don't. Move."

No problem. She was pretty sure her spine was somewhere on the hay-strewn floor below her.

He slapped his hands on her ass cheeks hard enough to make that one swat sting. His two fingers, wet with her juices, trailed down her butt crack to her anus. He swept his fingers across her hole until the nerve endings flared to life and the rim was sticky.

She stilled. They'd talked about anal sex, even done a little anal play back and forth, and she knew he wanted to shove his cock in her ass. She wanted that too, but she needed to be more prepared than just a couple of swipes of her come to ease the way.

Wynton's tight grip on her ass relaxed. She felt the damp heat of his breath on her lower back right before he kissed the spot and started to drag his tongue down the split in her ass, making a soft growling noise as he followed the trail he'd made with her juices. And when he reached her anus, he licked and lapped and sucked that tight ring before he plunged his tongue inside.

"Oh, God." He did it a few more times, driving her crazy with the raunchy sensation that she loved.

Then he tilted her hips and inserted just the tip of his cock into her pussy. He dangled something rough against her right leg that caused her to twitch before he slid it into her hand. She squeezed her fingers around it. It felt like...rope.

Holy fuck.

Still breathing heavily, still just resting his cock an inch inside her, Wynton guided her hand between her thighs.

Keeping his hand circling her wrist, he dragged the rope across her clit.

Mel arched up. She tried to pull her hand away, but Wynton wouldn't allow it.

"Ride that line between pleasure and pain."

"I-I...what if it's too much?"

Once again he layered his chest to her back. "There's no such thing." He sucked on her earlobe, impaled her fully, and pulled the rope across her clit all at the same time.

She screamed.

Wynton fucked her as rough and fast and hard as he'd warned he would. His harsh grunts, the sucking sounds of her pussy with his every stroke, the *thump thump thump* of the bench legs echoed around her.

Even before she started to come, Mel drifted to that place where anticipation met intent. She furiously rubbed her clit, her stomach tight every time the twine scraped over that swollen nub. But she couldn't stop. It was so close... It was right...there.

The orgasm ripped through her. Her clit throbbed like she'd never felt it. Her pussy clamped down so hard on Wynton's cock that she swore she could feel his heart pounding as he plowed into her. Every part of her body tingled. Her ears rang, her head went muzzy. She sucked in a deep breath and the last thing she heard before she passed out was Wynton roaring like a beast.

* * * *

She'd blacked out.

Now Wynton had to know something was wrong with her. Women didn't just pass the fuck out during sex—even as mind-blowing as that sex had been. At least she hadn't checked out before the orgasm that would forevermore be "the orgasm" that all others would be judged by.

She wiggled her naked body. She turned her head. The pillow smelled like him. The scent immediately soothed her. As did the rough-skinned palm that skated down her arm.

"Hey, sleepyhead."

"Uh, how'd I get here?"

"You were seriously out of it after we…you know."

The man was embarrassed? Get out.

"So I carried you into the house, undressed you, and tucked you in my bed."

"How long have I been here?"

"Half an hour." A soft kiss landed on her shoulder. "I fucked you so hard that you passed out, baby." Another kiss. "I've never had that happen before."

Now he sounded so smug. "It's never happened to me before either."

"One for the record books, Amazing Slut-Girl."

Mel smiled in the dark. "True dat, Super Man-Slut." The more conscious she became, the less it felt like she'd had an…episode. Maybe she was just thirsty, hungry, and tired because she'd worked all day, followed by getting spun inside out and upside down by one of the most intense sexual encounters of her life. What woman wouldn't pass out from being exposed to Wynton Grant's pheromones and sating his beastly sexual appetite after he'd made her come so hard she'd screamed? Twice?

"You all right?" he murmured.

"Mmm-hmm. I need to eat something and I'm really thirsty. But besides that…" She stretched. "I feel thoroughly fucked."

He chuckled. "Me too. You sore?"

"A little."

"My fault. Lemme fix that." He slipped beneath the covers and positioned himself between her legs. He planted the softest kisses on her abraded clit.

"Wynton—"

"I just fucked you hard, fast, and rough, Melissa. Now let me make love to you slow and sweet."

Like she could say no to that.

Chapter Eight

In the last three weeks, Wyn's life had changed completely.

He'd fallen in love.

With a hookup.

A *wedding* hookup, no less.

It's been more than a hookup since the first time you kissed her, dumbass.

True.

Wyn was done denying this was a *one and done* or *hit it and quit it* scenario. Melissa was meant to be his. Not for just a few lousy weeks, either. Now he just hoped that Melissa could see he was "the one" she'd been looking for.

How had he gotten so lucky? She was everything he'd wanted and feared he'd never find. She was perfect.

Perfect.

She'd proven it so many times, in so many ways.

She could ride a horse like no woman he'd ever seen.

She liked to just sit around and bullshit.

She liked to play video games.

She liked to play darts and pool.

She liked to curl up on the couch and watch TV.

She liked to cook.

She had a great sense of humor.

She loved sex—anytime, anyplace. She was as inventive in her suggestions as she was adventurous with his.

With each new thing he discovered about her, he fell harder for her.

Why was he reminding himself of all these awesome things about her?

Because Melissa had been a little...grouchy since yesterday. It wasn't his fault that she'd fallen asleep in his bed after he'd made love to her. When she woke up—cranky as hell—she stormed off to her bed, insisting she slept better alone.

How would she know that if she hadn't actually tried sleeping in his bed an entire night?

Maybe he'd man up and ask her that when he got home. He grinned. That'd get her riled up—and that was how he loved her best.

He slowed down and pulled into Cres's driveway.

Cres was out of his house as soon as Wyn killed the ignition. As Wyn wandered up the driveway with a six-pack of Fat Tire beer, Cres said, "That's your *we've gotta talk* look. So it's finally time to deal with Dad's bombshell?"

"I didn't want this to be a pressure thing, Cres. I guess we could've discussed this while we were movin' cattle."

Cres dropped the tailgate on his truck. "Mel's been around and it didn't seem right to talk in circles or exclude her from our conversation. And every other time we've been together it's been with Dad and Mom."

Wyn hopped onto the tailgate beside his brother and handed him a beer.

"Thanks." Cres said, "Does it surprise you that Dad hasn't been bugging us to make a decision?"

"Dad's got other things on his mind for a change. I'm happy to see that. Mom is too. So to be honest, I don't think they care one way or another what our decision is because they've already made theirs. Make sense?"

"Yeah. And Mom's too busy harassing you about what's going on with you and Mel." Cres sipped his beer. "Speaking of Mel...you two seem very happy to be playing house."

Wyn scowled. "I *hate* that fucking term."

"What else can you call it if it's not a trial run for the real deal?"

"Piss off. And her name is Melissa, not Mel. Mel...well, that's more in line with your tastes."

Cres laughed. "True. I like her. She's good for you."

"So if I wanted to play house with her for real?"

"I'd probably come over more often since she's a better cook than you."

"Again, Cres, piss off." Wyn cracked his beer. "I want her there for the long haul. Not just because she's a good cook but because she's…everything. I just feel in my gut she's it for me."

"Does she feel that way too?"

"I hope so."

"Man, Sutton is *so* gonna rub it in your face that you're pussy-whipped."

"I deserve it." He grinned. "I *welcome* it. Anyway, you've had a couple of weeks to think about Dad's offer. Made any decisions yet?"

Cres looked at him oddly. "It never really was a decision for me, bro. I like ranching with you. It'd suck to do it by myself. I say let's keep it together. Same as it's always been."

Wyn held his bottle to his brother's for a toast. "Amen."

A few moments of silence passed.

"Since it seemed like *you* were dragging this decision out, I thought maybe you were gonna suggest we divvy it up."

Wyn pinned him with a sharp look. "Why in the hell would you say that?"

Cres shrugged. "I came out last year. Everyone in the family has been supportive—even more than I expected. But supporting me in my personal life and bein' offered a chance to cut ties with me professionally because of *how* I live my life… We both know it might affect who wants to do business with both of us, Wyn. I could see that dividing it would be an easy out for everyone. I think that's why Dad offered it as a suggestion."

"Bullshit. I thought *you* might be lookin' for an out from ranching completely," Wyn said. "Trying to figure out a way to sell your portion to me."

"And what would I do if I wasn't ranching? I've got no interest in doin' anything else, so selling never even crossed my mind," Cres said. "Besides, knowing us, even if we divided it up, we'd still work together most days anyway."

"True." Wyn swallowed a mouthful of beer. "So we good?"

"I reckon. Be weird not havin' Dad around day-to-day. I'm gonna miss him and those fucked up curse word combinations he uses when he's frustrated."

Wyn smiled. "I'm gonna miss him too. He and Mom deserve a chance to spend the money he's been saving all these years. As for us...dividing the profits by two instead of by three will take some getting used to."

Cres grinned. "That extra cash will come in handy for you since you're playin' house."

"Asshole. What about you and Mick? Any thoughts of playin' house with him?"

"It's casual," was all Cres said. "He's comin' to help load for the Denver trip tomorrow."

"That's an overnight trip."

"Yep. If you gotta problem with that, let me know."

Wyn shot him a *don't be an idiot* look. "I don't."

"Good." Cres exhaled. "Thanks. Christ. I don't know fuck-all about havin' a boyfriend, bro."

"Mick keeps comin' back around, so you must know how to do something right." As soon as that left Wyn's mouth, he groaned. "Shit. I didn't mean it that way."

Cres laughed. "How 'bout we don't go there. *Ever.*"

"Deal." He smirked. "Although...Melissa said you and Mick together...that'd be live porn she'd watch."

"Jesus. No wonder you love her. She's as perverted as you."

* * * *

After almost three weeks of ranch life, Mel hadn't gotten used to waking up at the butt crack of dawn and hauling her carcass out of a toasty bed.

So Wynton's way-too-early, and way-too-chipper summons, "Up and at 'em, Kentucky," as he beat on her door annoyed the crap out of her.

Mel forced herself to respond, "I'll be there in five," somewhat politely, instead of yelling at him to get the fucking battering ram away from her door.

Yeah. She was punchy and cranky.

After taking her shot of insulin, she shoved a glucose pill in her jeans, packed her coat pockets with snacks and filled her water bottle.

The last day of shipping cattle meant everyone was in a hurry, so she didn't have time for coffee or breakfast.

Mistake number one.

Once she'd saddled up and the sun had come out, she'd immediately overheated. She took her jacket off and tossed it over a fencepost.

Mistake number two.

Since this was the largest group of cattle going to market, of course everything went wrong. Which meant she spent four hours chasing down runaways and culling cows from the milling herd.

Four hours without a break, without water, and without her trusty snacks.

Mistake number three.

But rather than tell Wynton she hit the hypoglycemic stage and was about to crash, she decided it'd be better to just go off and crash alone.

Mistake number four.

The edges of her conscious began to shrink in on her like a camera viewfinder that starts out close, but objects get smaller and farther away until everything is fuzzy and ringed with black.

She rode to the barn and dismounted. If she could just have a few minutes of clarity to unsaddle her horse while those guys—loaded or unloaded the cattle?—she couldn't remember, she could probably make it to the house before she collapsed.

Wait. The house was collapsing? Why?

She was so confused.

Where was she? What happened to her horse?

Mel spun around and that action caused a quick spike of pain. She tried to pat the top of her head to see if some asshole had buried an ax in her skull, but she ended up smacking herself in the face.

Fuck that hurt.

Take a pill for it.

Good plan. She dug in her pocket—why weren't her fingers working?—and found a round, white thing. She squinted at it. After enclosing it in her fist, she went to find water. She took two steps forward and swayed.

Whoa. When had she gotten on the carousel? Why was everything spinning so fast it was blurred? What was that loud, whooshing noise?

She made it to a bale of straw before the darkness overcame her.

Chapter Nine

After the cattle truck rumbled down the driveway, Wyn did loading chute maintenance—his least favorite part of shipping cattle. But if he didn't fix the problems now, they'd have issues the next time they used the chutes because he wouldn't remember what needed done.

He'd welcomed Mick's help today. Wyn was especially grateful that Mick was riding with Cres to the sale barn, so Wyn could catch up on the piles of paperwork that always accompanied selling cattle. Cres and Mick planned to stay overnight in Denver before heading home. He wouldn't begrudge his brother a little personal time since he'd come to realize how much he needed that in his own life.

Speaking of…he wondered where his hot, redheaded cattle cutting expert had gone. She'd been acting a little weird toward the end.

He saw Plato in the corral, but it looked like he still wore a bridle and bit. Melissa would never turn him out like that.

"Melissa?"

No response.

An eerie feeling rippled down his spine. "Melissa?" he called into the barn.

No answer.

If his head had been turned the other direction, he might've missed her. But the red in her corduroy shirt snagged his attention. He sauntered up to the hay bale she sat on and noticed her eyes were closed. "Napping on the job, Kentucky? For shame."

Melissa didn't acknowledge him at all.

Man, she was really asleep. But as soon as he stood in front of her, he knew she wasn't napping. Something was wrong with her.

He crouched down and took her hand. Holy shit, it was like ice. But he saw her forehead was damp with perspiration and her face was flushed. He tried to shake her. "Melissa?"

She mumbled something.

"Baby, you're scarin' me." Wyn noticed her other hand was closed in a tight fist. He pried her fingers open and saw she'd clutched a white pill. He remembered her complaining of a bad headache last night before she'd gone to bed in her own room. How many of these had she taken?

When her body started to shake uncontrollably and even that didn't wake her up, he dug his cell phone out of his pocket and dialed 911.

After he'd given them the information, hearing the word overdose—which he vehemently argued against, he decided to buck the operator's judgment and move Melissa to the ground.

He'd just propped her head on his jacket when he heard the unmistakable sound of a cattle truck rumbling up the driveway.

His annoyance that Cres had forgotten something *again*, was immediately replaced with a sense of urgency. Mick had medical training.

Wyn carefully lifted Melissa into his arms and carried her out of the barn. He'd made it halfway to the house when both men jumped out of the cab of the truck and ran toward him.

"What happened?" Cres demanded.

"I don't know. I found her like this. Mick, help her," he pleaded.

"Completely unresponsive?"

"Yes. Then she started to shake, almost like she was having a seizure."

"Take her in the house. You called 911?"

"Just got off the phone with them, but they said it'll be at least fifteen minutes."

Once they were inside, Wyn laid Melissa on the couch. He hovered over her as Mick poked and prodded her.

"Is she on any medication?"

"I don't know." He paused. "Wait, she had this in her hand." He passed over the pill.

Mick held it up to the light and frowned.

"What?"

"It's a glucose pill."

"What's that?"

"Diabetics take them when their blood sugar levels are low." Mick looked up at him. "Wyn, is Melissa diabetic?"

"I have no idea. She's never mentioned it to me."

"You haven't seen her testing her blood sugar levels first thing in the morning? Or the last thing before she crawls in bed at night?"

Suddenly, her secretiveness, her insistence on sleeping in her own bed at night and even locking her damn door in the morning made sense. Wyn said, "Fuck. We don't sleep in the same bed. She claimed she's a restless sleeper and needs her own space, so she's been sleeping in the guest bedroom. But obviously it was so she could keep this from me. Why would she do that?"

"Worry about that later. Right now, go into her room and see if you can find a blood glucose meter, some kind of insulin injection instruments. Hopefully she's got a Glucagon rescue kit."

Wyn looked at Cres with utter confusion. "What did he say?"

"Mick, under the circumstances it'd be better for you to do it since you know what to look for," Cres said.

"Where's her room?"

"Last one at the end of the hallway."

Mick took off.

Wyn dropped to his knees beside Melissa. He picked up her hand and kissed her knuckles. "You and me are gonna have a serious talk when you're not goddamned unconscious."

"Promise me you won't yell at her for this when she comes around."

He turned and glared at Cres. "Why the fuck would you even say that to me?"

"For that reason right there. You get angry first and maybe you'll try reasonable later. I'm askin' you not to do that this time. There's a reason she kept this from you. If you want to understand why, don't scare her off with your blustering and accusations." He softened his tone. "I know you care about her. And I know she's crazy about you. So don't wreck this. Just…tread lightly okay?"

Mick jogged back into the room. He held up a kit. "She's got one."

"You know what to do?"

"Yeah. You gotta move, man," Mick said to him. "Oh, and I found her medic alert bracelet. She is diabetic. Type 1. She's insulin dependent."

Wyn was absolutely poleaxed. This woman that he'd bared his soul to, opened his home to, made love to and had fallen for...hadn't trusted him enough to share this with him.

"This will help her out a lot," Mick said.

"Should I call and cancel the ambulance?" Wyn asked.

"No. The paramedics will need to assess her. They might even take her to the hospital since it sounds like she might've had a seizure."

Seizure. That word twisted his guts into a knot. He couldn't watch as Mick...did whatever he did, because Wyn would be tempted to ask a million questions. The time for questions would come later.

Time passed in an endless void as he paced.

Finally, he heard Mick say, "No, Mel, don't try and sit up."

Melissa said something too low for Wyn to hear. But Mick's response was loud and clear. "Yes, he's here."

She was asking for him?

Wyn crossed the room and stood behind Mick. A sick feeling twisted his stomach again. Until he heard her whisper...

"Tell him I love him."

Say what?

"I'm sure he'll appreciate hearing that." Mick sent Wyn an apologetic look. "She's babbling."

But I want her to mean it.

Mick kept up a running dialogue, if only to keep Melissa from talking. "It's only been twenty minutes since we left. We had to turn around because Cres left the paperwork and his wallet in the tack room."

"Wyn?"

What the hell? She never called him Wyn. She always called him by his full name. It appeared she didn't know what she was saying. "Yeah, baby, I'm here."

Melissa's skin was blotchy, red in spots, pasty white in others. Her eyes were vacant. But when she saw him? Her eyes held fear. And then a film of tears. Her lips started to wobble after she mouthed "sorry" and then she turned her head into the couch cushion, away from him.

The fuck that was happening. She was goddamn *done* hiding anything from him. Wyn stepped in front of Mick and braced his hand on the wall above the back of the couch, so he loomed above her. He reached down and gently turned her face toward him. "Kentucky, look at me."

"Wyn," Cres warned.

"Butt out, bro. This is between me and my woman."

That got Melissa's eyes to open again.

He stroked his thumb over her cheek. "There she is, my beautiful, stubborn filly. Fair warning, darlin'. After the EMTs get here and tell me what steps I need to take to get you back to normal, you and me are gonna have a serious talk."

"You're mad at me," she choked out.

"No, I'm scared for you. Big difference. Now I'm gonna let Mick do his thing. I just wanted you to know I'm here and I ain't goin' anywhere."

Her eyes teared up again and she nodded before she closed her eyes.

The paramedics arrived.

Wyn hung on the periphery and tried to decipher what they were saying as they spoke to her and Mick. Even when he knew it was ridiculous, he had a flash of annoyance that the EMTs were talking to Mick about Melissa's condition when they should've been talking to him. He should know this stuff. Every single bit of it. He vowed he'd never be kept out of the loop again when it came to Melissa's health issues. He'd read everything he could get his hands on so he knew exactly how to help her. And figure out how to prevent this from ever happening again.

The female EMT finally took Wyn aside. "We're not admitting her to the hospital as long as you're comfortable keeping a very close eye on her the next twenty-four hours."

"Absolutely."

"Mick indicated that you weren't aware she was diabetic."

"No, but I can promise you I'll be up to speed on everything about this in the next few hours."

"There's tons of information online—most of it is excellent. Thankfully she had an emergency kit. You'd be surprised how many diabetics aren't so well-prepared. Anyway, she said she took her dose of insulin this morning, so this…episode isn't due to negligence—aka 'forgetting' to inject herself. It sounds like she overexerted herself the past few days."

Wyn experienced a punch of guilt over that. He *had* been working her hard. "The tablet she had in her hand. Is that part of her daily medication?"

"No, it's supposed to be a quick fix when she feels the effects of low blood sugar. That's just one of many choices to get her glycemic index back in balance. She can fill you in on what foods/drinks/snacks usually work best for her when her body tells her she's hypoglycemic."

He should be recording this conversation—all the words were jumbling together.

"As soon as she's feeling up to it, she needs to eat. She'll need to check her blood sugar levels more often. And if rest, liquids, and food don't get her levels back down into the normal range? Bring her to the ER."

"I will."

She patted his shoulder. "I know you will."

Wyn shot a quick glance over his shoulder. "Can I ask…have you seen this before?"

"What? A diabetic starting to go into diabetic shock?"

"No, people close to the patient bein' in the dark about their condition."

She looked thoughtful. "For some people, talking about having diabetes is an embarrassment because of all the misinformation and misperceptions about it, so it's easier to keep it under wraps. I had a friend in high school that went to great lengths to hide it because she didn't want our classmates or teachers to treat her differently or feel sorry for her. Even at age seventeen, she worried that she'd never find love because it would be daunting for a guy to take on a woman with a chronic illness. Maybe that sounds stupid to us, but the truth is, we don't have to be vigilant about food intake, watch physical activity, take insulin shots, do blood sugar monitoring that the people who have this disease have to deal with every day. And like it or not, type 1 diabetes is an incurable disease. That's not to say it's not manageable, but it is a lifelong condition." She paused. "Did that answer your question?"

"Yes. More than you know. Thank you."

By the time the EMTs left, Melissa was sitting up.

Cres and Mick waited in the kitchen. That's where he went first.

"I know you've gotta take off, and this is one time, baby bro, that I won't chew your ass for forgetting paperwork. I'm thankful that you were here, Mick."

"Glad to help. But you need to get to the bottom of why she kept this from you. Show her you're a standup guy, Wyn. Maybe she's never had anyone show her how to stand your ground when the going gets tough."

"I hear ya."

Cres clapped him on the shoulder. "See you tomorrow. You need anything, call or text."

Wyn followed them out and watched the cattle truck drive away for the second time. Then he went back inside to deal with his woman.

Melissa looked so…frail sitting on his couch with an afghan draped over her.

He crouched in front of her. "You feel like eating anything yet?"

"No. The beef jerky and orange juice will hold me over for a bit."

"Good. You ready to get some rest?"

"I thought I'd stretch out on the couch."

He stood. "You thought wrong." He scooped her into his arms. "Hang on."

She didn't speak until she noticed they weren't going in the direction of her room. "Wynton?"

"From here on out, you're sleepin' with me."

"But all my stuff—"

"Will be moved into my room." He set her on the bed and pulled the afghan away. "In my bed is where you should've been all along and you damn well know it."

Melissa didn't argue.

"Now, do you need me to help you take your clothes off? Or do you wanna do it?"

"Stop it," she snapped. "I don't want you to baby me."

Wyn got right in her face. "Tough shit. I want to take care of you and you'll let me, understand? " He exhaled a slow breath. "I need to do this as much as you need to let me do it."

She reached up and touched his face. "Okay. But no funny business when you help me take my clothes off. I don't have the energy for it."

Do not snap at her for believing you're such a sex fiend that you'd take advantage of her after she had a diabetic episode.

"God, I'm sorry for saying that. I was trying to make light of the situation and it didn't come out that way."

Wyn kissed the inside of her wrist. "You and me are gonna have to come up with a whole new way to communicate, Kentucky."

"Agreed."

He popped the buttons on her pearl snap shirt and tugged it off. He pulled her T-shirt over her head, glad to see she'd taken his advice to dress in layers. He unhooked her bra. He forced himself not to focus on how quickly her nipples puckered into tight points.

"Are you stripping me down completely?"

"Yeah."

"What if I get cold?"

"I'll keep you warm. Stand." He dropped to his knees and undid her belt, then her jeans. He peeled the denim down her thighs and held onto her arm as she kicked them aside. He pressed a soft kiss to her belly as he pulled off her panties. Then he wrapped his arms around her, breathed her in and released all the tension he'd carried in the past hour and a half. She was all right. Soft and warm and in his room, with him, where she belonged.

"Wynton."

"Give me a sec."

Melissa sifted her fingers through his hair. "I'm okay."

"You scared me."

"I scared myself." She clamped her hands around his jaw and tilted his head back. "I'm sorry I scared you. And we'll talk about everything after I've had some time to recover. But for right now, can I please get under the covers? I'm freezing my ass off."

He smiled against her stomach.

When he reached down to remove her socks and she said, "Huh-uh, cowboy. I'll let you strip me naked, but one of the fun side effects of diabetes is my feet are always cold, so the socks stay on."

"Yes, ma'am." Wyn rolled back the bedding. Then he stood and shed his clothes.

From beneath the covers, Melissa stared at his crotch and said, "You're hard."

"Seein' you naked does that to me. It'll behave, I promise."

"You sound like *it* has a mind of its own."

Wyn slipped in next to her. "Sometimes, I swear it does." He tucked her head under his chin and wrapped her in his arms. A sense of peace settled over him as he drifted off.

"Wynton?" she murmured.

"Yeah, baby?"

"I never want to sleep away from you again."

He kissed the top of her head. "Same here."

Chapter Ten

When Mel woke up, she had that same panicked sense of disorientation as she did when she came to on the couch in the living room.

"It's okay. You're still in my bed."

She shifted toward his voice and noticed he was propped up against the headboard, a laptop open on top of a pillow. "Surfing porn sites while I sleep, Super Man-Slut?"

He grinned. "Dammit. Why didn't I think of usin' the Internet to find porn sites? I'm usin' it for pesky research."

Her chest tightened. "What kind of research?"

"Small engine repair for this motor I plan to rebuild."

"Really?"

Wynton rolled his eyes. "No, not really. I'm finding out everything I need to know about type 1 diabetes. You got a problem with that?"

"No." She flopped back into the pillows. "I'd tell you that you could ask me anything you wanted to know, but that's sort of the whole point, isn't it? I *didn't* do that."

"Yeah." He set her blood glucose meter on her chest. "And so the fun begins. It's been two hours, so time to check those levels again."

Her eyes narrowed. "You want to watch?"

"I need to watch so I know how to do it if I ever have to. I also want to watch so I know what you deal with every day. How it's part of your routine."

Stupid, sweet man. Now he was gonna make her cry. "I need the box of glucose test strips, the box of lancets, and the alcohol swabs." She went through the process, poking herself, putting the drop of blood on the glucose test strip, putting the strip in the meter and showing him where the results appeared and explaining what the number meant.

"Wait, I know what that number means. You're still on the low end, so you need to eat or drink something to boost your count and then retest in fifteen minutes."

"Wow. You are a quick study."

Wynton stroked her cheek. "I am when it matters to me."

He definitely was testing her tear threshold.

"Do you want juice? Or raisins? Or honey? Or regular soda? Or a glucose tablet?"

"Juice would be great."

He leaned over and kissed her forehead before he popped out of bed. "Don't move. I'll be right back." The man hustled out and he didn't bother to put on pants.

She loved that about him.

She loved *everything* about him.

An odd sense of…déjà vu niggled in the back of her mind.

Tell him I love him.

The few times she'd gotten to the point she had today, she'd heard from others she'd been spectacularly nasty. She'd also heard of instances where a person blurted out secrets with no recollection of it. So had she confessed her feelings for him? To him?

Given how unbelievably close they'd gotten in the last three weeks, it wasn't a surprise that she'd fallen head over heels in love with Wynton Grant. The man was beyond amazing. But she hadn't wanted him to find out that way, when she wasn't even aware of what she was saying.

But on the other hand, it would be weird if she asked him if she'd confessed her love for him. *Hey, sexy rancher man, I'm not sure if you caught it before because I'm not even sure that I said it, but I love the fuck out of you.*

Ugh. No. That would *not* be cool.

Wynton returned with a tray. He set it on the dresser and handed her a glass of juice.

"Thank you."

"You're welcome. I'll just…" He blew out a breath. "I don't know what the fuck to do. I have so damned many questions but I don't want to bombard you."

Mel sipped the cranberry juice. "Bombard away."

"How long have you had diabetes?"

"Six and a half months."

That surprised him.

"Yeah, it's a new thing to me too. Several months before I was diagnosed I had all the classic symptoms—excessive thirst, weight loss, irritability, no appetite. I chalked it up to the end of the season stress. Then I blacked out, much like I did here today. It scared me and I went to the ER. They ran tests. The results surprised the medical staff as much as it did me because at my age it's almost always a diagnosis of type 2 diabetes, not type 1. So I spent two weeks learning that burying my head in the sand and pretending it would go away isn't the best way to deal with it."

"What happened before?"

She took another swig of juice. "I was lethargic but I competed anyway. I did great in the first go. I did fine in the team penning round. But I was the next to last competitor of the day in the cutting competition and I almost passed out. Hearing people describe the run, they said I sat atop Plato as if I'd been hypnotized."

Wynton brushed her hair out of her face. "Is that how you remembered it?"

"That's the thing. I *don't* remember anything at all. Not dealing with my horse or even getting back to my horse trailer. I woke up the next morning and it was a worse feeling than a blackout drunk."

He kissed her forehead. "Keep goin'."

"That's when I went to the ER. After my diabetes crash course, I took Plato back to Gradsky's because I knew I had to give up competing. I blurted out everything to Berlin. She swore she'd keep it between us. But she insisted I stick around there until I got a better handle on how to live with diabetes and what was next in my life. I avoided everyone in the world of rodeo. I even avoided London when she came home."

"So that's what Breck meant when he said you were—"

"All plumped up again? Yes. I'd lost thirty pounds over the course of three months, so I probably did look anorexic."

"Still makes him a fuckin' ass for sayin' that shit to you." He absentmindedly stroked her arm. "So you've been hiding?"

"Pretty much."

"You don't gotta hide from me."

Please don't ask me right now why I didn't tell you. Because you're not running scared after finding out makes me hope this isn't the end. She pointed to the tray.

"Could I get some beef jerky and one of those hard candies?"

"You bet."

"You really did do your homework."

"Like I said, I pay attention when it matters." Wynton pinned her with a look. "And in case that ain't plain enough for you, I'll repeat it. You matter to me, Melissa Lockhart. A whole heckuva lot."

She burst into tears.

Wynton thought he'd said the wrong thing, and Mel tried to get him to quit backtracking, at least until she got control of her emotions.

But the man didn't let her sob into her pillow. He simply picked her up and hauled her onto his lap, forcing her tears to fall on his chest. He murmured unintelligible things, but they soothed her with their intent.

After she settled, Wynton kissed the tears from her face. "It wrecks me to see you cryin'. Guts me like nothin' else. Except seein' you unresponsive in the barn." He rested his forehead to hers. "I still have a ton of questions, but I'll let it be for now. You test your level and then rest a little longer."

"Will you stay in here with me?"

"If you want."

"I do."

He grinned. "See? That wasn't so hard, was it?"

Chapter Eleven

Wyn had thrown a roast, potatoes, and veggies in the slow cooker before they'd loaded cattle earlier this morning, so at least he could feed her properly.

While she'd slept he'd texted Cres, letting him know she was doing better.

He'd done a little more research online.

But the answer he needed the most he could only get from her.

Melissa wandered into the kitchen. "Hey. You let me sleep a long time."

"You needed it." He kicked out a stool. "Have a seat. We can eat whenever you're ready."

"Smells good. What is it?"

"Roast. My mom's recipe. I followed it to the letter so I didn't screw it up. I'm not so good at improvising."

She gave him a smug look. "Maybe not when it comes to cooking."

"True. Is there anything you need to do before we eat?"

"No. I'll shower after dinner. Is there anything I can help you with?"

Wyn shook his head. "It's a one pot deal so I'll just plop it on the counter and dish it up."

Although they sat side by side, they didn't talk during the meal. He kept sneaking looks at her to see if she was really enjoying the food or if she was just pushing it around on her plate. But her plate was nearly empty.

"Stop looking at me out of the corner of your eye. I'm fine."

He faced her. "It's not that."

"Then what?"

"I'm embarrassed that this is the first time I've cooked for you in my home. I never thought I'd be the type of guy who'd take for granted that you'd cook for me when you stayed here because you're a woman."

She set her hand on his arm. "I cooked for us because I like to cook. And since you've been stewing about this you probably know that the other reason I did it was because I have dietary restrictions."

"So you wouldn't set off my warning bells if I made something that you couldn't eat. And then I wouldn't ask questions if you were doin' all the cooking."

Melissa shoved her plate across the counter. She wiped her mouth and turned her barstool toward him. "We're having this out now? Fine. Ask me."

"Why didn't you tell me?"

"Because you were supposed to be a one-night wedding hookup, Wynton."

He counted to ten. "But it didn't turn out that way. You've been livin' in my house, we've been workin' together, sorting cattle almost every day for three weeks, we've been fucking like bunnies…and not once when you were scurrying off to your room to test your blood sugar and inject yourself with insulin did it ever occur to you to tell me that you're diabetic? And that you could have some sort of serious episode that might send you into a coma? I keep thinking how goddamned glad I am that Mick came back here and had the experience to know all wasn't right with you. Do you have any idea how it made me feel that I didn't know my lover has a life-threatening disease? That I wouldn't know what the fuck to do if something like that happened when we were alone? That you could've died because I wouldn't have known how to help you? That flat out sucks, Melissa. And I know this ain't about me, but goddammit, you *know* it was wrong to keep this from me for even a day, let alone fuckin' weeks!"

Wyn's voice had escalated and he shrank back away from her. Shit. He hadn't meant to yell at her. He scrubbed his hands over his face. "Fuck. Sorry. I just…" He pushed back from the counter.

"Wynton—"

He held up his hand. "Just give me a minute." He walked to the back door. The day had stayed warm and although the sun had set, he welcomed the breeze blowing through the screen, needing something to cool him off because he hadn't gotten a handle on his temper like he thought he had.

Soft arms circled his waist. Melissa rested her cheek on his shoulder blade. "I'm sorry. I can't say that enough and mean it enough. I never wanted you to see me like that."

"Which is why you didn't tell me?"

Her sigh warmed his shirt where her mouth rested. "No. I didn't tell you because I worried that it'd spook you."

"Why in the hell would you think that?"

"Um, I was at the hospital with you during your dad's ordeal, remember? And we had a few conversations about how you didn't know how to deal with health crises situations. You said you either shut down or used avoidance. You admitted you were freaked out by Sutton's injuries—both times—and how relieved you were that he made a full recovery because you weren't sure you could handle him being permanently damaged. So tell me, I was just supposed to blurt out that I have a condition that might end up blinding me? Making me lose a limb? That I had to deal with medication and monitoring every day for the rest of my life? You would've said, 'Thanks for telling me, Melissa. I know we haven't even been on one date yet, but I want to learn everything about your condition on the off chance that I'm not freaked out by helping you deal with this every day forever.' That's bullshit and you know it."

She was right. Fuck he *hated* that she was right. She hadn't even mentioned how horrified he'd been that she had dealt with a permanently injured sibling. And she hadn't called him out on his less than grateful attitude that he'd been spared that.

"Do you want to know how my mother reacted when I told her? She tried to convince me that I was mistaken. I couldn't possibly have 'contracted' type 1 diabetes as a thirty-two-year-old woman. She got all haughty and informed me that what I meant was I had type 2 diabetes. And well, she had little sympathy for me because everyone knows that type 2 diabetes is a disease fat, lazy people and alcoholics bring on themselves by not taking care of themselves."

Wyn didn't know if he could stomach any more of this.

You will listen, asshole. You're the one who demanded to know why she hadn't told you. Now that she has the guts to do so, you ain't gonna puss out.

"Then she said she couldn't believe I was making such a big deal about it. That there were people like Alyssa with real physical problems that couldn't be fixed by a change in diet and exercise. And it was sad that I needed attention for a situation of my own making, and I should be ashamed. That I shouldn't contact them again until I got my life in order."

He spun around and gathered her into his arms when the sobs broke free. "Baby, I'm so sorry."

"So you can see why I'd be less than eager to relive *that* experience."

"No offense, but your family is a bunch of fucking idiots."

"It still hurts."

"I can't imagine." He kissed the top of her head. "Did your sister react the same way?"

"I haven't told her."

"I'm sensing a pattern here, Kentucky."

Melissa head-butted his chest. "I'm sorry I didn't tell you. I haven't told Alyssa because she's been in Europe for fucking ever and I haven't talked to her." She looked at him. "Are you ever going to forgive me for not telling you?"

"Yes. If you'll let us start over."

"Meaning what?"

He took the biggest chance of his life. "As much as I'd like to pretend this has only been about sex between us, that's a lie. It's been about more than that since the second you walked into the hospital and stayed with me all night. I like being around you. I like having you in my house and part of my life."

"I-I don't know what to say."

"Say you'll give me a chance—us a chance."

"I'm supposed to leave tomorrow."

Wyn kissed her. "I know. I'm askin' you to rethink that."

Those soulful brown eyes searched his. "What happened today hasn't scared you off?"

"Exactly the opposite." *It makes me want to hold on to you tighter. It makes me want to prove to you that I can love you like no one else can. It makes me think I've been single all these years because I was waiting for you.*

She sighed and snuggled into him. "You make my head spin, Wynton Grant."

"Is that a good thing?"

"A very good thing. Now, can we curl up on the couch and watch *South Park*?"

"Yeah. Hearing you laugh will do me a world of good, Kentucky."

"I was thinking the same thing about you, cowboy."

* * * *

When Mel felt so restless she thought she might crawl out of her skin, she told him she needed an orgasm to relax.

He told her to take a shower. And he insisted she clean up in his master bathroom since his huge shower had a bench seat in case she got tired.

The man was still babying her.

She sort of loved it.

As hard as she tried to convince him he didn't have to sit on the vanity and watch her, the stubborn man didn't listen.

After she'd washed and conditioned her hair, shaved and loofah-ed her skin with her favorite lavender vanilla body wash, she rinsed off and decided to put her plan to get a little action into action. But the man usurped her intent to give him a show—rubbing one out while sitting on the bench, her legs spread wide—when he entered the shower completely naked with that wicked gleam in his eyes.

"I could tell by the way your ass twitched that you were up to no good, Amazing Slut-Girl. So if you're feelin' up to teasing me then I figure you're up for this." He dropped to his knees and pulled her to the edge of the bench. "Brace yourself, arms behind you." Then he nuzzled her patch of pubic hair and slid his tongue up and down her slit.

"You are so very, very good at that, Super Man-Slut." Melissa felt dizzy for an entirely different reason, but she wouldn't tell him because he might stop doing that swirling thing with his tongue.

Wynton wasn't in a teasing mood. He ate at her as if he was starved for her. The water from the shower flowed over her skin like a dozen softly caressing fingers. Tiny sparkling droplets beaded on his face, the ends of his hair, and those amazingly long eyelashes. His fingers tightened on her ass and he stopped sucking to growl, "Fuck. I know where all the sugar in your body has gone to. Right here. Christ. You're as sweet and addictive as candy."

She trembled at the power behind his meaning. "Wynton. Please."

"Give it to me."

"I am."

"You're holding back. I wanna feel you explode on my tongue."

"Then stop talking and put your mouth back on my clit," she retorted.

His laughter vibrating on her swollen tissues had her gasping.

And the man knew just how to use that skilled tongue.

She shattered—the pulsing, pounding, dizzying orgasm sent her soaring to that other white void.

When she floated back down and opened her eyes, she saw something she'd never wanted to see on her lover's face. Concern.

He opened his mouth—probably to ask if she was okay—and she placed her fingers over his lips.

"Don't. I feel great. I want to feel even better. So get up here and fuck me. I want to lose myself in you for a little while." She scraped her fingers across the dark stubble on his cheeks, loving how the water had softened those bristly hairs. "There's something else I didn't tell you."

"What?"

"You're the first man I've been with since I was diagnosed."

"Why me?"

"Because you're like me—or the me I used to be before. Unapologetically sexual. I liked the way you just took over. I've never had that. Never needed it. Never wanted it. So once we got past the first couple of times we were naked together, I thought if you noticed the insulin injection sites while we were rolling around in the sheets then it wouldn't be as big a deal. That I could tell you the truth and maybe you wouldn't kick me out of bed. When you didn't notice them, for the first time in six months I felt like myself again. You have no idea what that meant to me."

"Yeah, baby, I think I do." Wynton kissed his way up her body, stopping to lick the water off her nipples. When he reached her neck, he sucked and nuzzled the spot that made her wet, made her wiggle, made her moan. "When I was in your room earlier I noticed a package of birth control pills on the dresser. You've been taking the pill?"

"Yes. Why?"

"Because I want you bare. No barriers between us. I'm clean. I haven't been with anyone in eight months." He brushed his lips over her ear. "I've never had sex without a condom."

She pushed him back to stare into his eyes. "Never?"

"Never. I've haven't been interested in a long-term relationship. Until now. Until you, Melissa."

It took every bit of control for her not to burst into tears. She managed to keep her tone light. "Lucky for you I'm so wet we won't even need lube since we won't be using a lubed up condom."

He kissed her then. Kissed her and pulled her into his arms. He maneuvered them so he was sitting on the bench and they were face to face. "You're beautiful."

"You don't have to flatter me. I'm a sure thing, Wynton."

"You're still beautiful." When he kissed her like she was precious to him, and not as if he was being careful because she was fragile, she understood his tenderness came from his strength. And she loved him all the more for it.

Locking her ankles around his lower back, she draped her forearms on his shoulders. When she felt him position the head of his cock at her entrance, she whispered, "Go slowly so I can watch your face."

Wynton kept one hand on her ass and the other cupped her neck as he eased into her fully. "Oh yeah. That feels fucking fantastic."

"Make this last. I want to feel you fill me every single time."

He groaned. "Babe. Cut me a break. The first time with no condom. I don't know how long I can last."

They moved together slowly, taking time to kiss and taste and caress. And when he couldn't hold back any longer, she slipped her hand between their bodies and got herself off the same time he bathed her pussy in his liquid heat.

Only after he kissed her did she notice he'd turned the water off.

"Did you mean it?" he whispered.

"Mean what?"

"Mean it when you said, *tell him I love him.*"

Her heart raced. "I didn't think you heard that."

"I did. And I want to know if you meant it."

"Yes, I meant it."

He smiled against her neck.

"Wynton. This is where you tell me this isn't logical. That it's crazy I fell in love with you in three weeks."

"I can't do that. I'm suffering from the same lack of logic, Kentucky, because I fell in love with you too."

Mel eased back and looked into his eyes.

"Don't go tomorrow. Stay with me."

"For how long?"

"Just until the end of time."

She laughed. But her smile faded when she realized he wasn't joking. "Are you sure? Everything is up in the air with me."

"Those things would still be up in the air regardless if you were here or in Timbuktu."

"You do have a point."

He rested his forehead to hers. "Let's figure some of this out together."

"No rush?"

"None."

"Okay."

Chapter Twelve

One week later...

Mel's phone rang and her pulse jumped, as it always did when she saw her sister's name on the caller ID. "Hello?"

"What the hell, sis? I just found out that you have type 2 diabetes?"

"Hi Alyssa, long time no talk. How are you?"

"Pissed. God. I've been gone to Europe for eight months and I don't hear from you at all—we'll get into that bullshit in a minute. So when I ask Mom how you're doing, she just casually fucking mentions that you have 'contracted' diabetes, like it's some kind of venereal disease?"

Mel laughed. She loved her sister. Over the years, Alyssa had taken total control of her life. She didn't take shit from anyone, including their parents, and she'd plow over anyone who got in her way of achieving her many goals. The woman was a muscular beast—on her upper half anyway—and she could inflict some serious damage on anyone dumb enough to assume that being paralyzed from the waist down meant that her brain was somehow impaired. "I can say this to you because you understand, but Mom was a stone-cold bitch when I told her about my diagnosis. And I don't have type 2 diabetes, I have type 1. Which means I'll be insulin dependent for the rest of my life. Of course, Mom being the medical expert on all things insisted I didn't know my own diagnosis."

"Are you kidding me?"

"Nope." And because it felt good to get all of this off her chest with Wynton, she did it again, detailing the entire conversation between her and their mother.

Alyssa was so quiet for so long afterward that Mel thought they'd gotten disconnected.

"Hello?"

"I'm still here. Checking my blood pressure because I'm fuming so hard. First of all, it sucks that not only did you discover you have a serious health issue, you didn't have family support after you found out." She paused. "You didn't keep me out of the loop about your diagnosis to pay me back for bein' such a sorry-assed cunt to you after my accident?"

Mel snorted. How had she forgotten that bloody cunt and sorry-assed cunt were her sister's favorite words? "God, no. I knew you were rolling across the globe, being the world spokeswoman for impaired athletes and inspiring millions. I didn't want to burden you."

"Burden me," Alyssa repeated. "That's horseshit. You've supported me through more than I care to think about. You should've let me rot in my own misery, but you didn't. And it sucks that you wouldn't allow me to be there for you. You didn't have the right to take that away from me. Yeah, I probably wouldn't have flown home, but goddammit, Mel, I have a fucking phone. We could've talked about it."

"I never knew what time zone you were in and international calls are expensive."

Alyssa snarled, "Expensive? What the ever-loving fuck? Jesus, Mel, we both have a damn trust fund! Money hasn't ever been an issue, nor will it ever be. Try again."

Wynton strolled into the kitchen and smiled at her. But his smile dried when he saw she was on the phone. He mouthed, "You okay?"

She nodded.

"Still waiting *Mel-is-sa*." Alyssa singsonged her full name like their mother used to.

"After I told you how Mom reacted, you're honestly surprised that I didn't break my finger trying to dial you up to sob on your shoulder?"

"Fine. You've got me there. But the fact is, I'm back in the States now. I missed you. I want to catch up on your wild, on-the-road rodeo tales. Isn't it about time for national championships to start?"

"Yeah, but I sorta...gave up competing after my diagnosis."

Silence. "Gave up. Please don't tell me it's some kind of stupid safety rule the organization enforces and you're being discriminated against due to your health impairment. Because you know I have a team of lawyers who love to go after those kinds of cases."

"Simmer down, crusader. I had a couple of episodes where I put myself, my horse, and the others in the corral with me in danger. It spooked me. So I've been taking stock."

"That better not be Mel-speak for quitting."

"And if it is?"

"I'll harass you endlessly. And you have to listen to me because I'm *paralyzed* and I still compete."

"Omigod, Alyssa. You do *not* get to play the paralyzed card with me!" She shot Wynton a look and he seemed...shocked by the conversation. Most people would be, but this is how it was between her and her sister, and she wouldn't have it any other way.

Alyssa laughed. "Wrong. I *always* get to play the paralyzed card." She paused. "The question is...do you miss competing?"

Mel locked gazes with Wynton. "Actually, no. I don't miss it as much as I thought I would. I'm thinking about getting my teaching certificate so I can torture teens with words instead of a riding crop."

"You'd kill at that, sis. Good for you."

"Oh, and I *am* utilizing all the equestrian skills I've learned over the years. I've been helping out at this beautiful ranch in Colorado. I've even got this smokin' hot cowboy rancher who wants me to stick around and be his personal ranch hand. He's the lucky one I've been showing all my best riding tricks."

Wynton grinned.

"You have a boyfriend! Is it serious?"

"Yes, it's serious."

"I want to meet this guy," Alyssa demanded.

To Wynton, Mel said, "Alyssa is demanding to meet you."

"She's welcome here any time. I'll even install a wheelchair ramp for her."

She melted. She mouthed, "I love you," at him before she said, "Did you hear that?" to her sister.

"Yes, I heard that and I think I'm a little bit in love with him. Does he have a brother?"

"He has two brothers, but one is married and the other one is gay."

"Story of my life. I'm happy for you sis. Truly."

"Thanks."

"Take care of yourself. You've been feeling okay?"

How weird to have her sister asking about *her* health. "I still miscalculate sometimes, but I'm in the beginning stage of learning to live with it."

"Call me whenever you need someone to listen."

"I will."

"Okay. Love you, and be expecting a phone call from Mom at some point this week because I am going to ream her—and Dad—a new one. It's going to be fucking epic."

Mel was still smiling when she hung up.

Then Wynton was right there, curling his hands around her face. "Sounded like that went…well."

"Alyssa is pissed on my behalf. She can lay on the guilt trip to our folks way better than I can, so I'll let her."

"I can't wait to meet her." He paused. "You're serious about looking in to getting a teaching certificate?"

"It's something I always wanted to do, but I've been too unsettled to follow through with it. Being with you…I feel settled for the first time ever, and not because I settled. But because I'm finally where I'm meant to be."

"I couldn't agree more." He kissed her and chuckled against her mouth.

"What's so funny?"

"Remember one of the first nights you stayed here and we were talking about the difference between love and lust? I told you I warned Sutton that no one falls in love in a month? And you admitted you told London the same thing?"

"Yes. Why?"

"Because we beat them by falling in love in three weeks."

Mel sighed. "Is everything always going to be a competition between you and your brothers?"

"Probably."

"You know, London and Sutton are going to take full credit for us getting together."

"Let 'em. You and I will always know the truth."

"Which is?"

"Super Man-Slut and the Amazing Slut-Girl were destined to hook up and then hang up their unopened packets of condoms for good so they could become the one and only for each other, forever."

"I love a happy ending."

"Me too." He scooped her into his arms. "Speaking of happy endings…you owe me one, woman."

"Hey, I thought you owed *me* one."

Wynton gave her a depraved look that sent her pulse tripping. "You thinking what I'm thinking?"

"Uh-huh."

Then they said *sixty-nine* simultaneously.

And they both got their happy ending…

Strung Up

Prologue

Cres

I believe that love is stronger than death.

That had become my mantra, my focal point in the last seven days, ten hours, and thirty-four minutes since the highway patrolman had knocked on my door.

I'm sorry to inform you that Michael Darby was involved in an accident and died at the scene. He listed you as his emergency contact.

The rest of what he'd said had been a blur.

At first I thought there'd been a mistake. Michael Darby and Mick Darby. I'd never called him Michael. He never called himself Michael. So maybe the cops had it wrong. Maybe there was another person's life they should be destroying with this bad news that their lover was dead.

So I argued.

Then the officer calmly pulled Mick's driver's license out of the leather wallet I'd given him for Christmas.

And then I knew it was true.

Mick was dead.

How could he be dead?

How was that fucking fair? He'd survived four wartime deployments overseas during his military career. Four years in hell. Only to be killed by a jack slipping and crushing him beneath the wheel of a car.

The injustice infuriated me. Mick being a good guy once again. The Samaritan who always stopped to help. Only this time his helpful nature had gotten him killed.

I wanted to yell at him for being so stupid.

But I'd never get to yell at him again. Or laugh with him. Or touch him. Or tell him I loved him.

He knew. Because you reminded him of that every day.

"Let us pray," the minister announced.

I bowed my head. But my focus wasn't on the minister's pointless platitudes. Instead I studied the shoes of the other four people in the front pew with me, all with one commonality—each pair was black. Mick's father wore polished dress cowboy boots. Mick's mother had opted for closed-toe pumps. Mick's sister Aria had chosen wedges. Mick's brother Sam had donned loafers.

I had Mick's favorite pair of boots on my feet. It'd been a joke between us that since we were the same size in clothing and footwear, we'd doubled the size of our wardrobes when he'd moved in with me.

I'd felt the need to wear him today. His boots, his socks, his belt, his T-shirt beneath his white dress shirt. The suit was mine. The tie was his.

Had been his.

Fuck. Would I ever get used to thinking of him in the past tense?

"Amen."

I raised my head.

Music played behind us. The organ made the tune nearly unrecognizable until the singer started "Let It Be" by the Beatles.

I closed my eyes. *Please be a shitty rendition that's way the fuck out of tune. Please garble the words so I can't understand them.*

But short of jamming my fingers in my ears and singing *la-la-la*...I couldn't tune it out.

It was beautifully sung. Poignant. I wouldn't cry. Not because I thought I was too tough to publicly show that I'd had my guts and my heart ripped out. But because if I started to bawl, I might not be able to stop.

Finally, the song ended.

Then the service ended.

I felt as if my world had ended.

Everyone stood as the urn was wheeled out. Now we'd make the sixty-mile drive to the veteran's cemetery in Miles City. Mick would have the military burial he deserved. Then we'd return to the Darby's house for the repast with his friends and his family that I didn't know, talking about "Michael," the man I hadn't known at all.

Outside on the sidewalk in front of the small white church, I looked up at the steeple as the bell eerily clanged a death toll. Mick's family had told me this was where Mick had been baptized and confirmed. They'd probably hoped he'd be married here. Instead he'd been eulogized.

I had a hard time wrapping my head around the fact Mick had decided on all of his funeral details prior to his first deployment. It didn't matter that ten years had passed. It didn't matter that I was his lover and partner now; I'd had no input regarding the ceremony.

What would you have done differently?

"Cres? You ready?"

I glanced at my brother Wyn. Both my brothers and their wives had driven to Montana for this, even after I'd told them they didn't have to come. But now, as I watched Mick's family climb into the limo—they claimed there was no room for me—I was glad my family was here. I wouldn't be forced to make the drive to Miles City by myself.

If you were here by yourself you wouldn't go to the cemetery. You'd jump in your truck and haul ass back to Colorado. Because Mick isn't in that urn. He won't know that you skipped out on the interment. Mick's family would rather you weren't there because then they won't have to justify why they're being handed the folded flag instead of you.

But would he have wanted me to have it? Since my presence and my role in his life had come as a shock to his family?

They believed—Mick had told them—that I was his roommate.

His fucking roommate.

The lie—his lie—had sliced a jagged cut to my soul that left a scar straight down to the bone.

I heard Mick's justification in my head as clearly as if he'd been in our bed next to me, whispering it in my ear. *What does it matter?* You *know who you are to me.* You *know what you mean to me. They are my past.* You *are my future.*

And so I'd forgiven him before I had a chance to be mad at him.

After today, it wouldn't matter. I'd never see Mick's family again, so I didn't give a rat's ass what they thought of me.

"Creston? Are you ready?" my mom prompted.

I shook my head. "I'm not going."

"Of course you're going, sweetheart," she said gently. "This final stage will be hard, but we're all here for you."

"Fine. You go. I'll meet you at the motel afterward. Or better yet, I'll see you at home on the ranch."

"Don't be ridiculous—"

"Sue," my father said sharply, "drop it. If he doesn't want to go, he doesn't have to go."

Having my dad's support meant everything to me. I looked at Wyn and Sutton.

They nodded in solidarity.

To keep myself from breaking down, I turned away and repeated my mantra.

I believe that love is stronger than death.

But I knew I'd never give love a chance to break me again.

Chapter One

Cres
Two years later...

"I don't see why I need to go to this thing. It has nothin' to do with me."

My brother Wyn paused long enough that I was forced to meet his gaze.

I saw a hard look in his eyes and I knew I was totally fucked.

"You *are* goin' because more than half of your family is involved in this new venture. And you will show support for it and for your brother and sisters-in-law, Cres, if I have to hogtie you, prop you up in the corner and paint a goddamned smile on your face myself."

"Fine. Whatever. I'll be there." I slapped Petey on the rump and turned him out into the pasture to graze. I hefted the saddle off the fence and hauled it inside the barn. When I returned for the saddle blanket and the rest of the tack, I saw that Wyn still rested against the corral, his arms crossed, probably waiting to rip into me some more.

I ignored him.

Wyn followed me into the tack room.

I continued to ignore him.

I took my time putting everything away in its proper place, hanging up the saddle blanket to dry before I faced him. "What? I said I'd be there."

"Good. We miss you," he said softly.

"You see me every damn day, Wyn."

He shook his head. "I work with you every day. Outside of that, we don't see you."

I turned away. "You've got your own life with Mel and your son." I didn't point out it was the same situation with our other brother Sutton, his wife London, and their little boy, Brennen. I was the odd man out—in so many ways.

"I'll pick you up at six-thirty."

"I can drive myself."

"Nope. You're goin' with me. This is not negotiable."

Anger made me snap, "I *said* I'd be there. I don't need a fucking escort."

"You brought this on yourself, Cres, since you haven't shown up for any of the other family get-togethers in the past year after you promised you would. Not takin' a chance this time. Besides, I need you to drive my truck back here. Melissa drove her car earlier today and we don't need two vehicles there since we're stayin' overnight."

"So in addition to bein' forced to attend this thing, I'll also have to stay sober?"

"Yep." Wyn moved in behind me and squeezed my shoulder. "Clean yourself up. I'll be back in an hour. Don't make me come lookin' for you."

I stayed in the barn until I heard my brother's rig drive off. Then I grabbed a beer out of the fridge and headed toward the house.

Clean yourself up. I had half a notion to stay in the same stinky-ass, manure splattered clothes I had on. Why did it matter what I wore? The shindig was being held in a barn. A three-million-dollar-barn, but a barn nonetheless.

But showing up as the dirty, bedraggled, surly brother would bring unwanted attention to me. Better to clean up, blend in, and play the part they demanded.

I stripped down as I walked through my house and was naked by the time I reached the bathroom. I stepped into the shower, letting the tepid water run over me for a long time. It'd been a hot and dusty day moving cattle and the cool water felt good. Keeping my eyes closed, I remained under the spray as I finished my beer. Then I grabbed the soap and lathered up. Rinsed off. Dried off. As I shaved, I figured any day now my mom would say I needed a haircut. Maybe I oughta just grow a beard and go with the whole mountain-man look.

Don't you mean hermit?

Standing in front of my closet as I towel dried my hair, I scowled at my clothing selection. They'd better not expect me to wear a damn suit.

My stomach bottomed out when I remembered the last time I'd worn one.

Mick's funeral.

Blindly, I thrust my hand into the closet and grabbed a long-sleeved shirt. I slipped it on over my T-shirt and tucked it into my jeans. Belt on, boots on, dress hat by the door, I snagged another beer and parked myself on the couch to wait for my babysitter to arrive.

* * * *

Wyn arrived on time.

After I hopped into the passenger side, I turned around to look in the back of the double cab, expecting to see my nephew Evan happily kicking his chubby legs in his car seat. But the car seat was empty. "Where's the rug rat?" I asked my brother.

"Mom and Dad are watching him and Brennen."

Brennen, Sutton and London's son, was only two months younger than Evan. Our folks were in heaven with their two adorable grandsons. "So they get to skip this event? Shoot, if I'da known that was an option, I would've volunteered to babysit."

He snorted. "Standin' around sipping beer and listening to speeches is a cakewalk compared to chasin' after a couple of two-year-olds. Consider yourself lucky."

"How long is this thing supposed to last?"

"No idea. They invited like a thousand people."

That shocked me. "A thousand people? Jesus. Why so many?"

"Grade A Farms jumping into the rodeo school arena is a big damn deal. You oughta know by now that the Gradskys don't do anything half-assed."

"When does the rodeo school open officially?"

"Next month, I guess. They're workin' out the scheduling since they'll have to utilize all three arenas on the property. They're already near full capacity for enrollment. I'm betting that after tonight they'll have a waiting list. They keep expanding operations and they'll own the entire southeastern corner of Colorado."

The Gradskys' main chunk of land, Grade A Farms, devoted to raising rodeo stock—both rodeo rough stock and horse breeding—was a hundred miles south of the Grant Ranch. "Why'd they build the school this far north? Wouldn't it be easier to have the breeding stock in the same place as they were teaching students?"

Wyn shot me an odd look. "Have you been payin' attention at all the past year and a half?"

I bristled. "What do you mean?"

"Gradskys relocated all their operations to this location."

"Everything?"

"Everything."

Shit. I hadn't been paying attention. "Why?"

"They outgrew the land faster than they'd planned. Plus, after London and Sutton gave Chuck and Berlin their first grandchild, they wanted to live closer. Their son Macon practices law in Denver anyway. And Stirling..."

"What's goin' on with Stirling?"

"She quit her fancy job and bought two hundred acres adjacent to her folks' place. Crazy girl has started an organic farm."

I frowned. "We're talkin' about Stirling Gradsky, right? The corporate executive is giving up power lunches in Lear jets to dig in the dirt like a common farmer?"

Wyn grinned at me. "Oh, don't kid yourself that it'll bother her to ruin her manicure. She's savvy enough to hire all the right people. But she's a control freak and has no problem doin' the dirty work so she keeps more of the profits."

"What's she growing?"

"Pot. Wish I'd thought of that," Wyn groused. "Now those commercial Ag permits are hard to come by. She skated in with all the applications the week that pot became legal in Colorado. She's gonna make a fuck-ton of money."

"Rather see her successful at it than these out-of-state fuckers."

"Amen."

"What did the Gradskys do with their other place? Sell it?"

Wyn shook his head. "Kept it. Turned it into a full-time cattle operation and a dude ranch. The Gradskys' nephews Lewis and Clark are running it. They're good guys. I feel bad their folks saddled them with those names. You met them at Sutton and London's wedding. But maybe you don't remember."

I didn't. Because I met someone far more important than them: Mick.

I got really quiet.

"What?"

"You're right. I haven't been paying attention to anything. It's just…" How did I say this? "Why haven't you all given up on me?"

"Because you're family, bro. All we can do is be here for you when you're ready to pay attention again."

I scrubbed my hands over my face. "If I haven't said so, I appreciate that none of you have nagged and told me I've been grieving long enough and it's time to move on."

Wyn actually looked horrified. "Cres, that ain't for anybody but you to decide. I wasn't bullshitting you earlier. We miss you. All of us do. We thought it'd do us all good to be together tonight, no kids, no talkin' about the ranch. Just the five of us hanging out."

I tried not to think back when it was the six of us hanging out. My brothers and their wives had accepted Mick and me as a couple and him as part of the family. "It still feels wrong that he's not here," I admitted.

My brother reached over and patted my leg.

The drive had taken a little more than half an hour. We turned down a dirt road and I saw hundreds of cars parked in a field off to the left side.

"Holy shit."

"I had that same reaction the first time I saw it too. Like I said, the Gradskys don't do anything half-assed. They arranged for buses to take guests up to the compound."

Berlin and Chuck Gradsky were my sister-in-law London's parents. Their business interests ran the gamut from horse breeding, to horse training, to cattle ranching, and they invested their all financially and personally in every venture they attempted, which was why it seemed everything they touched turned to gold. After Sutton became their son-in-law, Wyn and I became part of their family too. I'd understood why Wyn was in the inner Gradsky loop, since his wife Melissa worked as a teacher and a trainer for Grade A. But they'd accepted me too—welcomed me even—and that meant more than I could express.

Wyn bypassed the parking lot. He handed me a heavy piece of paper he'd pulled down from his sun visor. "VIP parking pass. Put that on the dash."

It was hard not to gawk at the structures as we tooled up the blacktop. We passed three indoor arenas, each with its own corral. The road forked and a sign marked "dormitories" pointed to the right. Behind the trees I could make out two buildings with a courtyard between them. The road split again and an arrow pointed to the left with a sign that read "classrooms and dining hall." Then we crested a rise. I blinked at what appeared to be a small town spread out at the base of the hill.

"They did all of this in a year and a half?"

"Actually, it's been less than a year."

"Did you know the Gradskys had this kind of money?"

He shook his head. "I don't think anyone knew, including their kids."

"Well, everyone will know after tonight, won't they?"

"Yep." Wyn parked in the VIP lot.

We hoofed it through the tall grass toward the biggest tent I'd ever seen—guess a three-million-dollar barn wasn't big enough to hold everyone. Beneath the big top were bleachers. I half-expected to see clowns making balloon animals, jugglers throwing flaming batons into the air, scantily clad women twirling on trapezes, and the trumpeting of elephants.

I muttered, "I need a damn drink."

"Staff and family have their own section with an open bar. We're almost there."

The moment we stepped through the curtained-off area, my sister-in-law Melissa threw herself at my brother, greeting him with a steamy kiss. Then she whapped him on the chest. "What took you so long?"

"I checked on Evan before I picked Cres up."

Melissa whirled around, noticing me for the first time.

I managed a smile at her look of shock that I'd actually shown up. "Hey, Mel. You're lookin'—"

"Round. I wasn't this big at the end of my last pregnancy." Then she wrapped herself around me as best as she could with the basketball baby between us. "I'm so glad you're here, Cres."

"I appreciate the invite. How are you really feelin', little mama?"

"I'm excited for everyone to see the facility. It's been crazy today, running all over the place, getting everything ready."

Wyn loomed over her as soon as she stepped away from me. "When was the last time you sat down?"

"I don't know. I'm fine. Stop fussing."

"Like that's gonna happen. Your ankles are swollen. You need to be off your feet until this shindig is underway."

His tone meant business. Mel's diabetes added to my brother's worries and she knew better than to argue.

"We're sitting at the far back table since it's closest to the bathroom."

"Let's go."

I trudged behind them. As soon as Wyn reached the table, he plopped down and scooped Mel onto his lap, kicking out a chair for her to put her feet up on. I made a beeline for the bar. I ordered two Fat Tires and brought one back to him.

"Thanks."

Mel toasted with her bottle of water. "London and Sutton will be along any minute."

"What time does this start?"

"The official program and introduction of the instructors begins at eight. Tours have been underway since about four."

"Now I wish we would've gotten here earlier," I said, surprising myself and them. "I'd like to check it all out."

"I'll give you a personal tour any time you want," London said behind me. Then she wrapped her arms around my shoulders and squeezed me tight. "So, so, so glad you came, Cres."

"Me, too."

My brother Sutton dropped into the chair next to mine. Not only was I the youngest of the Grant boys, at six feet two and one hundred eighty pounds, I was also the runt of the litter. Both Sutton and Wyn topped me by two inches.

Sutton's way of saying hello was to grin at me before he swiped my beer. "Thanks."

Some things never changed.

I got up to get another beer and just to be ornery, brought London back a double shot of tequila. London tended to get out of hand once the tequila started flowing and it was my right to encourage it on a night of celebration.

"Ooh, you read my mind, Cres. Thanks," London said and touched the plastic glass to my beer bottle before she downed the shot.

I said, "You're welcome."

"Really, Cres?" Sutton complained.

Wyn laughed. "You brought that one on yourself."

"Yeah," I retorted. "Next time, get your own damn beer."

And then it really did seem like old times. As if it'd just been last week that we'd all hung out, shooting the breeze and drinking beer. I even managed to laugh when London launched into a story about horse training that somehow shifted to potty training Brennen.

But our family time ended all too soon. Before I had time to ready myself for being in a crowd, we were surrounded by one. The Gradskys descended. Berlin hugged me, Chuck and Macon shook my hand, followed by a reintroduction to London's cousins who were running the dude ranch. That group expanded to include all the employees and their spouses until it seemed a hundred people were crammed into the space, all talking at once.

Would anyone notice if I snuck out?

Doubtful.

I sucked it up and stayed until Berlin and Chuck took center stage.

The crowd beneath the big top quieted as the introductions of the instructors began. I half-listened because I recognized knew a few names from the world of rodeo anyway.

When the lines opened to the buffet, the crush of people made it hard to breathe. I slipped out the back, the opposite direction of the food line. I'd never been one for crowds and after spending the last two years in isolation, this scene sent me searching for solitude.

A white catering van had been parked near the rear exit. It appeared I wasn't the only one seeking an escape. A big guy, roughly the same size as Sutton, rested against the side of the van, one boot heel hooked to the running board. He wore dark jeans and a plain white button down shirt with a logo on the left pocket. He'd angled his head down, obscuring his face. But with that build and that posture, I knew I was looking at a rodeo cowboy.

Something seemed familiar about him.

That's when I noticed the poker chip in his left hand. He passed it through his fingers over and over again. I recognized that nervous tic.

My gut tightened. I took a few more steps forward, alerting him to my presence.

He palmed the poker chip before he slowly raised his head and looked at me.

Then I was staring into that face. That handsome fucking smug face.

A face I used to dream of.

A face I hadn't seen in four years, since Sutton and London's wedding.

I waited for the dismissive sneer to distort that perfect mouth.

A mouth I'd dreamed of nearly as often as his perfect face.

But no sneer formed.

His compelling eyes met mine.

I saw his recognition in those arctic blue depths. Followed by wariness. But no hardness. Or the mean glint I'd unconsciously steeled myself against.

He didn't move.

Neither did I.

I found my voice. "Breck?"

"Hey, Cres."

"What are you doin' out here?"

"Same thing you're doin', I reckon. Avoiding the crowd." He paused and dipped his chin to the empty space beside him. "There's room if you wanna take a load off."

I waited for the innuendo.

None came.

Everything inside me cautioned me to beat a fast retreat.

Not everything. My long-dormant libido urged me to stay.

Chapter Two

Breck

I watched Creston Grant trying to decide whether to stay or go.

I didn't blame him for his indecision.

The Breck he remembered? Total fucking tool. As well as being a world-class asshole, a condescending prick, a sharp-tongued dickhead, and a douchebag.

Yeah, I'd been the posterchild for how *not* to win friends and influence people.

Little wonder I was back here hiding, wondering what the hell I'd gotten myself into again.

Cres heaved a sigh and shuffled forward. Then he turned and planted his backside next to mine—but not too close to mine.

I quietly exhaled.

He didn't speak right away. I remembered that about him—he weighed his words carefully before he spoke. At first I'd believed it was a family trait he shared with his brother Sutton, the stereotypical quiet gruff cowboy. But then I discovered the reason for his caution—his sexual orientation. I might be in a different situation if I'd acted more circumspect.

But I also remembered finding a fissure in that tough outer shell of his. And how easy it was to apply the perfect amount of pressure until that fissure widened into a crack—a crack I used to open him up fully to all the naked possibilities between us. I should've felt guilty; Cres was a decade younger and hadn't built up defenses against a guy like me.

Yet, of all my conquests, Cres Grant had been the one I'd regretted letting go.

"I'm surprised to see you back here alone," he said, interrupting my silent contemplation. "I thought you preferred to be in the thick of things."

"I used to."

"What changed?"

"Everything."

"That's cryptic."

"It is what it is."

From the corner of my eye I saw Cres turn his head and squint at me. "So why are you here, Breck?"

"Here in Colorado at the grand opening of Grade A Rodeo Academy?"

He nodded.

"Sutton, London, or Mel didn't fill you in?" I asked.

"Nope. I've been out of the loop since…" He paused. "For a while."

I shoved the poker chip in my front jeans pocket. "I remember you tellin' me you didn't follow rodeo even when your brother dominated the leaderboard."

Cres shrugged. "Not my thing. So you're here as a guest?"

"Nah. I'm a staff member."

He frowned. "I didn't hear your name called or see you go up to the podium when Chuck and Berlin introduced the staff."

"That's because I asked to remain anonymous."

"Right. Because you're still way too fucking cool for all this bullshit."

His response wasn't unexpected but it still stung. The old me would've gone off on him, belittling him, berating him until he slunk away with his tail between his legs, allowing me to feel superior. I didn't have it in me to be that guy anymore.

"Yeah. That's it. You've got me pegged." I pushed away from the van. "Nice seein' you, Cres. Take care." I skirted the front end of the van and kept walking along the raised ledge of the small ravine until the noise faded and I could breathe.

Heedless of the dusty surface, I found a flat spot and let my feet dangle over the edge. Wasn't a huge drop, but it'd be a bitch to climb out of if I slipped. Good thing I hadn't been drinking. Scooping up a handful of rocks, I thought about the last time I'd seen Cres—at Sutton and London's wedding. So much of that time was a blur of booze. I'd managed to scrounge up a date because back then it'd been paramount to keep up appearances.

Nothing to see over here, folks. Just a horny single cowboy adding a new notch on his championship belt by bedding yet another hot woman.

I'd had a huge ego back then too. It'd been heady stuff, knowing guys wanted to be me; on fire in the arena and burning up the sheets with a different buckle bunny every night.

But it'd all been a lie. A house of cards about to tumble and crush me like a bug.

I might've been able to survive rumors of fucking anything with a pulse if I'd had a winning season. In previous years, officials, sponsors, and even rodeo fans chalked up the rumors of my insatiable sexual appetite as blowing off steam after my many wins. The whispers of my sexcapades with same-sex partners were written off as drunken experimentation after too many Jäger shots. Even the wildest rumors worked to my advantage and added to my status that I could have any woman I wanted on her knees with just a look.

Problem was it wasn't a woman I wanted on her knees.

When I began to lose on the circuit, the females I'd counted on to flock around me as camouflage began to flit away. I should've become more cautious at that point, not more reckless. Somehow I believed my oversized championship belt buckle had become a shield. That I was invincible. Impervious. That with three All-Around world titles I could be forgiven anything.

Wrong.

When you're on the highest rung of the ladder, hitting the bottom leaves you far more broken than you ever imagined.

It'd been a long, slow recovery and no climb back to the top. And for me, there'd been no privacy while I dealt with the various traumas—physical and mental. There'd been no one to lean on, no one to talk to.

That had been the reality of my life the past three years. Humbled and lonely.

I tossed a pebble at a flat rock and watched it bounce down into the ravine.

Boot steps shuffled behind me.

Had I really thought he'd let me go without poking his nose into my business?

You were hoping he wouldn't.

Cres crouched next to me. "What happened to you?"

"Depends on who you ask," I said.

"I'm askin' you, Breck."

I turned my head and met his gaze. Brown eyes the color of cinnamon stared back at me. I let my focus drift over Cres's face. Damn man still had the power to render me incoherent. All those rugged angles that made up his face epitomized magnificent. Seeing his curiosity and not pity allowed me to say, "Pull up a rock."

He shifted from a crouch into a sitting position. "You couldn't have stormed off to a table by the bar instead of the edge of a cliff?"

"I didn't storm off," I retorted. "And it's hardly a cliff."

"I remember you always had a flair for drama."

"I've had enough drama to last a lifetime." I shot him a sideways glance. "And if you use the word *queen*, I'm pushing you over the edge."

"Whoa." Cres put up his hands in mock surrender. "Never crossed my mind. So am I the only person at the open house that doesn't have a freakin' clue as to what's goin' on with you?"

"Probably. In the words of the reporter who wrote the article, 'this story rocked the very foundation of the rodeo community.'"

"That bad, huh? What'd you do? Shoot a jealous lover in self-defense or something?"

I snorted. "Sad to say I'd be forgiven for that. Really sad to think that homicide is preferable to bein' a homosexual in the pro rodeo world."

That admission startled him. "That's what's goin' on with you? Jesus. I had no idea." He paused and studied me.

"No one did."

Cres reached for a small rock and chucked it at the other side, sending up a puff of dirt. "What made you decide to come out?"

"I didn't. The decision was taken out of my hands."

"Really? How?"

"Cockiness on my part. I'd been seeing this guy Carlyle off and on. He wasn't part of the rodeo scene so I thought I was safe. He knew I was in the closet and he seemed fine with it…until he wasn't. He hated the bunnies, even when nothin' was happening between them and me.

He went from waitin' for me in the motel room to waitin' for me outside the stock pens. And if I tried to dodge him, well, he cranked the gay on high and threw a major sissy-hissy fit. To make matters worse, I had the shittiest run of my career. I wasn't even in the top twenty in my circuit. So I broke it off with him, telling him I needed to concentrate on getting back on top—which wasn't exactly a lie. I thought he understood what was at stake for me. I thought he'd keep his mouth shut and move on."

"What'd he do?"

"Called *Country Times Today* magazine, that piece of crap rag devoted to gossip in the country music scene that also regularly reports on CRA and EBS standings. Carlyle spilled his guts and my secrets, all in the guise of helping us find our way back to each other because he believed 'our love shouldn't have to be hidden away.'" Yeah. No sarcasm there.

"Lemme guess. This guy was a pretty-boy model type? From one of the coasts?" Cres said with a sneer in his tone.

I couldn't even bristle at that presumption because he'd hit it right on. "Everyone has a type. A pretty boy happens to be mine." I started to remind Cres that's why he and I had hooked up—his pretty face with those high cheekbones, chiseled jawline, aristocratic nose, and full lips did it for me in a bad way. The passing years had just fine-tuned his features and he'd grown from a pretty boy into a beautiful man.

"So the country tattler printed the story and then...?"

My neck and face burned hot, as it always did whenever I thought about the day my life as I'd known it had ended. "It wasn't just a small paragraph buried in the back of the rodeo stats page. I'd scored the front cover and an eight-page spread with other 'secret male lovers' coming forward. Christ. They even had pictures. One picture in particular of me and Carlyle in bed. I was asleep with my head on his chest, so I had no fucking idea he'd even taken it.

"I'd finally started winning again and that's why I thought there were a bunch of reporters waitin' for me after I'd won the tie-down and bulldoggin' events in Prescott. The appearance of the article completely blindsided me. As did all the questions about my perversions as a liar and a sodomite who'd hopped on the express train to hell."

He whistled.

"Yeah. And it gets better. Although I never figured out which one of my competitors had a hand in getting the article published, all the rest of them took advantage of running me down when the AP got ahold of the story. The national news services interviewed anyone who would talk smack about me—which was everyone. Guys I'd never met claimed they'd always known something was 'off' with me. Each quote was another blow, knocking me so deep into the dirt…" *I feared I'd never dig myself out.* I paused and swallowed hard. "Not a single person on the circuit stood up for me, Cres. Not one. I'd been friends with some of them for a decade. I'd helped them out professionally. Several of the guys…I'd been at their ranches workin' as a hand during calving and branding. I knew their wives and their kids and they all turned their backs on me."

"Man. That is harsh. I'm sorry. I don't know what else to say."

"Most people thought I got what I had coming to me. There was talk for a few months of the CRA stripping me of my world titles. It never happened, but my name was tarnished beyond repair at that point anyway. My sponsors dropped me. The rodeo organizations, even at the county level, banned me from competing. People laugh about bein' blackballed, but it is a very real and a very ugly thing." I couldn't admit to him that even the "rainbow" circuit for gay cowboys wouldn't have me because I refused to publicly state my sexual orientation.

"What'd you do?"

"Went home to South Dakota. Or I tried to go home. My brother was waitin' for me at the end of the road, blocking me from stepping foot on the family farm. He didn't say a word to me when he handed me the paper that cut all ties and connections to the Christianson family."

"You're fucking kiddin' me."

I shook my head. "Mom and Dad, my brothers and my sister—they disowned me. They wrote letters denouncing me and had them notarized and everything. The last bit of paperwork denied me any future claim whatsoever on any part of the Christianson farm or the land despite the fact I'd sunk three quarters of a million dollars into keeping it afloat over the years. Since they were family, I never asked for a legal contract, so I was fucked."

"Didn't the magazine at least give you a chance to tell your side of the story? Or interview you?"

"Nope. They told the story as they saw fit. The following month they'd moved on to something else. By then, I had no choice but to move on because the article had destroyed my life as I knew it. I lost everything."

"What happened to the Carlyle guy who sold the story to the magazine?" he demanded.

"He left me a voice mail full of self-righteousness, pointing out I'd brought everything on myself by denying my true nature."

"That wasn't for him to decide."

"True. But he wasn't wrong. Maybe everything would've blown up in my face eventually. It just happened sooner rather than later." I knocked my shoulder into his. "Enough about me. What's goin' on with you?"

Cres stiffened up. "Not much. Ranching with Wyn."

"That's it?"

"Yep." His face fell into shadow when he lowered his head and focused on brushing the dust off his jeans.

"I pour my guts out about the shitshow that my life has become and 'not much, ranching with Wyn' is all I get from you? Fuck that, Cres. Do they know—?"

"That I'm gay? Yeah. I came out after Sutton and London got together."

Something about that timeframe sparked a memory. "A few months after we hooked up in Denver?"

"Yep." Cres fastened his gaze to mine. "It's because of you that I had the balls to start that 'I'm gay' conversation with them."

"Why?" Hopefully I hadn't given him some stupid drunken speech about honesty when I hadn't been honest with myself about who I was until I'd been forced into it.

"Because I didn't want to live my life like you."

My jaw tightened.

"Don't get me wrong," he said apologetically. "I know why you chose that. In a sport like rodeo where the motto is 'God and country first,' bein' openly gay just ain't done. Not surprised you didn't have any support when you were outed; more than a few guys on the circuit were probably sweating bullets that they'd be found out too."

"I was so goddamned angry about the breach of privacy that I'm ashamed to admit I considered takin' some of them that I'd been with over the years down with me."

"But you didn't, did you?" he asked alarmingly.

I shook my head. "How would takin' their choice away make me any different than what Carlyle did to me?"

Cres seemed relieved. And surprised.

Because I acted like a decent person? At one time I'd been proud of my asshole reputation. No wonder I'd isolated myself.

"Anyway, back to you. Did anything else besides seein' me livin' a lie prompt you to come out?"

"I'd gotten tired of the fix ups. Tired of women coming onto me and creating excuses about why I wasn't interested. Tired of the questions about when I planned to settle down. I wanted to be done pretending."

"You showed more maturity than I did. At an earlier age than I did."

"Yeah. Well, we're all different." He readjusted his hat.

Even a basic compliment still made him squirm and that just got to me. And charmed the hell out of me.

"Was there any fallout from the women you'd been linked to?"

"I'd only had two girlfriends during my years on the circuit who could be considered long term. They both knew I preferred dick and had their own agenda as to why they let me use them as cover. Celia Lawson—Celia Gilchrist now—wanted to build a reputation for bein' wild. And Lally Bunker..." I smirked. "She happily joined in threesomes—as long as it involved girl-on-girl time for her. So I got the rep for demanding girl-on-girl action from the bunnies chasin' after me, which worked as cover for both of us."

Cres studied me. "That week we spent together, you told me you were bisexual."

I rubbed the back of my neck and gave a sheepish chuckle. "I was an idiot, okay? I thought if I said it enough times then maybe I'd start to believe it. It would've been an easier road, refuting the 'you're gay' accusations by telling people I liked sexual variety and hated sexual labels."

"You still could've taken that tack after the article released," he pointed out.

"But like *you* said, I wanted to be done pretending. So your family was okay with you when you told them about batting for the other team?"

"They were surprised, but it didn't change anything. I still had a job on the ranch. A home near them. And yeah, I do know how lucky I am to have that family support when I hear that others don't. So speaking of family…" Cres stood. "I'd probably better get back to the party. My brothers will wonder why I disappeared again." He offered his hand to help me up.

"Thanks."

Cres pulled a little too hard and I nearly knocked him over when I popped to my feet. I kept ahold of his hand and circled my arm around his lower back to steady him.

At that moment a breeze from the ravine eddied around us, gifting me with a whiff of his skin and the lime scent of his shaving cream. During our time together in Denver, I spent hours kissing and nuzzling that strong jawline and the smooth contour of his throat. Now, with my hand on his strong back and his scent beckoning me, I wanted to haul that hard body against mine and surround myself with him.

Maybe only your dick is hard right now. Maybe this lust is one-sided.

But Cres tilted his head back, almost as if he was offering me a taste of his mouth or his throat and murmured, "You're not as heavy as I remember."

The heat in his eyes when straight to my balls. "No need to maintain all that bulk if I'm not usin' it to take down a steer."

"How is it that less looks good on you?" he said huskily.

My eyes searched his. I liked what I saw when I looked at him—eagerness, which hit the perfect mark between shy and sexy. "You flirting with me, Cres?"

He blushed and tried to retreat. "That isn't why I followed you."

I softened my stance and my tone. I didn't want to scare him away. "Why did you follow me?"

"To apologize for making assumptions about you. I understand probably more than anyone that people do change."

There was another thing I remembered about him that I'd found so damn appealing besides that muscular body honed by honest labor—a genuine sweetness. "I appreciate you sayin' that."

"Besides, it's been so long for me, I'm pretty sure I've forgotten how to flirt."

"Trust me, you're doin' fine." I cocked my head. "But you have changed."

"I ditched the passive persona."

Cres was so freaking intense with the way he studied me and my reaction to his declaration. "You weren't passive with me."

"But I wasn't assertive either."

"Is that how you are now? Assertive?"

He waited a beat to make sure he had my full attention when he said, "Very."

Fuck. Me. That one word. That determined look proved time hadn't cooled the red-hot attraction between us.

The head in my pants urged me to step forward, but the head on my shoulders resisted, reminding me that I'd learned the hard way not to make the first move.

"You couldn't have gotten ugly and bitter after your forced coming out? Let yourself go to hell?" he said lightly.

I laughed. "I'm sorry you're disappointed."

"I'm not." Cres gave me a very thorough once-over. "So not. You still pack one helluva sexual punch, Breck."

When our gazes clashed again, I said "fuck it" to myself about not making the first move. I inched closer. "Did you come to this open house alone?"

"I rode with Wyn."

"That's not what I meant."

He jammed his hands in the back pockets of his jeans and admitted, "I'm here solo."

"You're not involved with anyone?"

"Nope."

The relief I felt must've shown because Cres smirked. "Are you?"

"As you can imagine I've developed some serious trust issues, so no."

"Then I'm glad I came," he said huskily. "Even if it was too late to take any of the tours."

I tipped my head toward the arena. "I could show you around the complex if you want."

"Sure. If you don't mind stopping at the food tent first. I skipped out on supper."

"I oughta check in anyway and see if there's anything I'm supposed to be doin'."

We started walking, close enough that our shoulders nearly

brushed. I'd missed this zing of sexual tension. The spark of attraction that crackled below the surface, ready to ignite at any moment. The silence between us allowed me to hear his rapid breathing and for him to hear mine. I couldn't help but sneak looks at him. That long, lean body. That strong profile nearly hidden beneath the shadow of his hat. I wanted to reacquaint myself with every hard muscle, tease every soft spot that made him growl and groan, beg and buck.

Cres stopped. His head slowly came up and our eyes connected.

"Wait here for me?" I asked.

For a moment when he hesitated, I thought he'd changed his mind. "I'll grab some food. Come find me when you're done."

Chapter Three

Cres

I kept my head down, my focus firmly on my boots eating up the dusty ground as I headed toward the smaller tent.

What are you doing, Cres? This isn't smart.

Maybe it wasn't, but making plans with Breck didn't feel wrong.

Probably nothing would happen anyway.

Whatever you want to happen, can happen. Especially with him.

That wasn't an arguable point, so even my brain didn't bother to try and counter it.

One thing about Breck Christianson hadn't changed; the man was hot as hell. That coal black hair. Those piercing blue eyes. That mouth.

Christ that mouth could do me in. Seemed I couldn't look away from it regardless if Breck was sporting a smile or a sneer. Lust hit me with another one-two punch when I recalled how those full lips alternated between being cushiony soft, skating down my torso, or hard and firm during a breath-stealing kiss. Or a combination of both when he worked my cock over.

It'd been ages since I'd thought about that week I'd spent with him in Denver. After Sutton's career-ending rodeo injury, he'd been searching for a buyer for his temperamental—but highly prized—horse, Dial. As my brother's rodeo buddy, Breck had offered to give Dial a trial run and I'd volunteered to take the horse to the stock show.

I hadn't expected my brother's big-time rodeo buddy to be into guys.

I really hadn't expected a charismatic guy who looked like Breck to be into *me*.

Around my twenty-first birthday, I'd accepted my attraction to men wasn't a phase and that actually made me...gay. By age twenty-four I hadn't come out of the closet. I'd been cautious with hookups, sticking with blowjobs and hand jobs. I'd fucked a couple of guys and had let a couple fuck me. Pretty straightforward stuff.

Then I'd met Breck.

He'd taken my carnal education to a whole other level. It'd been an eye opener for me, experiencing that kind of deep passion and intimacy with another man. It'd given me hope that someday I'd find that same connection again, but something permanent I could be open about.

The last time I'd seen Breck had been at my brother Sutton's wedding. He'd shown up with a date—she was trashy and he was testy and surly with everyone. Even my sister-in-law mentioned Breck was quickly running out of friends on the circuit due to his recent attitude and actions.

At the time I'd wondered how much longer he could continue to live the lie. I'd intended to take him aside and try and get him to open up to me, but that night my father had suffered a near-fatal heart attack. And much later that night, I'd ended up with Mick.

My body flushed hot with guilt. I'd never told Mick about Breck. It hadn't seemed relevant. Breck had been a sexual mentor. That was it. And after Mick and I were a couple, I hadn't thought about Breck at all.

Maybe that's why you haven't told Breck about Mick either.

More guilt kicked in. Telling Breck about the death of my lover and that I'd spent the last two years in a fog would definitely put a damper on tonight's possibilities. I still wasn't sure if I could be with another man.

But wouldn't Breck be the perfect guy to test out that theory on?

"Cres?"

I glanced up and realized London's sister, Stirling, was standing in front of me. "Hey. Sorry. My mind was elsewhere." I smiled at her. "I hoped I'd get to see you since I heard you were living in the area and had become a farmer—which I see is a lie because you are not rockin' the overalls."

Standoffish Stirling actually hugged me and laughed. "It's true. I feel like a different person after I tossed off the shackles of corporate

America. I've gone completely country, back to my roots."

I gave her bohemian outfit—jeans covered in rhinestones and a sheer, floral top—a quick once-over and whistled. "Overalls or not, farmer looks good on you." Stirling was one of those tall, willowy Nordic blondes with an icy outer demeanor that scared off most men. She and I had always gotten along great because I wanted nothing from her except friendship.

She kept a hold of my arm and squeezed my biceps. "Ranching has always looked good on you, Creston Grant. Are you sure you're gay? Because a dude with your looks and physique should definitely reproduce."

Just then Breck sauntered in on the other side of the tent.

Our eyes met.

Heat from his hungry look rolled through me in a wave of want so strong I had to lock my knees.

Yeah, sweetheart. I am one hundred percent about the dick.

"Have you eaten?" Stirling said. "I got stuck waiting for Liam the Lab Loser to show up and missed the chow line."

"Actually, I was headed that direction."

"Let's dine together." She looped her arm though mine.

I felt Breck's eyes on us. I could almost feel his impatience pulsing through the air.

It won't hurt him to wait a little longer. And it'll make you seem less desperate.

So I remained fully aware of Breck pacing on the other side of the tent as I loaded up a plate.

However, Stirling was blissfully unaware of the way my pulse jumped every time my gaze connected with Breck's. Or the coiled tension in every inch of my body as I imagined his rough-skinned hands gripping my ass as I thrust my cock into that Hoover of a mouth of his.

"You are starving," Stirling said as we sat at an empty picnic table. "You just made a growling noise."

I forced my gaze away from Breck and concentrated on chatting with London's little sister. "So who is this Liam guy? And why did you call him a lab loser?"

Stirling sighed and signaled to the bartender closest to us. Immediately a server dropped off two Fat Tire beers.

Handy to be dining with one of the Gradsky princesses.

"I've spent the last seven years literally working in the corporate meat market, using my animal science degree to breed better beef cattle on a large-scale commercial level without growth hormones."

A concept I was familiar with since we didn't use growth hormones.

"Now I've partnered with my brother Macon and we've jumped into the organic farming market."

I said, "What organics are you growing?" even when I already knew.

"Marijuana, man. It's what all the cool farmers are doing."

I snorted.

"But seriously, only three quarters of our total acreage will be devoted to pot. The rest is slated for organic vegetable production, concentrating on 'heritage varieties' that haven't been crossbred."

"I knew that cold, corporate hard-ass persona of yours was totally fake." I pointed at her with my beer bottle. "I always suspected you secretly wanted to be a professional pothead."

"Busted." Stirling smirked at me. "What kind of farmer doesn't regularly perform quality control tests on their crops?"

"So this Liam dude is in charge of quality control in the lab and he's blocking your access to product testing?"

"Not hardly. Dr. Liam is my brother's former client, supposedly a brilliant Ag bio-engineer and our secret weapon in advanced splicing technology. But he lives in his own little bubble. He doesn't write anything down. He doesn't follow instructions. He's conceited. And he's utterly lacking in any social graces. Lucky me has been tasked with teaching him to be a team player."

"I take it he's resistant?"

She rolled her eyes. "He's a know-it-all jackass with an IQ of like a billion but he is incapable of learning basic clerical duties. He refuses to even try."

"Did you try getting high with him and see if that mellows him out?"

"Twice. When that didn't work I even tried to bribe him with a five-hundred-dollar bottle of scotch." She shook her head. "No go there either."

"I'm guessing money isn't a factor since you probably pay him plenty."

"We pay him a fuck-ton. So that left me with sex as an incentive. I hired this super-sweet, super-smart, super-hot college student with a porn-star mouth and a pair of DD's."

For the first time ever, stick-in-the-mud Stirling reminded me of her wilder older sister London. "How'd that go?"

"The woman might as well have been wearing a sackcloth and ashes or a nun's habit for all the attention he paid to her," she complained.

I laughed.

"Cres. This is not funny. This is part of what's holding up production. Neither his formulas nor his gene splicing technique can be a secret from *us*. We need the ability to recreate in case something happened to him."

Keeping my attention on Breck, I pressed my lips to my bottle of beer and took a big swig, swallowing thickly and making a show of licking my lips when I finished.

His wicked smile promised retribution.

Bring it.

"Cres. Are you even listening to me?" Stirling demanded. "I need your help."

I refocused after discreetly readjusting the crotch of my jeans. "What can I do? High-grade pot didn't work, booze didn't work, dangling a juicy, young coed didn't work—"

"Maybe because I dangled the wrong *flavor* of juicy coed," she said. "Maybe he prefers beefcake."

Now she had my full attention. "Are you suggesting that I—"

"Show up in the lab wearing a pair of running shorts with your bare chest and abs glistening with sweat? Absolutely."

I choked on my drink of beer.

"I just need you to recheck my gaydar."

Before I could answer, a tray slammed down on the table.

Stirling's eyes widened.

A tall, lanky man stood next to me, his posture regal. If he hadn't worn a lab coat and glasses, I never would've guessed him to be an academic. He hit the mark between a hipster and an indie rocker, seriously freakin' hot in that nerdy way with his dark brown hair secured in a ponytail at the base of his neck.

"I assure you, Miss Gradsky, there is nothing wrong with your gaydar. I am entirely heterosexual." He turned and pinned me with eyes that reminded me of quicksilver. Then he offered me his hand and tight smile. "Dr. Liam Argent."

His heavily tattooed hand was smooth and his grip strong. "Cres Grant."

"Pleased to make your acquaintance, Mr. Grant. And if I had any inclination toward a dalliance on the other side of the fence, so to speak, I'd be more than happy to see you in my lab, half-naked and glistening with sweat."

"Uh. Thanks?"

Dr. Liam angled forward so he had Stirling's full attention. "You know my conditions for taking clerical instructions, Miss Gradsky. *You* are the one who has refused to comply with the terms."

"Because I am not taking dictation as your personal secretary, dickhead," she retorted.

Yep. That response totally reminded me of London.

"It's not as if I demanded you wear thigh highs and stilettos with a Catholic schoolgirl outfit as you're receiving my oral direction," he said in a silken drawl.

And...I'd heard enough. I had my own sexual tension to deal with. I didn't need a front row seat to theirs. I stood and mumbled good-bye.

Breck waited for me by the rear exit. "Did you get enough to eat?"

"I guess. Sort of a bizarre dinner conversation so I don't really remember what I ate."

He chuckled. "That's Stirling for you."

Once we were outside, he briefly placed his hand on the small of my back to guide me. "Let's start the tour this way."

Even that single touch caused my stomach to cartwheel.

Blue light glowed from the big top. An electric guitar strummed once. Then twice.

"Sounds like the dance is about to start," Breck said.

"I didn't know there was a dance."

"I don't think it'll go late. Most of the guests left as soon as they finished eating." He walked closer to me. "You ever danced with a guy, Cres?"

"Like gone out two-steppin'? Nah. No clubs that cater to that around here. Gotta go into Denver to find that. What about you?"

"I've hit a gay dance club a time or two. Slow dancin' is easier with a guy because there's no fighting about who's gonna lead."

I smiled. "True. So if you don't mind me asking…how'd you get this job workin' for the Gradskys?"

"Macon Gradsky contacted me. We've stayed in touch over the years." A funny look must've crossed my face because he clarified, "Macon isn't gay. He and I were competitors. We met for the first time at the National High School Rodeo finals. He was the All-Around champ for Colorado and I was All-Around champ for South Dakota." He flashed that megawatt grin. "I whupped his ass in tie-down ropin' and bulldoggin'. He beat me in saddle bronc ridin'. We both ended up attending University of Wyoming and were teammates on the college circuit. I went pro after I graduated and he went to law school."

"Sounds like you've known the Gradsky family for quite a while."

"Rodeo is a small world." He smiled sadly. "A small-minded world too."

"So was it your decision not to go on the podium and introduce yourself tonight? Or did your bosses ask you to hang back?"

"Fully my decision. The focus tonight needed to be on them, not on me." He blocked the path so I couldn't race away. "The Gradskys know you're gay?"

"Kind of a hard secret to keep with London as my sister-in-law." I said dryly. "But yeah, they know."

None of the yard lights were on around the buildings. Probably to keep guests from wandering. A tiny sliver of moon did little to slice through the darkness. I wondered if that darkness made it easier for Breck to take my hand.

My heart jumped into my throat. It'd been so long since I'd had that simple connection it felt foreign.

That's because it's not Mick's hand.

Breck's hand was bigger. Rougher. Stronger from years of handling coarse ropes. He locked his fingers more tightly to mine. Mick's hands had always been cold and clammy—and it bothered him enough that we rarely held hands. Even when we were home alone.

Why are you thinking about that? Every comparison you make will add to your uncertainty. If you can't follow through with simple handholding, let him know now.

Fuck that. I could do this. I *had* to do this.

And I'd take it far beyond handholding.

As soon as we cleared the corner of the next building, I dropped

Breck's hand and pushed him against the bricks. "Take off your hat."

He removed his hat with his left hand and let it fall to his side, holding it lightly against his thigh. Automatically his right hand came up and he ran his fingers through his dark hair, trying to get rid of the mark the hat band had left.

It shouldn't have been a sexy move, but with him, it was. Because I knew even when it was dark, Breck retained his pride that he wanted to look good for me.

"Aren't you ditching your hat too?" he asked in a raspy tone.

"Not yet. Keep your right hand by your side too."

"Fuck, Cres, I wanna touch you."

With me standing on the cement curb, we were eye to eye. Mouth to mouth. I flattened my palms beside his head and leaned in until we were groin to groin. "You'll get your chance, just not right now."

A soft grunt escaped him and gusted across my lips when I rocked my pelvis into his.

His cock was already hard.

So was mine.

I pressed my lips to his and held them there. Then I slowly started to move them. A little to the left. A little to the right, keeping up that easy glide until his lips were fuller. Softer. Wetter. I dipped my tongue in the seam, licking the inside edge of his upper lip and then his lower. Getting a taste of him.

Like smoke and whiskey. Not the minty taste I associated with Mick.

That's good. Keep going.

I convinced myself I was anticipating, not stalling. That I was treating this tease as a test to see if Breck could control his dominant nature and let me set the pace.

Are you sure it's not a test for you? To see if you freak out when you remember that the lips clinging to yours aren't Mick's?

Stop.

Breck deserved my full attention.

When I allowed our tongues to touch, he growled, "Fucking kiss me already."

That's all I needed. I dove into his mouth like I owned it.

Greed overwhelmed me.

Yes. *Yes.* This.

Fuck. I needed so much more of *this*.

My head spun as I went at that lush mouth from every angle. My hand cupped his jaw so I could open him up wider, get deeper. Our tongues stroked. Our lips pursed and pressed and glided and teased.

Harsh panting breaths echoed around us and mingled together. Soft groans. The click of teeth. The sounds of passion.

I could not get enough.

I'd missed this urgency. Craved it.

How had I survived without it? It hadn't ever been this way with Mick. Not even in the beginning.

It'd only ever been this way with Breck.

Seemed I'd forgotten that too.

I broke my mouth free, sliding across Breck's smoothly shaven skin to drag my teeth down his jaw, nipping at his chin and the tender flesh of his neck.

Breck let out a muttered, "Christ." Then he tilted his head to the side, giving me full access to his throat, and I nearly snarled with satisfaction. I'd never had his surrender.

Now I did.

Now I wanted it all.

And I'd take it all.

Pushing back on my heels, I reached for his belt buckle, my mouth continuing to maraud his neck and jaw as I unbuttoned and unzipped his jeans. Hooking my fingers inside the waistband beside his hipbones, I tugged his jeans and briefs down to the middle of his thighs.

He hissed in a sharp breath when I lowered to my knees.

I didn't tease. I brought the stiff length into my mouth in a single, greedy gulp.

Then I froze.

That's when the "this is wrong, this isn't Mick" voice became louder.

My thoughts warred with reality. The unfamiliar—yet it was familiar—taste on my tongue. The additional girth stretching my lips. The musky aroma filling my lungs that was all man…but wasn't my man.

My eyes watered.

Not because I wanted to cry.

I gagged.

Not because I didn't want to do this.

I fisted my hand around the base of his shaft and slid my mouth up, my lips catching on the rim of his cockhead. Then I twisted my hand up that meaty cock as I bobbed my head down, hollowing my cheeks with every suctioning pull.

A surprised, "Jesus," exploded above me, followed by a rush of ragged exhales.

Lean hips pumped away from the wall toward my mouth.

Then strong fingers curled around my throat, stopping all motion. His dick slipped free when those fingers latched onto my jaw and tilted my head back.

My gaze collided with Breck's as he squeezed his shaft in the middle, creating a makeshift cock ring. He continued to drag the wet head of his cock across my lips.

"If it hadn't been so long since I had my dick sucked I'd tell you to slow down. But when I'm this close I need to know if I'm coming in your mouth."

I nodded.

"Take your hat off, Cres," he murmured huskily. "Keep your eyes on mine."

A shiver worked through me as I set my Stetson on the ground.

Just like that, he'd taken charge.

Just like that, I'd let him.

For now.

Breck tenderly ran his fingers across my scalp before grabbing a fistful of my hair and directing my head to where he wanted it. His eyes glittered with lust as he began to fuck my mouth, each measured stroke faster and faster until that moment when he shoved in so deep my teeth dug into the root of his cock.

Breck groaned and his dick jerked on my tongue.

Thick bursts of come coated the back of my throat. He didn't have to tell me to suck hard and swallow; I knew exactly what he needed.

That's what I needed too. The heady rush of power. The give and take of control. Of surrender. The suspense of whose will to be on top would win out.

He released my hair and pulled out of my mouth, slumping back against the bricks, eyes squeezed shut, his chest heaving.

In the distance I heard music. In my peripheral vision I saw headlights sweep across the tall grass bordering the fence. Whoops and hollers drifted from someplace.

Resting on my knees in the dark, with my painfully hard dick pressing against the button-fly of my 501s, my jaw sore, I felt entirely disconnected. An overwhelming urge to escape had me blindly reaching for my hat and pushing to my feet.

"Don't run off," Breck said gruffly, when I took a step back off the curb. "I ain't close to done with you tonight." He situated his hat on his head and righted his clothing, never taking his eyes off mine. Then he reached for me. "The tour can wait."

"Okay."

"I can't." Breck loomed over me. "Christ, I want you." He shoved his left hand in the front of my jeans and latched onto me by my belt, his knuckles brushing my erection as he held me in place. He angled his head above mine without banging our hats together—a trick I'd never managed when I locked lips with another cowboy. This kiss was all sweet seduction and gratitude.

My free hand landed on his chest. I was bowled over by his tenderness—something I never expected from a guy who considered fucking an endurance sport.

He murmured, "Come to my place. Even for just a couple of hours."

I slowly licked his lower lip. "If that's what you want."

"Oh, I want all right."

His wicked grin sent my pulse tripping.

We walked hand in hand up the road and cut through the last open area before the tree line. The path grew steeper. By the time we crested the hill, we were both breathing hard again.

That's when I noticed we were in a campground, complete with electrical hookups for each unit space and a private picnic shelter.

"What's this place?" I asked.

"Campground for staff."

"You live in a camper?"

"Yep. The one on the end is mine." Breck stopped in front of a motor home too damn fancy to be called a camper. I'd seen rock star tour buses on TV that were trailer trash compared to this.

"You win the lottery?" Or maybe he'd won a lawsuit. Since he indicated he was buddies with Macon Gradsky, it was a possibility they'd sued the magazine for damages and gone after the CRA for discrimination. From listening to London talk about her brother, Macon was one sue-happy motherfucker.

"This isn't mine from lottery winnings—either from the state or a lawsuit lottery. When I decided to wander, I needed someplace to call home. I bought this with the money I had left." He opened the door and a motorized step popped out. "Go on in."

The inside was ten times more impressive than the outside. I sort of stood there with my mouth hanging open.

A *whoosh* sounded after I watched Breck poke a button that shut the door. The blinds were already down, obstructing the view out the windows. But no one could see in either.

Breck stalked me. "Tell me what you want, Cres."

I stood my ground, even when my heart jackhammered and the first flutters of panic made breathing difficult. Then we were chest to chest, groin to groin. "What are my options?"

He removed my hat and set it on the table next to his. "You want seduction? Rolling around on my bed naked for an hour of foreplay before I fuck you?" He brushed his lips across the top of my ear. "Or should we skip that and I suck you off before I bend you over my table and fuck you?"

"Maybe I want option C. You already got yours; I take mine by bending you over the arm of the couch."

"You are more assertive than you used to be," he murmured in my ear. "I like that. It's hot as hell. Means you're gonna make me work for it. I love a challenge, so let's see where this goes."

I didn't argue as Breck propelled me backward, his mouth plastered to mine, his hands on me everywhere. Making me hard. Making me dizzy.

We stopped when the backs of my knees connected with a solid surface. He broke the kiss and placed his hand on my chest, pushing me until my ass hit the mattress.

"You look good on my bed, Cres."

When Breck leaned over, I grabbed ahold of his shirt and pulled him on top of me. Yeah, he was a big guy, but I wasn't exactly a 98-pound weakling.

Still, the move surprised him.

It really surprised him when I rolled him beneath me and nestled my ass against his groin. Keeping my gaze on his, I said, "Still wanna see the aggressive side of me?"

"Fuck, yeah."

I rocked against the thick length of his erection pressing between my butt cheeks.

Breck groaned and reached for my hips. "Shift back. I wanna feel your cock rubbing on mine."

I laughed softly. "Topping me from below ain't happening."

A devilish gleam entered his eyes. "I already got off once. I just wanted to even things up, but whatever. You're on top."

"Damn straight. Now unbutton your shirt," I said, still grinding against him.

His hands went to his throat and he undid the first button. "You did have a thing for my chest."

"Let's see if I still do. Hurry up."

Once he'd reached the last button above the waist of his jeans, I lifted up so he could untuck his shirt. Then he spread the two sides open, gifting me an unobstructed view of his upper body.

My dick went harder yet and a growl of approval rumbled out.

A thick mat of dark hair furred his chest. He'd lost some of the bulk, but his pectorals were still beautifully defined, as were his abs. The flat brown nipples—almost invisible unless he was aroused—poked up, as if begging for my mouth.

"Jesus, Cres. Stop licking your lips like that. You're gonna make me shoot my load in my damn jeans."

I pressed my thumbs on his nipples, spreading my fingers outward, digging the tips into his sides between his armpits and his ribcage. As I angled forward I had to shift down his lower body so we were nose to nose. "Touch me."

Breck clamped his big mitts onto my butt. He squeezed the flesh and pressed down, adding more pressure to our cocks grinding together. A confident grin tipped up his lips before he fused them to mine. His voracity pulsed through our bodies like a sonic wave each time he sucked on my tongue. My mouth throbbed when he slowed the kiss and tasted the underside of my top and bottom lips with lazy sweeps of his tongue.

That's when the tingling started at the base of my spine.

Too soon. I wasn't ready for this to end. It felt like we'd just started.

"Cres." Breck nudged my chin up and nipped my jawline with firm-lipped bites. "Undo our jeans. Rub your cock against mine. Skin on skin."

I wanted the heat and hardness. The urgency. The musky scent of spunk and sweat.

He knew I was about to give in and he did the one thing that'd guarantee it. He whispered, "Please."

I pushed myself up and scooted back so my knees bracketed the outside of his thighs.

Breck rose up to rest on his elbows, so he could watch me unbuckle and unzip him. His chest was damp, billowing in and out as he rolled his pelvis so I could tug his jeans and briefs down to his shins. My knuckles smacked into the top of his boot shaft, startling me. We'd been so crazed for each other we hadn't taken off our boots.

Time to rectify that.

I hopped off the bed.

His right eyebrow winged up. "Goin' someplace?"

I grabbed the heel of his right boot and lifted, yanking it off his foot. Repeated it on the left side.

Grinning, I pantsed him.

Then I undid my belt and unzipped before I crawled back between his legs.

His smile faded. "Why am I mostly naked and you're not?"

I flattened my palms by his head, keeping my body in a pushup position over his as I brushed my lips over the divot in his chin. "I want you feelin' the friction from the denim scraping the inside of your thighs as I'm grinding on you." My lips traveled up to his ear. "I want you to hear the buckle on my belt clanking as I'm moving above you." I sank my teeth into his earlobe and he arched up. "I want you to remember this. I don't want to be another anonymous quickie fuck, Breck."

Where the hell had that come from? I sounded possessive and commanding. As if I expected this to be more than a one-time blowjob and rub off.

"You never were that, Cres, even when that's all you were supposed to be." Breck jerked my jeans and boxer briefs down to the middle of my thighs. He followed the crease of my ass up, ending at my lower back.

When he reached between us and his knuckles grazed my balls, I started like a frightened rabbit. It'd been a lifetime since any hand beside my own had touched my cock.

He stroked me and stared into my face, his fierce eyes issuing a challenge. "You sure you don't wanna straddle my face so I can suck you off?"

"Still topping from below." I lowered my pelvis, forcing him to let go of my dick. I hissed in a breath when our cocks touched and adjusted my hips so the rim of his cockhead caught on mine with every upstroke.

"Oh, fuck. That's…" He groaned as I rubbed my rigid shaft over the sweet spot below the head of his cock.

"Still want me to stop and fuck your mouth?" I whispered against his temple.

"No. Goddamn you're good at this. Don't ever fucking stop." His fingers dug into my ass and he tilted his head to conquer my mouth in a sizzling kiss.

That dizzying sense of urgency assailed me and I began to move with more enthusiasm than finesse.

Wet mouths, hot, hard, damp bodies in motion. The heated scent of his skin, the addicting taste of his mouth proved to be too much and I teetered on the edge.

He pumped his hips, his body shaking beneath mine. "I need it faster."

"Do it."

Clamping his big fist around both of our dicks, he jerked us off. "Fuck. Yes."

I started to come, his name on my lips as I shot my load in hot bursts of ass clenching pleasure.

His sexy grunts of satisfaction followed.

After my cock quit twitching and the buzzing in my head faded, I collapsed on top of him. Burying my face in the crook of his neck, my lips searching for the spot on his throat where his pulse always jumped wildly.

But it wasn't there, next to his voice box.

I murmured, "That was a nice change of pace."

The body below mine shook with humor. "Nice? That was fucking spectacular."

I froze.

Not Mick's voice—he never swore.

I inhaled.

Not Mick's scent—he always wore cologne.

And because I was either losing my mind or a fucking masochist, when I licked the skin beneath my lips, it wasn't the clean taste of Mick's sweat. This was earthier. More...primal.

I scrambled upright so fast my cock jerked free from the hand surrounding it with enough force my balls stung from the sharp pain.

Then I was staring into slumberous blue eyes, not brown.

The smile on the full red lips was decidedly cocky, not sweet.

Holy fuck.

Since Breck wore that sated look...maybe he hadn't heard me saying another man's name when I spurted all over his hand.

Shame burned through me.

I was off the bed and fastening my jeans and belt before Breck knew anything was wrong.

So very wrong.

"Cres? What's goin' on?"

"I can't do this. I'm sorry. I've gotta go."

"What? Jesus. Just wait a damn minute."

But I didn't.

I ran out like a fucking coward.

Chapter Four

Breck

The next morning I went looking for Sutton Grant.

Most of the staff had stayed over after the party last night. And I knew from Berlin's complaints that London wasn't an early riser so chances were good they were still around.

The tricky part would be asking Sutton what was wrong with his brother without rousing his suspicions. I wasn't sure Cres would appreciate being linked to me given the fact he'd run out on me.

Chapped my ass every time I thought about it.

The construction workers had already disassembled the biggest tent and were packing up chairs. I cut across the road to the cafeteria.

Sure enough, Sutton held court by the buffet.

I sauntered over to the industrial coffee urn and filled a cup.

The guys wrapped up their conversation as soon as I approached them. The paranoia still lingered that people were talking about me when a discussion abruptly ended if I was within earshot.

"Morning," I said to Sutton.

"Hey, Breck." He pointed with his chin to my cup of coffee. "Fair warning that London made the coffee. It's got a serious kick."

I looked around for her. "Where is your better half?"

"Helping Grandma Berlin fill my truck with more shit for Brennen. I swear we could open a damn toy store with all the stuff both sets of his grandparents buy him."

"You're not really complaining, buddy."

Sutton smiled. "Only when I have to haul it and set it up. But the look on my boy's face is worth it." He paused. "What's goin' on with you?"

"Just wandering around. It appears the open house was a success."

"Thank God it's over. Now I'll get my wife back. She's been stayin' here three nights a week getting ready for it."

"Shame she's not teachin'." I hid my smirk behind my cup.

"Bite your damn tongue," he shot back. "The woman's temperament is better suited to workin' with horses than people."

"Looked like London was tearin' it up last night."

"Cres's fault. He started her on the tequila."

There was the angle I needed. "So Cres didn't stick around last night?"

"He drove Wyn's truck home since he had to feed cattle this morning. Why?"

"He forgot to give me his number last night after"—*he came all over my hand and took off like his ass was on fire*—"we spent time talkin' and stuff. Wondered if you'd give it to me."

Sutton's eyes narrowed. "I saw you two *talkin'*."

"You say that like we were doin' something besides talkin'," I said evenly.

"Were you? You both disappeared for a while."

"Not exactly what I asked. Not any of your business either."

"Along those same lines, if he'd wanted you to have his number, he would've given it to you, doncha think?" Sutton retorted.

That was a little hard to do when he had my cock in his mouth. "Look. If you don't want to give it to me, that's cool." *I'll just get it from someone else* went unsaid.

Sutton studied me before he sighed. "I'm protective of him."

"Why? I get that he's your younger brother, but he is an adult."

"Cres has had a rough go of it and I don't want you takin' advantage of him." Sutton's gaze hardened. "Like you did a few years ago when I sent him to you to deal with my horse."

"Cres was an adult then too. He made his own choices. And fuck you if you think his bein' with me back then somehow turned him gay."

"Whoa. I never said that and I sure as hell didn't mean to imply it." He paused. "Let's start over. This isn't meant to be accusatory. But when you were talkin' with Cres last night, did you tell him about bein' outed and all the crap that happened afterward?"

"Yeah. I always thought you were bein' humble when you said not everyone in your family rabidly followed rodeo." I sipped my coffee. "He didn't know anything about it."

"Not surprised. People outside the world of rodeo would likely shrug and wonder why it'd been such a big deal." He folded his arms on his chest. "So part of me wonders why you'd willingly put yourself back into this world, Breck."

My cheeks heated. "It's not like I have another skill set. And besides, don't think I don't know that *you're* the one who suggested me as a possible instructor for the Gradskys' rodeo school. Macon made the call, but that happened at your urging, Sutton."

He grinned. "I figured if they couldn't have me, they'd want the second best champion bulldogger…which is you."

"You're hilarious. And if I haven't said it, I appreciate your faith in me." Before things got sappy or awkward, I added, "So why didn't you take the job? Since your wife is here all the time anyway?"

"After I survived that last run, during my stint in the hospital I swore that I was done throwing myself off the back of a galloping horse onto a steer. It's a promise I've kept."

"Bein' a teacher doesn't mean you have to actually demonstrate," I pointed out.

"Maybe not for you and the way you teach, but it does for me. I've told my in-laws I'll fill in if the need arises." Sutton gave me another shit-eating grin. "So if you want a *four*-time world champion bulldogger as a guest lecturer, I'd be happy to swing by your classroom."

"Don't be surprised if it ends up bein' permanent for you. The students—or their parents—might run me out on a rail anyway."

Sutton shook his head. "Ain't gonna happen. Chuck and Berlin will stand behind you, Breck. Whether you have a chick or a dude in your bed at the end of the night has no bearing on your past credentials and shouldn't be allowed to diminish your expertise."

"Thanks."

"No problem. And I'll go you one better than giving you Cres's phone number. I'll give you his address so you can drop off the pneumatic drill I borrowed from him. I've got too much baby junk in my truck."

I'd take any excuse to talk to Cres and find out what had happened last night.

"I'll drive over to your campsite and drop it off. Say…fifteen minutes?"

"Sounds good."

I was leaning against my Jeep when Sutton pulled up. The pneumatic drill wasn't big, so I recognized his excuse of not having enough room in his 350 diesel truck was total horseshit. I tried not to dissect why Sutton had changed his mind about me corrupting his younger brother.

He handed me a scrap of paper. "Here's Cres's address for you to punch into the GPS." He slammed the hatchback door on the Jeep. "Like I said before, Cres had a rough go the last two years so I'm glad to see him…" He sighed. "Sounds clichéd to say livin' again, but it's true."

"What's been goin' on with him?"

Sutton's head snapped up so fast his hat nearly tumbled off his head. "He didn't tell you about Mick?"

A bad feeling rolled over me. "Not a word."

"You really didn't do a lot of talkin', did you?" He held up his hand. "Sorry. None of my business."

"We talked a lot, Sutton. Just not about Mick." I'd asked Cres what he'd been up to and he'd hedged. Even when I'd called him on it, he'd managed to sidestep any conversation about his life. And I'd let him.

"That little shit. I'm gonna wring his damn neck."

"Who's Mick? An ex or something?"

"Mick was his boyfriend. They met at our wedding and moved in together. Two years ago Mick was killed in a freak accident. Cres shut down after that. And I hate to admit this, but Wyn and Mel had a baby a few months before Mick died, and then me and London had Brennen. We were busy with our lives and didn't butt into his. Last night was the first time we forced him into a social situation that wasn't only our immediate family. And he wouldn't have come if we'd given him any advance notice or if Wyn hadn't driven him."

Now Cres running out on me made sense. It also gave me an odd feeling of loss—like I'd already lost Cres because he belonged to someone else. "I'm glad you forced his appearance."

"And now I'm forcing yours." He glanced over his shoulder. "Good thing Wyn didn't notice you and Cres talkin'."

"Why?"

"Wyn ain't your biggest fan. He'd discourage…hell he'd probably campaign to keep Cres from spending time with you."

I frowned. "I'm confused. I don't know Wyn. I've met him like once."

"But he thinks he knows you. Do you even remember bein' a total prick to Mel at our wedding?"

I shook my head. "I barely remember bein' at your wedding. My date drove; I drank and ended up passing out in the motel room. I woke up to discover she'd snuck out at some point during the night with all of my cash." I felt the heat of shame spread across my face and neck. "I understand why Wyn would have a problem with me if I acted like a drunken fucktard."

"Pretty much," he said with far too much glee.

"Does Mel feel the same way about me?"

"I don't know. You always were a cocky, manipulative, condescending asshat. I know you've changed. London and her family have embraced the changes you've made. They've accepted the man you are now. As far as anyone else…including my brother? You'd better brush up on the charm that used to come so naturally."

"Awesome."

He clapped me on the shoulder. "Good luck."

* * * *

I pulled up to Cres's place around lunchtime. He lived in a log house— not the norm in Eastern Colorado. Off to the left side by the garage stood a row of evergreens. On the right side was a corral and a metal barn. I gave the rest of the area a passing look after Cres ambled out of the house and paused at the top of the steps on the front porch.

Immediately after I climbed out of my rig, a dog tore out of the barn, snapping and snarling as it barreled toward me.

Cres bounded down the steps, yelling, "Banjo, knock it off."

By the time the Australian shepherd skidded to a stop by head-butting my knees, he'd lowered his hackles and was wagging his tail. I crouched down to pet him. "Banjo, huh? Bud, I'm afraid your bark is worse than your bite."

Banjo yipped and tried to lick my face.

I grinned and let him. I missed having a dog.

"Banjo, go lay down," Cres commanded.

The dog circled me one more time before he trotted up the porch steps and out of sight.

I stood and propped my hands on my hips. Let him take the first stab at conversation.

He said, "Let me guess. You were just in the neighborhood."

"It's a hard place to find without GPS."

"It's an even harder place to find when my name, address, and phone number are unlisted."

"Sutton asked me to return your pneumatic drill. Blame him for breaching your privacy. But he refused to give me your cell phone number, so it's kind of a wash." I paused. "Then again, he did tell me about Mick. So you might want to chew his ass about that."

His posture stiffened. "What'd he say about him?"

"More than you did, that's for damn sure. So I'm here because I wanna hear it from you, Cres. I'll even tell you where I want you to start. Back to our conversation last night when I asked what you'd been up to and all you said was ranching with Wyn."

Cres turned and focused on a spot beyond the horizon, giving me his profile. The muscle in his jaw bunched and I could almost hear him grinding his teeth together.

Seemed like an hour passed, but when I glanced at my watch, it'd only been five minutes. Still, that was a long time to exist in silence.

You don't need this. Sure, you like Cres. Maybe you've always liked him a little too much. But right now, he's a former hookup. That's all he sees you as. Take the hint and move on.

Cres remained in the "stare at nothing" state when I took the drill out of the back of my truck and carried it to the porch.

I paused behind him and said, "Take care." I'd almost made it to the sanctity of my truck when Cres spoke.

"I loved Mick. We were inseparable almost from the moment we met. He died just over two years ago when a car slipped off its jack and crushed him."

An ugly death. Accidents left survivors with too many "what if" scenarios and guilt the accident could've been prevented. I ached for him.

"When you told me that you lost everything after you were outed on the circuit, my first thought was…you don't really know what it's like to lose everything."

The anger in his tone? Not a surprise. The derision? Unnecessary and unfair. I faced him. "Death trumps everything. Got it. Sorry that I burdened you with my insignificant life problems. Don't worry. You're still the champ in the 'shittiest life event' contest that I didn't realize we were playing." I stepped closer to the driver's side door. "Sorry for your loss, Cres."

"Don't go."

I paused with my boot on the running board.

"I know I sound like a dick. But I didn't get to finish that train of thought before you jumped in," Cres said testily.

"I'm listening."

"For a year and a half, I believed I'd lost everything when Mick died. It's just been in the past few months that I could face the truth. *I* gave up everything as a result of Mick's death. He's the only thing I lost. But I can't go back and I've been fucking petrified to try to go forward. I haven't talked to anyone about it."

That admission smoothed the rough edges of my anger.

"Seein' you last night…was the first time I felt like movin' on." Cres jammed his hand through his hair. "Trauma, grief, whatever is not a competition. I'm sorry if it sounded like I one-upped you."

"Why didn't you tell me about Mick last night?"

His head snapped up. "Because I wanted to see if I could be a normal single guy again. Acting on an attraction to a hot guy who knew nothin' about what I'd been through."

"And?"

"And you were there. I fucking ran out on you when it got to be too much."

"You also gave me one helluva blowjob. You almost had me coming in my jeans before you stripped them off and made me come again." I locked my gaze to his. "From where I'm standing, you had no problem acting on your attraction to me."

Cres broke eye contact. "I said his name."

"What?"

"When I started to come, I said Mick." His gaze returned to my face. "That's why I ran out."

"And you thought I'd what? Knock you on your ass if you told me that?"

He erased the distance between us and got right in my face. "Why the hell are you bein' so reasonable about this, Breck?"

I have no fucking idea.

I fisted my hand in his shirt and hauled him closer. "Because I want more of you, dumbass. A whole lot more." My mouth crashed down on his and I kissed the shit out of him. He had an aggressive streak, but it was nothing compared to mine. Nothing.

He wasn't the only one who'd had a recent revelation. I'd stared at the damn ceiling for three fucking hours after he'd left last night. Not only wondering what had happened to make him run, but wondering when I'd lost my goddamned balls and hadn't chased after him. When had I turned into the mild-mannered gentleman cowboy who hid in his motor home? I'd always been the guy who went after what he wanted— men, women, championships, sponsorships. I'd let the system, a goddamned system that failed me, dictate the kind of man I became after I'd risen from the ashes of my spectacular crash and burn.

No. More.

Cres eased up on the kiss. He kept one hand twined in my hair and the other hand flattened on my chest. "Sorry I fucked up and didn't tell you about Mick."

"I'm not the same asshole guy I used to be."

"You never were an asshole to me, Breck."

There was that sweetness again.

Cres confessed, "I'm still a little screwed up."

"Aren't we all screwed up about something?"

"I guess." He sighed. "I gotta admit, this isn't goin' like I envisioned when I saw your Jeep pull up. But I am really glad you chased me down."

"I should've done it last night. But bein's I was buck-ass nekkid and you weren't, you had a head start." I slid my hand beneath his jawbone and feathered my thumb across his bottom lip. "It turns me the fuck on when your lips get like this, full and red and shiny. I could get used to seein' them like that all the time."

Cres's body went taut.

Even when I had good intentions, I somehow messed up by saying or doing the wrong thing. "What's wrong?"

"Just because I said I was testing the waters to see if I'm ready to move on, I'm not lookin' for a relationship ever again."

"Never?"

"Love ain't worth the trouble of the heartache you get when you lose it."

I should've run then. Instead, I shrugged as if my heart wasn't hurting for him. And hurting for myself since I'd never been lucky enough to have that kind of love. "I'm not here for the long haul anyway."

His gaze turned shrewd. "How long are you here?"

"For the first session, which is nine weeks. Then I'll decide if I'm cut out for teachin'. But I'll warn ya, I've still got itchy feet even after spending twenty years livin' on the road. I like it. It's part of who I am so I don't see that changing any time soon."

"What are you saying?" he asked.

"We'll be in the same area for nine weeks. We could have a lot of fun together exploring this. If it gets boring, we'll end it, no harm, no foul." That wasn't entirely true. I'd pull out all the stops to ensure we'd spend every free moment of those nine weeks together.

"Just fucking? No relationship?"

I continued to stroke his lip as my gaze wandered over his face. "Even if we're just fucking, Cres, we *are* in a relationship. That can be whatever we want it to outside of the hot sex. My days of sharing are over." I figured it'd be hard enough sharing him with the ghost of Mick.

He tried to drop his chin to hide his eyes, but that was bullshit.

I forced him to meet my gaze. "No more half-truths or secrets. Talk to me. Even if you think it'll piss me off."

"I haven't been with anyone since Mick," he blurted out. "That's the other reason I ran out. I wasn't sure how far I could go."

"Guess we'll see if I can convince you to go all the way with me." I grinned. "It wasn't too difficult that week you came to Denver...I had your cock in my mouth within two hours of us meeting. I had you bent over with my cock in your ass that same night."

He groaned. "Smartass. Be serious. This could be a problem."

"If we get to a point that you're freakin' out, tell me. I ain't gonna get mad or jealous about Mick. I don't have a right to it. But I ain't gonna lie. I want the rights to this." I reached down and palmed his hard-on, letting my fingers slide back and rub his balls. "If I had my way? I'd blow you right here against the side of my Jeep to remind you how good it is between us."

His cock jumped beneath my palm and his eyes burned hot. Interesting.

"What ranch chores you doin' this afternoon?"

"Nothin' pressing this week. Why?"

"I thought I'd give you the tour of Grade A Rodeo Academy if you weren't busy later. Then I could fix us supper and we could hang out for a while tonight."

Cres's eyes narrowed. "You cook?"

"I'm a thirty-eight-year-old bachelor. Of course I cook." I leaned in and dragged my lips across his ever so slightly. "We did more than fuck and suck that week in Denver."

"Then why did you bail on me? I showed up that last morning and you'd already gone."

It'd sound like I was pandering if I told him our connection had spooked me because it'd happened so fast. Cres deserved more than the man I'd been at that time of my life—secretive and on a path of self-destruction. Being my usual dickish self, I'd left him first before he could leave me. "I'm not tryin' to charm my way into your jeans when I say I thought about you a lot over that next year."

"Same here. I intended to talk to you at Sutton and London's wedding. I'd heard you were on a destructive path and when I saw firsthand how bitter and angry you'd gotten, I thought maybe I could get through to you. But then..."

"Then you met Mick."

"Yeah."

"Was it lust at first sight?"

"He was buff as fuck, so that part of the attraction was a no-brainer. But he worked with Sutton and I hadn't been out long enough to know if it was..." He scratched his chin. "Acceptable, I guess...to go after a guy if I wasn't sure that he preferred sucking a prick to eating a pussy."

I laughed. "Crude. So how'd you figure out he was a dick-smoker?"

Cres held his fist up for a bump. "Equally crude. And if I would've said that to Mick? He would've blushed and stammered. For bein' former military, he had few vices."

"Besides lovin' the D," I said slyly.

"Yeah. Anyway I think we were at a community barbecue and we got to talkin'. He asked me out for coffee. We had a few dates. I hadn't been too sure about him in the beginning since he didn't have much experience. But he was eager. And the more I got to know him, the more I realized Mick was just one of those genuinely good guys. Honest, brave, and true. Helpful, loyal, obedient."

I didn't point out it sounded like he was describing a dog.

"He stuck around after my dad had his heart attack. He helped Mel when she had issues with her diabetes. His sweet nature appealed to me, you know? Then after the first time we fucked, he moved in." Cres blinked. "Shit. Sorry. Didn't mean to go off on a mangent."

"Mangent?"

"When you don't shut up about the guy in your life."

I chuckled. "Never heard that one before."

He smirked. "Because you're old."

"Hilarious. Guess I'll toddle off to the old folk's home, sonny boy, and drink my Metamucil before *Wheel of Fortune* comes on."

Cres laughed. I liked to hear it because I suspected there hadn't been much humor in his life in recent years.

I fished my phone out of my back pocket. "Hit me with your number." As soon as I had the info saved, I sent him a text. "Now you have mine."

"Good. I'll be there about three."

"That'll work. Text me if anything changes."

Chapter Five

Breck

Patience—a trait I'd never had much use for.

Practicing restraint? Not a natural reaction for me either.

But I had no choice but to implement both from the moment Cres had shown up for his personal tour of Grade A Rodeo Academy.

When I'd shown him the empty classrooms I'd exercised restraint, even when my brain kept replaying the image of me on my knees between Cres's legs, my head bobbing as I noisily sucked him off as he braced himself against my desk.

I filed that away as a future possibility. That counted as patience, right?

Hour two into the tour, after I'd introduced him to the other instructors as Sutton's brother and we'd chatted with Berlin and Chuck Gradsky, I decided I deserved a fucking medal for patience, restraint, and circumspection for not dragging his sexy ass into the boiler room and fingering his prostate until he jizzed all over my chest.

Yeah, that scenario would shock the stuffing out of Bill, the groundskeeper. But I'd put a note in the suggestion box that maybe the boiler room door needed a proper lock.

I was getting the hang of this "being a team player" shit.

By hour three—Cres's patience had worn thin.

And that tested the fuck out of my restraint because we were near the end of the tour.

In the first arena, he'd grabbed me by the shirt and kissed the sense out of me.

I'd kissed him back because I sure as hell wasn't shooting for sainthood.

In the second arena, he'd stood behind me and started rubbing his groin into my ass, suggesting a hand job to relax me.

My cock had pouted when I resisted the temptation.

In the third arena, Cres warned me if I didn't end the tour in the next seconds he was going home.

It might've been the only time in my life I gave in to an ultimatum with zero resentment.

He asked, "How far is the campground from here?"

"A ten-minute walk." Or a four-minute run.

Then again, running with a hard-on sucked.

When my motor home came into view, I clicked the key fob that unlocked and opened the door.

My eyes were on his butt as he jogged up the steps.

As soon as my boot hit the top step, Cres was on me, his mouth ravenous, his fingers at the hollow of my throat as he undid all of the pearl-snap buttons on my shirt with one vicious tug.

I circled my hand beneath his jaw, breaking free from that tempting mouth so I could think. "Hey, horny toad, how about you let me close the door before you tear off my clothes?"

"Then hurry the fuck up. You've been shaking that tight cowboy ass at me the last three hours and I want it now."

I shut and locked the door and darkened the blinds, while Cres attacked my neck.

He peeled my shirt down my arms, carelessly tossing it to the floor. He groaned with frustration. "Why are you wearin' another shirt?"

"I always wear an undershirt."

"Next time don't. I hate havin' to strip another layer off you to get to the good stuff."

In the back of my mind I wished I could take the time to bask in Cres's lust for me. I couldn't remember the last time I'd been wanted with such near desperation.

Then he hooked his fingers in my belt loops and towed me down the hallway to my bedroom so fast we nearly tripped.

He laughed. "Keep up."

Normally I'd be the one urging us to get naked as I assumed the dominant role.

So it was a fucking rush to let go and follow Cres's lead.

Once we cleared the doorway to my bedroom, Cres shoved me against the wall and held my arms by my sides, plastering his body to mine. His lips grazed my ear. "Fast and dirty, Breck. That's how I'm gonna fuck you."

"Whatever you want."

He pushed back and dropped his ass to the mattress, keeping his molten gaze on mine as he grabbed the heel of his right cowboy book and yanked it off. A smirk curled his lips when he tipped the boot upside down and two strips of condoms fell on the bed.

I laughed. "Interesting place to keep them."

"Too many to keep in my wallet. Didn't want to run out." He lifted his left foot.

"Got lube in that one?"

Cres tugged his boot off and tipped it on the bed. Individual packets of lube landed on top of the condoms.

I laughed again.

Then Cres was back on his feet. The hunger in his touch, in his eyes, undeniable.

He rid me of the pesky T-shirt. He braced one hand beside my head. "Take off your boots."

Damn difficult to do with his lips leaving wet trails across my collarbones, but I persevered.

He went into full-on attack mode after the first touch of his tongue to my nipple.

My head *thunked* against the wall. The hours working out were worth it to get this reaction out of him. He kept at it, rubbing his face in my chest hair, licking and sucking my nipples, biting them, turning me inside out.

He dropped to his knees and had my jeans around my ankles and my cock in his mouth while I still reeled from his expert nipple play.

I glanced down and cupped his gorgeous face in my palms. "You look really fuckin' hot with my cock in your throat. But I don't wanna come in your mouth, Cres. I wanna come with your cock in my ass." There was power in admitting that I wanted to let go of the fierce control I maintained in every aspect of my life—especially sex—and I trusted him to give me what I needed. Keeping a tight grip on his head, I pushed him back, letting my dick slip out so just the tip rested on his lower lip. Then I thrust in deep, fucking his mouth with fast, confident strokes so he understood that while I had no issue with him fucking me, I'd *never* be a fucking bottom.

When I released him, he said, "Get on the bed. Hands and knees."

I brushed the condoms aside and looked over my shoulder to see him striding forward, buck-ass nekkid.

Whoa. Fifteen seconds ago he'd been fully dressed.

And I saw no sign of the playful man who'd dragged me into my own bedroom. I saw a primal male, oozing raw sexuality and pulsing with conquering greed.

Holy hell. I nearly nutted right then.

Cres rolled the condom on and stroked himself. "Face forward and move your knees closer together."

The bed jiggled as he climbed on.

Immediately he caged me beneath his body—something I wouldn't have believed possible since I had more height and breadth. He nested his cock into the crack of my ass and peppered hot kisses from my left shoulder to my right. Then his lips found my ear and he taunted, "Fast and dirty."

Christ. I was already dangling on the edge and he'd barely touched me.

His tongue followed the line of my spine down.

And down.

And down.

And surely he wasn't going there.

Please, please be going there.

Then his hands were spreading my ass cheeks and his tongue lapped at my hole.

Oh fuck oh fuck oh fuck.

Don't come yet, don't come yet, or he'll stop.

I could hold off if he didn't…and then he did.

Cres gently sucked on the ring of muscles and alternated between soft kisses and tender licks on the clenching pucker. His grunting growls of pleasure vibrated across my skin, sending tingles straight up my spine and down to my balls. His fingertips dug into the globes of my ass with enough pressure to leave bruises.

I'd never wanted the marks of a man's possession as much as I needed his.

Then he plunged his tongue into my ass.

The edges of my consciousness went a little hazy.

Cres must've sensed I couldn't take much more before I'd blow, so he backed off.

I felt a cool smear of lube and the slow press of one finger inside me. I groaned and pushed back, signaling I was ready for more.

He added more lube and another finger, his breath hot in my ear as he prepared me with the patience and suretly that kicked my anticipation even higher.

Then the head of his cock rested against my hole.

He didn't ask if I was ready. One hard snap of his hips and his cock was fully embedded in my ass.

My dick slapped against my belly from the driving force when he started to fuck me.

It'd been a dry spell the last year and I should've been wincing in pain. But he'd prepared me well enough that all I felt was the sweet ache of pleasure.

"Gonna have to jack yourself this go," he panted. "Because fuck...I'm almost done in."

I had a moment to bask in the sense of satisfaction that he already teetered on the brink of unraveling—that he'd needed this as much, or maybe more than I did. Balancing on my forearm, I fisted my cock, too far gone to do anything but watch my hand between my legs as I beat off.

I had a zip of warning before my balls tightened and I was spurting into my fist.

Cres grunted and stopped moving completely. The rhythmic squeezing of my anal passage was intense enough to pull his orgasm from him, and he shuddered above me.

Fuck, yeah. That's what I needed.

As I attempted to level my breathing, I snagged the undershirt I'd left on the bed and wiped my sticky hand.

That's when I heard it. An odd-sounding, wounded noise.

A panicked noise.

No fucking way. He wasn't running out on me again. We'd deal with his guilt or sadness or whatever together.

When he started to pull out, to pull back, to pull away, I reached around and clamped my hand behind his quivering thigh. "Don't," I said gruffly. "I need a sec."

That brought him out of it. "Sure. Sorry."

I slowly pushed up onto my knees, keeping his cock—which hadn't seemed to have softened at all—lodged in my ass.

Immediately Cres slid his hands up the front of my body, over my abs, ribs, and chest. He curled his fingers over my shoulders, flattening his palms to my collarbones. He pressed his lips to the nape of my neck and squeezed me tight.

A funny tickle started in my chest and I closed my eyes. Although he had the dominant position, I knew I was holding him up.

Neither of us spoke. Cres clung to me and I continued to hold onto his thigh, letting my thumb sweep across the curve of his ass.

Finally he heaved a huge sigh. "Thanks, man."

"You okay?"

Another sigh. "I am now. It's just…different." His lips whispered across my skin. "That was fuckin' awesome."

I grinned and turned my head to kiss his knuckles. "For me too, buddy."

"I didn't think of him," he confessed. "I was one hundred percent in the moment with you, Breck. I want to make sure you know that."

"You feel guilty about that, Cres?"

"No. And then I felt guilty for not feelin' guilty." He paused. "That's kinda fucked up, isn't it."

I didn't answer because he just needed to say what he was thinking out loud. What a huge feeling of relief that he trusted that I could handle his honesty.

"Thanks for stayin' with me during my little freak-out," he murmured against the slope of my shoulder.

"Well, to be honest, it was a selfish reaction. Because I don't think my ego could've handed it if you would've run out on me twice after we fucked around."

Cres chuckled.

"You wanna get your cock outta my ass now?"

"Not really." He sank his teeth into the spot on the back of my neck that made me goddamned weak in the knees.

Another chuckle vibrated across my back when I swayed against him.

I slapped his ass cheek.

"Okay. I'm goin'. But don't go anywhere."

I turned my head to look him in the eyes. "There's nowhere I'd rather be."

He kissed me with sweetness and surety and passion.

That's when I knew I was already in over my head with this man.

* * * *

Cres insisted we climb under the covers after he dealt with the condom.

My body temp ran hot, so I welcomed the coolness of the sheets as I stretched out on my stomach. I knocked the pillows aside and folded my arms above my head, resting the side of my face on my right biceps, still floating on that post-orgasmic high.

Snuggly Cres wormed his way right next to me. Then his hands were all over me.

Somehow I'd forgotten how damn handsy the guy was after fucking.

He planted a kiss on the ball of my shoulder, his lips soft and sweet.

For the longest time, he was content to drag the tips of his fingers up and down my spine while he rested his cheek on the back of my left arm, his leg hooked over mine. So when his fingers ventured outward and connected with the scar, every bit of my relaxation vanished.

"What's this?"

"A scar."

"No kiddin'. A scar from what?"

"Someone figured they needed to teach me a lesson with a whip." Why had I blurted that out? I should've given him some bullshit lie about a rodeo injury.

"It feels new." His fingers connected with the raised edges of the two scars below it. "How many of these do you have?"

"Not sure," I lied. "It's hard to look at my own back."

"Do you get distracted by your hot ass? Because I sure would."

"You've already had my hot ass. I'll need recovery time before you have it again."

"While I'm waiting, I'll check out these painful-lookin' marks, tough guy." Cres used the remote and cranked up the bedroom lights to full power, searing my retinas. I turned my head toward the wall to block out the light.

Right. That's why you're avoiding eye contact.

The heat of his breath flowed across my skin as he inspected every inch of my back. Every time he found a new mark, he counted it out loud.

I already knew I had twelve visible scars from that night.

Cres had found every one.

The mental scars…there were far more of them.

"How—where—did you get these?"

"They were a belated parting gift from a few guys on the circuit."

"Jesus." Cres swept his hand down my spine and back up. "You didn't consent to this."

"Who the fuck would consent to bein' trussed up half-nekkid while some drunken dude whipped you hard enough to break the skin?" I snapped.

Soothingly he said, "Tell me."

"How about we don't go here because it's one of the most humiliating things that I've been through." Yeah, that'll get him to drop it.

Then sweet Cres vanished. "I don't give a shit. I wanna know how the fuck this happened to you. And I'm as tenacious as a damn bulldog, so start talking."

I'd never told anyone this. I'd just dealt with it and then blocked it out. "After everything went down, and I had no place to go, I bought this motor home. I wandered the country, traveling the back roads."

"No one knew you'd joined the 'go RVing' movement?"

I snorted. "Nope. Although this is a nice ride, it doesn't stand out when you're tooling down the highway or parked at a campground with 200 other motor homes. Paying cash for camping meant I didn't have to register at any of the sites. For all intents and purposes, I disappeared."

"You didn't tell anyone your plans?"

"No one to tell, Cres."

"That sucks." He nuzzled the nape of my neck. "Were you lonely during your journey to the center of nowhere?"

"Solitude forced me to examine aspects of my life that'd been long overdue. I stayed in contact with a few people I trusted, like the Gradskys. I shut down all my social media. But because I'm also a creature of habit, I went to Vegas."

"During finals?" he said sharply.

"Yeah."

"Why the hell did you even care?"

"I went because I'd bought tickets and prepaid my hotel room a year in advance. When I didn't dress like a cowboy or act like king of the damn rodeo, I wasn't on anyone's radar. I'd had two days of anonymous in the stands. On the third day—night—whatever, I hit this dive diner that's off the strip. I sat up at the counter like I always did. Again, nothin' about me said cowboy."

I felt him smile against my skin as he pinched my ass. "Hate to break it to you, dude, but everything about you screams cowboy. Even when you're nekkid. But go on."

"So this hot young guy, probably your age, sits two chairs away and strikes up a conversation with me."

"You didn't think that was suspicious?"

"Nope. Bullshitting with strangers about random stuff is the hallmark of this diner. We kept talkin' even after our food arrived and he moved over to the seat next to mine. Just from the way he looked at me, I knew he was interested. And I hadn't gotten laid for six fucking months. I suggested we hook up and he immediately said yes."

As I struggled to get through this next part, Cres waited, keeping up those tender touches I could easily get addicted to.

"I followed this guy outside and around the back of the building and found myself in a blanket party."

My heart thundered remembering the scratchy wool saddle blanket being pulled over my head. The absolute darkness. The lack of air. The ball-shrinking fear I was about to pay the ultimate price for wanting a few hours of companionship and someone to touch me. "When they started to drag me to the empty field behind the restaurant, I fought back with everything I had."

"Do you know how many guys were involved?"

"Around ten. Took every one of those fuckers to take me down."

Stupid point of pride for me, but there it was. I forced myself to take a deep breath. "Even with the blanket over my head I recognized a few of the voices as guys I'd known on the circuit. Some of the shit they said to me…they were seriously sick motherfuckers. I didn't hear it all because they had the blanket around my neck too tight and I passed out. That part wasn't intentional because when I came to, they were arguing about not accidently killin' me. Before I felt any relief I wasn't about to die, they cut my shirt off, tied my wrists together in front of me and draped my arms over a fence post. I made the mistake of tryin' to get free and ended up slicing the shit out of my forearm on the barbed wire. So I knew whatever they'd planned to do to me, I'd just have to stand there and fucking take it." I flinched even now when I recalled the whistling sound of the bullwhip right before the loud crack of leather connecting with my flesh.

"Breck," he breathed in my ear. "You're safe here with me. You don't have to talk about it if you can't."

"I've never told anyone about this, Cres. So just…give me a second."

"Sure. Take your time. I ain't goin' anywhere."

Out of sheer mortification, I continued to face away from him. "One guy laid into me with the whip while his drunken cohorts laid into me about my perversions and bein' an embarrassment to all decent rodeo cowboys. One dickhead called the open gashes a 'bloodletting.' Assholes laughed like fuckin' donkeys about that. Another asswipe said our ancestors had it right. A sicko with my predilection would've been strung up as a warning to others."

"These are the same ancestors that thought slavery was A-Okay," he sneered.

"Right. Then they yanked me from the fence post and tossed me on the ground." Bile rose in my throat. My stomach churned and no matter how rigid I held my body, I started to shake when I remembered the thick taste of my fear and the loathing they leveled on me. "Their final humiliation was they each pretended to fuck me. Grinding their groins against my ass, pumping their hips into my face. Tellin' me I deserved to choke to death on a dick. Askin' if that was how I liked to get fucked. Calling' me a filthy butt fucker, a disgusting ass licker, a sinning sodomite, a cocksucking pervert…"

Cres rolled me over and wrapped himself around me. "Stop," he said hoarsely. "Take a break. Jesus, Breck, you're shaking like you're about to go into shock." He pulled the covers over us. "C'mere. For chrissake, let me warm you up."

I pressed my cheek against Cres's chest, letting the steady beat of his heart calm me.

That gave me the courage to skip to the end. "After these guys I'd once considered friends finished mentally brutalizing me, they kicked me a few times for good measure. My lip was split open. One of my eyes had already swollen shut. They left me tied up, helpless and bleeding in the dirt. I don't know how long I laid out there, but eventually I wiggled around enough to free my head from the blanket. I managed to stumble to the back door of the restaurant. I refused to let them call the cops. I'd walked to the diner from my hotel, so no way in hell was I goin' back there in case those fuckers had followed me. I called a cab to take me to my motor home I'd left at a campground outside of town. I guess I passed out after I crawled in bed.

"I woke up feverish. I went to one of those walk-in emergency clinics, got the infected wounds cleaned up, and they gave me antibiotics. After that…I must've slept for three damn days. But not long enough for the marks to scab over. I ended up with these scars."

Cres didn't say anything for the longest time.

But I wasn't panicked he'd pass judgment on me.

Finally he said, "I know gay-bashing happens." He pressed his lips to the top of my head. "I hate that it happened to you. *Hate* it."

"But?"

"But I have to ask why you even considered takin' this job. You're training guys whose main goal in life is to compete in the CRA—the organization that supports fuckers like the ones who destroyed your career and physically attacked you. After all you told me about driving under the radar and steering clear of the rodeo life that turned you into a guy you didn't recognize, why didn't you tell the Gradskys to suck it?"

"I like your dirty euphemisms, Cres."

"Answer the question."

I sat up. "Sutton asked me the same question this mornin'."

"What did you tell him?"

"It's not like I have another skill set besides rodeoin'."

Cres sat up too. "Bullshit. You have a college degree. There are a lot of other things you could do."

"Name one."

"Go to work for Stirling. You're a farmer with an Ag degree. You're perfect for her operation."

"I'd considered that. But she needs someone full time and permanent. I already told you I'm not a permanent guy. Itchy feet, transient nature, remember?"

That startled him. "Yeah, I remember."

"Spending three months in Colorado during the summer and bein' able to leave when the snow starts to fly appealed to me. Havin' a chance to mold a few of the guys in this younger generation appealed to me too. If they see me as a normal guy tryin' to make a livin', not the secretly gay former rodeo champion rocked by scandal…maybe I can make a difference and change their misperceptions."

"Christ, you're as altruistic as Mick."

Had he meant that as an insult?

"When do you start teaching?"

"Next week. I'm nervous as hell."

Cres scooted off the bed and started to get dressed. "I imagine you have set hours?"

"It's pretty fluid. I have specific things I'm talkin' about and then the other instructors and I are in group sessions with all the students. Berlin is emphasizing that we're a team."

"You don't agree with that philosophy?"

I watched him zip his jeans and fasten his belt. There was nothing sexier than a man wearing just a pair of jeans, his chest and feet bare. And Cres epitomized sexy with his ropy forearms, and long and lean build.

"Breck?"

My gaze traveled up his body until my eyes met his. "I've got it bad for you, rancher. You slipped those jeans on and all I can think about is tearing them off again."

He crawled across the mattress until we were face to face. "I've got it bad for you too, farmboy. So the point of all of my questions was to figure out when we're gonna see each other."

I said, "And?" because I knew there was something else on his mind.

"And if we're keeping this *9 ½ Weeks* just between us?"

"I'm not hedging, but a lot of this is a day-by-day, wait-and-see thing. My coworkers know I'm gay. If the students ask I'll be honest with them. But to me there's a difference between sayin' I'm involved with a guy and havin' a boyfriend who's part of my workin' life. Especially when I ain't exactly sure what all that workin' life entails." I reached up and ran my knuckles down his jaw. "I want to see you, to get to know you better, take full advantage of the time I'm here. So I don't have a problem with your truck bein' parked at my campsite. I don't care if the Gradskys know we're spending time together. If you wanna tell your brothers, I'm fine with that too. My natural reaction is to admit I want to keep you here in my bed and to shut out the world. That's the way I've always done things. So this bein' out and proud thing…I'm more inclined to take baby steps than a giant leap."

Cres beamed at me. "Right answer."

I let out a relieved breath.

"Now get dressed. You promised to cook supper and I worked up an appetite fucking you stupid."

Chapter Six

Cres

As I entered the gates of the Grade A complex, I waved to Tammy and Trent, who were out for their pre-dinner walk.

I stopped to let Annie and her black lab, Shadow, cross the road.

Bill flagged me down and asked if my hardware store had a decent parts department since he was having a devil of a time getting what he needed from his local Mom and Pop place.

I slowed when I reached the recreation area.

Two groups of boys were shooting hoops on the basketball court.

Half a dozen girls played sand volleyball.

Most of the boys were more interested in watching the girls' parts bounce than they were in bouncing the ball.

I waved to Mitzi and Bob in the feed truck, who were making the rounds and feeding the stock.

Breck and I had been involved for four weeks. Since I was here almost every night after work, I'd become familiar with the facility and the staff.

So far Breck had an easier go of being the "gay" bulldogging instructor than he'd expected.

But if he did have problems, would he tell you?

That…I wasn't sure of.

Sexually, we meshed. It helped we were both horny as fuck all the time. The newness of being lovers hadn't worn off and the heat between us hadn't cooled a bit. In fact, now that we knew each other's preferences and kinks, we were even more eager to get naked and raunchy. Even with all of that…we were keeping it just sex between us.

Sure you are. That's why you know the comings and goings of ninety percent of the staff. That's why you keep his refrigerator stocked with groceries since he cooks supper for you almost every night. That's why your toiletries are in his bathroom. That's why you ironed his work shirts when he didn't have time. That's why you surprised him with a PlayStation since you hate gaming on his Xbox. That's why you've stopped running unless the two of you are running together. You're doing all of that stuff because it's keeping it "just sex" between you.

I shot a quick look at the envelope on the seat.

Undeniable proof, bud, that you've gone over for the man. If this was just a sexual relationship with an end date, you wouldn't need to get blood tests done so you can ditch the condoms.

Annoying that the voice of reason picked today to point that out. Even more annoying that I'd chosen this day to listen to it.

I'd been so adamant about not starting a relationship—even after Breck had pointed out "just sex" was a relationship. I'd naively believed I could keep feelings out of the equation. That physical release would be enough. Like I could get off and get gone.

Right.

I got off plenty. I just couldn't seem to yank up my boxer briefs after we finished fucking and get gone. I liked Breck, and spending time with him clothed held almost as much appeal as being body to body, skin to skin, mouth to mouth with him. We'd been able to build on, expand, and go beyond the physical attraction. The caring, open, and honest person Breck had become following his long journey to his self-acceptance was just the damn cherry on top. Yet, within those changes, he'd retained his sense of humor and his pride that he wasn't just a dumb cowboy. Seeing him transform from a selfish guy into a thoughtful man blew my mind. He pulled me out of the dark place I'd been in for too long, but he let me decide when I was ready to cross the next boundary. He remained by my side as I approached another hurdle—stopping the guilt because I was alive and Mick wasn't. That I deserved a second chance at happiness.

I wanted that happiness with him.

So he'd helped me come to terms with aspects of myself and my life that I could change.…how did I help him see that by jumping back on the road when the semester ended, that he was hiding as much as I'd been? How did he know he wouldn't like a more settled life if he never tried it?

Not something I could solve today, but hopefully each day we spent together would make him want more days until he couldn't see a day without me in it. Because that's where I was.

I pulled up to the office building and parked. Sutton had sent a box of paperwork for me to deliver to Berlin since both London and Brennen were down with a stomach bug.

Berlin and Chuck bounded down the steps before I'd reached the end of the sidewalk.

"Here, lemme take that," Chuck said, plucking the box from my hands. "We appreciate you bringing this by."

"No problem. I'm usually in the neighborhood."

Chuck smiled. "And we're happy to have you here, Cres."

As soon as my hands were empty, Berlin hugged me. This family was the hugging-est bunch I'd ever met. "Have you seen my daughter and grandson?"

"Sutton is keeping them quarantined. This stomach flu is nasty stuff. It knocked him down for a week."

"I'm not surprised London and Brennen caught it."

"Us either. Luckily, Wyn, Mel, and Evan haven't been around them for a couple of weeks. It's hard on my folks, though. But we don't need them getting sick."

"Amen to that." Berlin's eyes scanned my face. "No one is worried about you catching it?"

I grinned. "My family claims I'm too ornery to catch it."

"Then London shouldn't have gotten it either."

"Ooh, I'm tellin' her you said that, Mama B."

She whapped me on the arm. "Come on. I know why you're really here. I want to see it too, so let's walk over to the arena."

Tonight the instructors were demonstrating their rodeo skills for their students. As much as I wanted to see my man in action, we were still stumbling our way through public appearances as a couple, especially when it came to his job. It'd been really sweet that the big, tough rodeo cowboy had acted shy when he'd asked me to come to the demo. As if I could refuse that.

It's not like you can refuse him anything.

Maybe I'll start with refusing to let him go when this session ended in six weeks.

Whatcha think about that, voice of reason?

My voice of reason got suspiciously quiet.

"So we received some great news today that you'll be interested to hear about."

Please tell me that Breck signed on for another teaching session.

"What's that?"

"Mel's sister Aly has agreed to teach an equestrian class next semester!"

I stepped around a cactus. "Mel will be thrilled. But is Grade A set up to handle that? I mean, is there specialized equipment you'll have to buy?"

"Believe it or not, Aly is donating most of it. And because this whole complex is brand new, it's completely ADA compliant."

My sister-in-law's sister Aly had been paraplegic since age sixteen. Being wheelchair bound hadn't prevented her equestrian pursuits. The woman was a total badass on a horse. After winning a bronze and a silver medal, last year she'd finally won gold in the Paralympics Games. Earlier this year Mel mentioned Aly had decided to retire from professional competition, but she wasn't sure what Aly would do next.

"We will have to change a couple of things," Berlin continued. "Starting with adding asphalt paths that connect all of the outer buildings to the arenas. It'd be too dangerous for wheelchairs to use the road."

"Aly has the contacts to bring in students?"

"Yes. But for that program, enrollment will be very limited. If it's successful we can always bump up the numbers."

I draped my arm over her shoulder. "Mama B, you are amazing. The more time I spend here, the more I'm impressed by the kind of place you've built. Not in terms of the best of everything—although that does apply—but it's an inclusive atmosphere when it could easily be exclusive. High-five for that."

Berlin stopped and faced me. "Thank you. It's been a labor of love."

"It shows."

We walked into the arena and I wasn't sure where I was supposed to go.

"Breck said you should sit at the rear since that's where you prefer to be."

I fought a blush. That jackass loved to tease and see if others picked up on his innuendo. "Thanks."

Berlin jogged down front and I scaled the bleachers until I reached the top row. I'd have a great view from here.

The kids I'd seen shooting hoops and playing volleyball started shuffling in. I watched DiDi, head chaperone, count heads and then do a roll call. When she spoke into her walkie-talkie, I suspected some dumb kid had tried to skip out.

I settled in to watch the show and snickered when Macon Gradsky's voice boomed through the sound system. It killed me that the buttoned-up attorney was a total ham when he filled in as an emcee, rodeo announcer, and DJ.

The school ran these demos like a rodeo, with the bucking horses first. The only difference was they'd do two run-throughs, allowing each instructor to demonstrate twice. I'd learned from Breck these past few weeks that rodeo competitors were making constant adjustments. Arena conditions, the quality level of the rough stock events impacted each round. So showing the students two rounds allowed them to see successes and failures—another unique aspect of this particular rodeo school.

Since Breck had stopped vying for the All-Around title after winning three world championships, he'd dropped saddle bronc from his competitive events. I was glad I didn't have to watch him tie himself to a mean-tempered bronc determined to toss him on his ass. Seeing him launch his big body off a galloping horse and onto an animal running away from him and then wrestling it to the ground provided enough white-knuckle moments for me.

I hadn't seen him compete in tie-down roping, but his championship status indicated he excelled at that too. Two nights ago the cheeky asshat had told me after he'd blown me that tie-down roping was the only real skill he could bring to ranch work.

So my head had been spinning, my balls were still tight, my cock was still throbbing when he'd dropped that gem on me. Or had it been a hint? Like he'd wanted me to be aware that he had the experience I needed in a ranch hand? Or was it wishful thinking that my lover was showing interest in becoming a long-term partner with a rancher?

I still hadn't sorted all that out yet.

Macon's announcement that Breck Christianson, three-time CRA All-Around World Champion, was on deck to demonstrate steer wrestling—aka bulldoggin' in the world of rodeo—pulled me out of the fantasy of Breck riding the range beside me for many years to come.

I squinted at the chute below me. On the left side I could see the top of Breck's hat and the ears of his horse. I didn't know who'd agreed to be his hazer—the guy riding on the right side during the run that kept Breck's horse in a straight line—but I knew he preferred to have Sutton doing it.

The gate opened, the steer got a head start, and then Breck chased after him.

My gut clenched when Breck leaned over the right side of his horse, with just his right foot in the stirrup and his left hand on the saddle horn. His left leg practically stuck straight up as he slid it across the back of the saddle.

Most people thought bulldoggers launched themselves forward, but they actually leaned back. So once they grabbed ahold of the steers' head, they could pull backward when both their feet hit the dirt. That balance to power ratio allowed them to twist their bodies and use their weight and strength to slam the steer on its side.

I'd listened to my brother discuss dismount strategies, complain about flexibility training and conditioning. I understood there was more to what steer wrestlers did than what rodeo spectators saw in the few seconds they spent in the arena.

When it all came together like clockwork? It was a sight to behold. Danger and precision that looked effortless.

That's how my man's first run went.

Breck had that steer down in 3.9 seconds.

Applause and whistles echoed throughout the arena. I had such a burst of pride for him to hear the entire school's acknowledgment of his skill—an affirmation he hadn't heard for far too long.

I saw him glance at the judge to see if there were flags for breaking the barrier or an illegal takedown. When he saw nothing but the impressive time on the scoreboard, his cocky grin made my dick hard.

And I paid particular attention to how he walked across the dirt. Not only because his rear view was damn fine with that tight cowboy ass and his broad shoulders, but I wanted to see if he favored his right leg. He'd mentioned having a sore knee last night. When I saw him hitch his shoulders and twist to the side, I figured he'd probably prefer a backrub to a blowjob tonight.

My voice of reason snorted disbelief.

After the bulldogging event was tie-down roping, and I noticed Breck served as hazer for the tie-down roper. Team roping followed, then barrel racing, and finally bull riding.

There was a fifteen-minute intermission before the next round started. I didn't move, although I exchanged a few friendly waves with other instructor's significant others as we killed time in the stands.

Breck's second run resulted in just a tenth of a second faster than his first time. If this was a real competition, his combined score was good enough to land him in the payout slots.

After the demo ended, a quick thank-you to teachers served as the closing of the event. The arena emptied quickly but I didn't rush out. Breck would track me down when he finished with his official duties. The school had horse handlers, so he didn't have to deal with that, but he never trusted anyone to take care of his tack—a habit I respected.

Twenty minutes later I heard the *clang clang* of his boot heels on the metal steps as he climbed the risers. The happy grin, the light shining in his eyes when he looked at me...just did me in.

Yep. You are so dick-whipped over this bulldogger.

I stood when he reached me. He didn't look over his shoulder to see if anyone was watching before he hooked his hand around the back of my neck and brought my mouth to his for a kiss.

"Hey."

Another thing that made me so crazy about him? He kissed me hello. Every single time. Usually before he uttered "hey"—the standard cowboy greeting.

"Hey, yourself. Nice runs. You looked good. Smooth. Like you're still competing a few times a week."

He shrugged, but I knew he was pleased I'd mentioned it. "Thanks. You hungry?"

"Starved."

"Good. I had a little extra time today so I went into town and picked up that ice cream you like so much."

"You did?"

"Yep. Course, you're gonna have to share."

A mental image flashed of Breck licking the sweet white stuff off my stomach and cock.

"I also saw the new Lee Child paperback, so I snagged that for you too."

Yeah. Not just about sex for me anymore—if it ever was. "Aw. Thanks. Is that a hint you need a break tonight and you're actually gonna let me read?"

Breck growled and gave me a hard kiss. "Fuck, no. We're gonna eat. Then fuck. Then I'm gonna school you on Madden, boy."

"You wish. I have a surprise for you too."

"What?"

"Not telling. That's why it's a surprise."

He shrugged. "I know what it is anyway. Blood test results."

Of course he'd gotten his too. "Mine were all clear. I brought them with me."

"Mine's all clear too."

We grinned at each other.

Then he said, "Think it'd be obvious we're impatient to fuck if we run through the crowd and back to the campsite?"

"Maybe just a tad. Besides, I'll meet you. I left my truck in the office parking lot."

"I'll walk with you."

I didn't point out that would put us in direct view of the cafeteria and the dorms and everyone would know we were headed back to his place.

But Mr. Popular had to stop and chat with everyone. As much as I wanted time alone with him, it thrilled me to see the return of charismatic Breck, the confident cowboy, the guy in the thick of things. The joy on his face, like he truly felt their acceptance…was worth the wait.

Chapter Seven

Breck

"I suck as a teacher."

Jerry, my colleague, the saddle bronc instructor, grunted and crushed his empty Coors can beneath his boot. "What makes you think that? Did one of your students say something to you?"

"No. It just seems none of them are makin' any progress."

"Progress." Jerry snorted. "These kids are here to learn the basics. Think back to when you were seventeen. Did you give a hoot about *makin' progress*? Or were you more focused on if the pretty girls were watching you acting like a rodeo cowboy stud?"

A beat of silence passed and the campfire popped, sending a flame of orange sparks into the air.

"Shoot. Sorry. Sometimes I forget that you're..." He gestured distractedly. "You know."

I grinned. "You have no idea how happy I am to hear you say that you forgot I'm...*you know*..."

"Smarty."

"Anyway, yeah, I had an ego and liked people watching me become a rodeo stud and All-Around Cowboy contender. But I also had discipline and drive to get better in all three of my events. And I can't get these boys to focus on just one event when they're in class."

"Discipline and drive is why you've won more championships than the whole lot of these students—combined—ever will." He paused. "There's only one student here with the potential to win big."

We both said, "Etta Geyer," at the same time.

"See? You know talent when you see it, Breck. You can't feel guilty because none of your kids have talent."

"Lucky for Sharla, she knows she's got a gem in Etta." Sharla, the barrel racing instructor, had twenty years on me and Jerry age wise. She'd retired from competition before I'd started competing. I'd never met anyone who knew every nuance of the sport like she did.

"Etta may have to give it up because of her family situation." Jerry cracked open another Coors. "I ain't a gossiping old fart, but this is her last year to prove herself on her high school team and snag the eye of one of them college rodeo team recruiters."

"Where's she from?"

"Nebraska."

"So she lives too far to use Gradskys' stock to make a splash."

"Yep. Damn shame. But I think the school officials would call it an unfair advantage." He sent me a sideways glance. "Etta's been clocked below eleven on Whistler's Dream."

I shook my head. "That's unheard of."

"That's why I hope that little gal gets to make a name for herself."

We watched the fire for a while. I kicked the closest charred log deeper into the embers.

Jerry swallowed a mouthful of beer. "The last three weeks of this session are gonna drag out forever."

God, I hoped so. I couldn't believe how fast time had flown by and I'd been in Colorado for two months. Cres and I had been together for seven of those eight weeks. When I realized I only had three more weeks with him, tightness banded across my chest and I felt as if I was slowly suffocating.

"If you think you're a sucky teacher, does that mean you won't be back next session?"

I wasn't sure how to answer.

Then Jerry's cell phone rang. He said, "Sorry, I gotta take this," and swung his legs over the other side of the log, disappearing into the darkness.

Staring into the flames, I brooded about my uncertain future. I didn't trust my ambivalence toward teaching because I was a master at self-sabotage. Maybe I considered this teaching experiment a failure so I had an excuse not to sign on for the next session. Then I could stick with the "I'm a ramblin' man" warning I'd given Cres and return to the blacktop.

But I didn't want to go back on the road. Facing miles of empty highway day after day…I knew firsthand it was as lonely as it sounded.

Loneliness hadn't been an issue since I'd rolled into the Grade A complex. I spent my days surrounded by students and staff and my nights wrapped up in Cres.

Sexy, funny, sweet Cres.

I'd been such a fool to think I could work him out of my system. The more time we spent together the more I wanted. Yet Cres hadn't mentioned extending our time.

Maybe because you've done a bang-up job convincing him of your "itchy feet."

Only because he'd been so insistent about never getting into another serious relationship, and I didn't want to be the pathetic hanger-on, trying to convince him that I was worth the risk to his heart, because I wasn't sure I was.

There was some confidence. I'd gotten my mo-jo back in the arena, but I didn't have the same certainty with Cres unless I was fucking him.

Why did this have to be so fucked up? Why couldn't I just tell him my feelings had changed and I needed more than "just sex?"

Because I was worried that his feelings hadn't changed. He'd made some strides in letting go of his guilt for moving on from Mick, but I knew he was still hung up on the guy. In all the weeks we'd been together, Cres hadn't asked me to sleep over at his house. Which made no sense…unless he considered the bedroom he'd shared with Mick a sacred place he never wanted to share with another man. By denying me access to his personal space, he believed he was keeping to his original declaration he didn't want anything but a physical relationship.

As much as it bugged me that I hadn't gotten an invite into his bed, I had too much fucking pride to ask for one.

Boot steps stomping across the underbrush had me shaking off the melancholy. I expected to see Jerry reappear, but Macon stepped out of the dark woods.

"Breck! What are you doin' out here?"

"Enjoying the campfire, the stars, and the clean Colorado air." *While I'm wallowing in uncertainty of where "what is" intersects with "what could be."*

Jesus. Where had that hippie-dippy philosophy come from? I

sounded like I'd been sampling some of their product.

Macon eyed Jerry's empty beer can. "Are you enjoying an icy cold beer? Because I'd take one if you were offering."

"Sorry. Fresh out."

"I forget you're a teetotaler now."

I shrugged. "I don't miss it, to be honest. I really don't miss the bad decisions I made when I was liquored up." I'd been hesitant to mention my non-drinker status to Cres, but he'd been fully supportive. He didn't drink around me—his choice, not something I'd asked of him. He'd told me he'd rather have the taste of me in his mouth than beer anyway.

"I hear ya. So where's Cres?"

"At his home, I reckon. Why?"

He lowered onto the log. "No reason. You two are usually joined at the hip."

"He's hit the busy season at the ranch now, so he'll be around less."

"Sucks for you," Macon said. "So what's this bullshit I've heard from Mom that you're not re-upping to teach next session?"

"I'm not...*not* re-upping. I haven't decided yet."

"No need to get defensive. I get that dealing with teens isn't for everyone. I thought you'd give it more than one session. Especially now that you've found someone worth sticking around for."

"Me'n Cres haven't discussed makin' this relationship permanent, so we'll see."

"Yeah, right." Macon smirked. "After seeing you two together, you're feeling the burning need to go back on the road?"

I didn't need him grilling me on things that were already pissing me off. "What are you doin' here, counselor?"

"Babysitting, apparently."

"Lemme guess. Stirling and Liam got into it again."

He touched his nose.

"What is the deal with them?"

"They were both used to bein' the alpha dog in their previous positions and neither is willing to be the beta even for one damn day." He pinned me with a look. "Organic farming was my little sister's bright idea, not mine. If I had my way, we'd use that acreage for pot. But it's too late in the season to build grow houses. If she intends to plant anything next season, she has to prep that soil now before it snows so it's ready to go in the spring."

"What needs done before it's ready to go?"

"Plowing, tilling, taking soil samples, figuring out what needs to be added to adjust the PH levels for each heirloom variety. Hiring a certifying agent. But instead of getting a jump on that, she thought it'd be funny to put powdered purple Kool-Aid in Liam's favorite lab gloves."

I winced. "Shit."

"Yeah. His hands are stained the most hideous shade of purple. She bought him new gloves only after I chewed her ass, but she refused to apologize. She said he needs to grow a sense of humor. Then she added that next time she'll dump blue powder in his cup." He sighed. "Now I have to worry how Liam will retaliate, because there's no way he'll let this slide."

Kool-Aid reminded me of the summers I'd spent toiling on the farm in South Dakota. I'd never minded the work—it was working with family that drove me away. I'd known from age ten that I wanted to rodeo and farm, so I'd practiced my rodeo skills during the day and pored over Ag magazines at night. I'd taken great satisfaction in the purple ribbons I'd won in 4H and for FFA at the state fair for the produce I'd grown in my section.

"What were you thinking about just now?" Macon asked.

"Sorry." I shot him a sheepish look. "Didn't mean to tune you out. I was just thinkin' about farming and college. Lost opportunities."

"Or ones that were taken from you?"

"I've had enough distance to admit that goin' back home and helping run the family farm hadn't ever been in the cards for me."

Macon leaned forward, resting his forearms on his knees. "So if you really hate teaching, would you consider coming to work for us on the organic farming side of Grade A?"

"You askin' me because you wanna pass off the babysitting duties?"

He laughed. "I'm pleading the fifth on that one. But I am serious because if you would've said no to the rodeo school, I planned to ask if you'd be interested in the Ag side."

Maybe I did have options besides hitting the happy trail to nowhere. "Why?"

"I've known you since college. I trust you and you've got the background to be a real asset. And I don't think you'll find anyplace else that suits you better on a personal level either. You have acceptance and respect here, Breck. That's something you were looking for the past couple of years."

He'd poked every one of my "Yes! Where do I sign?" buttons. That was the perfect example of Macon being the Gradskys' secret weapon in negotiations; he wouldn't walk away unless he got what he wanted.

Maybe you should adopt that philosophy.

"I'll think about it."

A log popped with enough force it sounded like a gunshot and I jumped.

"Is this a private party?"

I jumped again and my head snapped up.

Cres stood on the other side of the campfire, his hands jammed in the front pockets of his jeans.

Macon chuckled and stood. "It is now."

"Hey, Macon. How's it goin'?" Cres asked.

"I can't complain. How've you been?"

"Busy and cranky."

Macon pointed at me. "Maybe you can pull each other out of your bad moods." He hopped over the log and vanished into the forest.

I refocused on Cres. Firelight created a glow as if he were a mythical woodland creature.

"You're lookin' at me like I'm a ghost, Breck."

"Since I hadn't expected to see you tonight, I worried you were just an apparition I'd conjured up."

"Nope. I'm flesh and blood and bone."

I cocked my head. "Did you say you had a boner?"

He laughed. "Not yet."

"The night is still young." Except it wasn't. It was after eleven and past the time early rising ranchers were usually in bed. "So you were in the neighborhood?"

Cres plopped down on the log across from me. "Nah. I was restless. So I took a drive."

"And ended up here." Why? Because he wanted to watch the next episode of *Archer* on Netflix with me? For a fast goodnight fuck to take off the restless edge?

If he was here to get fucked, I'd oblige him. Happily. At least twice if he did a little sweet talkin'. Or better yet, dirty talkin'.

Then he shocked the hell out of me by saying, "I took a drive here because I missed you, dumbass."

The tightness in my chest loosened. I crooked my finger at him. "Prove it."

He sauntered over, intending to sit next to me.

"Huh-uh. Down there"—I pointed to the ground—"so I can put my hands on you."

"Bossy bulldogger wants me worshipping at his feet," he said with a sly grin. "Not a surprise." He situated himself between my legs, propping his forearms on my thighs.

"Forget something?"

Cres tilted his head back. "What?"

"This." I lowered my lips to his and we kissed for a good long time. We needed that connection since Cres's working hours had kept us apart of late.

"This is romantic," he said softly.

"Only now that you're here." I leaned closer. "I wanna fuck you by a fire sometime. I'll bet your ass looks hot with a red glow to it."

Cres cranked his head around and narrowed his eyes at me. "Was that a hint that you want to spank me? Get my ass glowing red from these big hands of yours?"

"No. I never wanna hit you. Even when it's supposed to be fun or hot and sexy or whatever." The idea of touching him with anything except reverence—even the roughness that exploded between us wasn't borne out of violence but passion—turned my stomach.

"Hey. I'd never ask that of you, okay?"

Sensing my tension, he nuzzled the inside of my thigh until I relaxed and said, "Okay."

"I'd like to see you nekkid by firelight too, farmboy."

"Maybe someday soon we'll both get our wish." I laced our fingers together and rested our joined hands on my knees. I dropped my chin onto the top of his head. "So tell me about your day, rancher."

As Cres filled me in with the details about his long-assed day, while he was warm and pliant in my arms, I had a sense of rightness I hadn't felt...maybe ever.

And I knew I'd do whatever it took to keep it.

Chapter Eight

Cres

Buzzing on the nightstand at four a.m. woke me and it wasn't the alarm on my phone. I immediately reached for my cell and blinked at the caller ID.

Wyn.

"Bro, did you butt dial me again when you got up with Evan?" I said groggily.

"No. Melissa's water broke."

The panic in my brother's voice had me sitting up. "She's not due for another two months."

"I know. I'm dropping Evan off with Sutton and London and takin' her to the hospital."

"What can I do?"

"I don't know when I'll be back so you'll probably be doin' everything by yourself the next couple of days at least."

"Wyn, I'll be fine. Take care of your wife and baby."

He blew out a breath. "I'm not calling Mom and Dad—no reason to wake them up when there's nothin' they can do. I'll give them an update when I know more."

"Sounds good. Keep in touch as best as you can. Give Mel my love."

"I will. Thanks." He hung up.

I eased back down into the pillows, but I was wide awake and worried so it'd be pointless to try to go back to sleep. I got up, dressed, and shuffled to the kitchen to make coffee. Guess I'd get chores done early today.

If you're doing them by yourself? Wrong.

In the past four years since our dad had retired and turned the ranch over to us, Wyn and I had doubled our herd. We'd leased grazing land instead of buying it outright to see how difficult a larger herd was to manage. Some times of the year one person could handle it all. But this time of year, Wyn and I both could stay busy from sunup to sundown. After Mick died, I'd willingly taken on more responsibilities because working until exhaustion had been easier than being alone in an empty house.

Before I'd met Mick it hadn't bothered me to live alone.

That's because you hadn't known what you were missing.

Over the past few weeks that Breck and I had been together, I'd realized he'd exaggerated his contentment about being a lone wolf. We were together nearly every night. If we weren't physically in the same space, we were on the phone. Or texting.

The pink and orange glow of sunrise spread across the horizon as I started down the porch steps. Banjo greeted me, his tail wagging crazily. I scratched behind his ears. "Let's get you fed so we can start the day."

He yipped in agreement.

I finished my coffee as Banjo chowed down. It'd be faster to check the herd on horseback than going over to Wyn's and getting out a 4-wheeler. Then I could return for the truck before I started baling the grass we'd cut last week. I hoped the baler cooperated. Damn thing was old and touchy as hell. Only Wyn seemed to have the magic touch with it. We were babying it, trying to eke one last season out of it before we upgraded.

Banjo scrambled down the steps and rolled in the dirt. Then he shook himself and barked at me.

"Okay, okay, let's get Petey saddled and we'll be on our way to check cattle."

Had I always talked to my dog this much?

Yes. Mick complained you talked to the dog more than you talked to most people.

For the first time in a long time, thinking about Mick didn't cause me pain.

Hours later, I returned to the house and checked my cell phone for news from Wyn. Sure enough, he'd left me a voice mail. As had Sutton. And my dad.

Shit.

I listened to Wyn's message first.

"Hey. I'll get to the point since I ain't got a lot of time. The docs performed an emergency C-section. They put Melissa out for it and she's still in recovery with some minor complications. Since the baby was eight weeks early and he only weighed two pounds, and he'd gone into distress prior to birth, and there's no neonatal care unit here, they immediately flew him to Denver Children's via Life Flight. Melissa can't travel after the surgery for several days, depending on when they get her blood sugar levels managed and her blood pressure stabilized. Which means I'm on my way to Denver right now to be with the baby. I had to leave Melissa here. Christ, I didn't even get to see her, Cres. And neither of us has even seen our son."

My guts twisted at hearing the anguish in his voice.

"Between Sutton and London and Mom and Dad, Evan will be looked after. I hate for Melissa to be alone in the hospital, but she needs to take advantage of this time and freakin' rest. So I'm sorry, bro, but you'll be a one-man band while I'm dealing with all the family medical stuff."

Like that was something he needed to worry about with his premature baby in one hospital and his wife in another.

"Text me when you get a chance and I'll check in later when I know more."

I saved the message and played the one from Sutton.

"Hey, Cres, I know Wyn called and filled you in on what's goin' on. I don't have anything new to report except to say holler if you need help. I'm sure you'll be hearing from Dad and he'll try and convince you he's up to the task of mowing, but he's not and we all know it."

My dad had been a rancher all his life until a heart attack had forced him into early retirement. We'd had to adjust our lives then, and it looked to be the same thing now.

"Mom will be helping London out with the boys as well as spending time with Melissa in the hospital. Once Melissa is able to go to Denver, Dad will drive her. If we keep Dad busy then he won't insist on helping you with ranch work. Sucks, but it'd be best for everyone if you're on your own."

No shit.

"Anyway, Wyn forgot to tell you your nephew's name is Truman. It's hard for him to stop calling Tru 'the baby' since they weren't ready for him and it'll be touch and go as far...his odds. But the sooner we all call Truman by his name, the more it'll show the world that we believe he's a fighter and he *is* gonna make it. He has to make it. Has to."

Sutton's voice broke on the last couple of words.

"Text me when you get back from checking cattle."

I saved Sutton's message and played my dad's next.

"Cres. I know what your brothers are doin' with havin' me be a glorified damn gopher and chauffeur—tryin' to keep me from helping you on the ranch. But if you have problems with the baler, call me. If you need a gate opener, call me. I'm not a damn invalid."

That made me smile.

After I slapped together a couple of sandwiches, I hitched the baler to my truck and headed out.

Luck was on my side and the baler didn't break down. I finished the last bale just before sunset.

On the way home I managed to talk to both of my brothers and my parents. No change in Truman's condition was considered good news because they'd gotten him stabilized. And Mel had been moved into a regular room—more good news.

I hesitated to call Breck. This was the last week of class and he'd warned me his schedule would be tight. I missed him.

Our agreement of no relationship and just indulging in a nine-week fuckfest...had lasted maybe one night. The last couple times we'd hung out, we hadn't fucked. We binge watched two seasons of Breck's new obsession *American Ninja Warrior*.

He'd tried to teach me how to roll a poker chip through my fingers. When he questioned my dexterity after the hundredth unsuccessful attempt, I proved my dexterity was above average with an outstanding hand job.

After that he hadn't uttered a single crack about my fumbling fingers.

He'd even set up a moonlit horseback ride for us. Breck had a romantic streak, which I loved, but he also balanced that with his dirty, adventurous side. He'd fucked me with such possession and intensity I'd had a hard time getting back on the horse.

I loved every second of it.

Shaking off that train of thought, I left the baler hooked up to my truck and trudged into my house. Exhaustion set in as soon as I took my boots off. I conked out on the couch in front of the TV.

The next morning I woke up starving since I'd skipped supper. Banjo whined at the door. I'd forgotten to feed him too. "I'm coming, dog."

Day two was nearly identical to day one.

The next three days were a blur of work and family phone calls.

The fifth day Breck pulled up at dawn just as I exited the house.

My belly fluttered and I felt a ridiculous sense of happiness that he was here.

Banjo yipped and jumped all over Breck as soon as he got out of his Jeep.

Smart dog. I wished I could get away with being all over Breck too.

My eyes drank him in because my man looked like a million bucks in faded jeans, a long-sleeved plaid shirt, and a cream-colored summer-weight cowboy hat. His handsome face was smooth and his smile genuine as he petted my dog.

"You're a good boy, aren't you, Banjo?" He straightened and propped his hands on his hips. "The dog gave me a more enthusiastic welcome than you have. Oh, and he's texted me just as many times as you have too, Cres."

"Ha, ha. I've been busy, you know, running the ranch by myself and all."

When he started toward me, my pulse skyrocketed.

"Berlin told me some of what's goin' on." He stopped in front of me. "How are Mel and the baby?"

If I concentrated on answering, maybe I wouldn't be enticed by the scent of his cologne. "They're releasing Mel this morning, if her numbers hold up. Then my folks will drive her and Evan to Denver. Wyn's been there with Truman. Mel hasn't even seen him yet."

"Is the baby okay?"

"They're doin' everything they can to help him survive. He'll have a long stay in the hospital. So Wyn and Mel and Evan will be living in Denver until Tru is healthy and ready to come home." I sighed. "It's rough on everyone."

"I imagine. But it sounds as if it'll be really rough on you." That beautiful blue gaze encompassed my face. "You look like hell, Cres."

"Thanks, Captain Obvious."

"Here's something else that oughta be obvious—I'm pissed off at you. But before we get into that..." Breck curled his hand around the back of my neck. "I need this." He slanted his mouth over mine and kissed me. First with the passion that made breathing difficult, then with the sweet longing that had me swaying against him.

He didn't touch me except for maintaining the iron grip on my neck. But he held me one hundred percent in his thrall with just his kiss.

When he finally had his fill of the lip-lock, he buried his face in the crook of my neck. "Why didn't you call me? I've been worried about you and your family."

"Besides the fact you warned me not to bug you during this last week of the session?" *Besides the fact I worried you'd already heard the siren's call and had returned to your life on the road? And the thought of driving to the campground and finding you gone, like you'd done to me in Denver—made me physically ill?*

He lifted his head and blinked at me. "I don't remember sayin' that."

"You did."

"When?"

"The night we sat by the campfire with Stirling and Macon."

"I was in a sugar coma from those damn s'mores she insisted we eat and I wasn't thinking clearly."

"Or...they weren't s'mores at all, and those sneaky Gradskys were secretly product testing us."

"You were especially horny after that, so it's a possibility." Breck rubbed his mouth down my throat. "Fuck. I just want to take a bite outta you."

I groaned. "I'd let you bite me wherever you want, but once you start, I won't have the willpower to stop you."

"We'll pick this up later." He stepped back. "What are we doin' first today?"

I raised my chin to look at him. "We?"

"I'm here to help you."

"I don't need—"

"Bullshit. You do need me—would it kill you to admit it?"

Had he intended for that to have a double meaning?

You're exhausted, Cres. Let it go.

He cocked his head. "Okay, we'll talk about why you dodged that question also. Get it through that thick cowboy head of yours that I ain't goin' anywhere, so let's get this done. Cattle check first, right?"

I nodded.

"You still haying after that?"

"Yeah."

"I don't know that I'll be much help with the haying, but I can help with the cattle. Then later on we can get to the other reason I showed up at the crack of dawn."

"Which is what?"

"I missed you, dumbass."

I smiled. "Let's see if you can keep up, farmboy."

Breck flashed me that megawatt grin. "Bring it, rancher."

"You have your own tack?"

"Always. And don't even think about giving me a shitty old horse."

I raised an eyebrow. "Snobby about your horseflesh?"

"I'm used to the best."

"Unfortunately for you, the best is my horse Petey. You can't have him so you'll have to make do with second best."

"Better to make do than to be second best," he muttered.

I squinted at him. "What'd you say?"

"Nothin'. Let's round 'em up."

"We're not 'rounding them up,' bulldogger."

He smirked at me. "So it'd be against the rancher's handbook of clichés to say 'get along little doggie' to Banjo?"

"You are punchy."

"That's because I'm spending the day as a *cow puncher.*"

"Jesus." I groaned. "I missed you."

Within the first half an hour of working with Breck, I knew two things. One, my cock would spend the next five hours in agony because watching him ride made me hard as a fucking fence post. And two, his abilities on a horse weren't just for show. He was a good ranch hand. I appreciated the fact he didn't yammer on and that he followed my directions.

Over the course of the morning, the sky had transformed from watery blue, to dismal gray to almost black. The air had cooled considerably and hung heavy with humidity.

"Let's try and beat the storm," I said just as the first fat raindrops fell.

"Too late," he said as the skies opened up.

Once we'd reached the barn, we took off the saddles and draped the tack over the sides of the pens. We brushed the horses down and turned them loose in the pasture.

I removed my wet hat and hung it on a peg. When I turned around, Breck was right there.

"Shame about the rain keeping you from haying this afternoon."

The smolder in his eyes burned off any residual chill. "Yeah, I'm really broken up about it." I angled my head and licked a bead of water in the hollow of his throat. Then I attacked the buttons on his shirt. "You'd better get these wet clothes off." I pushed him against the support beam and sucked on his neck, grinding my groin into his.

He was already as hard as I was.

I peeled off his wet shirt. The nearly see-through undershirt clung to every ripple of muscle on his chest. I lowered my mouth to the dark nipple, the tip already hard enough to bite, and I started to suck through the fabric.

He hissed out a breath.

But when I began to work his belt, he stayed my hand.

I moved to the other nipple and knocked his hand away, reaching down to palm his cock.

Again, he pushed my hand aside.

I lifted my head and looked at him. "You got a problem with me touching you?"

Breck locked his frustrated gaze to mine. "No. Unless this is another attempt to keep us from finishing this inside. In the house you shared with Mick. In the bed you shared with him."

"Whoa." I stepped back. Way back. His accusation quickly snapped me out of my horny state. "What are you talkin' about?"

"Why haven't we ever fucked in your house? Goddammit, Cres, we've been together two and a half goddamned months and I've never made it past your front porch."

That startled me. "What? That's...not true." Or was it?

"Come on. You can't possibly be surprised by that," he snapped.

"Well, I am. I didn't realize we were supposed to be keeping track of our overnights on a calendar," I shot back.

"Maybe if we had, you'd see that yours is completely blank. You always come to my place, which is great because bein' with you is the high point of my day. Since you have to get up at the ass crack of dawn to do chores, wouldn't it make sense for you to ask me to spend the night here sometimes? But you've never asked me. Not one time."

I stared at him, absolutely poleaxed.

"I'd even gone so far as to justify your lack of an invite into your house and your bed as you avoiding a confrontation with Wyn. Bein's you ranch together, I imagine he's here early in the morning. If he saw my Jeep, then you'd have to confess you're fucking a guy he can't stand."

"How do you know that Wyn can't stand you?"

"Sutton told me." He snorted. "But it's never had a damn thing to do with Wyn. It has everything to do with Mick."

Goddammit. He could be so self-righteous…even when he was dead wrong. I got in his face. "I don't need this shit from you today."

"Tough. You're getting it. I'm tired of avoiding the ghost in the room. Or maybe I should say the damn ghost still living in your house."

He did *not* just say that.

"You're an asshole. And a fucking clueless one at that. Go home, Breck." Fuming, I spun on my heel and walked out.

From that first night, being with him had made me so happy that was all I focused on—getting to him as soon as my workday ended, seeing that special dirty smile as he leaned in the doorway of his motor home waiting for me. I hadn't cared where we were together, just that we *were* together.

I stepped outside. The gloomy angry sky fit my mood. The rain had gone from a steady drizzle to a torrential downpour.

I'd barely made it fifteen feet when a hand landed on my shoulder. "Cres. Wait."

I turned to face him. "What?"

Even soaked to the skin, standing in the rain, Breck didn't look like a drowned rat; he looked like a male model at a photo shoot for a vacation in the tropics. Water streamed down the angles and planes of his face. Tiny droplets sparkled on the ends of his long eyelashes. His hair, without his cowboy hat to smash it down, had become a riot of black curls.

Yeah, he's gorgeous, but he's about to tear into you without just cause, so focus.

"Don't shut me down when I finally have the balls to admit that I'm jealous of him. He gets a place of honor in your house and I get the barn."

"Breck. What the hell are you even talkin' about?"

"I'm talkin' about you messing around with me in the barn because you don't want to bring me into your house—the sacred space you shared with him."

"Sacred space? That doesn't have fuck-all to do with anything. I wanted to mess around in the barn with you because nothin' like that ever happened with him."

I shouldn't have relished his expression of shock, but I did.

"I'm sick to death of keeping all this inside and worrying I'm tarnishing his memory by admitting the truth."

"What truth?"

"What you and I have? Passion, need, lust…I never had with him. Mick wasn't spontaneous or adventurous. It drove me crazy that he kept his military attitude even when it came to sex. We fucked on the bed in the bedroom—because that's where you were supposed to fuck. We might've had sex in the shower once, but he never would've blown me in the barn or the kitchen or the truck. He wouldn't have let me suck him off on the first fuckin' date, outside with a thousand people partying in a tent behind us. He had some rigid ideas about roles and refused to consider other options."

"Like what?"

"Like he bottomed. Period."

His eyes went wide with shock. "Mick never fucked you?"

I shook my head. "He said 'Not my thing' and that was that. We fought about it, but I knew he wouldn't change his mind."

"So you just accepted it?"

I looked away.

"Answer me."

"I accepted it then. I wouldn't now."

"Fuckin' *look* at me when you're talkin' to me."

My defiant gaze met his. "What do you want me to say?"

"The truth."

"The truth that I settled for Mick? Because it was easy and comfortable? Maybe I did. But it didn't feel like that at the time because I loved him." I ignored the pained look on Breck's face and soldiered on. "And bein' with you is different in every way I needed it to be. Nothing...no one...has ever come close to giving me what you do. No boundaries, no limits, and no goddamned way is it fair that I have to give it up."

"You are confusing the fuck outta me."

"What don't you understand? I don't want you to go. You know why you didn't hear from me this week? Besides the fact I was too damn tired to even take my boots off when I stumbled into my house at night? Because I was afraid you'd already moved on."

"Moved on," he repeated. "To another guy? Fuck you if you think I'd do that when—"

"Literally moved on, in your motor home, tooling down the road like you repeatedly warned me you planned to do as soon as your teaching job ended."

"I would never do that to you!" he yelled over the thunder.

"Bullshit. You did it to me in Denver. No note, no nothin'. You just hitched up your horse trailer and you were gone, Breck."

"I am not that guy anymore. And I'm still here."

"For how long?" I demanded. "Because I want this to be long-term with you—"

"Since when?" he demanded back. "You've never indicated anything has changed from the first time you told me about Mick. You've maintained that you never want another relationship."

"I didn't think I did, but fuck, *you're* the one who told me that us fucking made it a fucking relationship! So we've been in one from the start. And I don't want to give it up. *Ever.* Do you hear me? I want it all from you, Breck, not just sex. I'll buy medicated powder for your itchy feet if that's what it'll take to keep you here with me—"

His mouth crashed down on mine.

He devoured me.

Breck kissed me so often I thought I'd known every type of kiss in his arsenal.

But nothing that had been between us before had prepared me for this: his brutal, beautiful possession and his onslaught of emotion that transcended words.

I clung to him as if my life depended on it, because in a way it did.

When we came up for air, Breck curled his hands around my face. "Right here in the wind and the rain, in the mud, on my knees and on yours, I'm gonna give you what you want, Cres, and then I'm gonna take what I need."

"Breck, wait—"

But he didn't hear me—or didn't give a damn—because he was already on his knees, working my jeans open, yanking the wet denim down to my ankles.

Then his mouth hovered above my cock for the briefest moment.

I loved watching him blow me, seeing that beautiful face lost in bliss as my dick tunneled in and out of his hungry, sucking mouth.

He swallowed my cock in one greedy, suctioning pull, groaning like a starving man, and then it was on.

No teasing.

No finesse.

Just speed.

Lots and lots of speed.

I fisted his black silk curls and held on.

More thunder rumbled. Rain continued to beat at us. The wind rose and fell.

I came as quickly and with as much force as the storm.

Immediately Breck brought me to the ground in a show of dominance.

We rolled. Him on top, then me. Our bodies were bucking and grinding together as we fought each other.

Fighting for deeper kisses.

Fighting for a better position to taste and touch and bite.

I pulled his hair when he sucked on my neck.

His fingernails gouged my back when I gifted him with the same openmouthed suck mark.

Rain pounded down.

Thunder pounded above us.

Breck flipped me onto my knees and elbows, lifting my ass into the air, using a combination of spit and water as lube and then he was pounding into me.

I'd never been fucked with the elements leaving as much of a mark on me as my lover.

The air crackled—not with lightning but with the energy flowing between us.

He roared when he came.

I let him have his beastly moment.

Because I was going to get mine.

And I did.

I pushed him back, spun him around and pinned him down, driving my cock into his ass with the same driving force as the rain.

My body should've been cold after spending this much time in the rain, but I radiated heat.

And power.

God, I fucking loved this explosion of need between us that had us fucking in the mud.

After having *this*...I couldn't ever go back to not having it.

Breck bore down as I plowed into him.

One, two, three strokes and I erupted.

Water dripped into my mouth when I tipped my head back and howled to the sky.

As I caught my breath I half-expected—half-hoped?—Breck would be ready to go at me again.

But he grunted and bumped his ass into my thighs as a hint to climb off.

I pulled out and flopped on my back, closing my eyes.

Gravel crunched beside me and then it was quiet.

Breck spoke first. "You okay?"

"Fuck, no." I paused. "Are you?"

"Fuck, no."

I smiled and figured he was smiling too.

"Ask me again," I said a few moments later.

"Are you okay?"

"Fuck, yeah."

He snickered.

I said, "Are you okay?"

"Fuck, yeah."

I'd like to say we were smart enough to come out of the rain after that, but we weren't.

We didn't move.

Maybe because we couldn't move.

"You howled," he said almost conversationally.

"Your beast roars, mine howls. No fucking judgment, dude."

"Christ, I think I just fell in love with you."

"Ditto." I groaned. "I've never said ditto in my life."

Breck said, "Ditto."

That word struck me as wrong and funny. And I started laughing—the hold your gut, slap your knee, wipe your eyes kind of laughter.

"What's so funny?"

That almost set me off again. "Besides the fact we're both laying in a puddle on the driveway with our jeans around our knees, after we fucked each other so thoroughly during a thunderstorm that we can't even fucking crawl into the house?"

Next thing I knew Breck started laughing as hard as I was.

After the hilarity died down and we still faced the sky, our dicks flapping in the wind, raindrops spattering around us, Breck reached for my hand.

"I'm sorry."

"Me too."

Still, we didn't move. Weird that it almost seemed...peaceful.

"You were wrong," I said after a bit.

"About what?"

"About my house bein' a sanctuary filled with memories of Mick." I turned my head and looked at him to find he was already looking at me. "Mick never lived here."

"I thought you lived together."

"We did. Just not in this house. I had a trailer. After Mick died...I got rid of it. Then I bought this. It's one of those pre-fab modular homes that's built on site, but I still ended up doin' a ton of work on it—"

Breck loomed over me. "Why didn't you tell me?"

"You never asked." I brushed his sodden hair off his forehead. "So it really was just a stupid oversight that you've never been in my house or in my bed. Would you like to come in and see my place?"

"I'd love to." He smiled and then he winced. "You have a first aid kit? Because I'm pretty sure there's gravel embedded in my knees."

"Yeah, my elbows are feelin' a little raw." I kissed his smirking mouth. "But it was worth it."

"Definitely."

Chapter Nine

Breck

Somehow we dragged our sodden, love-drunk asses into the house.

I didn't look around. I'd have plenty of time for that later. Years, I hoped.

Neither of us lingered beneath the spray of hot water when we had the option of curling up in Cres's warm, dry bed.

Probably made me a prick, but I had a surge of satisfaction knowing I was the first—and only—man Cres would share this space with.

No surprise we dozed off after the intensity of the storm we'd dealt with.

But as soon as Cres stirred, half-awake in that sleepy-eyed state, I took him again. Face to face, our hands clasped together above his head.

It was a sweet reconnection.

It was a necessity that I could show him my loving side I'd never shared with another man. He accepted that part of me without a moment's hesitation. I whispered the words I'd held inside my heart and he whispered them back with equal conviction.

I came when he did, my name spilling from his lips as I poured everything of myself into him—my heart, my body and my soul.

Afterward, Cres had sprawled on his stomach beside me.

I couldn't help but trace the scratches I'd left on his back. "So…it's later."

"And?"

"And...can we talk about a couple of things?"

"Of course I'll let you fix supper in my kitchen. In fact, head out there right now and get crackin'."

I pinched his ass and he swore at me.

"Fine. What's on your mind?"

"The first session ended at Grade A day before yesterday."

"I know. What's that mean?"

"I'm not sure if I'm cut out to teach, but there's no rush for me to sign a contract."

"Why not?"

"The Gradskys are numbers people. They have to assess and reassess, so they're delaying the second session until next spring. In the meantime, I did sign on to head up the soil prep and organic certification process for Stirling's organic farming experiment."

Cres pushed up onto his elbow. "Really? I thought you were done with farming."

I shrugged. "I liked farming. I didn't like workin' with my family. So I'll be using my Ag degree for the first time since I graduated."

"That's exciting for you."

"But?"

He smirked. "But I'll take shit from my brothers for bein' involved with a *farmer*."

"Maybe they'll cut you some slack when they hear I'm offering to be your ranch hand until Wyn is back in action." I swept my thumb across the dark circle beneath his eye. "You can't continue to do this alone, Cres. If it's not me, you'll have to hire someone anyway, right?"

"Probably. But won't you be busy enough with your new job?"

"Macon and Stirling said I can set my own hours. I figured some days you'd need more help than others. On the slower days, I'll head to Grade A."

"But you'll be here at night?"

"Yep." I pecked him on the mouth. "I'm lookin' forward to sleeping with you the whole night."

"Me, too." Cres ducked his head, acting as if he was concentrating on smoothing out my chest hair.

"What else is on your mind?"

"If you're not workin' on Sunday, would you wanna go to Denver with me? I need to see for myself how Wyn is holding up and I want to meet Truman."

"I'd love to come along and let your family know that I'm not goin' anywhere. Think Wyn will be okay with us bein' together and with me helping out on the Grant Ranch?"

Cres looked up at me. "He'd better be okay with it since Mel worked as his ranch hand for a couple of weeks and that's how they ended up playin' house for real. This is just as real to me. Plus, I want you to meet my Mom and Dad." He snickered. "Our nephews will wear you out. They are wild. It's so fun riling them up and then handing them back to their folks. I'm betting Tru will be the same way."

Everything he'd said after *our nephews* was hazy.

He had no idea the power those words had for me.

Our.

He was mine and I was his.

I almost felt my feet getting heavier, as if they were finally ready to set down roots.

"Breck? You okay?"

I looked at him and grinned. "Fuck, yeah. Never been better."

* * * *

Also from 1001 Dark Nights and Lorelei James, discover Tripped Out.

Sign up for the 1001 Dark Nights Newsletter
and be entered to win a Tiffany Key necklace.

There's a contest every month!

Go to www.1001DarkNights.com to subscribe.

As a bonus, all subscribers will receive a free
1001 Dark Nights story
The First Night
by Lexi Blake & M.J. Rose

Turn the page for a full list of the
1001 Dark Nights fabulous novellas...

Discover 1001 Dark Nights Collection Four

ROCK CHICK REAWAKENING by Kristen Ashley
A Rock Chick Novella

ADORING INK by Carrie Ann Ryan
A Montgomery Ink Novella

SWEET RIVALRY by K. Bromberg

SHADE'S LADY by Joanna Wylde
A Reapers MC Novella

RAZR by Larissa Ione
A Demonica Underworld Novella

ARRANGED by Lexi Blake
A Masters and Mercenaries Novella

TANGLED by Rebecca Zanetti
A Dark Protectors Novella

HOLD ME by J. Kenner
A Stark Ever After Novella

SOMEHOW, SOME WAY by Jennifer Probst
A Billionaire Builders Novella

TOO CLOSE TO CALL by Tessa Bailey
A Romancing the Clarksons Novella

HUNTED by Elisabeth Naughton
An Eternal Guardians Novella

EYES ON YOU by Laura Kaye
A Blasphemy Novella

BLADE by Alexandra Ivy/Laura Wright
A Bayou Heat Novella

DRAGON BURN by Donna Grant
A Dark Kings Novella

TRIPPED OUT by Lorelei James
A Blacktop Cowboys® Novella

STUD FINDER by Lauren Blakely

MIDNIGHT UNLEASHED by Lara Adrian
A Midnight Breed Novella

HALLOW BE THE HAUNT
A Krewe of Hunters Novella by Heather Graham

DIRTY FILTHY FIX by Laurelin Paige

THE BED MATE by Kendall Ryan
A Room Mate Novella

NIGHT GAMES by CD Reiss
A Games Novella

NO RESERVATIONS by Kristen Proby
A Fusion Novella

DAWN OF SURRENDER by Liliana Hart
A MacKenzie Family Novella

Go to www.1001DarkNights.com for more information.

Discover 1001 Dark Nights Collection One

FOREVER WICKED by Shayla Black
CRIMSON TWILIGHT by Heather Graham
CAPTURED IN SURRENDER by Liliana Hart
SILENT BITE: A SCANGUARDS WEDDING by Tina Folsom
DUNGEON GAMES by Lexi Blake
AZAGOTH by Larissa Ione
NEED YOU NOW by Lisa Renee Jones
SHOW ME, BABY by Cherise Sinclair
ROPED IN by Lorelei James
TEMPTED BY MIDNIGHT by Lara Adrian
THE FLAME by Christopher Rice
CARESS OF DARKNESS by Julie Kenner

Also from 1001 Dark Nights

TAME ME by J. Kenner

Go to www.1001DarkNights.com for more information.

Discover 1001 Dark Nights Collection Two

WICKED WOLF by Carrie Ann Ryan
WHEN IRISH EYES ARE HAUNTING by Heather Graham
EASY WITH YOU by Kristen Proby
MASTER OF FREEDOM by Cherise Sinclair
CARESS OF PLEASURE by Julie Kenner
ADORED by Lexi Blake
HADES by Larissa Ione
RAVAGED by Elisabeth Naughton
DREAM OF YOU by Jennifer L. Armentrout
STRIPPED DOWN by Lorelei James
RAGE/KILLIAN by Alexandra Ivy/Laura Wright
DRAGON KING by Donna Grant
PURE WICKED by Shayla Black
HARD AS STEEL by Laura Kaye
STROKE OF MIDNIGHT by Lara Adrian
ALL HALLOWS EVE by Heather Graham
KISS THE FLAME by Christopher Rice
DARING HER LOVE by Melissa Foster
TEASED by Rebecca Zanetti
THE PROMISE OF SURRENDER by Liliana Hart

Also from 1001 Dark Nights

THE SURRENDER GATE By Christopher Rice
SERVICING THE TARGET By Cherise Sinclair

Go to www.1001 DarkNights.com for more information.

Discover 1001 Dark Nights Collection Three

HIDDEN INK by Carrie Ann Ryan
BLOOD ON THE BAYOU by Heather Graham
SEARCHING FOR MINE by Jennifer Probst
DANCE OF DESIRE by Christopher Rice
ROUGH RHYTHM by Tessa Bailey
DEVOTED by Lexi Blake
Z by Larissa Ione
FALLING UNDER YOU by Laurelin Paige
EASY FOR KEEPS by Kristen Proby
UNCHAINED by Elisabeth Naughton
HARD TO SERVE by Laura Kaye
DRAGON FEVER by Donna Grant
KAYDEN/SIMON by Alexandra Ivy/Laura Wright
STRUNG UP by Lorelei James
MIDNIGHT UNTAMED by Lara Adrian
TRICKED by Rebecca Zanetti
DIRTY WICKED by Shayla Black
THE ONLY ONE by Lauren Blakely
SWEET SURRENDER by Liliana Hart

Go to www.1001 DarkNights.com for more information.

About Lorelei James

Lorelei James is the *New York Times* and *USA Today* bestselling author of contemporary erotic romances in the Rough Riders, Blacktop Cowboys, and Mastered series. She also writes dark, gritty mysteries under the name Lori Armstrong and her books have won the Shamus Award and the Willa Cather Literary Award. She lives in western South Dakota.

Connect with Lorelei in the following places:

www.LoreleiJames.com

www.Facebook.com/LoreleiJamesAuthor

www.Twitter.com/LoreleiJames

www.Instagram.com/LoreleiJamesAuthor

Discover More Lorelei James

Tripped Out
A Blacktop Cowboys® Novella
By Lorelei James

Coming September 12, 2017

Where there's smoke...

Stirling Gradsky abandoned the corporate rat race for a more laidback lifestyle. So it's ironic she's partnered with a hard-bodied, know-it-all scientist who treats her like a stoner instead of a stone cold business woman capable of running a large scale marijuana farm. Dr. Hot and Tattooed with the big...brain needs to stop sampling their product; he's under the half-baked idea that he's the boss.

Dr. Liam Argent's doctorate isn't in chemistry, but from the moment he meets his sexy new coworker, there's enough heat between them to short out all the grow lights in the greenhouse. First item on his agenda? Clearing up the sassy, blunt blonde's hazy notion that she's in charge.

Sparks fly as their attraction blazes. But can they weed out their differences without getting burned?

On behalf of 1001 Dark Nights,

Liz Berry and M.J. Rose would like to thank ~

Steve Berry
Doug Scofield
Kim Guidroz
Jillian Stein
InkSlinger PR
Dan Slater
Asha Hossain
Chris Graham
Pamela Jamison
Jessica Johns
Dylan Stockton
Richard Blake
BookTrib After Dark
The Dinner Party Show
and Simon Lipskar

Made in the USA
Columbia, SC
26 June 2021